Lisa Shearin

National Bestselling Author
of *Armed & Magical*

The Trouble
with Demons

Be careful what you seek…

ACE

$7.99 U.S.
$9.99 CAN

ISBN 978-0-441-01712-6

5 0 7 9 9 >

EAN

Praise for

Armed & Magical

"Fresh, original, and fall-out-of-your-chair funny, Lisa Shearin's *Armed & Magical* combines deft characterization, snarky dialogue, and nonstop action—plus a yummy hint of romance—to create one of the best reads of the year. This book is a bona fide winner, the series a keeper, and Shearin a definite star on the rise."

—Linnea Sinclair, RITA Award–winning author of
Hope's Folly

"An exciting, catch-me-if-you-can, lightning-fast-paced tale of magic and evil filled with goblins, elves, mages, and a hint of love interest that will leave fantasy readers anxiously awaiting Raine's next adventure."   —*Monsters and Critics*

"The kind of book you hope to find when you go to the bookstore. It takes you away to a world of danger, magic, and adventure, and it does so with dazzling wit and clever humor. It's gritty, funny, and sexy—a wonderful addition to the urban-fantasy genre. I absolutely loved it. From now on, Lisa Shearin is on my auto-buy list!"

—Ilona Andrews, national bestselling author of
Magic Strikes

"*Armed & Magical*, like its predecessor, is an enchanting read from the very first page. I absolutely loved it. Shearin weaves a web of magic with a dash of romance that thoroughly snares the reader. She's definitely an author to watch!"   —Anya Bast, national bestselling author of
Witch Heart

"Intriguing."   —*SFRevu*

continued . . .

Magic Lost, Trouble Found

Ace Books by Lisa Shearin

MAGIC LOST, TROUBLE FOUND
ARMED & MAGICAL
THE TROUBLE WITH DEMONS
BEWITCHED & BETRAYED

The Trouble with Demons

Lisa Shearin

ACE BOOKS, NEW YORK

THE BERKLEY PUBLISHING GROUP
Published by the Penguin Group
Penguin Group (USA) Inc.
375 Hudson Street, New York, New York 10014, USA
Penguin Group (Canada), 90 Eglinton Avenue East, Suite 700, Toronto, Ontario M4P 2Y3, Canada
(a division of Pearson Penguin Canada Inc.)
Penguin Books Ltd., 80 Strand, London WC2R 0RL, England
Penguin Group Ireland, 25 St. Stephen's Green, Dublin 2, Ireland (a division of Penguin Books Ltd.)
Penguin Group (Australia), 250 Camberwell Road, Camberwell, Victoria 3124, Australia
(a division of Pearson Australia Group Pty. Ltd.)
Penguin Books India Pvt. Ltd., 11 Community Centre, Panchsheel Park, New Delhi—110 017, India
Penguin Group (NZ), 67 Apollo Drive, Rosedale, North Shore 0632, New Zealand
(a division of Pearson New Zealand Ltd.)
Penguin Books (South Africa) (Pty.) Ltd., 24 Sturdee Avenue, Rosebank, Johannesburg 2196,
South Africa

Penguin Books Ltd., Registered Offices: 80 Strand, London WC2R 0RL, England

This is a work of fiction. Names, characters, places, and incidents either are the product of the author's imagination or are used fictitiously, and any resemblance to actual persons, living or dead, business establishments, events, or locales is entirely coincidental. The publisher does not have any control over and does not assume any responsibility for author or third-party websites or their content.

THE TROUBLE WITH DEMONS

An Ace Book / published by arrangement with the author

PRINTING HISTORY
Ace mass-market edition / May 2009

Copyright © 2009 by Lisa Shearin.
Map illustration by Lisa Shearin and Shari Lambert.
Cover art by Aleta Rafton.
Cover design by Judith Lagerman.
Interior text design by Kristin del Rosario.

ISBN: 978-0-441-01712-6

ACE
Ace Books are published by The Berkley Publishing Group,
a division of Penguin Group (USA) Inc.,
375 Hudson Street, New York, New York 10014.
ACE and the "A" design are trademarks of Penguin Group (USA) Inc.

PRINTED IN THE UNITED STATES OF AMERICA

10 9 8 7 6 5 4 3 2 1

As always, for Derek

Thank you for encouraging my dream, for understanding the hours I spend at the computer, and for knowing when to take me to Dairy Queen for a Blizzard. Chocolate ice cream and M&M'S make any plot snag (or author crankiness/stress) go away. You're the perfect author husband. I love you more than words can say.

Acknowledgments

To God, who makes all things possible and who made my dream come true.

To Kristin Nelson, who in my opinion is the best agent on the planet. Period. And to Nelson Literary Agency assistant Sara Megibow, who always gets me what I need even before I know I want it.

To my fabulous editor, Anne Sowards. You share my vision for Raine's stories and probably know what I'm thinking before I write it down.

To Aleta Rafton, my amazing cover artist. Thank you for bringing Raine to demon-butt-kicking life.

To Cameron Dufty, Ace editorial assistant (and in my opinion the best editorial assistant in New York), and my new Ace publicist, Rosanne Romanello. Thank you both for all of your hard work and endless energy.

To Shari Lambert, for bringing artistic flair to the map of Raine's world. I can't draw a tree or mountain to save my life.

To Todd and Elyse, my splendid webmaster and designer. Thank you for making www.lisashearin.com such a cool place to visit and hang out.

To the cherished members of my Yahoo! Group fan club— Raine's Rangers. I can always go there for support, encouragement, and a good laugh. You guys are the best. And *mucho* thanks to David, Marie, Megan, Patty, and Renee—the moderators who keep the party under control. Save me a bar stool in the tavern and pour me a pint.

To simply the best fans any author could ever hope for. Your e-mails, blog posts, cards, and endless enthusiasm keep me going. These books are for you.

Chapter 1

I knew there was evil in the world. Death and taxes were all necessary evils.

So was shopping.

"I hate shopping," I muttered.

"Of course you do," Phaelan said. "You're a Benares. We're not used to paying for anything." Phaelan was my cousin; he called himself a seafaring businessman. Law enforcement in every major port city called him "that damned pirate," or less flattering epithets, none of them repeatable here.

I really hated shopping. More to the point, I hated the aggravation of having to go into one shop after another to actually find the things I needed, things I had to have. Which was really strange considering what I did for a living.

My name is Raine Benares. I'm an elf and a seeker—and then some.

Two weeks ago, I found the Saghred—an ancient stone of cataclysmic power, an annihilator of armies, a stealer of souls, an eater of spellsingers, and the bane of my existence. The soul-sucking rock attached itself to me like a psychic leech. My magical skill level used to be marginal. Now I don't think I have any limits.

So I came to the only place with people who could possibly help me.

The Isle of Mid was home to the most prestigious college for sorcery, as well as the Conclave, the governing body for all magic users in the seven kingdoms. My new talents put me at the top of every power-hungry mage's most-wanted list. They wanted to kill me, or kidnap and use me, or keep me locked up for the rest of my life. I just wanted to get rid of the damned rock.

Since arriving on the island, I'd stepped hard on some faculty toes, assaulted the number-two mage on the island (he started it), single-handedly stormed the elven embassy, then topped it off with a walk on black magic's wild side with a sexy goblin dark mage. It was a good way to make a bad first impression.

If that wasn't enough, now I had to go shopping. I had one good set of leathers, and I was wearing them: trousers, above-the-knee boots, and my favorite doublet, all in formfitting, supple brown leather. I liked the doublet because it had steel links woven between the outer leather and inner lining. It also had leather sleeves to hide my weapons, a pair of knives in forearm sheaths I carried when I knew someone was going to jump me, but I just didn't know when, which over the past few weeks had become the story of my life.

My leathers had taken a beating since I'd arrived on Mid, and as little as I liked it, I had to replace them, hence the need to shop.

"Have you considered something in scarlet leather?" Phaelan mused from beside me.

"Have you considered just painting a bull's-eye on my back?" I retorted.

My cousin wasn't with me because he liked shopping. He was by my side because being within five feet of me was a guarantee of getting into trouble of the worst kind. Phaelan hadn't plundered or pillaged anything in weeks. He was bored. So this morning, he was a cocky, swaggering invitation for Trouble to bring it on and do her worst.

Phaelan ignored my irritation, and his grin flashed white against his tanned face. "Raine, everyone knows who you are, what you are, and where you are. It's not like you're trying to hide."

"Ma'am, there are mages on this island who could kill you without even seeing you."

That cheerful insight came from Vegard Rolfgar, Conclave Guardian, my bodyguard, and my personal shadow. He was big, blond, bearded, and human—classic Myloran sea-raider stock. The Guardians were sorcerers and warriors, and had the dubious honor of being peacekeepers on an island packed with mage bureaucrats, mage professors, and teenage mages in training—a volatile combination any way you looked at it.

"Yes, I've got a price on my head and every other body part," I said. "Do either one of you have a point?"

Phaelan's laugh was more like a bark. "Live fast, die young, and leave behind a damned fine-dressed corpse."

My cousin favored scarlet, but today he was a vision in royal blue. His trousers were leather; his doublet was suede slashed to reveal the whitest of linen shirts. High leather boots matched his belt and baldric, all of black leather, and his dark hair was tied into a short ponytail at the nape of his neck. Phaelan's favorite rapier swung comfortably at his side, with a brace of long daggers behind his back. There were plenty of other bladed weapons out of sight, but within quick reach. Our family didn't like to be caught short.

I made a show of looking him over. "Much like yourself?"

Phaelan leveled those dark eyes on me. "Cousin, you can slink around this island in black or brown, or you can show the bastards that your balls are bigger than theirs. You're the Saghred's best friend; they're scared shitless of you."

The aforementioned bastards also wanted what I had—potentially unlimited power without the insanity and death side effects that typically went with Saghred exposure and use. But just because contact with the rock hadn't turned me into a cackling loony or killed me yet didn't mean that a padded room with level twelve wards wasn't in my not-so-distant future.

I had to be careful; more than careful—vigilant. Of the Saghred, but mostly of myself. As long as I tapped its power, the rock didn't give a damn what I did with it. Even though I had done only good things for the right reasons—like refusing to stand by and let innocent people be killed—using the Saghred's power to prevent those deaths had probably brought me one step closer to crazy. Or not. Everyone else who had used the Saghred had quickly gone off the deep end. I hadn't. And no one, including me, knew why.

I wasn't sure which was more dangerous anymore, me or the rock.

"How do you think Dad and I control those mangy, homicidal maniacs we call our crews?" Phaelan was saying. "There's always one or two that step out of line. We simply turn them into a well-publicized example, and the rest behave themselves."

I just looked at him. "How about they're just mangy, *money-grubbing*, homicidal maniacs who put up with your crap to get a cut of the gold a Benares ship brings in?"

Phaelan flashed a crooked grin. "There's that, too."

At least Phaelan knew who'd be planting daggers between his shoulder blades. I had no freaking clue. Don't get me wrong; I knew the names and faces of most of the mages or bureaucrats who wanted me dead or snatched. But I also knew that they'd never dream of getting my blood on their lily-pure hands. They'd hire someone else to do it for them.

Generally the rich and powerful were tighter than a banker's fist on their purse strings, but if they wanted something done badly enough, they'd be willing to cough up the coin. They also did their homework before they hired help to ensure they'd be getting their money's worth. So chances were any assassin or kidnapper they sent after me would be pros who knew their business. Phaelan knew the cream of the crop by name and on sight. I knew a couple of them myself—some a little too well.

Phaelan had men staking out the docks who knew whom to look for, and runners who would bring news of any sightings to his flagship, the *Fortune*. So if a pro stepped off of a ship, boat, or dinghy, Phaelan and I would have his or her name within minutes, but that didn't stop the space between my shoulder blades from itching.

I had Phaelan and Vegard with me and four uniformed Guardians around them. They were close, but not too close. Other Guardians in plain clothes mingled with the crowds. Most women go shopping with their girlfriends; I go with an armed escort.

Within the hour, the armorer had taken my measurements and would be making me some leathers a woman could be proud of wearing and safe being seen in—or shot at. I'd ordered three ensembles: one in black, one in brown, and one in midnight blue. To his credit, the man didn't balk at the rush job. I knew he wanted me to be wearing his work as soon as possible. When someone finally did take a shot or stab at me, he wanted to make sure it was his leathers that saved my hide. There was nothing like a foiled hit to boost business.

Phaelan was less than thrilled with my choice of colors.

"You wear red," I told him as we left the shop. "I don't. With my red hair it'd make me look like a lit match."

Something blue darted on the edge of my vision. Several blue somethings, man-sized, about a quarter of a block ahead. A blue so bright that it gave Phaelan's doublet a run for its money.

One of them stopped and stared at me.

I stopped breathing.

The thing was standing in the middle of the street, people flowing around it as if it weren't even there.

It was blue, all right. From its clawed feet to the top of its bald and horned head. Blue.

It was also naked.

I couldn't tell if it was male or female, and I really didn't want to get close enough to find out. But it didn't appear to have anything to indicate that it was either sex. Creepy.

It grinned at me and darted down a side street.

I think my mouth fell open. "What's bright blue and buck naked?" I never took my eyes from where it'd gone.

"Hmmm, I don't know," Phaelan mused. "I haven't heard that one. Vegard?"

The big Guardian shrugged. "New joke?"

"No joke," I told them both. "You didn't see it, did you?"

At the tension in my voice, Vegard moved in front of me. Protectively. Annoyingly. Now *I* couldn't see anything. I ducked under his arm and headed for that side street. Vegard reached out to push me behind him and I ducked out of reach and ran. Phaelan and the Guardians were right on our heels.

"They were blue, naked, claw-footed, with horns on their heads," I told Vegard.

"What?" The Guardian stopped, pulling me with him. "Ma'am, are you sure you haven't been—"

I drew breath to retort, but a scream from that side street answered him better than I could.

It's been my experience that nothing clears a crowded street quicker than a scream. In this instance, I approved of crowd cowardice. Fewer people on the street meant fewer people hurt. It also meant fewer people between me and where I was determined to go. And if I had to drag a big, blond Guardian behind me, so be it.

Vegard drew a massive battle-ax from the harness on his back, the steel blade shimmering pale blue with magic.

He insisted on looking around the corner first. I let him.

He took a look and relaxed the arm holding the ax. "Ma'am, there's nothing there." He said it as if nothing was precisely what he expected to find.

I wasn't giving up. "What about the scream?"

"One scream, no victim—at least not here." Vegard turned to a pair of Guardians in plain clothes. "Erik, take Dacan and see if you can track down where—"

I stepped around Vegard to look down that street myself. "I

can't believe there's no . . ." I looked, saw, jumped back, and flattened myself against the stone wall beside Vegard.

There were nearly a dozen of us. There were more of *them*. A lot more.

"Vegard, there are definitely—"

The scream turned into a shriek, and it was coming from that street.

Phaelan had his rapier in his hand and stepped around the corner. In a split second, his face went from combative to confused. "What the hell?"

"I don't have it!" a terrified voice shrieked.

Vegard and I looked where Phaelan was looking. An elf in mage robes was rolling around in the street, cringing and trying to cover his head. Just him, no one else. Apparently that was what Phaelan and Vegard saw.

I saw a gang of blue monsters mugging a mage.

I tried to duck past Vegard. The big Guardian moved with me this time, completely blocking my way.

"But they're beating the crap out of him!" And I was tempted to beat the same thing out of Vegard.

"Who are *they*, ma'am?"

I swore. The creatures had to be using a cloaking spell of some kind. I desperately looked around for something, anything. There it was. A broken piece of cobble. Perfect. I bared my teeth in grim satisfaction, took aim, and threw that chunk of brick as hard as I could at the closest blue head.

It hit. The pain made the thing drop its cloak, and it turned, thin blue lips curling back to show me a collection of jagged, unnervingly sharp, and entirely too many teeth. One by one, the others did the same as they left the elf lying motionless in the street and turned on us.

Sometimes it was bad when a plan worked. The "I told you so" on my lips turned into the four-letter word that I rarely use.

Now Phaelan and Vegard saw what I saw.

Phaelan didn't say anything; he just blanched.

"Demons!" Vegard bellowed to his men.

The Guardians drew weapons shimmering with magic, magic that would slice through anything it touched. Vegard picked me up and forcibly put me behind him. I didn't stay there. Thanks to me, we had the undivided attention of over two dozen blue and now angry demons, so Vegard didn't have time to argue with me.

Some of the demons cloaked again.

Vegard's pale blue eyes darted. "Dammit!"

"It's a cloak," I told him.

I drew the pair of swords strapped across my back. The longer my steel, the farther away I could stay from those things. In theory.

"You can see them?" Vegard asked.

"Yeah, I'm just lucky that way." I centered my attention on the demon that had focused his yellow eyes on me. He grinned. I didn't.

I felt Vegard's power building beside me.

"Shield your eyes," he ordered.

"What are you—"

"Street dust," he said with a vicious smile. "No cloak is that solid."

I half covered my eyes, and with a simple gesture and word, Vegard kicked up a dust storm, coating the demons in dust and whatever else was in the gutters. The cloaked demons were still cloaked, but thanks to Vegard's dirt bath, everyone could see them just fine. I loved a man who could think dirty on his feet.

The demons charged. We spread out to give ourselves room to fight. I claimed a piece of street with a wall at my back. Better a wall than a demon.

"Want some company?" Phaelan's maniacal grin told me this was the most fun he'd had since last week, when he'd helped blast a hole in the elven embassy.

Phaelan wasn't the only one who wanted to keep me company. The demon who'd targeted me was closing distance fast. He didn't have a weapon. Those horns and talon-tipped hands *were* weapons. When he was within range, I opened his gut with the tip of one of my blades. I expected insides to fall out, not his hand to go into the hole I'd made, making it bigger.

Oh, that wasn't good.

The demon grinned wider and pulled out a fistful of something you'd think he'd need to keep. The stench was all too familiar.

I was almost too disgusted to move. Almost.

The demon flung it right at us.

"Incoming!" I yelled. I ducked and pulled Phaelan with me.

The glob splattered on the wall behind us, sizzling coin-sized holes in the brick. Coin-sized holes that could have been in us. The demon reached in and reloaded.

We weren't going to be here when that hand came out.

Vegard nearly sliced a demon in half with his ax. The demon healed. Immediately. One second he was almost in two parts, then he wasn't. Vegard coolly noted it and put his ax back in its harness. When he'd sheathed his weapon, his hands glowed incandescent white.

Change of tactics. One of the things the Saghred had done was to make me a fast learner when it came to magic. I didn't have to tap the stone, just use the power boost the Saghred had given the abilities I already had, letting me save my skin without risking my soul.

Phaelan was darting and weaving, trying to get in close enough to take out that demon's hands before the demon could take out more ammo.

"What the hell are you doing?" he shouted.

I kept my eyes on Vegard's glowing hands. "Learning."

It was the same concept as a lightglobe, times a thousand. Basic magic, multiplied into something lethal. I looked down at my hands and concentrated. Considering that two dozen demons had us pinned down, I did my concentrating real quick. I had almost conjured a respectable flare of light when one of the demons roared.

I damned near jumped out of my skin. "Son of a bitch!"

I tried again, this time through gritted teeth. The teeth

gritting must have helped, because in the next instant, I was lobbing fireballs along with Vegard. Mine weren't as big as his and didn't glow as bright, but they made up for it in tenacity. These weren't flames the demons could drop and roll to put out. It was sticking to them—and burning. Saghred-enhanced magic was saving my biscuits once again.

The elven mage was struggling weakly to drag himself out of the middle of the street. A demon blocked his way. He was taller than the others, his skin darker, almost purple. The mage looked up, eyes wide with panic, and said something I couldn't hear.

"Vegard, cover me!" I yelled.

I didn't wait for a response. Rage fed the fireballs in my hands until I could feel the heat. I ran toward the mage, hurling the fireballs at the demon as one clawed hand locked around the mage's throat, claws piercing his flesh, pulling him to his feet and tearing his throat out doing it. The demon simply raised his free hand, and one of my fireballs ricocheted off of it and came right back at me.

I swore and ducked. The fireball hit the wall behind me and burned straight through the brick. Seconds later, I heard flames crackling from inside. Crap.

The demon was staring at me, his eyes yellow with a vertical slit for a pupil, like a goat. But unlike any goat I'd ever seen, the demon's pupils glowed red.

A familiar fire bloomed in the center of my chest. The Saghred. I silently went through a litany of curses. I did *not* need this now. I braced myself for the surge of Saghred-spawned power that was coming. Power that would consume me, force me to fight it rather than the demon. Power that was going to get me killed just like that mage.

Nothing. No surge, no force, nothing. What the hell?

The demon smiled slowly, the tips of his needle teeth visible. I desperately called my magic for another fireball. Not a spark. All the fire I had seethed in my chest. It wasn't white-hot and raging; the stone's power wasn't fighting to get free. It burned bright, warm, welcoming.

For the demon.

The demon looked at me, unclenched his hand, and negligently tossed the dead mage aside. Then he stepped back and bowed deeply and respectfully.

"We are honored by your presence," he told me.

Then he cloaked, invisible to all but me, and with one leap was on the wall like a big purple spider, the talons of his claws and feet clicking and gouging chunks out of the bricks as he scuttled around the corner, right over the clueless heads of a crowd that was forming at the end of the street.

I knelt over the mage. His dead eyes stared sightlessly at the sky as blood pooled and spread beneath his ruined throat.

I heard murmurs from the far end of the street. Most of the people had just arrived, waiting until the fight was over to come out of hiding.

I was kneeling over the mage, his blood on my hands. They were looking at me, grim-faced, angry, and accusing.

"Murderer!" someone yelled.

Oh shit.

Chapter 2

Running sounded like a real good idea. As a Benares, I'd been taught that there's no shame in running, only in being caught.

I ran, but not to get away from the mob. I ran to catch a murdering bastard demon. I didn't know if it was what they thought they'd seen me do, or the fact that I was running straight at them, but the mob who'd just called me a murderer got out of my way. Vegard shouted for me to stop. I ignored him and kept going; he'd catch up. He always did. Phaelan was already beside me. What I was after didn't make any difference to my cousin; I'd found trouble and he wasn't about to miss a second of it. When all this was over, I needed to have a long talk with Phaelan about his mental stability.

While I was at it, I might want to check into my own. Tall, naked, and purple wasn't trying to get away from me; he wanted me to follow him, and I was obliging him. That wasn't healthy, mentally or otherwise. But I didn't have any choice. He was back on the street, running through innocent bystanders and heading toward campus. There were hundreds of young magic users there; some knew how to defend themselves, but most hadn't learned yet. I had to take him down before he got there. Problem was, I had no freaking clue how.

The demon knocked people aside and slashed others with his claws. I didn't even need to keep the demon in sight; I only had to follow the grisly trail of fallen and bleeding people.

"What are we chasing?" Phaelan panted. He'd sheathed his rapier. Smart man. Crazy, but smart. The street was too crowded, and he didn't have a target. I did.

I dragged some air into my overworked lungs. "Purple demon," I rasped.

"You can see him?"

"Yes!"

"You sure?"

I had plenty of responses to that, but didn't have time or the breath for any of them. If we survived, I could always smack Phaelan later.

What I thought were ridges on the demon's back unfolded into a pair of batlike wings, and the thing went airborne above the people crowding the narrow street. I swore, and ran faster.

I caught sight of him again where the maze of buildings emptied into an enormous city square bordered with coffee-houses, pubs, bookstores—places students liked to go between classes. The kids called it the Quad. If the demon wanted victims or hostages, he'd just found hundreds to choose from.

It was a sunny day, midmorning, and the beginning of the semester. The Quad wasn't just full; it was packed. Hovering above it all, his leathery wings keeping him about ten feet over the unsuspecting students' heads, was my quarry. The kids felt the whooshes of air from his wingbeats and looked up and around in confusion. They had no clue what was right over their heads and I didn't want them to know. With knowledge would come fear, and with fear could come a stampede. That did not need to happen.

The demon looked at me and grinned, exposing a mouthful of needle-fine teeth, and gestured with spidery fingers at the bounty spread below him. His for the taking, and the bastard wanted me to know it.

Unless I stopped him.

So that was it. He wasn't trying to get away; he wasn't even trying to snatch a student for a snack. Though he wouldn't mind taking one with him for later. He wanted me to fight him, and he wanted me to use the Saghred to do it.

No way, no time, no how. And especially not here. I didn't believe in collateral damage.

The demon knew. He shrugged elaborately, his lips split into a feral grin, and he dove into a group of students.

I screamed the word I rarely used except in cases of extreme rage and near-death experiences. That word and the half a dozen armed Guardians who'd caught up with me made the kids around us scatter in a panic.

The demon was snatching up students, taking them about a dozen feet into the air and dropping them on the crowd below. The kids couldn't see him, but they knew their classmates weren't jumping and falling by themselves. Some of the ones he dropped landed on other students, knocking them to the ground; others he dropped landed unmoving on the cobblestones. All of them were in danger of being crushed underfoot if the students stampeded.

I felt Vegard and his boys pulling together some serious kick-ass magic behind me. It got the demon's attention, as he dangled a young student by the scruff of the neck. A pretty, dark-haired human girl. I recognized her. Katelyn Valerian, the archmagus's granddaughter.

The demon looked at me.

And then he roared and materialized in all his demonic glory in the middle of the Quad.

The students' screams were deafening as they panicked and ran—or tried to. There were too many of them and too little open space. I didn't blame them for running, but I also didn't want to be trampled. I wanted that demon.

Someone beat me to it—and that someone wasn't Vegard.

I knew that voice.

A rich baritone of staggering strength and power pierced the chaos, his spellsong dark and discordant, the notes booming and harsh. A long-fingered hand extended above the crowd toward the demon, fingers spread, helping him focus his spell-song.

Piaras Rivalin.

Oh no.

Piaras had just turned eighteen, but the young elf had the pipes and talent of a spellsinging master. Youth and lethal skill were a dangerous combination. Piaras's voice was a weapon; he was in college to learn how to control it. Last week he'd inadvertently knocked out half the Guardians in the citadel. Right now, the kid had that demon—a demon that had his girlfriend's life clutched in his claws—tacked to a piece of sky like a bug pinned to a board.

The demon snarled and tried to break free, but Piaras held firm. He'd reacted instinctively without realizing what he had bitten off. He knew now. His normally pale face was strained with effort, his lean chest rapidly rising and falling, struggling to keep air in his lungs to keep that spellsong going. He spotted me, his large brown eyes relieved and imploring at the same time. Poor kid had never seen a demon before. Now he'd caught one and had no idea what to do with it.

That made two of us.

I didn't know what I could do to help, but I wasn't going to let him down. I'd think of something.

The students who had been sitting at the café table with Piaras had knocked over their chairs and scrambled out of the line of fire should that demon be able to strike back. All of them ran except for one young goblin student—Talon Nathrach. Piaras's friend. The son of a more-than-good friend of mine, Tamnais Nathrach.

Piaras's expression turned from fear to fierce determination; the demon's sharp features contorted with raw hatred. If Piaras's spellsong faltered, that demon would fry him where he stood—or rip his throat out like that elven mage.

No way in hell or anywhere else.

Vegard swore and kept his fireball in readiness, but didn't launch it. I knew why. Interrupting another magic user's spell with one of your own was potentially deadly for anyone in the general vicinity—especially the spellcaster. Piaras was in enough danger without me or Vegard making it worse.

Piaras's song held the demon immobile, but the thing was strong enough to snarl and tighten his grip on the back of the Katelyn's neck, puncturing the girl's skin with his claws. Katelyn screamed. Piaras snarled and redoubled his attack.

Talon hissed a low countermelody in Goblin to run under Piaras's spellsong, merging seamlessly into his spell. The unwholesomely handsome goblin was a spellsinger and dancer at Sirens, his father's nightclub. I had thought his songs were limited to making the clientele horny. Apparently I was wrong. Piaras's spell held the demon; Talon's spellsong told the demon in no uncertain terms what was going to happen to him unless he let Katelyn go.

Piaras and Talon were both scared to death, but they were doing what needed to be done, and damned if they weren't doing a fine job. I'd worry about how they were doing it later. But they couldn't keep it up for much longer.

Vegard extinguished the fireball and carefully stepped into the area beneath the demon and the dangling girl.

Phaelan swore under his breath.

"Miss Valerian," Vegard said, "I'll catch you; you're going to be fine. Just try to relax."

"Good luck with that," Phaelan muttered.

I elbowed him in the ribs.

The big Guardian's voice was calm and commanding, but most important, he pitched his voice low, carefully avoiding vocal conflict with Piaras and Talon's work.

I stood there feeling worthless, desperately trying to come up with a way to help without making matters fatally worse.

With visible effort, the demon unclenched his fingers, letting Katelyn fall into Vegard's waiting arms. Vegard pushed her in the direction of a coffeehouse. The demon's thin lips stretched in a mockery of a smile. He had wanted to be rid of her; now he could focus all of his attention on Piaras and Talon.

Steel weapons wouldn't work and neither would fireballs. Dammit. Those kids couldn't hold him all day.

"Can the boys let him go and dive for cover?" I asked.

"He'd roast them before they could blink," Vegard said. "We need a demon trap."

"So get one!"

"I've sent Dacan, but he won't be back in time."

A voice brushed against my mind, its familiar intimacy like a caress of dark silk against bare skin. I didn't need to see him; I knew who he was.

Tamnais Nathrach. Goblin dark mage, former chief shaman for the royal House of Mal'Salin, ex–magical enforcer to the goblin queen—but right now, Tam was a really pissed-off father whose son was in mortal danger.

"Get behind the demon where he can't see you!" Tam commanded. *"Quickly! He can't turn while the boys still have him."*

Tam and I had spoken mind-to-mind many times, but never like this. Never this close. Tam wasn't just speaking to me; Tam was *inside* of me.

"How . . . What the hell are you—" I blurted out loud.

"Just do it, Raine!"

Vegard glanced sharply at me.

"It's Tam," I told him.

We had a demon on a rampage; Tam was a dark mage. It was clearly a match made in hell. I didn't know what he could do to help; but whatever it was, I was all for it.

"Tell Talon to stop," Tam ordered. *"Then you can take the demon from Piaras."*

"I can *what*?"

"I've fought demons before." His words came in a rush. *"I can work through you; tell you what you need to do."* Silence. *"Raine, my power is your power."*

I froze, thoughts running in panicked circles in my head. I knew what Tam was saying, but worse yet, I knew what he meant.

Last week, when I'd used the Saghred to keep innocent people from being slaughtered, Tam and his potent black magic had been right there with me. We'd worked together, combining our power, doing what had to be done. That had earned us both a lot of unwanted attention and accusations. That six lives had been saved didn't mean a rat's ass to our high-ranking accusers.

"Raine!"

"I'm here," I snarled. My breathing was shallow and rapid. What I was about to do through Tam—with Tam—scared me more than the demon did. I didn't like being scared; it pissed me off. Tam was asking me to unleash some demon whoop-ass, and I had no idea how.

Piaras was weakening; the intensity of his notes wavered. The demon howled in gleeful anticipation.

"Tell me. Now!"

Tam did, and I understood. I didn't have the skill or experience to do it, but Tam did. He told me what to do, and if I used his power, I could.

In theory. I hated theories.

"Find a mirror, thick glass, something you can force him inside of," Tam ordered.

Mirrors were too dangerous to keep out in the open, but several of the shops had glass in their windows, diamond panes. I didn't need Tam to tell me that wouldn't work. Then I saw them. Some of the kids had gotten an early start on their drinking. They'd run, but they'd left two bottles of wine behind. Two empty bottles—with corks. Let's hear it for partying college students.

"Would a bottle work?" I quickly asked Tam.

Silence and some fast thinking. *"Yes. Is there a stopper of some kind?"*

"Cork."

"Get it."

I snatched a bottle and cork off the table. The demon saw and laughed, a deep rumbling that vibrated through my chest all the way down to my toes.

"You are no demon master." He smiled, slow and horrible, and held out a clawed hand. "Come to me, elfling, and I will let the young ones live."

"Shove him in!" Tam growled.

"And just how the hell am I—"

"Visualize him flowing into the neck of that bottle and it will happen."

I froze. "Do I have to hold the bottle?"

"Yes!"

Dammit.

"Tell the boys to release him." Then Tam's voice turned imploring; Tam didn't implore anyone. *"Raine, I will help you. You can do this. We can do this."*

I felt as if I were about to step off a cliff. I swallowed. "Talon, stop." I tried to keep my voice calm and rational. "Ease your song away from Piaras and run."

The kid looked at me as though I had lost my mind.

I wasn't entirely sure I hadn't.

"Trust me."

Talon hesitated, then carefully did as I said. He'd seen me in magical action before.

"Let him go," I told Piaras. "I've got him."

Piaras couldn't believe what I was telling him to do. His song faltered and the demon thrashed and lunged. I swore. He thought I was going to use the Saghred. The kid was going to hold that demon and get himself killed to protect me from that damned rock.

"Let him go!" I screamed.

Piaras did and dove behind some overturned tables.

Free of all constraints, the demon roared in triumph and turned on me.

I had the bottle and cork in one hand, and Tam's power coiled inside me ready to strike.

We were ready for the son of a bitch.

I thrust my empty hand toward the demon, fingers spread, much like Piaras had done. Piaras had only focused a spellsong; I was focusing Tam. My arm shook with the effort and my shoulder was on fire. Tam's power exploded through my body, my own surging upward to meld with it. Tam's dark magic rushed up from the deep, primal core of him. My own magic coiled and flared through my body, seeking and triumphantly finding the source of Tam's power. It was like a well, dark and deep. I dove in headfirst.

The demon's roar turned to a scream of rage and disbelief, and finally to a thin shriek as Tam's magic shoved him face-first into the bottle with enough force to knock me on my ass. I shoved the cork in and grabbed the bottle in a two-handed death grip, holding it as far away from me as possible. Purple mist writhed inside.

I really wanted longer arms.

Chaos surrounded me. Vegard was barking orders, and Guardians were running out of the Quad to carry them out. Meanwhile, more Guardians were arriving, and so were officers of the city watch. From Vegard's expression and all the armed men shouting and running around, you'd think we were under attack. And here I was sitting on my ass holding a demon in a bottle. I got to my feet. My knees were a little shaky, but I made it.

"I've got him!" I yelled to Vegard over the din. "What's the problem?"

"You have *one*, ma'am. There'll be more just like him."

I gripped the bottle tighter. "More?"

"It's a Volghul, Raine," said Tam's voice in my head, as if that explained everything. It didn't. Tam sounded as though he was running. I don't know how I could tell, but I could.

"What the hell's a Volghul?" I asked Tam, Vegard, or whoever could tell me what was going on. And why were Guardians in full battle armor running into the Quad?

"There will be more of everything," Vegard told me.

I was incredulous. "Some lunatic is summoning these things?"

"*Volghuls aren't summoned,*" Tam said. "*They cross over by themselves. Vegard knows this.*"

"Cross over?"

"*Through a Hellgate.*"

I stopped breathing for a few seconds. "You mean a gate to Hell? Literally?"

"*If by Hell you mean the dimension in which demons reside, then yes, I mean a gate to Hell. Volghuls are advance guards.*"

I froze. "Guards in advance of what?"

Vegard and Tam answered me at the same time. "A legion of demons."

Chapter 3

We were in the headquarters of the Isle of Mid's city watch. Bars on the windows, bars on the cells, and wards just about everywhere. Most people would feel safe, but I wasn't most people. One, I was a Benares, and we didn't feel safe anywhere there were bars, unless it had bar stools and a lot of rum, which I could use a shot or two of right now. Two, according to Vegard, things were on their way here that iron bars and wards couldn't hold, at least not for very long. Every Guardian and watcher was now on full alert. Anyone on leave was being recalled, and a day off had just turned into on duty. The demonology department faculty was aware of the situation and was taking steps. I hoped they were big ones.

I hadn't seen any demons on the way here. Aside from a lot of heavily armed men, daily life and classes seemed to be business as usual. Word had to be getting around about the demon in the Quad, but as of yet, there was no terror in the streets. Then again, on an island full of magic users, seeing a demon might not be all that unusual. If we were lucky, people thought that a demonology grad student's class project had escaped or something. The last thing the authorities on Mid needed right now were panicked citizens.

The possibility of an impending demon invasion did deflect some uncomfortable questions. Vegard told the chief watcher that I didn't murder that elven mage. It was Vegard's word and the word of his Guardians versus the groundless accusations of citizens with an overdeveloped mob mentality. My accusers had come out of hiding only after the fight was over; what they had seen was me confirming that the dead elven mage was indeed dead. It wasn't my fault they mistook confirmation for carnage.

My being wrongly accused of murder wasn't anyone's biggest concern right now, and fortunately, neither was the other thing that I'd done.

I'd just taken out a demon in front of hundreds of people using a magical skill that obviously wasn't mine. My enemies would think I'd used the Saghred. Actually, having them think that was better than what I'd really done. I was linked in some way with a goblin dark mage. To certain powerful and influential people on Mid, that was an even worse offense. It wouldn't matter to them that I'd saved student lives. I'd be declared elven public enemy number one within the hour, if not sooner.

The purple demon was imprisoned in the wine bottle like an evil genie. The bottle was sitting in the middle of the floor in a jail cell so heavily warded it crackled. I wholeheartedly approved of the city watch's security precautions; I didn't think they were in the least bit excessive. I just hoped they held.

And I thought shopping and an attempt on my life would be the worst that could happen to me today. Though I shouldn't complain, I wasn't the one who'd had my throat ripped out. That dead mage was downstairs on a slab in the morgue. Some of the students were in the infirmary—a few had broken bones, but none had been killed. Katelyn Valerian was one of those in the infirmary. Considering that a demon had her neck in his claws, she was doing surprisingly well, though we'd almost had to drag Piaras from her side to come here.

We were sitting outside the corner office of Chief Watcher Sedge Rinker. Piaras sat on one side of me, Talon on the other.

The room was one big office area filled with the usual: desks, chairs, file cabinets, watchers, accused perpetrators, and plenty of noise. Cells lined one wall. Some had bars, some had wards, and some had both. If the city watch had gone to the trouble to apprehend someone on an island full of magic users, I guess they wanted to make sure they stayed put. One cell held a couple of students who looked as if they'd done something last night that'd sounded like a good idea after a few rounds. A few hours behind bars and killer hangovers were giving them second thoughts. The Guardians had captured four of the blue demons that had attacked that mage and then us. They were in a warded cell. The wards were thick, but not thick enough for me. The demons hadn't taken their beady, yellow eyes off of the three of us since we'd arrived. With Piaras and Talon, I couldn't tell what their interest was, but having demons interested in the boys was bad enough. I didn't know anything about demonic facial expressions, but from what I could see, I think they were either afraid or in awe of me. I'd take either one, even though I knew it wasn't me they were terrified or intimidated by. When I'd taken on their purple leader, they'd gotten a good whiff of the Saghred. I didn't blame them one bit for being afraid—that damned rock scared me, too. But what Tam and I had done had scared me more.

I glanced at Piaras. Being escorted to headquarters by watchers and Guardians was yet another first for Piaras that was a direct result of knowing me. Most of the trouble I'd gotten into, Piaras had been sucked into right along with me.

Phaelan was still in Sedge Rinker's office with Vegard. I had given my statement, then the boys had come in and told Sedge their part of the story. While they did, I'd stayed with them. For all intents and purposes, I was the closest thing Piaras had to family on the island. He was the grandson of my landlady back in Mermeia. I had lived in the apartment above her apothecary shop. Piaras was like the little brother I never had. And since Tam was the closest thing I had to a man in my life, I felt compelled to keep an eye out for Talon's rights, too.

Not that Sedge Rinker was going to violate anyone's rights. Sedge wasn't just Mid's chief watcher; he was also good people. He didn't get to be chief by sitting behind a desk all day. He was a consummate professional, knew his business, and cared about the safety of his citizens. Sedge did tell me that before the elven mage's fatal run-in with the demons, he had been the chairman of the college's demonology department. I hoped one of those steps the department faculty was taking right now was finding themselves a leader who stood a better chance of survival than their recently deceased predecessor.

I sighed and slouched in my chair, crossing my legs at the ankles. I think even my bones were tired.

I glanced sidelong at Piaras. He'd been running a nervous hand through his dark curls, making them even more tousled than normal. Though if he stayed around me for much longer, he'd probably get some white hairs to go with the dark. Piaras was tall and lanky, and he didn't quite know what to do with his height, so he had a tendency to slouch, which was about the only comfortable position in these torture devices that passed for chairs. I guess watchers didn't care if accused criminals were comfortable or not.

"Sorry, sweetie," I told him.

Piaras still looked straight ahead, but one corner of his lips curled upward, trying for a smile. "We're making this a habit, aren't we?"

He tried to sound casual, but I wasn't buying. The kid had a death grip on the arms of the wooden chair he was sitting in. I didn't think he even realized it. Probably his first time in a watcher station, along with being his first time latching on to a demon.

"No, *I'm* making this a habit," I told him. "*You* just keep coming along for the ride."

His lips twitched again and his grip lightened. A little. "You'd think I'd know better by now."

"Hey, at least this time we weren't kidnapped, tied up, and

blindfolded. The watchers asked us nicely and there were no handcuffs involved. *And* we're not in a cell."

Piaras almost grinned. "That is an improvement, isn't it?"

"Damn right, it is."

"So, how many times have you been arrested?" Talon piped up, his aqua eyes sparkling.

We both just looked at him. Piaras was normally the nonviolent sort, but was clearly entertaining thoughts about his new friend and spellsinging classmate.

"I've never been arrested," I told him. I didn't mention that the Benares family had the best lawyers in the seven kingdoms on retainer. That little benefit alone had kept my bacon out of the clink at least twice. Not that I had been guilty of anything; well, not exactly, but other people had thought otherwise. Kind of like today, my inner pessimist reminded me.

I told my inner pessimist to shut up. "You're looking quite at home here," I told Talon.

The goblin shrugged. "I've had a few unfortunate misunderstandings with watchers in my time."

Considering that Talon's time only amounted to about nineteen years, those must have been some misunderstandings. He was slender and sleekly muscled with waist-length black hair. His silvery gray skin was lighter than normal for a pure-blooded goblin, which Talon most definitely was not. His aquamarine eyes were from his mother, an elf. Tam liked elves, Tam liked me, and Talon was the living proof that I wasn't the only elf who Tam had liked.

When the boys had given their statements, Sedge had asked them the usual questions, but not the one I expected him to. I was glad he didn't, though my inner pessimist wondered why he hadn't. I wondered, too, but I wasn't about to turn down what could amount to a gift on a silver platter.

Piaras and Talon had taken on a demon that a troop of Guardians couldn't stop, and I had only been able to bottle him with Tam's help—a dark mage, highly trained in black magic. Piaras and Talon were too young to be highly trained in anything, yet they'd held that demon until Tam and I could take control of it. What they had was natural talent: raw, powerful, and dangerous. That kind of talent also got you noticed by people you didn't want to have notice you.

"The two of you worked well together," I said quietly. Piaras and I weren't the only elves in the room. Some of the watchers were, too. Elven ears did more than just look good.

Talon shrugged. Piaras didn't say a word.

"You've been reading new spellsongs again, haven't you?" I asked Piaras.

His hesitation told me everything I needed to know.

"A few," he admitted.

I swore silently.

Piaras wanted to be a Guardian more than anything and was studying with Maestro Ronan Cayle, a legend among spellsinging masters. When Tam and I had joined forces to save those six lives last week, Piaras had destroyed some nasty magical beasties before they could destroy us. He'd used a spellsong that was damned near suicidal for someone of his age and inexperience to attempt. He'd seen it once in a spellsong book, read it, and had instantly memorized it. He'd gambled and won—that time. Today he'd gambled again, and if Tam and I hadn't been able to take that demon from him, this time he would have lost.

I took a breath and silently counted backward from ten. It took all the way to one before I could trust myself to talk without yelling. "That was quite a risk the two of you took." My voice came out amazingly calm. If I hadn't been so tired, I would have been impressed.

I saw Piaras's jaw clench under a faint shadow of stubble. Jeez, the kid had stubble; when had that happened?

"Would you have had us do nothing?" His voice was tight.

"No, I would not have had you do nothing." I took another breath and let it out slowly. I'd better say what I needed to say quickly, because calm and I were about to part ways. "That's not what I mean—at least not entirely. You acted when no one else would and stood your ground when everyone ran. Both of you were very brave." I paused and resisted the urge to grit my teeth. "You also had no idea what you were latching on to, but you grabbed it anyway, and neither one of you were trained to handle it."

Piaras drew breath to retort, and I quickly held up my hand. "I'm not saying what you did was wrong. You have the skill, but not the experience. It would—"

Talon interrupted. "It would have been better if we'd just sat there, while that thing mauled its way around the Quad?"

I turned on him. My calm was officially gone. I held my thumb and forefinger a hairbreadth apart in front of Talon's face. "The two of you came this close to getting torn to shreds! Your father just found you, and he doesn't want to lose you. Do you have any idea what he has been through to protect you since you got here?"

The normally cocky Talon looked taken aback. You'd think I'd slapped him. A couple of the watchers were suddenly interested in our conversation. I glared at them until they found something else to do.

"No." Talon's voice was subdued, but only slightly. Teenage defiance still seethed beneath the surface. "He didn't tell me."

I leaned back in my chair, blew out my breath, and closed my eyes. "And he probably won't." Tired had surrendered to exhausted. "He wouldn't want you to worry. Because he loves you."

When Talon didn't respond, I opened one eye and looked at him. "He hasn't told you that, either, has he?" I asked wearily.

"Not exactly."

My elbow was resting on the chair arm, and I dropped my head onto my upraised hand. I snorted. "Not exactly." I shook my head. "Men." I didn't lift my head off my hand; it felt too good to be resting on something. I turned it about an inch and I could see Piaras just fine.

His face was a shade or two short of a full, blazing blush. "I know you do." His words tumbled out in a rush. "You don't have to tell me."

I grinned slowly. "What? You don't want me saying the 'L' word in public?"

"I'd rather you didn't." He looked around uncomfortably. "At least not here."

I sat back and crossed my arms. "Okay then, I'll make you a deal. You tell me where and how you picked up what you did in the Quad, and I won't yell 'I love you!' and plant a big, wet, sloppy kiss on your forehead in front of half the watchers on Mid."

"I told you; I read it in a spellsong book."

"Does Ronan Cayle know about your extracurricular reading?"

Piaras hesitated, then in the span of two seconds, he winced, grimaced, and looked queasy, as though what he was about to tell me was the last thing he wanted to say.

"Yes, he does. It was part of a lesson."

I blinked. "What?" My voice was quiet, the kind of quiet that said Ronan better be glad he wasn't in the room with me right now.

Piaras turned to face me and lowered his voice to a bare whisper. "Raine, I may be the age of a first-year student, but I've long known what they're just now learning. Maestro Cayle did some testing with me to determine what level of study I should start at—"

Now I was the one who felt queasy. "And what I saw today was it."

Piaras nodded. "I've been working on a confinement spellsong for the past two days in class. One of the things it works on is demons."

"And after only two lessons you used it today."

"When I saw that thing fly into the Quad, I had to do something."

I froze. "Wait, you *saw* it fly in? It didn't materialize until it snatched up Katelyn."

Piaras's brow furrowed in confusion. "I could see it." He leaned forward and looked around me at Talon. "Could you see it?"

"I heard it." The goblin wrinkled his nose. "I sure as hell

could smell it. But no, until it popped up over our heads, I couldn't see it."

"Vegard couldn't even see it," I told Piaras. "And I could only see it because . . ." I didn't want to finish that sentence, at least not out loud. I didn't know it for sure, but I strongly suspected that my demon-sighting ability was the Saghred's doing. I had a link with the Saghred; Piaras didn't. So what did Piaras have that a senior Guardian, a highly trained, elite magical warrior, didn't?

Piaras turned his face toward me and away from the squad room. "You think you could see it because of the you-know-what?" His voice was barely audible.

"I suspect so, yes," I told him. "And you seeing it is probably just another talent you didn't know you had." I didn't believe it for a second, but I didn't want Piaras thinking otherwise.

And speaking of manifesting new talents, there was the not-so-small matter of Talon needing to come clean with his father.

"Does Tam know you can do what you did?"

Talon winced. "I think he's starting to suspect there's more to me than meets the eye. Are you going to tell him what happened?"

"No, I'm not. Unless you don't do it first."

"But—"

"Talon, there were witnesses," I told him point-blank. "Hundreds of them. Tam will find out, if he hasn't already."

Talon was a half-breed, and that was reason enough for the old blood of both races to despise who he was, what he was, and the very fact that he existed. The kind of power he'd thrown around today wasn't about to change anyone's mind. Talon was probably in more danger than he'd ever been in his young life—and the kid didn't have a clue. He had to know there'd be rumblings, but not that some of the Conclave would be calling for his blood—and his head. Especially considering who and what his father was.

Talon thunked his head against the back of his chair and hissed a chain of obscenities in Goblin. I had to admit, if you needed to do any quality swearing, Goblin was the language to use.

Then Talon turned on the charm and grinned slyly, fangs peeking into view. "You of all people should know what a burden it is to be gorgeous *and* a magical prodigy. People just don't understand."

"You didn't answer my question," I said blandly. "Are you going to tell Tam?"

The kid's grin widened. "I'll tell him if you'll give me that big, wet, sloppy kiss."

"No kiss, and you'll tell him anyway."

His aqua eyes glittered devilishly. Damn, but he looked like Tam.

"You're no fun," he told me.

"Yeah, kid, that's the burden *I* carry."

Phaelan came out of Sedge Rinker's office then and slouched in a chair next to Piaras. His body language said he was calm and confident. The twitch in his left eyelid said otherwise. My cousin, the scourge of the seas of seven kingdoms, was in the same room with at least fifty sworn officers of the law. It didn't matter that he hadn't broken any laws today (at least not that I knew of). When your daily life was steeped in as much criminal activity as Phaelan's was, there was always someone somewhere who wanted your neck in a noose for something. His eyes flicked to a bulletin board covered with wanted posters. He mouthed an obscenity and quickly looked away.

I looked at the board. Yep, one of them was Phaelan. I'd seen a lot of wanted posters of my cousin. Unlike most of them, this one actually bore a resemblance. Kind of.

I chuckled, as did Piaras.

"Shut up!" Phaelan's teeth were clenched, his lips didn't move, and words still came out. Impressive.

My chuckle turned into a snort. "Sorry."

"No, you're not."

"You're right. I'm not. But you should be."

"Hey, I'm just a man making a living."

Talon leaned forward and squinted at the poster, then

grinned until his fangs showed. "I don't think that's what it says."

"Quit staring at it!"

"I'm not staring at it. Don't worry; it's not that good a likeness."

I felt someone staring at me then. I didn't need to look; I knew who it had to be.

Paladin Mychael Eiliesor, the commander of the Conclave Guardians, was standing across the room, his eyes on me, his face a calm, professional mask. I knew better. When Mychael didn't show emotion, it meant he was experiencing some strong ones. I'd felt them the moment he'd walked through that door. Or more to the point, I'd felt him. Mychael was a master spell-singer and healer, but first and foremost, he was a warrior. The aura of danger and controlled power surrounding him had nothing to do with healing and everything to do with his lethal skill in battlefield magic. The air around him virtually crackled with it, and I knew what stirred the hair on the nape of my neck was just the leftovers. I'd be willing to bet that demons had crossed Mychael's path on the way here, and they probably weren't alive anymore to regret it.

I'd been expecting him. From a law-enforcement standpoint, Mychael had ultimate control over the Isle of Mid and everyone on it. As paladin, protecting the Saghred was his responsibility—and since the Saghred and I were a package deal, all that protecting extended to me.

The noise level in the squad room abruptly decreased, and it wasn't because Mychael had walked through those doors. As paladin, he'd been here many times. I hadn't. The watchers shut up because they wanted to hear what happened next.

I didn't.

I stayed right where I was. Mychael cut through the squad room with long strides to where we sat, a man on a mission. I was that mission.

Talon swore again; Piaras made his own contribution, and Phaelan nonchalantly sat up straighter.

"Think we should make a run for it?" my cousin asked.

"I think that'd be a bad idea."

He shrugged and sat back. "Had to ask."

When Mychael was within ten feet of me, I stood up. Call it a primitive dominance response. I was a head shorter than Mychael, but I wasn't about to keep my butt in a chair while he loomed over me.

Close up gave me a nice view of Mychael, and as always, he was damned good to look at. His eyes were that mix of blue and pale green found only in warm, tropical seas. His hair was short and auburn. His handsome features were strong, and his face scruffy with stubble. Very nice. Sexy nice. I guess having demons on your island didn't give you time to shave. Mychael was an elf, and the tips of his ears were elegantly pointed. I'd felt the urge to nibble those tips on more than one occasion, but I didn't think now was the time or place.

"We need to talk," he told me. It was his paladin's voice. His words weren't a direct order, but he wasn't giving me a choice, either.

"Hello, Mychael. We're all fine. No demon damage. Thank you for asking."

He just looked at me. "We need to talk." He glanced over my left shoulder. "Sedge, may we use your conference room?"

"Of course." The chief's basso rumble came from his office doorway. "I'll see to it that you're not disturbed."

Mychael almost smiled. "I appreciate that, but I brought my own lookouts." He glanced down at Piaras and Talon. "And men to escort the two of you out of here and back home right now."

I tensed. "Now?"

"Now. They need to leave."

Sedge Rinker stepped forward, his lips a grim, narrow line. "Anyone in particular I should be looking out for here?"

"You'll know him when you see him."

"You mean *if* I see him?"

"No, *when*."

Sedge took a breath and let it out with a quiet "damn."

Mychael nodded grimly. "Exactly."

Chapter 4

Mychael and I were inside the conference room; four Guardians were outside the conference room. Piaras was being taken under Guardian protection back to the safety of the *Fortune*. Talon was being escorted back to Sirens, Tam's nightclub. The conference room door was closed. So it was just me, Mychael, and enough tension and sizzling magical leftovers to fill the rest of the room. Cozy.

Like an increasing number of his men, Mychael was wearing full battle armor. For Guardians, that didn't mean clunky, shiny plate mail. Mychael's armor was steel and then some, and sleek was the best way to describe it. Matte finish, dark gray, and custom fit—Mychael's armor conformed to his leanly muscled body almost like a second skin. No armorer was that good; there had to have been magic involved when it was forged.

I made myself stop staring at Mychael's conformities and helped myself to a chair. "The reason you're rushing those boys out of here wouldn't happen to be named Carnades Silvanus?"

"It would."

"Shit," I spat.

Mychael nodded. "That's why I made sure I got here before he did."

"You know for a fact he's coming?"

"Without a doubt. And Piaras and Talon not being here will cause two less complications."

I raised an eyebrow. "So that's what you're calling me now? A complication."

Mychael pulled up a chair and sat facing me, mere inches separating us. He almost smiled. "You don't think it fits?"

"Oh, it fits. I just think you could've done better. Carnades has got some downright colorful names for me."

"Carnades has more time to think than I do."

"And plot," I reminded him. "Don't forget the plotting and scheming."

Carnades Silvanus was second only to the archmagus in terms of position on the Conclave's Seat of Twelve. The archmagus had the top spot and absolute authority over the Isle of Mid and everyone on it. Last week, Archmagus Justinius Valerian had nearly been assassinated. Until the old man recovered, Carnades had gone from second in command to sitting in the big chair, and he was determined to turn his temporary promotion into his permanent job.

When Mychael didn't respond, I thought I'd just cut to the chase. I had a knot in my stomach, but I went for casual and leaned back in the chair, tipping the front legs off of the floor. "Since I was there, I know what happened. I won't even pretend to understand any of it, but—"

"More demons have been spotted across the city," Mychael said quietly.

I swore. "Blue and naked?"

"The very same."

"Any more purple ones?"

"No Volghuls—not yet." His tone indicated that he didn't expect that good fortune to last for long. His lips curved up in a tired grin. "I hear you made quite an impression in the Quad."

I snorted. "At what? Finding a wine bottle?"

Mychael's blue eyes gleamed. "Vegard came right out and called you magnificent; he said you didn't give one inch of ground to that monster."

"I didn't know it was an advance guard to a freaking horde of demons."

He chuckled. "It wouldn't have made a bit of difference. If you'd known, you wouldn't have budged out of sheer stubbornness." In a blink of an eye, his good humor was gone. "There have been five Dagik sightings in the past two hours."

"Dagik?"

"A species of demon. The blue ones," he clarified.

"Oh. There's probably more than five; they're cloaking. We had over two dozen in that street with us, and they were cloaked until I hit one of them in the head with a brick."

I got the treat of seeing Mychael momentarily speechless. "You hit a Dagik in the head with a brick?"

"It wasn't an entire brick, just a chunk. And it wasn't like I had a choice. I couldn't get Vegard or Phaelan to believe I saw anything, so I figured pain would make the thing drop its cloak." I tried a grin, though I didn't find anything funny about what had happened in that street. "Turns out I was right. Then Vegard gave the rest of them a dirt bath. Then everyone could see them."

The corner of Mychael's mouth quirked in a quick smile. "So I heard. Vegard is a very resourceful man." The smile vanished. "Do you know why you were the only one who could see them?"

"The way my luck's been running, it's probably a Saghred thing." I paused. "Did Vegard tell you what Piaras and Talon did?"

"He mentioned it."

I proceeded to do more than mention it. I told Mychael what they'd done, what Ronan Cayle had deemed Piaras qualified to handle, and exactly how I felt about all of it.

"Ronan came and spoke to me before he started those lessons," Mychael told me. "He told me the results of his testing. He was right to start Piaras where he did."

"He could have been killed—or worse."

"Raine, Piaras wants to be a Guardian. There will always be risks, and some of the biggest risks can come during training. Every precaution is taken to protect—"

"But accidents happen," I snapped.

"Yes."

"And inexperienced kids can get in over their heads."

"Unfortunately, also yes. Raine, it was Piaras's decision. He's eighteen; he's a man now. His decisions and choices are his own."

Mychael was right and I knew it. But just because I knew, it didn't mean I had to like it. I didn't say anything; I let my glare do my talking for me.

"I didn't come down here just because of what happened in the Quad," Mychael told me. "Though there's a good chance that they're related. I needed to talk to you. The containment spells around the Saghred have been decreasing over the past few days."

My stomach tried to do a flip. "How?"

"The only explanation we can find is that the stone is absorbing them. The Conclave's best spellweavers haven't been able to restore them." His blue eyes were intent on mine. "Have you experienced anything unusual?"

"Unusual?" I resisted the urge to laugh. "As opposed to my normal, everyday contact with the thing? And seeing naked, blue demons in the middle of a crowded street in broad daylight?" Don't forget the flying purple one over the Quad, my gloom-and-doom pessimist reminded me. My stomach flip turned into full-fledged queasy.

"Raine, it's important. I wouldn't ask if it wasn't."

I took a breath and slowly let it out. "Okay, I was in the street, lobbing fireballs at the purple one, the Volghul. Suddenly it was like the Saghred got a whiff of that thing and decided to say hello."

"It wanted you to use it against the Volghul?"

"I wish. I couldn't make another fireball if my life depended on it, and it did. I figured the Saghred was gathering up its energy for the usual—the white-hot, raging command to kill. That's not what I got. The rock was burning, all right; it was downright warm and welcoming—for the demon. That's when the Volghul bowed to me and said he was 'honored by my presence.'" My voice felt the need to get louder, and I let it. "Just what the hell is that supposed to mean?" I shot a glance at the still-closed conference room door and lowered my voice to an outraged whisper. "I thought the Saghred was a goblin rock."

"The goblins were simply the most recent to possess it."

Wonderful. "So what you're saying is that the demons could have had their collective claws on it at some point."

Mychael nodded. "The recorded history of the Saghred only dates back about a thousand years."

Crap. "And those were goblin records." I was all too familiar with them; I'd read them myself in my ongoing effort to rid myself of the rock. "Let me guess: demons aren't big on keeping journals."

"It's highly unlikely." Mychael leaned forward, resting his elbows on his armored knees. His hands hung loosely. He wasn't wearing gloves, and the backs of his hands were scored with deep scratches. Demon claws.

I grimaced. "Mychael, shouldn't you get those taken care of instead of talking to me?"

"Talking to you is more important." He glanced down at his hands and smiled a little. "They look better than they did. I'm a healer, remember?"

"Aren't demon claws poisonous or something?"

"Not a Dagik's. I'll be fine."

He said that as if I were the one in bad shape.

"Has anyone inside the Saghred been talking to you?" he asked.

I knew who he meant. Sarad Nukpana. A goblin, the blackest of dark mages, and a proverbial mad genius. He wanted the Saghred and me to wield it for him. Thanks to me, he was trapped inside the rock. Thanks to him, I was now at the top of the goblin king's most-wanted list. But Nukpana hadn't been the one speaking to me.

"I've been dreaming about my dad," I murmured.

My father, Eamaliel Anguis, was an elven Guardian whose soul was trapped along with thousands of others inside the Saghred. He'd been the stone's protector until about a year ago when the Saghred decided to turn its protector into its next meal.

Mychael's voice was low and controlled. "What kind of dreams?"

"Just talking kind of dreams." I held up a hand, stopping his next question. "No, I don't remember any of them. And no, I haven't felt manipulated by 'evil forces.'"

"I didn't imply that you were."

"Then you're the only one on this island who wouldn't think so." I sat up, the front legs of my chair slamming into the floor. "That demon had himself an audience when he said he was 'honored by my presence.' I think Carnades won himself a dozen or so more converts to his Lock-Up-Raine Club." I ran my hand over my face; it came away with dust from the dirt storm Vegard had kicked up. Great. "And the Volghul said that if I came to him, he'd let Piaras and Talon live."

Mychael went dangerously still. "He wanted you?"

I waited a few heartbeats before answering, a little taken aback by his intensity. "He didn't tell me what he had in mind, and I didn't ask. From the look on his face, he was going to enjoy it and I knew I wouldn't."

The air around Mychael flared with power. It was magic, definitely lethal, and its target was that purple demon. Then in a blink of an eye, the aura was gone, clamped down tight by the sheer force of Mychael's will, only to be replaced by something more primitive, more male.

"Are you all right?" he demanded.

"Shaken up, but he didn't lay a claw on me."

The power still flowing from him swept over my skin, and I forced back a shiver of pure sensation.

Mychael realized what he was doing and resisted touching me, even though not touching me seemed to take as much effort as not going after that demon. "Raine, I want you to come back to the citadel with me. You're not safe on Phaelan's ship."

I'd stayed in the citadel since arriving on Mid a few weeks ago, but the past few days I'd been on the *Fortune*. The accommodations Mychael had provided for me had been luxurious, but with guards posted outside my door, a gilded cage was still a cage. My family doesn't do cages very well.

"Mychael, I'm not safe anywhere, and you know it. Vegard never leaves my side, but if it makes you feel better, post a couple more Guardians, though with literally all hell about to break loose, I doubt if you can spare them. I may not be any safer on the *Fortune*, but I'm happier. If I can't be safe, I'll take happy."

Mychael sat back and raked his hand through his hair. I knew I'd been one exasperation right after another since the day we'd met.

"I won't allow myself to be locked up," I told him.

"I would never lock you up. You know that."

"If I went back, you wouldn't let me leave, so what's the difference?"

"You'd be alive."

"Possibly."

"No, definitely." Mychael said it as if he dared Death to defy him.

"Mychael, I can't let you—"

"Can't let me what? Protect you? Save you? Keep the next Volghul from carrying you off? Dammit, Raine, I won't stand by and—"

He took my hand and the shock of his magic raced up my arm. My breath exploded in a hiss, not of pain, but of every nerve ending suddenly and sharply aware. The air was crisp and alive and filled with scents magnified a hundredfold: the wood of the chair and table, the metallic tang of Mychael's armor and weapons, and his unmistakably masculine scent. My magic surged forward to meet his, matching him, giving as good as I got. Our magics coiled and twisted, weaving us together, and I was keenly aware of his every pulse, every muscle, the surging of blood through his veins.

And he was just as aware of me—all of me. I was transfixed as his eyes darkened from sun-kissed tropical seas to ocean depths. As his power filled me, I saw what he'd done to the demons that had ambushed him and four of his men. When my magic rose to meet his, Mychael felt what I had done to that Volghul.

And he knew that Tam and I had done it together.

That thought broke whatever hold our powers had on us.

I pulled my hand away, dragging air forcibly into my lungs. "What the hell was that?"

Mychael's eyes were like twin sapphires. "Magic most potent." His deep voice was rich and vibrant; it was his spellsinger's voice. He wasn't doing it on purpose; it was simply remnants from the power that still roiled within him.

I was about to say "no shit" to his assessment, but the memory of what Tam and I had done froze the words on my lips.

It was my magic that had focused Tam's power, and my magic that had just surged into Mychael. The Saghred hadn't had a thing to do with either one.

I felt my hands start to shake and I let them. At least they knew what to do next. "What did you do?"

In response, Mychael tentatively reached out to touch me, but stopped when the air between us crackled with static. The sensation ran up my spine like a warm hand in a velvet glove. Damn, but that felt good. Too good. I held the breath I'd just taken and flattened myself against the back of my chair.

"Stop," I managed. "No touching."

Mychael slowly pulled his hand back.

We had touched more than each other's hands before, but absolutely nothing like this had ever happened.

In that exact instant, Mychael had the same thought; I felt the echo from it flicker inside my mind.

My own thoughts skittered in panicked circles. "I can hear you thinking."

Mychael sat unmoving. "It's fading, but I can sense your thoughts, too."

Damn.

"I agree," he said.

I hadn't said it out loud. Double damn.

"Anything like this ever happen to you before?" I asked him.

"Never." Mychael's eyes were on mine; they were slowly returning to their normal color. "Was this similar to what happened with you and Tam?"

I hesitated before answering. "Yes . . . and no. Yes, my magic felt the same as when Tam and I bottled that demon." I paused. "But Tam didn't feel anything like you."

"I'm not Tam." Mychael's voice was deeper, huskier.

I swallowed. "I noticed."

The air between us thickened, and then crackled with pent-up magic, among other things. With visible effort, Mychael pushed back his chair and stood. He put a few steps between us, then turned and leaned against the conference table, crossing his arms over his chest. To avoid temptation, get away from what tempts you. The paladin was back and he had a job to do.

"What happened with Tam in the Quad?" he asked.

"You just saw what happened—"

"Only flashes of image and sound."

I told him everything, starting from spotting the blue demons in the street, to the elven mage's murder, to the Volghul.

"I've never taken down a demon," I said. "Tam said he had, so he told me how to channel his power." I stopped. It took me more than a few moments to say what I didn't want to acknowledge, let alone admit. "Tam and I seem to have some sort of connection since what happened last week."

Mychael nodded, his expression grim. He knew only too well what had happened.

Six spellsingers had been kidnapped and held in a prison block deep under the elven embassy. They were intended as sacrifices to feed and reactivate the Saghred. There was a chance that Tam and I could save them, but only if we worked together. The Saghred had wanted to get its figurative hooks into Tam, and saving those spellsingers had given the rock a taste of Tam's black magic. What we'd done had torn down the magical barriers between us. Tam had said that we weren't separate anymore. Until today, I hadn't realized what that meant.

And now, with a single touch of his hand, Mychael's magic had merged with mine, and we could hear each other's thoughts. It was only for a few intensely intimate, breath-stopping moments—but it had happened. It was similar enough to what had happened between me and Tam to scare me, but the Saghred hadn't stepped in to join me and Mychael. It was only the two of us. Mychael was white magic; Tam was dark—it could be as simple as that, but I didn't think so. Nothing the Saghred ever did was simple.

I blew out my breath. It was a little shaky. "What's happening to us?"

Mychael's face showed no emotion. He knew that "us" included Tam. "I don't have an answer, but we will find one."

"Best plan I've heard all day." I stood; I couldn't sit still anymore, either. "Vegard said that Volghuls are advance guards for a legion of demons, and implied that we have ourselves a Hellgate opening on the island." I didn't mention that Tam had told me the same thing in my mind. If Mychael didn't know, I didn't need to tell him. "What does it take to open one?"

"Dark mages using the blackest of magic."

I didn't take my eyes off Mychael's. "You have suspects?"

"I do."

I met his response with silence. He knew one of the names I was thinking—no magic-linked mind reading necessary.

"It wasn't Tam," I said quietly.

"I know that."

"Others won't be so sure."

"I know that, too."

"Carnades despises goblins," I said. "Especially ones as powerful as Tam."

"Tam's not the only dark mage on this island," Mychael said. "I'm ashamed to say it, but more than a few of the Conclave's mages and the college's professors practice black magic. The vast majority of our mages and faculty want nothing more than to do research or teach. But some can't take the temptation of that much power. Practicing black magic is illegal, but that doesn't stop experimenting behind locked and warded doors. If they're caught and convicted, they will be executed."

"You'd think that'd be a deterrent."

"The punishment is harsh, but it has to be. I'm responsible for the safety of thousands of students, mages, and citizens on this island. No one, or no *thing*, will endanger the people I'm sworn to protect."

One of those people had gotten himself endangered right onto a slab in the morgue.

"Sedge Rinker said the dead mage was the chairman of the demonology department."

Mychael nodded. "Professor Laurian Berel."

"Those demons wanted something and they were convinced the professor had it," I told him.

I didn't know what "it" was, but recent near-death experiences had taught me that when bad guys wanted something, things would generally go to the lower hells in a handbasket if they got their hands—or in this case, claws—on it. And considering that the bad guys were demons, that trip to the lower hells could be literal.

"The professor said he didn't have it," I said, seeing the scene replay itself in my head, complete with the professor getting his throat ripped out. "And I believed him. I didn't know this Professor Berel, but from what I saw, he didn't strike me as the type to give his life to protect something."

"He wasn't."

"But he must have known what it was; otherwise, he couldn't have said that he didn't have it. Unfortunately he's dead, and the demon that killed him is stuffed in a bottle."

"Some of his colleagues aren't," Mychael reminded me.

I jerked my head in the direction of the cells. "You're going to question the blue ones out there?"

"I am. If they don't know anything, I'll have to let the Volghul out of the bottle."

"I don't think that's a good idea."

"It might be necessary. And since I've interrogated demons

before, and I am the paladin of this island, it's my duty to do it. But if I did have to interrogate the Volghul, I couldn't do it here. Sedge has top-notch shields and wards on his cells, but they're nowhere near strong enough for a Volghul. I'd have to take him to the demonology department for that."

"Let's hope the blue ones are talkative."

Chapter 5

All naked, blue demons looked the same to me. Perhaps that opinion offended delicate demonic sensibilities, but somehow I doubted this bunch had anything delicate. An hour or so closed up in a warded cell had given their collective aroma ample time to seep out. Believe me, there was nothing delicate about that. Wards and shields would hold in or keep out most anything— unfortunately a stomach-turning, gag-inducing stench wasn't one of them.

Vegard saw my grimace. "Brimstone."

"What?" I tried unsuccessfully to talk and breathe through my mouth at the same time. Must have been a gift I didn't have.

"The smell," he clarified.

"So that's what Hell smells like."

"I assume so; never been there myself."

"Not many have," came a woman's voice from behind us. "Afternoon, Sir Vegard."

The big Guardian turned and smiled. "Professor Niabi, good to see you."

"Considering how today's gone so far, it's good to be seen."

The woman was human, about my height, with nut brown skin, and black hair pulled back into a serviceable braid.

"So Hell's not a top-ten vacation spot?" I quipped.

Her teeth flashed in a good-humored grin. "The beaches suck." She put out her hand. "Sora Niabi, professor of demonology."

I hesitated only a moment before taking it. Her hand was warm and calloused. Sora Niabi had done more work than just turning pages. I might have to adjust my opinion about academic types.

"I'm Raine Benares, seeker and . . ." I looked up at Vegard. "What else are people calling me now?"

The big Guardian chuckled and shook his head. "A lot of things, ma'am. Some you've heard, most you haven't, but I'm sure you could guess."

"No titles necessary," Sora Niabi said with a grin. "I know who you are."

She knew, and she wasn't afraid of me. She also didn't want my power or want me locked up. I could sense it, and my instincts about people had never been wrong. Well, at least not yet.

"After this morning, Professor Niabi's also the new department chair," Vegard informed me.

Sora Niabi blew her breath out in disgust. "Looks that way. Though if Laurian Berel hadn't been such an idiot, I wouldn't be." Her robes were a riot of bright colors. They were also slashed up the side, exposing practical trousers underneath, and good, sturdy boots.

She noticed me noticing. "When you study demons for a living, Miss Benares, it's healthy to be able to haul ass when you have to."

That did it; I liked her.

"Call me Raine."

"Only if you'll drop the 'professor' and call me Sora."

"Done."

Mychael joined us. "Professor Niabi, thank you for coming on such short notice."

"Not a problem, Paladin Eiliesor. The coroner needed me to officially identify Professor Berel, so I had to be here anyway."

"He was a talented mage."

"Laurian was a better fool, and you know it as well as I do. You should have been a diplomat, Paladin. You actually managed to say that with a straight face. I was hardly surprised to hear he'd gotten himself killed; I've been expecting that news for years. In our line of work, talent can get you into trouble, but arrogance will get you killed and eaten—and not always in that order."

I nodded toward the warded cell. "Those four and their buddies were after something and they thought Professor Berel had it. He said he didn't. Any idea what it was?"

"Not a clue. Laurian kept a lot of bizarre artifacts around. We all do. Certain objects have power against demons. Everybody in the department has their own collection and their own favorites. It's safer to have your own when you need it. Chances are if you need it, you don't have the time to go borrowing."

Mychael lowered his voice. "He was killed by a Volghul."

Sora's only reaction was a raised eyebrow. "Nothing he had would have saved him from that. Apparently when the demons didn't get what they wanted from Laurian, they went to his town house. The place has been demolished from the inside out, like somebody got really frustrated."

"Frustrated demonic searchers?" I asked.

"The brimstone smell gave it away." Sora squinted through the thickly warded cell. "Is that a wine bottle?"

"The Volghul is in there," Mychael told her.

Sora whistled. "In a *wine* bottle? Damn. Who stuffed it in there?"

I half raised my hand. "That would be me."

"You?"

"Me. With a little help."

"That's some help."

I tried not to wince. "Yes, it was."

"Good work."

"Thanks."

Mychael nodded toward the demons' cell. "Do you have everything we need to question those?"

Sora gave the knapsack slung over one shoulder a shake. I heard something metal clank heavily inside. "Never leave home without it."

"And traps for transporting them out of here?"

"Got my two best grad students checking out a pair from the lab. They'll be here any time now."

"Good. Let's get started."

The demon's enraged screams had subsided to low growls.

Sora Niabi had wrangled it out of that cell and into a binding circle in an interrogation room. There was a ring of silver about three feet wide permanently embedded in the stone floor. Sora had added a thick silver chain on top of that. Both inside and outside the circle, she'd carefully placed objects I couldn't identify, and judging from how the demon had reacted when Sora forced him inside, he knew perfectly well what they were, and he didn't want to be anywhere near them. The professor knew her business. Good. Any interrogation room I'd ever seen was just a table, two chairs, no windows, and a barred iron door, with the obligatory big, burly, and heavily armed guard standing right outside.

Of course they did things differently on Mid.

There were still big and burly types outside the door, but that was where the similarities ended. Sure, these boys could stop an escapee with a fist or steel; they could also spit a spell that'd tack a miscreant to the nearest wall like a bug. The door and all four walls were kept warded. Nothing was leaving that room unless it was let go. Mychael and Sora had no intention of releasing that demon. Her grad students were stationed on either side of the door—on the inside. I didn't know if Sora had asked them to stand by the door in case they needed to make a quick getaway, or if they were there to make sure the demon didn't do the same. They honestly didn't look old enough to fight acne, let alone a demon, but I guess when it came to battling demonic forces, brawn didn't matter. Brains did—that and nerves of steel. From what I'd seen so far, Sora Niabi had both in spades. Before they'd gone in and locked the door behind them, those two kids had looked like they were still in training.

Phaelan and I waited outside the door, about ten feet away and slightly off to one side, should that door suddenly decide to blow off its hinges. I'd seen it happen before. Better safe than squashed.

Phaelan leaned close to my ear. "Why are we still here?"

He was talking through clenched teeth again, a sure sign my cousin wasn't happy in his present surroundings. I guess I really couldn't blame him; a couple of the watchers were glancing at Phaelan's wanted poster and then back at Phaelan. Sure, Mychael had given my cousin immunity from prosecution for any past legal indiscretions while on the Isle of Mid, but Mychael was questioning a demon right now. He wasn't here. It was just me and Phaelan and a roomful of increasingly alert watchers.

Phaelan cleared his throat impatiently. I hadn't answered his question yet.

"I could see those demons, but no one else could," I told him, keeping my voice to a bare whisper. "A man is dead, and his killer said that he was honored by my presence and wanted me to go home with him. I want to know why."

"Hmmm, let's see . . . That makes you a possible demon ally and accessory to murder. So you thought you'd stand in the middle of city watch headquarters."

I hadn't thought of it that way. "It doesn't sound too bright, does it?"

"No, it doesn't."

"Well, Sedge may not be through questioning us yet."

"Did he say he wasn't?"

"No."

"Then he's probably finished. I've talked to him. You've talked to him. The kids have talked to him. Vegard's talked to him. I'd call that finished."

"And if he's not?"

"It's easier to ask for forgiveness from a ship, than permission from a jail cell."

I couldn't argue with that logic.

The front doors opened and in strode the man Mychael had been expecting.

Oh crap in a bucket. I did not need this.

Carnades Silvanus wasn't the type to drop by watcher headquarters for a friendly visit. He had a reason for being here, and that reason was me. And judging from the people who'd come in with him and the fanciness of their robes, it looked like he'd brought along some high-powered—or at least self-important—friends. Fancy robes just meant a mage had money. Fashion had nothing to do with firepower.

Either way, I wasn't flattered that they'd all come to see me.

Carnades Silvanus saw himself as the champion of the elven people. I saw him as an uptight, self-righteous, narrow-minded jerk. Unfortunately, he also had the influence to convince a lot of powerful and dangerous people to see things his way.

Even before I'd set foot on the island, word had already arrived and spread about my link with the Saghred. Mages liked good gossip the same as everyone else. Some of those mages thought I had too much power. They couldn't control me. I was a risk. I had to be stopped. Some favored a permanent solution. The squeamish ones wanted something less drastic. I didn't think the five men and women behind Carnades were the ones with the weak stomachs.

No doubt Carnades considered himself the pinnacle of elven good breeding. The hair that flowed over his shoulders was the color of winter frost, eyes the pale blue of arctic ice, an alabaster complexion, a cold, sharp beauty. Pure-blooded high elf. His black and silver robes were understated and elegant, and clearly cost a small fortune. His only visible weapon was a curved and ornate silver dagger tucked into a silk sash. I knew better. Carnades Silvanus *was* a weapon.

With the archmagus temporarily out of commission, Carnades was in charge and he wasn't about to let anyone forget it, starting with me—especially after that incident last week in the Conclave's library. He called it assault; I called it entirely justified self-defense.

"Ma'am," came Vegard's tense warning from beside me.

"Thank you, Vegard. I see him."

"I know you see him. That's the problem."

"I'll behave if he does."

"He won't."

"Then there's going to be a problem."

Vegard came to reluctant attention. He had to. The Guardians' main duty was the protection of the archmagus and the mages of the Seat of Twelve. That included Carnades Silvanus.

Carnades crossed the room to me. He was as tall as Mychael, which put the top of my head level with his jaw. The elf mage had always looked down on me—in more ways than one.

Those arctic eyes gazed over my head and leisurely surveyed the squad room, taking in the accused perpetrators, the cells, and lastly the demons, who interestingly enough were crowded against the front of their cell looking at Carnades like he was some kind of new snack.

Finally Carnades's eyes came to rest on me. "Mistress Benares," he murmured, "how appropriate that I should find you in such surroundings."

I didn't take the bait. He'd have to do way better than that to get a reaction out of me.

I actually smiled at him. "Magus Silvanus, I don't believe you've met my cousin Captain Phaelan Benares." My tone was graciousness itself. Since I knew Phaelan was going to get into this, I figured I might as well introduce him to the man he'd probably be trying to stab within the next minute.

Phaelan stepped forward and smiled, baring all of his teeth. My cousin didn't offer his hand, and wisely, Carnades kept his to himself.

Phaelan spoke. "It's a pleasure to finally meet the man I've heard so many things about." From the feral glint in my cousin's dark eyes, the pleasure he referred to involved visualizing Carnades with a Benares blade sticking out of his back.

Carnades glanced over Phaelan's shoulder at the bulletin board—and the wanted posters. "It is reassuring to see that our city watch's artist created such an accurate rendering. The resemblance is truly uncanny."

I felt Sedge Rinker standing at my right shoulder. "Magus Silvanus, would you like to step into my office? You and your guests would be more comfortable there while you wait to speak to Paladin Eiliesor."

"Ah, yes. Where is our good paladin?"

An enraged demonic roar from the interrogation room answered that question.

"Questioning one of Professor Berel's attackers," Sedge clarified. "He will be finished shortly. If you would like to wait in—"

"No, I would not like to wait, Chief Rinker. I do not wish to wait in your office, nor will I wait for Paladin Eiliesor."

Carnades looked down at me and I met his stare. He'd have to blink first, because I sure as hell wasn't going to.

"What I came for is right here," he said softly. "At least one of them. Where is Piaras Rivalin?" His lip curled back in distaste. "And the *other* one?"

I made a show of looking around. "It doesn't look like they're here. So you brought your audience all the way down here for little old me. I hope they're not too disappointed."

"Hardly. Since we won't be leaving empty-handed." He glanced over at the cell containing the wine bottle and its demonic contents. "Only the blackest of magic could have subdued a Volghul. I knew you were in league with dark forces, but I now have irrefutable proof that Piaras Rivalin has been tainted by your influence."

I clenched my hands at my side. It was the only way I'd keep them away from Carnades's throat. "Maestro Cayle is teaching Piaras to battle 'dark forces' as part of his lessons. I can hardly believe you never smacked a demon around for fun in your younger days."

"Piaras Rivalin should take care who he accepts assistance from," Carnades said in the barest whisper. "The half-breed he is associating with is tainted not only by mixed blood but by parentage. Though considering who its father is, it can hardly be blamed."

Carnades had sneered the words "its father." Those two words carried a whole world of insult. I considered punching Carnades's lights out. But we were in watcher headquarters, not the best place for punching lights or anything else. There were too many empty cells around here. I didn't want to be in any of them. I was sure I'd get another shot at Carnades. I was just lucky that way.

I put a hand on Phaelan's arm. I knew which dagger he was going for. Carnades saw and smiled slowly.

"By all means, *Captain* Benares. Give me an excuse to take you as well."

I took a step forward, leaving scant inches between the elven mage and me. I had to look up to meet his eyes, but that was fine with me. Carnades could have reached out and touched me. I wanted him to. I also wanted him to remember what I'd done the last time he'd made the mistake of touching and threatening me. I'd do it again, and this time I'd have a squad room full of watchers as witnesses.

He knew it and kept his hands to himself, but he didn't back down. I knew he wouldn't. That was fine with me, too.

"Paladin Eiliesor is questioning the demons; I merely want to question their accomplice," Carnades said loudly enough for everyone to hear. "The dark mage who used her Saghred-spawned power to open a Hellgate, releasing her demonic minions to do her dirty work. Though I can't imagine anything being beneath a Benares."

I laughed. I couldn't help myself. "*Minions?* I'd ask if you're serious, but no doubt you believe that you are."

Silvanus's pale eyes glittered. "You are a danger to everyone on this island. I've said that you should be locked up—and today I'm here to see it done." The elven mage smiled. "On the authority of the Seat of Twelve, you're under arrest for practicing black magic and consorting with demons."

Carnades's pronouncement lost some of its effect when a

man shouted in fear and surprise from a back room, then swore in utter disgust. It took me a moment to realize the man's disgust wasn't a reaction to Carnades's speech.

A watcher came through a door in the back of the room dangling something by a bony, yellow foot. It was about a foot long, mostly arms and legs, with a round torso that kind of merged into a head. No neck. It was naked, it was hairless, it was wrinkled, and it had to be the ugliest thing I'd ever seen in my life. And it smelled like—

"It jumped out of the latrine!" The watcher looked like he was about to be sick.

Yep, that was the smell.

"Damn," breathed Phaelan from beside me.

I couldn't have agreed more, especially considering that the thing was still dripping. And it looked just a wee bit larger.

I looked closer. "Am I imagining things, or . . ."

The watcher who was dangling the thing by its heel grunted at the abrupt increase in weight. The thing twisted and squirmed, and since it was still wet, the watcher couldn't hold on, and I didn't think he wanted to. The yellow beastie hit the floor and scuttled under the nearest desk. Around the room, weapons were drawn, my own included. Phaelan had drawn steel *and* jumped on a chair. Carnades retreated to where his mage cronies waited.

"Cowards," I muttered.

"Cautious," Phaelan corrected me. "Do you know how much these clothes cost? No way in hell that thing's getting near me."

Considering where it'd come from, I didn't exactly want it rubbing against me, either. Some smells just didn't come out.

The wood the desk was made of creaked and then groaned. That was not good. Then the desk's legs rose about eight inches off of the floor, lifted by something underneath. Something yellow, stinky, and growing entirely too fast.

That was very bad.

Most of the watchers did their duty and stood their ground; other watchers took the duty-be-damned approach and started backing away. I wasn't a watcher, I had no duty, but I stood my ground anyway. Sedge Rinker stepped up beside Vegard and me.

Sedge kept his voice down. "Ma'am, you and your cousin might want to take advantage of this to leave."

"Finally, a lawman I can agree with," Phaelan muttered.

The growing demon stood up, and then up some more. The damned thing was so big it was wearing the desk like a hat. Then it turned around, facing us. Its eyes were black, beady, and really, really angry. With a single shake of its head, the desk went flying, splintering against a wall.

Professional discipline was pretty much gone at that point.

The interrogation room opened, one of Sora's grad students looked, saw, squeaked, and slammed the door.

Smart kid.

Those angry demon eyes looked directly at me. And got even angrier. Then it growled, rattling the windows.

I shouted over my shoulder. I sure as hell wasn't turning my back on that. "Carnades, if you want to haul me out of here, I think you're gonna have to get in line."

Chapter 6

There were a few heartbeats of stunned inaction; the only sound was the wheezing in and out of the demon's breath like some sort of putrid bellows.

Then he roared—and half the people in the room ran. Half the people included most of the accused perps, some still in handcuffs. The watchers let them go; they had a bigger problem, and it was still growing.

While less people gave the rest of us more room to fight, it gave the demon less targets to hit and a greater probability of hitting those targets, namely us.

"You still curious about demons?" Phaelan asked me.

"Not anymore."

"Too bad you didn't decide that five minutes ago."

We had bladed weapons; the demon preferred blunt objects, like office furniture.

In the street we'd used fireballs. That was outside. This was inside, with entirely too many flammables like furniture, walls, and civilians. The watchers opted to go with crossbows with a little magical something extra glowing on the bolts that'd go through any living creature like hot butter. At least they should have. Apparently the normal rules of magic didn't apply to this particular demon. The bolts shattered on impact and the demon didn't even slow down, chucking a file cabinet at the bowmen. They dove out of the way before impact, and we had to rethink our strategy, such that it was. The demon wasn't warded, at least not with any ward I'd ever seen; it was just impenetrable. A bad quality for something that needed killing.

Even worse was the reaction of most of the watchers. As keepers of the peace on an island full of magic users, Sedge's people had probably seen it all. I don't think they'd ever seen anything like this. That made all of us. But the thing didn't want all of us.

It wanted me.

"Run!" I screamed at Phaelan.

"We go together, or we don't go!"

The demon tried to stomp Phaelan to reach me, but my cousin darted to the left as the massive foot came down. Phaelan spun with deadly grace to plunge his rapier through the thing's foot—and the blade shattered on its skin. My cousin gaped at the remaining hilt in his hand and his words blistered the air blue. He loved that rapier.

I was watching the demon's feet, not its hands. My mistake. Huge mistake. Next thing I knew I was snatched off my feet, dangling upside down, with one leg clenched in the demon's fist. He swung me around and I got a quick and blurry view of the entire squad room. Some Guardians were behind the thing with fireballs ready to launch. Fire safety must have gone out the window along with the furniture. The demon pulled me up to his face, I guess to get a closer look at what he was about to eat. I got a closer look at what was going to eat me. No teeth, just knotty, bony gums. That was really gonna hurt. I'd rather be bitten in half than gummed to death. At least that would be quick.

The demon's breath came out of his nose in a sulfur-scented, gag-inducing stench.

Nostrils. Open holes. No wards.

Hot damn.

My hands were free, and an instant later, so were the pair of short swords I wore in a harness on my back. A second after that, the demon was sporting a sword up each nostril.

His shriek shattered what windows were left. Then he dropped me.

Being dropped was good; landing was not. Vegard, bless him, was there to catch me, which meant he let me squash him flat when I landed.

The demon pulled out the blades, threw one, then had the bright idea to use the other like a skewer at a buffet.

"Sorry!" I called to the hapless watcher who almost became the demon's next snack choice.

There was a massive safe next to Sedge's office where the watch kept their deadlier weapons. I couldn't begin to guess how much it weighed, and one demonic kick sent it skidding across the floor, slamming into the interrogation room door, trapping Mychael and the professor inside.

I felt power building behind me. A lot of it. Expertly controlled, focused, and deadly. Had to be Carnades. I hoped all that effort was to take out that demon, but I wasn't going to hold my breath.

"You and your goblin lover summoned a demon to slaughter our watchers," the elven mage snarled from beside me. He was focusing his magic and attention on the demon. His rage was focused squarely on me. "Ruthless and very clever, but not clever enough. You are under arrest."

I couldn't believe this guy. "Gargantua here's on a rampage, and you're still trying to arrest me! You ever heard of perspective?"

We both hit the floor and rolled as a fist the size of an office chair slammed into the floor where we'd just been, cracking the stone and knocking half the people still in the room off their feet.

Carnades and I ended up in a tangle against a bookshelf. The elven mage flung a ball of incandescent white death that hit the demon square between the eyes.

The demon absorbed it, grew larger, and got a lot more angry.

The blue demons cheered from their cell.

Two strides put the yellow demon in front of his blue buddies' cell. Red-hot sparks flew as one swipe of its claw-tipped hand sliced through both wards and bars like wet paper. The blue demons poured out and made a beeline straight for Carnades and me.

Magic just made big, yellow, and pissed even bigger. But magic had torched the blue ones in that street and would have done the same now, except the blue boys were a lot keener on survival than they had been before. They moved in flashes of blue, faster than any mortal or demon had a right to move. The presence of their yellow friend must have been a morale booster.

An explosion shook the building as the safe blocking the interrogation room simply disintegrated. Mychael was warded and ready for whatever was out here, and Sora was right behind him.

The professor looked up at the yellow demon and cut loose with a string of obscenities that would've made Phaelan's crew blanch—or fall in love.

Mychael looked at me, and then up at the yellow monstrosity. He knew where the worst danger was, but he wanted to come to me. If he did his "white knight" thing now, watchers and civilians were going to die.

The demon had a watcher in each hand; one was limp and bleeding.

"Get *him*!" I shouted, pointing at the demon.

Mychael hesitated only a second before diving into the fray. I could hear him and the professor shouting orders.

Carnades and I still had a problem. That trio of blue demons was circling us like we were the entrée they'd been waiting for all their lives. Sedge was leading his watchers against the yellow demon; Phaelan was nowhere to be seen; and Vegard was fighting his way over to us. He wasn't going to get here in time. My survival was up to me and a mage who hated my guts.

The yellow demon picked up a desk and hurled it at a knot of watchers. They scattered, the desk shattered, part of it flew out a window, and a chunk the size of my fist hit Carnades in the temple. He went down like a rock, and the blue demons rushed him.

I dove between them and Carnades before I could think what I was doing. But I knew what I was doing. I didn't like Carnades, but if those demons shredded him, guess who'd get tossed in the deepest prison pit the Conclave could dig?

Besides, it'd gall the hell out of him if I saved his life. I grinned at the demons and bared my teeth.

"You hungry?" I yelled over the chaos. "You want a piece of this? You want a piece of me?" I had a ball of blue fire in each hand, and the demons were circling me. There was one of me, two fireballs, and three demons.

And a whirlwind of searing flame curling and twisting in the center of my chest.

The Saghred.

Oh no.

Not now. Not here. Please, no, not here.

The whirlwind turned into a tornado. My breath hissed in and out from between clenched teeth. My chest was on fire. The fire and the Saghred's power that fed it blazed under my breastbone, white-hot and raging.

Take the power, or the power will take you.

It wasn't a voice; it was the Saghred's desires manifesting itself in my head.

It was also the truth.

I shoved down the fire and my fear. I swallowed them hard and held them down. The fire flickered and writhed, trying to get around my will. I pressed harder and it just increased its struggle, wild and untamable. It knew it was stronger. It knew it was going to win this time. I was its instrument, its bond servant, and I *would* do its will, surrender to its desires.

No!

The sounds of battle faded until all I could hear was my own breathing, and the sibilant words of the demons who had backed off a step or two, but no farther. I couldn't tell if their words were death spells or demon-speak for "You first" and "No, you go first."

It didn't matter, the Saghred didn't care, and no one had asked me what I wanted. Those demons just *thought* they were hungry. The Saghred hadn't had a decent meal in nearly a thousand years. And as I'd discovered a few days ago, I was the Saghred's bond servant, and part of that job was accepting soul sacrifices to feed the Saghred. And right now, the Saghred had a hankering for blue demons.

There was no way in hell demon souls were flowing through me to feed that rock.

The demons knew, and one of them moved in a blurred flash to snatch up Carnades's quasi-conscious body as a hostage, the mage's bared throat clutched in talon-tipped hand. It looked at me and bared dozens of needle-sharp teeth in a smile that told me Carnades was about to be the second elven mage to die today.

Not going to happen.

Time slowed for me until the demon's fingers constricting around Carnades's throat barely moved at all—but they were still moving. One of the pointed nails punctured the mage's skin and a thin stream of blood flowed leisurely down his pale neck, vanishing into the collar of his robes.

I took a deep, shuddering breath. Then I clenched my jaw, gritted my teeth, and with every ounce of strength and sheer stubbornness I possessed, forced down the Saghred's starvation, its demands, its desires. Forced them down bit by struggling bit. When I had as much control as I knew I was going to get, I aimed the stone's power directly at the demon holding Carnades hostage.

The demon's eyes widened in terror and disbelief. You'd have thought I'd shoved him headfirst into the business end of a cannon. He knew the power I was packing, and he knew the barest touch of that power wouldn't leave enough of him to fill a dustpan. He froze. So did the other two. Everything and everyone in the room went dead silent. Waiting.

For me. For what I was going to do.

I slowly raised my arm and extended my hand, leveling it at the demon. I think it was glowing; I think *I* was glowing. Carnades's eyes opened and he saw the demon.

And then he saw me.

Rescue now; explain later, I told myself.

"Put. Him. Down." My teeth were clenched and my voice shook against the power I was barely holding in check.

But I *was* holding it. I had it under control.

And Carnades knew it. Now I saw a flicker of fear turn into raw, unreasoning hatred. He saw—completely and clearly for the first time—the level of power I had, and he knew its source. It didn't matter if I saved him. He didn't care. What I could do—what I *was*—was all that mattered to him now. I'd just sealed my fate. Carnades would not only see me arrested, he would see me executed. Today if he could get away with it. In his misguided and twisted reasoning, I had just become too dangerous to live.

Part of me was tempted to let the demon finish its job. The instant Carnades died, most of my problems would die with him.

I'd never liked that part of me. I knew it'd be the worst mistake I'd ever made, but I kept my hand—and the harnessed Saghred's power—on that demon where it belonged.

The demon may have been evil incarnate from the lower hells, but he wasn't stupid.

"Gently," I added, showing him more than a few of my teeth.

The demon complied. His movements were slow, jerky. I was making him do something he didn't like and he wasn't happy about it. His yellow eyes were glowing orange.

No, he definitely wasn't amused.

I didn't care and I probably should have.

Carnades took a step back, staggered, then steadied himself. His blue eyes blazed with hatred and every dark and twisted thing that lay beyond. He wanted that demon dead and cold, and me the same way beside it.

I felt them move before I saw them. In a blink, the other two demons were on me, then the third one joined them.

And Carnades did nothing to stop them.

Son of a bitch.

I released the hint of power that I'd held in check, and the three demons vanished in a hiss of steam and sulfur. Not just vanished.

Vaporized.

Sickened and gasping for air I couldn't find, I staggered to my feet. Releasing that power released the hold I had on the rest of it. I'd just pulled a rock out of a dam with a wall of water on the other side, pushing through the hole I'd made, punching against the dam that held it back. Cracks were spreading; nothing could hold that torrent back; nothing could stop that power.

I couldn't stop that power.

"Raine!" It was Mychael's voice sounding like it was coming down a well. I was at the bottom of that well, trapped, with no way out.

"You've got to discharge!"

I was going to implode or explode or something fatal and final if I didn't get rid of the power charge that had built up inside of me. I couldn't force it back where it came from. There was too much of it, a wall of power bearing down on me. It was coming, and I couldn't stop it. The Saghred and I were one. Mychael said the containments were failing.

Clearly, no containments held the Saghred now.

Or would ever hold it again.

"His magic grew him; your magic can destroy him," Sora was calling down that same well.

I had no idea what she meant, but I knew what I could do, what I *had* to do before the power that surged through my veins killed me—and everyone else.

Then on some level, I understood what Sora meant. It was so simple.

I extended my hand, fingers spread. The yellow demon was massive, but it was across the room, and my hand covered it completely, at least that's what it looked like. It was a distance illusion, but illusion was magic, too.

I began slowly curling my fingers closed. The demon began compacting like I was crushing a wet sponge in my hand. It roared, then those roars turned to screams, and finally a thin shriek as I closed my hand until it was the tightest fist I could make. I tasted blood in my mouth, and black blooms danced on the edge of my vision. I opened my hand and released what was left and heard a wet, sickening plop from across the room. Then came the retching noises from a few of the watchers.

That and awed—and horrified—silence.

The last thing I heard before silence and blessed unconsciousness took me was Carnades's calm, cold voice.

"Lock her up."

Chapter 7

I woke up in a dark, warm room. Not a cell. And I was tucked into a soft bed, not a prison cot with a threadbare blanket. Nice. And deeply wrong. When I passed out, I must have hit my head. Hard.

I was in my bedroom back home in Mermeia.

"Aside from bruises that most certainly will hurt when you wake up, you're surprisingly unharmed, all things considered."

My father sat in a chair half hidden in shadow near my window. That was one reason why I hadn't seen him. The other reason was even more unnerving than waking up in a place where I couldn't possibly be. Unnerving, but not unexpected. We'd spoken directly one other time.

I'd been able to see through him that time, too.

Eamaliel Anguis's elegantly pointed ears marked him as an elf, a beautiful pure-blooded high elf. His hair was silver, and his eyes were the gray of gathering storm clouds. Eyes identical to my own. I could see why my elven sorceress mother hadn't cared that he was nearly nine hundred years old.

Yes, nine hundred years old, and he didn't look a day over thirty. Elves had the same life span as every other race, so having a father who looked four years younger than me took weird to a whole new level. He'd spent the last year or so inside the Saghred, the other eight hundred and something years the result of an extended life span from too much contact with the Saghred. A fate I really wanted to avoid.

I knew I wasn't really at home in my bedroom. One, it was impossible. Two, this bedroom was way too neat to belong to me.

I felt my temple for the lump that had to be there. "No concussion?" I muttered to myself.

"Just unconscious from what you did."

I remembered and groaned. I'd just done the worst thing possible at the worst possible time in front of the last person I wanted to see me do it.

I was screwed. Royally, completely, and utterly.

"Yes, you did put on quite a show," my father agreed.

I sat up in bed, and surprisingly it didn't hurt. "How are we—?"

"You're dreaming. You picked the setting."

"Why are you—?"

"Because we need to talk."

"Stop finishing my sentences!" I didn't mean to snap, but apparently I needed to.

"I know your thoughts as you think them, daughter. Isn't communicating this way more—"

"Annoying," I finished for him. Two could play at that game.

The corner of Eamaliel's mouth quirked upward. "Since it's your dream we'll do it your way."

I threw back the blanket and got out of bed. I went to the window and yanked back the curtain. Instead of Mintha Row with its shops and cobblestone street, there was a gray void.

My chest tightened. "You're sure we're not inside the Saghred?"

"Positive. For some reason, your dream only includes this room."

"And you."

"Apparently you wanted to see me."

I could certainly understand why I'd want that. Get in trouble, go home to Dad.

I let the curtain fall back over the window. "I'm sorry I yelled."

"No offense taken, Raine. I, of all people, understand your frustration."

And fear. Let's not forget gut-clenching fear. I looked down at my wrists. Just because there weren't manacles on my asleep self didn't mean my real self wasn't sporting a pair right now courtesy of Carnades Silvanus.

"Thank you," I said, sounding as exhausted as I remembered my real body felt. "I've had more than enough magic today."

"I hate being the bearer of bad news, but magic is what we need to talk about. And we need to do it quickly because you're going to be waking up soon."

The tightness in my chest dropped into a knot in my stomach. "Waking up where?"

Eamaliel knew I didn't mean in bed in my dreams. "That I don't know. I only see what you see. And at the moment, you're unconscious and not seeing anything."

"Carnades could be taking you to prison," purred a cultured and silky voice I knew only too well.

Sarad Nukpana was reclining on my bed in the exact spot where I had been.

"And it's still warm," he murmured, running a long-fingered hand over the sheets. His voice dropped, low and intimate. "Eamaliel isn't the only one who knows exactly what you're thinking."

Sarad Nukpana had been the chief counselor to the goblin king Sathrik Mal'Salin, and grand shaman of the Khrynsani, an ancient goblin secret society and military order. At least Sarad Nukpana had held those titles before a little quick thinking by yours truly had gotten him sucked into the Saghred. Nukpana and his boss wanted to get their hands on the rock and bring back the good old days of conquering kingdoms and enslaving thousands. Sarad Nukpana didn't want me dead, just tormented for eternity.

Here he was on my bed, in my dream. It wasn't exactly torment, but it was close enough.

I just looked at him. "So, what am I thinking now?"

Nukpana smiled slowly, fangs peeking into view. "Such violence, little seeker. I don't think what you propose is physically possible."

I showed him a few of my own teeth. "I won't know until I try."

His black eyes glittered. "As always, I welcome your efforts."

Being trapped inside the Saghred hadn't diminished the goblin shaman's dark, exotic beauty one bit. His long black hair was shot through with silver and fell loosely around his strongly sculpted face; the tips of his upswept ears were barely visible through the midnight mass of his hair. Nukpana's pearl gray skin set off what was any goblin's most distinguishing feature— a pair of fangs that weren't for decorative use only.

"Since this is my dream, I say who stays and who goes," I shot back smoothly. "Guess who doesn't get to stay."

Nukpana's smile spread. "As I said, I welcome your efforts."

I tried to not only ignore Sarad Nukpana on my bed, but to cease any thoughts of him, forget my memories of him, and blot out his very existence. I knew the last one wasn't possible, but it never hurts to try.

The goblin was still there.

He laughed, a dark, rich sound. "Getting rid of me is easier said than done, little seeker. Perhaps dispatching those demons took more effort than you could spare." He paused suggestively. "Or perhaps, you want me to stay. You just can't say so in front of your father. I quite understand."

"You're a parasite, Nukpana," Eamaliel noted coolly. "You'll merely take more effort to detach. Though such extreme measures are usually fatal—to the parasite."

The goblin's dark eyes narrowed briefly, then he ignored Eamaliel, focusing all of his attention on me. Lucky me.

"You may find this difficult to believe, but I hope Carnades hasn't taken you into custody," Nukpana said. "His Majesty's lawyers and my Khrynsani would be disappointed if you were snatched from their grasp."

Sathrik Mal'Salin had sent lawyers to Mid to try to retrieve the Saghred and extradite me. When legal means didn't work, he'd sent Khrynsani shamans and temple guards. So far the goblin king hadn't gotten his hands on either me or the Saghred. The lawyers and Khrynsani were still on the island and still trying. I almost admired their tenacity.

"What can I say? I'm the most popular spellslinger in town."

I felt rather than saw my father stand up. I didn't blame him; I felt the same way. When a first-rate psychopath like Sarad Nukpana appeared in your bedroom, you didn't want to be caught anywhere but on your feet. I was glad I hadn't still been in bed when the goblin had slithered in. That would have gone way beyond creepy.

"You said you would stay away from her," Eamaliel said with quiet menace.

Sarad Nukpana swung his long legs over the side of my bed. "I lied. Surely you didn't expect me to actually keep my word. You're the man of honor, not me. Honor and morals are an inefficient, unproductive waste of my time. By the way, the board is still as you left it, should you want to resume our game." He turned to me. "Your father stormed off in the middle of a match; it was his move, and I wasn't even cheating. He may be a man of honor, but he can be rude." His fangs flashed in a quick grin. "Perhaps there's hope for him yet."

I blinked at my father. "Game? You're actually playing games with him?"

"What an appropriate choice of words," Nukpana said. "Your noble father plays games on many levels, little seeker. His powers of manipulation are admirable—and that says much coming from me."

"Chess, Raine," Eamaliel clarified. "And yes, it is a way to pass the time and to keep an eye on this one. At least I know that while he's sitting across from me, he's not plotting with his allies."

Sarad Nukpana sighed dramatically. "He still doesn't believe that my allies have all but evaporated. Literally."

I could believe that. Almost. The last time I'd been in the Saghred, I'd seen filmy figures, some more solid than others, most wasted away to wraiths. I'd also seen some who appeared to be as solid as Sarad Nukpana.

"Unfortunately, their mental capacity evaporates with them," the goblin was saying. "It's difficult to scheme with yourself. I'm all alone."

I was sure he wasn't. "I'm sure you're managing," was what I said.

"Even the worst enemies when imprisoned together form a kind of camaraderie," Nukpana said. "Your father and I have found some things in common. You, for one."

"You're wasting Raine's time, Sarad," Eamaliel warned.

"There's all the time in the world inside the Saghred."

"She's not inside the Saghred."

Nukpana smiled suggestively. "A goblin can dream, can't he?"

"What happened at the watcher station wasn't your fault," my father assured me. "If you hadn't acted as decisively as you did, innocent people would have died, and many more would have met the same fate if those demons had escaped."

"Decisive. So that's you call shoving one demon into a wine bottle and squashing another into a bloody pulp."

"I call it beautiful," Sarad Nukpana said.

Eamaliel shot him a dark look. "It was necessary."

"But I used the Saghred for the big, yellow one," I said. For the purple demon, I'd used Tam. Or Tam had used me.

"Because you had to," my father was saying.

I snorted. "Yeah, I could use it, or I could get ripped apart from the inside by the rock or from the outside by a demon. Some choice."

"That's not what I meant. There was a need, and you acted.

You did the right thing, the *only* thing. Yes, the Saghred is a force of death and destruction. But those things aren't inherently evil. War is death and destruction; war is not inherently evil. People who misuse power are evil." He shot an accusing look at Sarad Nukpana. "You used your power for the greater good."

And I had felt good using it. There, I'd admitted it. The Saghred's full power had been terrifying, overwhelming, but it had also been intoxicating. And deep down, some dark part of me wanted to do it again.

"And she took a couple of giant steps closer to insanity," Nukpana was saying. "Either that or being locked up for the rest of her life, or getting a dagger in the back, whichever comes first."

"If I punched him, would my fist go through?" I asked Eamaliel.

"It would. I've tried."

"Too bad."

"There were mages like Carnades in my time," my father said. "Men who were absolutely convinced that their beliefs were right and just. Going through a self-righteous life wearing blinders will do that. They can't accept that the world isn't only black and white—there are many shades of gray."

I thought of Tam and what we'd done. "Tam," I murmured.

Sarad Nukpana pulled his legs up to sit cross-legged on my bed, a grin of eager anticipation on his face. "Ah yes, Tamnais Nathrach." He rubbed his hands together. "Finally things are going to get interesting. What the two of you did was very naughty. It must have felt delicious. Tell me, just how good was it?"

My father looked like he wanted to knock Nukpana off the other side of my bed and through the wall. It wouldn't work, but that didn't stop him from entertaining the idea. I was thinking along the same lines myself.

"Tamnais Nathrach tries to be a good man," Eamaliel said quietly. "But his past begins to catch up with him. His training and the instincts that feed his power may prove too much for him to resist in the end."

"I want to help him."

Nukpana chuckled. "You're both going to need help."

"Shut up!" my father and I barked simultaneously.

The goblin lay back on my pillows with a smug and knowing smile.

I swallowed. "Carnades wants us both in prison and—"

"That's not what I mean," Eamaliel said. "How long have you known Tamnais Nathrach?"

"That's important?"

"Very."

"A little over two years."

"Have you heard the term 'umi'atsu'?"

"No. Should I?"

"Umi'atsu is a goblin word meaning 'life twins,'" Nukpana interrupted. He raised his hands in mock defense when my father shot him a scathing look. "Eamaliel, who better to tell her about goblin magic than me?"

My father hesitated then nodded tightly.

The goblin graciously inclined his head and continued. "An umi'atsu is a bond conceived between two powerful mages—usually goblin mages—binding them first through their magic, then hearing, sight, and finally their minds and souls. After that, an umi'atsu bond can only be broken by death." Nukpana looked entirely too happy about that last part. "Some consider it a magical marriage of sorts—body and soul become one, until death do you part, all that sentimental nonsense."

Marriage? My mind seized onto that one word and locked up in panic.

"What does that have to do with Tam and me?" I dimly heard myself ask.

"Just everything." Nukpana looked closely at me and smiled. "Why, Raine, are you getting cold feet? It's a trifle late for that, the ceremony's over."

"You're saying that we're . . ."

"Umi'atsu," Nukpana finished helpfully. "Magically mated, if you will. Though in my opinion Tamnais could have selected a more romantic location than under the elven embassy." Nukpana's black eyes glittered. "And I didn't even get you a gift."

I desperately looked at my father.

"What he says is true," Eamaliel told me. "Such a bond can only be formed if the two mages were emotionally close prior to the incident that caused the bonding. Obviously the two of you must have been very close."

Tam and I were definitely close—he wanted to be even closer.

My father's face didn't have much of an expression. I couldn't tell if he was pissed, but he sure as hell wasn't the proud father of the bride.

Bride. Oh *shit*.

I thought, considered, and concluded in the span of a few seconds. What I thought wasn't pretty, and my conclusion didn't make me happy. "When Tam said that we weren't separate anymore, he *knew* what had happened." He'd probably wanted it to happen. And if I found out that he'd done it on purpose, once I got my hands around his throat, I was going from bride to widow.

Then I froze, unblinking. My heart tried to do flips in my chest, and questions tripped over each other in my mind. I'd just experienced something entirely too similar with Mychael. Could I be magically joined to both of them? Was it possible? Merely probable? And if so, was it illegal? Or just immoral? Maybe it was both, or neither.

I felt really woozy all of a sudden. Either there wasn't any air in the room, or I'd completely forgotten how to breathe.

Nukpana was laughing. "Of course Tamnais knew. He was Queen Glicara Mal'Salin's magical enforcer for five years. I've seen Tamnais Nathrach in action, little seeker. He knows only too well what goblin magic can do, especially the dark variety. He's done enough of it himself." The goblin leered. "And if something was enough fun, he would do it again."

"Tam's not like that anymore." I said it but I wasn't entirely sure. I stifled a growl. For his sake, he'd better not be.

Nukpana's grin was slow and wicked. "Would you care to place a wager on that? A *private* wager?"

My father spoke. "The two of you did what you had to—and

unfortunately forged an umi'atsu bond. Tamnais is powerful enough to be one half of an umi'atsu. You are not. But you and the Saghred . . ."

"Let me guess: it was enough."

"The level of magical power you and Nathrach generated to save those spellsingers was more than enough. Have you seen him since that night? In person?" he added.

"No, we didn't think it would be a good idea just now, what with Carnades thinking we're forming our own league of darkness. Does he know about—"

Sarad Nukpana snorted. "Of course Carnades Silvanus knows about magical bonds, especially anything that could involve a goblin. His life's goal is to wipe every one of us from the face of the earth. So what if we conquered, tortured, and enslaved thousands of elves—that was hundreds of years ago. Ancient history. Some people don't know when to let go of a grudge."

When I'd first met Carnades last week, he'd told me that he was an avid student of goblin history, and that only through knowledge can your enemy be defeated. To Carnades, every goblin was his enemy. Unfortunately a lot of powerful elves, mostly pure-blooded high elves and military types, felt exactly the same way. Part of me didn't blame them; part of me actually sided with Sarad Nukpana. That was a scary thought.

"But elves have become more adept at protecting themselves over the centuries," Nukpana noted. "They may even be more intelligent than their rather dim ancestors." He sighed nostalgically. "It's not as easy to defeat and enslave elves as it used to be."

Cancel that. I agreed with Carnades, at least as far as eradicating this particular goblin was concerned.

Eamaliel's eyes met mine. "Raine, you have an umi'atsu bond with the chief shaman for the House of Mal'Salin—"

"*Former* chief shaman," I hurriedly corrected him.

"To those such as Carnades Silvanus, that technicality makes no difference."

"And if I'm in this bond, the Saghred is in it." I didn't ask it as a question; I knew the answer.

"Unfortunately correct," he said softly.

I plopped down in the chair. "Carnades is gonna love this. He'll get me and Tam on the executioner's block in one fell swoop."

And possibly Mychael along with us.

A prickle of cold panic ran up my back. The walls of my room were fading and the gray void was seeping in.

My father swore. "You're waking up. Have a care, daughter." His voice was fading, as was he. "And trust your instincts."

Sarad Nukpana's mocking laughter came as if from far away. "You can't trust anyone else."

I woke up, came to, whatever, as my eyes blinked their way open—and told me nothing. It was dark. I think I was under a blanket or cloak; however, I didn't feel any manacles on my wrists. Good to know. I was also upside down, over someone's shoulder, and that someone was moving fast. It felt like all the blood in my body had converged between my ears. My carrier adjusted my weight with a grunt. I knew that grunt. Vegard. If he was moving that fast and had to hide me under a cloak, yelling for him to put me down probably wouldn't be a good idea. I opted for pounding my hand once on his armored back to at least let him know I was conscious.

He responded by tightening his hold on my legs and running faster. That didn't fill me with the warm and fuzzies about our situation.

"Stop!"

The sharp command came from in front of us. I heard steel being drawn from all around us. My blanket fell off, but I still couldn't see jack squat.

Footsteps echoed on stone, leisurely walking toward us. Then they stopped. A voice spoke, his words calm, his expectation nothing less than Vegard's complete cooperation.

"Give her to us, or die."

Chapter 8

"Put me down," I whispered from between clenched teeth.

Vegard had one arm around my legs. If there was going to be a fight, he'd need all the arms he could get, including mine. I was still disoriented, but if Carnades had sent his personal guard goons after me, I was going to take some slices out of them before they got their hands on me. I still had the blades strapped to my forearms, and I wanted a chance to use them.

"Rolf, that's Vegard! Are you blind, man?"

Uncle Ryn?

The *Fortune* wasn't the only pirate ship anchored in Mid's harbor. Phaelan's dad, Commodore Ryn Benares, was visiting with three of his best ships. Uncle Ryn's definition of "best" was his ships and crews that were best qualified for the most ruthless work. He was here to motivate Mid's mages to find a way to free me of my link to the Saghred. As soon as that blessed event happened, he and his boys would be on their way. If the Conclave didn't want pirates in their harbor and town, they'd better get to work on my problem. Mychael had given permission for Uncle Ryn to have his ships drop anchor in Mid's harbor with the strict understanding that he was there as my concerned uncle, not as Commodore Benares.

I felt the Guardian's shoulders relax, but only slightly. "Commodore?"

"Aye, Vegard," came my uncle's amused rumble from somewhere in front of us. "You've wandered into my new home away from home."

"Put me down!" I didn't bother with quiet.

"Let's take it slow, ma'am," the Guardian cautioned. "You're going to be a bit unsteady on your feet."

"I can stand." Truth was I had no idea what I could do. Upside down wasn't the best position to make that assessment.

Vegard carefully set me on my feet. As soon as he did, somebody spun the room in a big circle and I promptly landed on the floor. I put my hand over my eyes and just lay there. I couldn't even see the room, and it still felt like the damned thing was spinning.

"Ooooo, not feeling so good."

"Sorry, ma'am," I dimly heard Vegard say. "The paladin had me get you out of there quick."

Everything flooded back, making me even sicker. The blue demons, Carnades, the giant yellow demon I'd squashed, my dream, my possible marriage—and all of them were the Saghred's fault.

I'd used the Saghred, but mostly the Saghred had used me. No wonder I wanted to toss my cookies. I also felt raw and exhausted and I had the worst headache of my life. The stone floor of wherever we were felt wonderful beyond belief against my flushed face.

A pair of massive black boots appeared in my line of vision.

"Hi, Uncle Ryn." My voice was muffled from half of my face being smushed against the oh-so-delightfully-cool floor that I never wanted to leave.

"Afternoon, Spitfire."

Spitfire. Uncle Ryn's pet name for me. Also the name of a

particularly ill-tempered breed of small dragon. Uncle Ryn had always meant it as a compliment, so I'd taken it the same way. I didn't feel much like my namesake right now, and I'd have chuckled at the irony except I was trying really hard not to move. If I moved, the contents of my stomach were going to do likewise. That's what my stomach was telling me, and I knew it wasn't bluffing.

"Sorry for the less-than-hospitable greeting, Vegard," Uncle Ryn was saying. "But the only chances I'm taking right now are at a card table. Rolf doesn't know you, and you had my niece over your shoulder like a sack of potatoes."

Swearing and sounds of a scuffle came from behind us. The scuffle concluded with three sharp punches followed by a quick succession of oofs and pained grunts.

"Sorry, Captain Benares, sir." The man sounded like he was talking through a bloody lip and possibly some loose teeth. "We didn't recognize you in the dark, and we've been ordered to—"

"Yeah, yeah, I know. Stop everyone by any means."

"Our apologies, sir."

"The boys are a little on edge, son," Uncle Ryn explained. "Most of them never saw demons before."

I slowly sat up, gingerly holding my head as motionless as I could. "They saw demons? What did they look like?"

"Like something that shouldn't be here."

"Blue or purple?" I hesitated, not really wanting to ask. "Or were they yellow?"

"None of the above. Red with horns and tails."

I swore. Just what we didn't need—variety.

Phaelan's boots joined his dad's in my line of vision. I hadn't tried looking any higher than footwear. I thought it'd help my stomach to keep my eyes on the floor. Generally, floors didn't move. That went well, so I tried looking up at my cousin and uncle, then ever so slowly over at Vegard.

"Okay, boys. Hit me with it. What happened?"

Phaelan grinned. "You did."

I would have kicked him, but that meant I'd have to move. Phaelan knew that, the bastard. "I mean after that."

"A couple of watchers got sick when they saw the pile of yellow . . . mush that used to be that demon, and Carnades started making completely unreasonable demands." Phaelan's grin grew wider. "Then that blue demon the paladin was questioning somehow managed to escape that metal circle thing that was keeping him—"

"*Somehow* managed?"

"The paladin glanced at the professor, the professor winked at the paladin, and next thing we all knew, that blue demon was free and hot on Carnades's heels. The blue ones like him for some reason."

"Can't imagine what that would be," I muttered. If I could ever show my face again without getting arrested, I owed Mychael and Sora Niabi a big thank-you.

"While Magus Silvanus was occupied, the paladin told me to get you out of there," Vegard said. "The quickest way was you over my shoulder." The Guardian winced in apology. "Sorry all that jostling around made you sick, ma'am."

"It wasn't you, Vegard. It was the rock."

He went a little pale. "The Saghred?"

"That's the one."

Uncle Ryn squatted down next to me, and I still had to look up at him. Elves were usually tall and leanly muscled. Uncle Ryn was just big. He wore his dark hair short, his beard trimmed, and had a booming voice that'd carry clear up to a crow's nest. He had a booming laugh to go with it and a sense of humor to match. He was somewhere around fifty, but he didn't look it, and he sure as hell didn't act like it. I was a firm believer in being happy doing your chosen work. If you had to make a living at something, you should enjoy doing it. Ryn Benares was still in his prime and basking in the benefits of his chosen calling— the most feared pirate in the seven kingdoms.

He took one of my hands in his and gently wrapped his other arm around my waist. "Let's get you off the floor, Spitfire," he rumbled softly.

"Careful."

"That goes without saying. My shirt's clean and I'd like it to stay that way."

Uncle Ryn got me on my feet and I didn't mess up his shirt. It was one of the first things to go right all day. I hoped it was a sign that things were going to improve, but I wasn't about to place any bets.

"You steady enough?" he asked.

"Only one way to find out."

Uncle Ryn slipped his arm from around my waist, but didn't step back. I didn't fall down or throw up. Two nice surprises.

"I'm good," I told him. "Thank you." I turned to Phaelan. "So what happened after that demon went after Carnades?"

Phaelan just looked at me. "Raine, I'm a wanted man standing in the middle of city watch headquarters with a demon running amok. What do you think I did?"

I grinned. "Ran like hell."

"Damn straight. But it wasn't running. It was a tactical retreat."

"Of course."

"I tried to catch up with you and Vegard, but his legs are longer than mine. And with that crazed blond berserker look he's got going, people got out of *his* way. Apparently I'm not scary enough right now." He glared at Ryn's men who'd tried to stop him at the door. "I'll have to work on that."

I looked around. We were in a warehouse that looked like it'd been abandoned until recently. Uncle Ryn had been in port for nearly a week, and it looked like he'd started stocking this place the moment he dropped anchor. Food, ale, weapons, black powder—and every bit of it in ample supply.

"Looks like you're all moved in," I noted dryly.

Uncle Ryn nodded. "And prepared."

I snorted. "For a war?"

"To finish whatever anyone here starts. Don't get me wrong; I respect what Paladin Eiliesor's trying to do, but I'm not staying on the *Red Hawk* when my son and niece are up to their pointy ears in trouble."

I stood on tiptoe and gave my favorite pirate a peck on the cheek. "You know how to make a girl feel loved, Uncle Ryn."

His smile was warm. "I do my best, Spitfire." The smile vanished. "I heard the high points of what happened this morning. Now what were the two of you doing picking fights with demons?"

Phaelan answered before I could. "I didn't pick a fight with anything. I couldn't even see the things. Raine's the one who bounced a brick off its head."

Uncle Ryn looked at me like I was a couple arrows short of a full quiver.

I raised my hands to stave off the obvious. "I know what it sounds like. But the demons were cloaked, no one could see them, and they were killing a mage."

"So the brick made them stop killing the mage?" Uncle Ryn asked.

"Well, unfortunately not. But it did make that one uncloak so everyone could see them."

"And pissed it off," Phaelan added. "And all of its friends."

Vegard cleared his throat uneasily. "The paladin needs to know that you're safe."

I laughed. It made my head hurt, so I tried to stop. "Vegard, I haven't been safe since I met Mychael. And if Carnades gets his way, I'll be safely behind bars as soon as he can find me."

Uncle Ryn scowled. "I've been hearing that name from the men working the docks. They always spit after they say it. Who and what is Carnades?"

I thought I was best qualified to answer that one. "Until the archmagus gets back on his feet, Carnades is the senior mage on the island. He thinks I'm dangerous."

"He thinks right."

"He also wants me locked up."

"Only over my dead body."

I resisted the urge to kiss him again.

Phaelan felt the need to elaborate. "Carnades thinks Raine's a dark mage who called her demon 'minions' here to do her dirty work, whatever the hell that's supposed to mean. He tried to arrest her for 'practicing black magic and consorting with demons.'" My cousin snorted. "I think someone's bounced a couple of bricks off *his* head. That or his ballast has shifted."

Uncle Ryn's scowl turned into something darker. "How much influence does this mage have?"

"Entirely too much," I told him.

"He could have you imprisoned?"

"And then some."

"Then you're staying here with me."

Uncle Ryn's voice said no arguments. I didn't want to give him any, but I had to.

"Sorry, Uncle Ryn, but I can't."

"And why not?" he rumbled.

"Let's just say that something's happened, and there's someone I need to have a heart-to-heart talk with." I said it through gritted teeth, and the threat of violence that came out with my words wasn't lost on my cousin.

Phaelan knew exactly who I meant and swore. "Tam Nathrach. Raine, he's trouble; always has been, always will be."

"So are you," I shot back.

"Touché. So what kind of trouble has he gotten you into this time?" His eyes widened and then narrowed dangerously. "He didn't get you—"

I just looked at him. "No, I am not pregnant."

But you might be married, chuckled the pessimist in my head. My pessimist was starting to think this was funny.

"Ma'am, I've been told not to let that happen," Vegard said.

I didn't move; I didn't even blink. "Not let what happen?"

"You get within half a mile of Tamnais Nathrach right now."

I blew out my breath in exasperation and relief. "Let me guess. It was Mychael, and he didn't tell you, he ordered you."

"Right on both counts, ma'am. He said bad things would happen if the two of you got anywhere near each other."

My little voice snorted, then chortled. If he only knew.

"Vegard, bad things have already happened, and they're going to keep happening until I can get a handle on what's going on. The first—and absolutely necessary—step to doing that is to see Tam."

The Guardian looked decidedly unenthusiastic.

"Did Mychael order you to sit on me again?" I asked.

"Just to try to discourage you."

"Next time you see him, tell Mychael I'm not easily discouraged."

Vegard almost smiled. "I think he already knows that, ma'am."

Chapter 9

Getting from Uncle Ryn's hideout—excuse me, land-based headquarters—to Tam's nightclub involved going to ground. Literally.

A rats' warren of tunnels ran under the entire island. There was no way I could show my face on the streets right now. With Carnades running around waving a warrant for my arrest and/or execution, the quicker I got myself underground, the better. I guess it was too much to hope for that the blue demon had caught up with Carnades and eliminated him and most of my problems in one fell swoop.

I'd never liked tunnels before; I didn't like tunnels now, and that feeling was unlikely to change in the next hour or so that we'd be spending underground.

Hours underground.

That thought made me breathe funny and put a twitch in my left eyelid. I tried telling myself that I'd just obliterated a couple of demons, one of which had been the size of a small house. We'd have lightglobes or torches, so it wouldn't even be dark.

Most of Mid's tunnels were natural; they'd been there for eons and weren't likely to collapse on our heads.

I could tell myself all that, but it wasn't going to improve how I felt. Nothing good had ever happened to me in a tunnel or cave. Multiple near-death experiences in a cave just a few days ago only further convinced me that Fate was going to finish the job the moment I set foot in the dank dark.

Think about the destination, Raine. Not the journey.

I had to get to Sirens, and when I did, Tam and I were going to talk.

I'd first met Tam at his nightclub in Mermeia. I was on a case to retrieve a client's ring that her husband was about to gamble away at one of Tam's high-stakes card tables. I came to Sirens that night as a customer; I conned my way upstairs as a seeker who was going to do her job come hell or high water.

Tam was overseeing the tables himself that night. He knew I hadn't come to play, and somehow he also knew I was armed. I didn't want any trouble, but I wasn't leaving without that ring. Tam behaved like the perfect host, welcomed me to Sirens, and asked how he could be of service. I wanted to tell him he could serve me just fine by getting the hell out of my way. I tried to step around him; he blocked me. I had daggers strapped to my thighs under my gown and I considered using them, but I was in a high-class establishment and told myself that I could resolve this in a civilized manner. I told Tam why I was there, simply and directly.

My client got her ring back; Tam delivered it to her personally. It was a public relations coup and he knew it.

Tam told me later he did it to impress me. He needn't have bothered. Being a Benares, I've always been attracted to rogues. Kind of like a moth to flame. And if Tam and I had really formed an umi'atsu bond, I wasn't just singed; I was fried.

The entrance to the tunnels was in the shipping office at the back of the warehouse. I guess if you did business with certain people and dealt in certain commodities, a trapdoor in the floor of your office that led to tunnels could come in handy. The shipping office wasn't large. It was no more than ten paces deep and not much more than that across. It had a desk and a couple of chairs with faded ledgers and maps scattered across the desk. The musty, cloying smell of old paper and mold made the air thick. Though that could be as much from cramming so many people into such a small space as anything else.

Uncle Ryn had assured me that this tunnel, after a couple of turns—and a little over an hour—would put us directly under Mid's entertainment district. Leave it to a pirate to find the nightclubs, bars, and brothels on his first day in port. Like father, like son. His men knew the way, so I could keep my spells to myself. Yes, I was a seeker and could have easily found my own way to Sirens, but since I didn't know who or what Carnades had looking for me, the safe thing to do was to keep my magic under wraps.

There would be nine of us going down into those tunnels and under the city to Sirens. It sounded like an unnecessary crowd to me; to Uncle Ryn it was barely adequate security. Phaelan, Vegard, and myself had an escort of six of my uncle's most levelheaded crewmen. Level heads were good when going into a place where heavily armed and murderous bad guys might run at you out of the dark. I hated it when that happened. My eyelid twitched again and I put my finger on it to make it stop.

"Nervous?" Phaelan asked.

My eyelid fluttered under my finger; I pressed harder. "Guess."

"Sarcasm won't help," he told me.

"It's all I've got."

"Tell me again why we're going into a rotting, dark hole in the ground rather than taking our chances on the streets."

"Carnades."

Vegard and a crewman moved the desk in the corner of the office, exposing an iron ring attached to a trapdoor in the floor. Vegard opened it, and Phaelan and I gingerly leaned forward and looked down. Way down. It was just your basic nonthreatening, perfectly harmless, yawning black pit.

"Maybe that demon's still chasing Carnades," Phaelan

ventured, still looking into the hole. "We're not all that far from Sirens. I'm always up for a good sprint."

"It's across town and you know it," I said. "It's just dark and damp. There shouldn't be anything down there, but if there is, we can handle it. There's nothing down there. Right, Vegard?"

The big Guardian shrugged. "Just the usual. Rats, spiders, salamanders, maybe some larger-than-normal crabs—"

Phaelan stopped looking down the hole and stared at Vegard. "Define 'larger.'"

"Just Guardian rumors," Vegard assured him. "Ruben was coming off leave and a three-day drunk when he said he saw it, so we've never put much stock in that one."

Phaelan didn't bat an eye. "You didn't answer my question."

The big Guardian sighed. "Supposedly there's some kind of crablike thing with pinchers the size of your head running around down there—at least in the 'down there' that's closest to the waterfront."

"Which coincidentally is exactly where we are." My cousin did not look amused, and Uncle Ryn's boys had become noticeably less thrilled with our choice of routes.

"Captain, it was dark and Ruben was wasted," Vegard assured him.

"I've been wasted and seen plenty of things that turned out to be real," muttered one of the elven pirates.

Time to put a stop to this. I slapped Phaelan on the shoulder. "We'll just refill one of our water skins with melted butter and we'll be good to go. You like seafood."

"Yeah, but I don't like seafood that likes me."

He did have a point, but I chose to ignore it. I jerked the strap tighter that secured my two new short swords across my back. Uncle Ryn had replaced the ones I'd stuck up the demon's nose. I pushed the crab out of my mind, prodigious pinchers and all. Of today's problems, carnivorous crustaceans ranked way down on my list of worries.

Vegard and I made a pair of lightglobes and sent them through the trapdoor and into the tunnel; their pale blue light illuminated walls of packed earth that didn't look all that stable. Vegard went down first, then the crewmen. I followed with Phaelan.

As I climbed down, the rickety wooden ladder creaked, but held. I looked around. Wooden beams supported a packed-earth tunnel. The beams had seen better days. Some had fallen away altogether leaving no visible means of support.

I shone my lightglobe down the tunnel a few yards. "I thought all the tunnels were natural—and rock."

"Most of them are," Vegard replied with a shrug. "Some of them aren't."

I had a spell in mind should this particular tunnel pick sometime in the immediate future to collapse. Considering recent events, I thought it prudent to be prepared.

"I should lead," I told Vegard.

"That wouldn't be wise, ma'am. I should go first."

"Then I would have to bring up the rear, because these men are experts with steel. They don't have enough magic between them to light a candle, let alone torch a demon—or whatever might come running at us. And, if I bring up the rear, you can't keep an eye on me—and I know you want to do that. So, do you want to cover our backs, or spend half your time looking back at me?"

The Guardian scowled. "You lead."

I turned to one of Ryn's men, a young elf named Galen. "I want the most direct way to the entertainment district, no scenic routes."

"Understood, Miss Benares." He flashed a nervous grin. "We know the quickest way to the best bars, including Sirens." He looked down the dark tunnel and swallowed. "We just didn't know there was anything down here."

"Hopefully you won't find out anything different this time. And if you do hear pinchers clicking, just walk faster."

"That goes without saying."

"Good." I sent my lightglobe ahead of us. "Let's go. And just tell me where to turn."

The tunnel was damp, moldy, and had things that slithered

and scurried into the dark ahead of our lights. But thankfully, there was no clicking or clacking. However, a series of white lines ran along the walls at various heights. Salt. I knew what that meant. We were close enough to the harbor that a storm or exceptionally high tide would put where we were under water. I'd just add drowning to my worry list under giant crabs.

Time was next to impossible to keep up with underground. I didn't know how long we'd been down here, but it'd been long enough for me. I was ready to see the sky or the inside of Sirens, anything but tons of rock and packed dirt looming only a couple of inches above my head. Vegard had to walk in a perpetual hunch; I knew he was ready to get out of here.

The tunnel ended abruptly in a small chamber. It didn't end so much as give us five more choices of tunnels. Though it did give Vegard a chance to stand up straight, which he did gratefully. While he cracked his spine and rolled his neck, I surveyed our options.

"Okay, Galen, where are we now, and which way do we go?"

"We're under the center of town, near the college campus."

"And which way?"

"Sirens and the other higher-class establishments are on Rathdowne Street. That would be down the tunnel to our left."

"Where does it come out?" I asked.

"It forks after a hundred yards or so. One tunnel comes out in a drainage pipe that runs under Rathdowne Street, the other one dead-ends at a door."

Phaelan and I exchanged hopeful glances.

"The door, what's it look like?" I asked.

"About this tall," Galen held his hand to the middle of his chest. "Looks like solid iron."

"Is there a knob or handle?"

Galen thought for a moment then shook his head. "Nothing. Not even a key hole."

Last time Phaelan and I had been down here, we'd left Sirens by a door that had a handle on one side, but not the other. It hadn't been a problem for us; we needed to get to the elven embassy, not back into Sirens. Tam didn't need a handle, knob, or key to open his basement door; he'd use magic. I was sure he kept it locked and warded. Tam had arranged it so that his wards in his nightclub in Mermeia always let me in. I'd find out soon enough if these wards liked me, too. Get there first, Raine. One problem at a time.

I smiled. "Things are going right. That's the place. Let's—"

Our lightglobes died, leaving us in the pitch dark.

Crap. Me and my big mouth.

"No one move," Vegard ordered, keeping his voice to the barest minimum to be heard.

I felt him try to conjure another lightglobe. Not one flicker.

I tried the same. Nothing.

"Galen, do you have a torch?" Phaelan kept his voice calm.

"Yes, Captain. We all do." He sounded scared to death.

"Get them lit. Now."

I heard flints striking. Not one spark.

Something was down here with us and getting closer, moving at a steady pace, as if it had all the time in the world. It negated magic, smothered fire, and sure as hell wasn't a crab. Then the bottom dropped out of the temperature, and I knew what was down here with us. It did have all the time in the world.

Death was eternal—and so were its Reapers.

I couldn't see my hand in front of my face let alone the frost from my breath, but I could feel it. I clenched my jaw to keep my teeth from chattering, and the long muscles of my back convulsed with cold, the violence of it sending a shuddering spike of pain through my entire body.

Death sent Reapers to collect the dead and the dying. I'd never seen a Reaper, but then I'd never been dying. Battlefields supposedly swarmed with them.

It flowed over us, and around us—but not through us. We were the living.

A Reaper sought the dead.

I swallowed. "Vegard?"

"I know." His voice was the barest whisper.

"Where?"

"All around us."

Not the answer I wanted. One of the elves shifted, ready to run, his terror a tangible thing in the dark. Another elf's teeth chattered with cold, fear, or both.

"Don't run." Vegard's voice was low and commanding. "Don't even move. It will pass us by. It hunts not for us." His words were oddly formal and awed. As a Guardian, Vegard would have done more than his share of time on battlefields. No doubt he'd seen Reapers in action.

It touched me. My breath caught in my throat, my heart faltered. The soothing and eternal cold that flowed over me was death in its purest form. It was the complete absence of life, that which drew the souls of the wandering dead into itself.

Like the souls in the Saghred.

Please, no.

I was the reason the Reaper had come.

Thousands of disembodied souls, not truly alive, not entirely dead. With the Saghred's containments gone, those souls had become shining beacons, irresistible lures. The Reaper's coils wrapped themselves around me, soft and soothing, welcoming and entreating. Seeking the source of those thousands, the wellspring from which it could draw them.

I was that wellspring. I was the bond servant. Souls could pass through me to the Saghred, so souls could pass out of me into the Reaper—and my own soul would be taken with them.

I was the vessel that Death had sent one of his own to empty. The Reaper wasn't evil, it simply was. And it had a job to do, and that job was me.

Vegard realized the danger. I heard him move, felt his fear for me.

"Stay back," I said quickly, my voice thin.

The Saghred knew what to do, and I did it without hesitation. It didn't want to give up its souls—and I wasn't giving up mine. I wrapped my arms tightly around my ribs and closed in upon myself, drawing every shred of my will, my essence, vibrant and burning with life, to encase myself in living armor. Life so strong that Death itself couldn't penetrate it.

The coils of soul-numbing cold hesitated, then renewed their efforts. Insistent, probing, looking of a weakness.

And finding none.

My defiance wasn't entirely my own. The Saghred's power helped me block every touch, every seductive entreaty. A Reaper could quell magic, but right now the Saghred wasn't magic. It was life. Imprisoned and tormented souls, but still alive. The stone had always existed beyond Death's clutches, and a flash of insight told me that this was not Death's first attempt to claim those it considered its own by right, a right that had been repeatedly denied.

The Saghred had shaken off its bonds this morning, and now Death had sent a Reaper to try to collect. Again.

"No!"

I screamed, terrified and defiant—and in smothered silence. My silent scream tore the coils that were weaving their way around me like a shroud. Death had been denied before, and it was not going to win now. My scream turned into a snarl as I held on to my life and clutched my soul; that single, screamed word channeling my rage into a white-hot fury. The Saghred had torn me from my home and turned my family and friends into targets for madmen. Mages and kings wanted my power and my freedom.

Now Death wanted my life.

"No!"

The coils loosened, the pressure became less.

"No."

I said it quietly into the darkness, then repeated it with confidence.

The cold receded. The Reaper was gone.

It would come back.

I took one breath, then another, drew warm air into my lungs. Air that smelled of earth, and water, and life. My life, Phaelan's and Vegard's, and the men with us.

We were alive.

Vegard's lightglobe flickered to life. Phaelan lit a torch.

"Is it gone?" Galen whispered.

"For now," Vegard said, his eyes on mine.

Death was eternal; it would always be back. Vegard and I knew what had almost happened; Phaelan and his father's men didn't need to.

"What the hell was that?" Phaelan directed his question at me. I wasn't going to answer him. Not now. Maybe not ever.

My throat was bone-dry. I reached for the water skin at my belt; Vegard passed me his flask.

"You take what you need, ma'am." His voice was quiet. His eyes awed.

I did.

I swallowed and the whiskey burned its way down. "Galen, get us to Sirens."

Chapter 10

For the rest of the way to Sirens, that tunnel was bright as day. We used every light we could strike from flint or summon from magic to keep the darkness and any creature lurking there where they belonged—away from us.

When the Reaper came back for me—and there was no doubt in my mind that would happen—he, it, or whatever wouldn't be alone. There would be more. And when they came, what I had done this time wouldn't be enough. The Saghred and I probably didn't run that Reaper off; its job must have been to find me. Mission accomplished. Death must be thrilled.

"Raine!"

Any hand that wasn't white-knuckled around a torch drew steel.

I knew that voice, but I still had a dagger in my hand, and part of me was tempted to use it. The other part wanted to run to the tall and lean goblin standing on the edge of our light.

Regardless of whether I decided to stab or hug Tamnais

Nathrach, he had a lot of explaining to do. But from the way he was garbed and armed, he was expecting more trouble than me to show up on his doorstep.

He was in black leather armor from head to toe, including boots that came up to mid-thigh. I saw a few blades on him, but with Tam there were always more that you couldn't see. The last time I'd seen him his hair had been pulled back in a long, goblin battle braid. Today his hair was loose, falling in a dark, silken curtain over his shoulders and down to the middle of his back.

Tam was silvery skinned, black eyed, and wicked sexy.

Beyond Tam was the open door to Sirens' basement. Standing just behind him were a pair of goblins I recognized. Tam called them friends and colleagues; our family would have called them high-priced, out-of-town talent. They were dark mages, they were powerful, and dirty was the only way they knew how to fight. I had to hand it to Tam; he knew how to pick good backup.

Tam stopped just beyond the glare of our lights, his dark eyes alert to any movement that wasn't us. "Inside. Quickly."

We didn't have to be invited twice.

I kept my mouth shut all the way upstairs to Tam's apartment above the theatre stage. I thought my restraint was nothing short of miraculous.

Tam walked in front of me, which gave me ample opportunity to stare daggers into his back—and to be reminded once again that Tam Nathrach had a great ass. Yes, I'd almost had my soul sucked out by one of Death's minions, but some things a woman just couldn't ignore. Tam was manipulative, secretive, and you couldn't get a straight answer even if you choked it out of him—but his leather-clad posterior was without peer.

Tam spoke without turning. "Enjoying the view?"

I put a whole winter's worth of frost into my voice. "It's the first thing I've appreciated all day." I didn't appreciate being attacked, used, or threatened—and I despised being terrified.

All of the above pissed me off in ways that I couldn't even begin to describe. Though when we reached the top of those stairs, I was going to give it a damned fine shot.

Vegard and Phaelan were going to wait on the landing below, and Uncle Ryn's six crewmen were standing guard at the foot of the stairs in the theatre. The moment we'd stepped across Sirens' threshold, Vegard expanded his job description to include chaperone. Mychael didn't want Tam and I in the same room. I understood his concern, but I needed to talk to Tam alone. I had some questions for him that I didn't want Vegard—but especially Mychael—to know the answers to yet. Vegard stayed on the landing, but he didn't like it.

I almost told him that Tam and I didn't need a chaperone, regardless of our umi'atsu bond, but I'd have been lying through my teeth. Tam and I have always needed a chaperone. He was a not-quite-recovered dark mage. Thanks to the Saghred, I was a dark mage magnet. The two of us were an apocalyptic, magical kaboom waiting to happen.

I've never been one for small talk, so when Tam closed the door behind us, that was my signal.

"When were you going to tell me?" I demanded.

Tam stopped and turned, and from his baffled expression, he honestly had no idea what I was talking about.

I was only too happy to enlighten him. I was still shaking from that Reaper wrapping itself around me, and all that rage and fear needed an outlet. "What we did with that Volghul, what we could probably do to any demon anytime or anywhere thanks to a certain umi'atsu bond—when were you going to tell me about *that*?"

Tam was silent for a moment. "Until this morning I didn't know what we had was an umi'atsu bond."

"But you knew it could happen." I didn't ask it as a question.

"I knew it was possible," he said quietly.

"And you didn't tell me."

Tam's black eyes locked on mine. "When I saw that Volghul through your eyes, I knew a Hellgate was open on this island,

and I knew how much danger you and the boys were in. At that point, I had more important things to do than—"

I stiffened. "What else have you seen through me?"

"Nothing. I knew we had a link since that night under the elven embassy, but I didn't know it was an umi'atsu bond until that Volghul showed up. Your fear for those students, for Piaras . . ." Tam stopped, and his jaw tightened. "And for Talon—was so strong that I felt it with you. Then I could see it. A connection that strong and clear could only happen with an umi'atsu bond. Once I realized what we had, I knew I could work through you to take down that Volghul."

I took a deep breath and let it out, trying to calm myself for what I had to ask next. I had to be calm because when I asked it, Tam just might shock the hell out of me with a straight answer for once, and I wasn't sure if I was ready for it. "I heard that it also makes us magically mated, married even."

Tam had been married once before in the normal way to a Mal'Salin duchess, making him a Mal'Salin duke. His wife's unsolved murder didn't change his aristocratic status, even after he left the goblin court. Somehow I didn't think the goblin royal family would be amused at one of their own being married—in any way, shape, or form—to an elf.

Tam stood in silence; he didn't even blink. I think I was witnessing Tam Nathrach caught completely off guard. It was a first.

"Some segments of goblin society consider it binding," he finally said.

"Binding as in close together, or as in legally binding?"

"Yes."

"Yes, what?"

Tam's dark eyes were unreadable. "Yes, as in both answers are correct."

I couldn't believe my ears.

Tam spoke quickly, but firmly. "But for it to be legally binding, both parties must be in agreement that the bond should be established. Such ceremonies are planned with great care."

My mouth was hanging open; I managed to get it closed.

Then it dropped open again and words made it out. "It *is* like a wedding." My voice sounded small.

"There are similarities," Tam admitted reluctantly.

I was totally speechless. Tam had never heard me at a loss for words. Today was just chock full of firsts. I felt a giggle bubbling up. I was probably two skips and a jump away from hysteria.

"I have never heard of an accidental umi'atsu bonding," Tam assured me.

My voice was lined with steel. "Was it an accident?"

"You know it was."

"Tam, I'm not sure of anything right now."

"Our bond took hold in that alley," he said. "What we did under the embassy probably completed the connection. The first was accidental; the second was necessary."

I remembered the alley all too well. Tam was trying to keep me from being captured by the Khrynsani; he killed one of their shamans with a death curse in Old Goblin. It was the blackest of black magic and Tam wielded it with a master's touch. The Saghred had responded to Tam—and so had I. We couldn't have stopped what had happened between us. Under the elven embassy, we had no choice. It had taken nearly all the power both of us had to free those spellsingers and survive, and we'd only been able to do it together.

I knew Tam was a dark mage, and I knew what being a dark mage meant. Part of me just refused to dwell on Tam having ever done any of those things. If you were a mage, you'd been born with magic as a part of you. Through study and hard work, that magic grew and developed into specific talent. I was a seeker, a mediocre one until the Saghred latched on to me. I'd been resisting its power ever since. A dark mage wouldn't have resisted. For them, power was an addiction, and the more power the mage got, the more they wanted—and the more they were willing to do to get it. Like use objects of power that only asked for a little something in return. Like the Saghred and its soul collection. Feed the rock; get the power. Supernatural creatures offered the same temptations, but demanded different payment.

Some still wanted sacrifices or suffering, others wanted freedom from all restraint, and some, like demons, wanted entry into our world. If you gave them what they wanted, they gave you more power; and if the monster you summoned took a liking to you, they might even teach you a thing or two—things that no mortal had any business knowing.

I'd always told myself that whatever Tam had done while in the goblin court, he'd done it to survive. Maybe. But no one had forced him to be the goblin queen's magical enforcer. He'd wanted the job and he'd gone after it; and by doing whatever he had to do, he'd stayed at his queen's right hand for five years. In constantly shifting goblin court politics, five years was an eternity.

When Tam left the goblin court, he'd gotten help for his addiction. He blamed his ambition for his wife's murder. Call it what you will—intervention, black-magic rehab—Tam had fought his way back from the brink. I wasn't going to be the cause of his relapse.

"How do we get rid of it?" I asked him point-blank.

Tam looked genuinely puzzled. "Get rid of it?"

"Yes, rid. We're not the only ones bonded," I reminded him, keeping my voice as level as it was likely to get anytime soon. "The Saghred's the glue. You're a dark mage and all-around magical badass. I'm not. I'm just Raine Benares, a good seeker, a not-so-good sorceress. You say you didn't do it, and I sure as hell *couldn't* do it, so that leaves the rock."

"I've never heard of an umi'atsu bond being successfully broken," Tam told me.

I didn't move. "It can't be done?"

Tam exhaled slowly. "I said *successfully* broken. It's only been done a few times that I'm aware of." He hesitated. "The powers of neither mage survived the process—and in some instances, neither did the mages. Their powers were so entwined that they had literally become a part of each other—they shared their magic like a vital organ."

I felt a sudden need to sit down.

"You can't cut those in half," I dimly heard myself say.

"No, you can't."

"But Sarad Nukpana implied it was a progressive bond."

Tam went utterly still. "You spoke with him?" His dark eyes narrowed dangerously. "He took you inside the Saghred again?"

"No one took me anywhere." I stopped. "Wait, if you're in my head, why didn't you know about my dream?"

"Our bond is still new, so I only know your conscious thoughts, and then only those caused by a strong emotion such as fear. I cannot see into your dreams."

"So anything I think while asleep or unconscious is still private."

"Correct."

That was a relief. I'd rather Tam not know my dreams. Especially since he had starred in some of them before.

I hit the high points of what had happened when I'd lost consciousness after using the Saghred, and the dream conversation with my father. Though with Nukpana in attendance, it qualified more as a nightmare. Then I told him about the Reaper.

"Sarad Nukpana did not lie to you," Tam said. "An umi'atsu bond is progressive. But since the Saghred's involved, that progression appears to be moving at a faster rate."

It was only a spark of hope, but I grabbed it. "So in theory, we could still be separated."

"A theory I do not want to put to the test—and considering your own situation, neither do you." His expression darkened. "Especially now."

"Meaning what?"

"We both have enemies—magically powerful enemies. If severing the bond didn't kill us, they would. I've been accumulating enemies since my time in the goblin court. Many of them would relish the opportunity to have me magically defenseless. I'd be dead within a week."

I hadn't thought of that. "With my popularity at an all-time low, I'd be dead within the hour. And Carnades would be at the front of the line."

"No, Raine," Tam said solemnly. "That Reaper would be at the front of the line."

His words chilled me. "I've never had a Reaper anywhere near me before, but I knew exactly what it was—and what it was going to do."

"The Saghred has protected itself for centuries, probably millennia. It knew."

"And it told me what I had to do," I said, voice tight. "If it hadn't told me how . . . Or if I hadn't been able to understand . . ."

"But it did tell you, and you knew what to do."

I slowly exhaled. "And I'm here, alive." I looked at Tam for a few silent moments. "I know it'll be back. When it comes, it'll bring more with it—and I have no idea how I'm going to survive when that happens."

"You'll survive because you won't be alone. I want you to stay here with me."

"I won't endanger—"

He almost smiled. "Raine, endangered is my natural state. I wouldn't know how to act if at least one person wasn't trying to kill me."

"What about Talon?"

"I can protect my son."

I shook my head. "I can't put anyone else—"

Tam was unyielding. "I have guest rooms, and I swear on what honor I may still possess that I will not take advantage of the situation."

Instead of an argument, I gave him a tired smile. "Tam, you have more honor than most of the mages on this island put together."

His dark eyes widened. I'd surprised him with that. Another first.

I pressed on. "I appreciate the offer; but if certain people found out that I was staying here with you, the two of us would have more trouble than we already do—if that's even possible."

Tam started to protest, but I held up a restraining hand.

"You aren't the only one I've said 'no' to today. Uncle Ryn wanted me to stay with him. And Mychael wants me to move back into the citadel. I turned both of them down."

"Both were generous offers." Smooth muscles worked in Tam's jaw. "You should have accepted Mychael's." He said I should have accepted it; he didn't say he'd have liked it. He wouldn't have, and I didn't need an umi'atsu bond to tell me why.

There was tension growing between Tam and Mychael, and the source, cause, and reason for that tension was me. Tam wanted me. Mychael wanted to protect me—and maybe more. My relationship with Tam, if you could call it that, had yet to progress much beyond the teasing and lust stage. However since Mychael stepped into the picture a few weeks ago, Tam's teasing had taken a turn toward the serious. There had almost been a confrontation, but I'd defused it by leaving. Two men couldn't exactly fight over a prize if the prize refused to stay around to be fought over. Tam was in enough trouble, and Mychael had too much on his plate. I wasn't going to add to either one.

I suddenly felt every bump and bruise I had, and I ached all over. Yes, the Saghred had kept that Reaper at bay, but if Tam hadn't used me to bottle that Volghul, I wouldn't be alive to feel aches and pains. I didn't like being used, but it had been for a good cause. A lot of people were alive because of what Tam had done.

"Thank you." My voice sounded as beat as the rest of me.

Tam's warily arched an eyebrow. "For what?"

"For offering me a place to stay, for seeing through my eyes, showing me what I needed to do, and keeping me, Piaras, and Talon from getting ripped apart. I didn't like how you did it, and I don't like what's between us, but it beats the alternative. I'm alive and, believe it or not, I am grateful."

Tam smiled slowly, showing a hint of fang. "You're welcome. I take it that means you've decided not to stab me today?"

I gave him a crooked grin. "Day ain't over yet."

"I'll bear that in mind."

"And the way my luck's running, with our bond, if I stab you, I'll stab myself. I'd rather not do that." I crossed my arms. "And by the way, you still haven't answered my first question. When were you going to tell me about our bond?"

"After we bottled that Volghul, I was coming to get Talon—and you. I ran into the Guardians escorting Talon home; they told me you were at watcher headquarters—and that Mychael was there. I knew you were safe." A bad-boy sparkle lit his black eyes. "And after what I did with you this morning, I knew you'd come after me."

"Did you get the treat of seeing what happened while I was there?"

"Just the fight—Carnades, the Dagiks, and a Wollek. You were scared, so I could see what you did."

"A Wollek?"

"The yellow demon."

I sighed. Why couldn't everyone just call the damned things by their colors?

"If you saw all that, then you know what the Saghred and I did right in front of Carnades."

Tam glowered. "I saw. You should have let those Dagiks kill him."

"On hindsight, that would have been the smart thing to do," I admitted. "Problem is I've got this thing called a conscience that won't let me stand by and watch someone get their throat ripped out if I can stop it."

"Even if that someone is Carnades."

"Yep, even him. I know. It's a character flaw; I'm working on it." I felt laughter bubbling up and gave in to it. "A demon tries to gum me to death, so I crush him like rotten fruit. Carnades wants me executed; there's nothing between me and the Saghred but a closed containment room door; and a Reaper just tried to suck out a couple thousand souls, including mine. And to top it all off, I actually managed to stop the thing."

Then there was what happened between Mychael and me.

I think that should have scared me a lot more than it did. When we had touched, his power and mine had become one, and for the span of a few heartbeats, so were we. The memory of Mychael's compelling voice resonated in my mind. *Magic most potent.* He could say that again.

Carnades knew Tam was a dark mage; he knew I was linked to the Saghred. I'd used its power today, unwillingly. But to men like Carnades, motive didn't matter. The moment the Saghred had come in contact with me, I was tainted and had to be destroyed. Men like Carnades also didn't give up until they got what they wanted.

Tam was speaking. "Raine, I think you should—"

"Find a hole and pull the dirt in after me?" I got out of that chair. I had to move, and keep moving. Running would feel really good right now.

"Raine, I—"

"Tam, I have so much power now, I scare *me!*" The panic I couldn't give voice to in the tunnel suddenly lashed out like a whip. I leaned my head against the glass wall. My breath frosted the cool surface. "I scare me." My voice was muffled by the glass and exhaustion.

One entire wall of Tam's apartment was floor-to-ceiling glass overlooking Sirens' theatre and stage below. Tam had the glass bespelled so he could see out, but no one could see in.

I heard the creak of leather as Tam came to stand directly behind me, the heat of his body warming me. Warm and nice. Except it wasn't nice; it was dangerous. Don't forget dangerous, Raine. Tam was dangerous to anyone who crossed his path, but mostly to me, especially now.

And I was dangerous to everyone, period.

Tam's strong hands settled on my shoulders and gently pulled me back against him. I knew it was a bad idea, but I leaned into him anyway, my head resting on his chest. Just a minute or two wouldn't do any harm. A little comforting never hurt anyone, and right now, I could use some.

Our reflections looked back at us out of the glass.

I watched Tam's hands slide from my shoulders to my arms. His hands were deliciously warm. My numerous brushes with death today had left me shivering—and not just from cold.

"I'm sorry," he whispered. Those two words said everything, but told me nothing.

Tam could be sorry for any number of things: the bond that linked us, using me to cram that demon into a bottle, me being accused of practicing black magic, or even the crap heap my life had become thanks to the Saghred. But it didn't tell me what I could do about any of them. The only thing I wanted more than to run was to do something, anything to find a way out of all of this.

Tam wrapped his arms around me, pulling me closer, his head bowed, hair falling in a silken curtain around us. The side of his face softly brushed against mine, like a cat—a big, dangerous cat. A shiver ran through me. This was about to go beyond comforting.

My heart sped up, and not just from Tam's touch and his scent of fire-heated spices, of cinnamon and cloves. Getting within arms' reach of Tam had always been risky; the kind of risk where your clothes somehow ended up on the floor. Now risk had turned to danger. Thanks to our bond, we were as intimate as two people could be and still keep their clothes on. The Saghred had forged our bond.

The rock never did anything without a reason—and no wards held it now.

I swallowed hard. "Tam, no."

"Raine, I would never hurt you." Tam's voice was a husky whisper against my ear. It was the whisper of a man torn between what he wanted and the knowledge that what he wanted could ultimately destroy him. Tam wanted me. Tam's black magic wanted the Saghred. Deep down, he knew it. He knew it and he didn't care—or he couldn't stop himself.

In one swift, smooth move, Tam turned me to face him. I didn't fight him; I needed to see his eyes, to see if Tam was the only one home in there. I looked up into twin pools in a midnight forest. Not the solid black orbs that they'd been under the embassy, no black magic glittering there, just desire. A woman could drown in those pools. I could drown in those pools. But if I did, I'd drag Tam under with me. It might not be tonight, but it would happen. The Saghred would see to it.

"No, Tam," I said quietly. "I'm the one who would hurt you."

His heart pounded beneath my hands as he pulled me tight against him, his body hard against mine, his breath warm against the tip of my ear. I expected his lips next, followed by a nibble of fang. Neither happened. We stood there, not moving, not speaking, not safe. Definitely not safe. And we both knew it.

Tam pulled back just enough to gaze down at me. "It won't happen yet." His denial was murmured on the barest breath. He bent his head, his lips poised above mine. "Not yet."

I didn't stop him, and I should have.

Tam's kiss was a brush of featherlight silk, tentative, cautious; but his breathing had taken on a ragged edge—for me and for the power that had slowed to a soft pulse inside of me, anticipating, waiting. The touch of his lips quickened that pulse, and my breath along with it. Suddenly I was returning his kiss, my mouth pressing insistently against his, my tongue touching the smooth sharpness of his fangs. Tam shivered at the contact, and his breath came in a quick hiss as his long fingers gripped my hair, holding my head still as he kissed me hard and deep, devouring. His other hand left my waist to explore other places. I heard a soft groan; I think it was me. A slim slice of my consciousness knew it was more than me, more than Tam.

Stop this, Raine. Stop it now.

I couldn't.

My hands took on a life of their own, sliding from Tam's chest to his throat. I lingered there, my fingers resting against the vulnerable pulse point, feeling it quicken and throb at my touch. Tam's arms tightened around me, and suddenly my feet weren't touching the floor.

This was more than sensation, more than Tam and me. Magic curled in a sensuous swirl of heat through my belly and lower, along my skin and through my mind, and I saw Tam and

I pressed together as if I were standing outside my body, a witness to passion that I had no control over. Tam's magic answered mine, his power responding, transforming those swirls into living vines, touching, entangling.

Binding.

Heat flared in the center of my chest, awake and eager, and I came back to myself, passion turned to panic.

I wasn't across the room; I was clenched tightly in Tam's arms. Our lips parted and we froze, pressed together, breathing fast, our hearts beating faster. Inside of me, the Saghred's burn went from an exultant blaze to a triumphant smolder.

The rock had just given Tam a sample of the ultimate fix and a taste of me along with it. For a recovering addict, it could be damnation. Tam might be willing to risk it; I wasn't going to risk Tam or myself.

I got my hands between us and pushed hard against his chest. "Tam, let me go."

I was panting, so was he. A shudder ran through his body and his hold on me loosened just enough that my feet touched the floor. I was ready to fight him if I had to, but Tam released me.

"I'm sorry," he managed between breaths.

I pulled air into my lungs, trying to clear my head, and took two steps back. I'd have retreated farther, but my back was against the glass wall. Tam made no move to come after me.

I exhaled and tried for some more air. "My fault. Shouldn't have . . . let you get that close."

Tam's lips were parted, breathing softly. "I should have had more control."

His dark eyes were still drowning pools, reflecting fear at what had happened, but desire at what we'd done. I looked away. I couldn't drown if I didn't go swimming again.

"Though control would be easier to come by if you didn't feel so good." There was still fear in Tam's eyes, but his sly grin was sex itself. "And if you hadn't tried to stick your tongue down my throat."

"I didn't try to—" Then memory collided with sensation. Oh yes, I did. Damn.

"Maybe next time we should just stand across the room and talk dirty to each other," he suggested.

"There can't be a next time."

Tam didn't answer. He might be a scoundrel, but he didn't make promises he couldn't keep.

"Tam," I said in a warning tone.

He raised his hands defensively. "I'll keep my hands to myself, but my thoughts are my own."

"Until your thoughts become mine," I shot back. "By then the damned rock will control us both. Permanently."

That reached him.

"Before that happens, we need help—high-powered and someone we can trust."

Tam frowned. "Mychael."

I nodded. "And he already knows we have a connection of some kind."

Tam didn't ask how Mychael knew, and I didn't tell him how he found out. With our umi'atsu bond, I didn't understand how Tam couldn't have known. When Mychael and I had linked, I wasn't asleep or dreaming, and I was definitely having some strong emotions. Tam should have seen, heard, and felt every second of it. But I wasn't going to question Lady Luck too closely. If she wanted to smile down on me, I'd take all of her goodwill that I could get.

I pushed on before Tam did ask. "And Mychael can help keep us out of a dungeon."

He frowned. "Or put us in one."

"He won't do that."

"Not you; it's always open season on me."

"He's not going to arrest you; he told me so. He knows you didn't open that Hellgate."

Surprise, suspicion, and then reluctant gratitude flowed across Tam's face.

I continued. "On the other hand, Carnades knows he's found the culprit. In fact, he tried to arrest her at watcher headquarters."

"You?"

I nodded once. "Little old me. By the way, you're just my accomplice."

Tam stood there in utter disbelief, and then he actually laughed.

"I'm glad someone thinks it's funny. Carnades thinks I have demonic minions."

That just made Tam laugh harder. It was rich, contagious, and I was relieved to hear it. "That is absolutely the first time that I've been accused of being a mere accomplice." His black eyes were sparkling. "And he thinks that *you* have minions."

"I could have minions," I said defensively.

"No, darling, you most definitely could not have demonic minions." The twinkle left his eyes and the laughter stopped. "And I don't care what cursed rock you're linked to, you would never open a Hellgate. I know it, because I have. Once. I'm not proud of it, but I did it. And I almost didn't live to regret my own arrogance. There are . . . rituals that have to be done first. Hellgates aren't accidents; they're intentional and malicious." His eyes softened, and I could tell he wanted to touch me again. "You could never be malicious."

I felt my face get warm, and I had to clear my throat before continuing. "Carnades Silvanus thinks I was intentionally malicious with you backing me up—and by now a lot of other people do, too."

Tam smiled, though it was more like a baring of fangs. "Carnades and I go back more than a few years. He was the Conclave emissary to the goblin court while I was there."

"Carnades was at the goblin court?" I'd have paid good money to have seen that. Though I shouldn't be surprised. He had made it his life's work to study his enemies.

"He's been having me watched the past few days," Tam said. "But he hasn't come knocking on my door."

"Give him time, he'll get around to you. I think he wants to scratch me off his list first. Right now he's running around with an arrest warrant with my name on it."

Tam shook his head and chuckled softly. "I can't believe he actually thinks you're practicing black magic."

"And consorting with demons. All topped off by using the Saghred to save his highborn ass." I laughed, a short bark. "I'm sure there's more he's accusing me of, but he probably ran out of room on the warrant."

"Carnades would never want to sully his mind with mere facts, but it takes *seven* dark mages to open a Hellgate—six to do the heavy lifting, so to speak, and one obscenely powerful dark mage to guide their efforts and keep the Hellgate stable once it's open."

I had to ask. "When you opened that Hellgate before, were you the guider or a lifter?"

Tam's eyes met mine. "I was the guider. I also had a reason, and at the time I thought it was a good one. I was wrong; I couldn't have been more wrong—and it almost cost me my life."

I cringed inwardly. Now you know, Raine. Are you happy? No, and you knew you wouldn't be, but you had to ask anyway. When are you going to learn to keep your mouth shut?

I knew the answer to that one, too.

I frowned. "Mychael said there are some dark mages in the Conclave and on the college faculty." Nothing says you're sorry like diverting the blame to others.

"Yes, there are. And a few of them are strong enough to do the grunt work. Maybe."

"That 'few' includes you and me."

"We have the power," Tam admitted, "and I have the knowledge. But I'd have to be ten types of insane to ever do that again. And the last time I checked, my sanity was completely intact. Not to mention we didn't do it."

"Tell that to Carnades."

Tam's eyes glittered with dangerous glee. "I just might do that."

Not only would I pay to see that, I'd want a front-row seat.

"Okay, so who's the ultimate evil, dark mage nutcase?"

I knew as soon as I asked it.

"Shit," I spat.

Out of the mouth of an idiot comes the truth. I could tell

myself that I'd been on the run for most of the day, fought demons, dodged arrest, defied Death. I hadn't exactly had time to think, let alone ponder a possible list of suspects. I didn't need a list; I had a name.

A thousand-year-old, goblin grand shaman, the blackest of dark mages who had used the Saghred to slaughter thousands and enslave thousands more.

And he was seriously nuts.

Rudra Muralin.

Chapter 11

I glared at Tam. "You knew that, too."

"I did. Because I know for a fact that Rudra Muralin got out of that cave under the elven embassy before the roof collapsed. He survived." Tam pulled a folded square of parchment out of an unseen opening in the leather armor on his chest and held it out to me. "And he's been a very busy young man."

I didn't really want to touch anything Rudra Muralin had touched, but if I didn't take it, I couldn't read it. At least it was actual paper and ink. A couple of weeks ago, Sarad Nukpana had sent his demands on paper made from human or elf skin and had used fresh blood for ink. Apparently opening a Hellgate didn't give Rudra Muralin any spare time for sadistic craft projects.

"His Khrynsani shamans didn't survive," Tam was saying. "Without his shamans, he would need powerful help to open a Hellgate." Tam's laugh was dark and humorless. "I imagine Rudra found all the new friends he needed when he told them that he planned to hold the island hostage for the Saghred. I know mages on this island who'd give their souls just for the chance."

And if Rudra Muralin ever got the Saghred, his mage allies would be his first sacrifices. Bet he hadn't included that in his offer.

I read the letter.

> *Tamnais,*
> *The demons you have seen today are but a taste of what is to come. You know what I want, and you of all people should know precisely what will happen if my demands are not met. Have your elf whore get the Saghred for me and deliver it herself to the location I will specify in my next communication. You have failed me once, Tamnais; fail me again and you will have only yourself to blame for the actions I will be forced to take. My associates will fully open the Hellgate. Imagine it, Tamnais. Legions of demons overwhelming Mid's defenses, the most magically gifted young people in the seven kingdoms at the tender mercies of the worst the lower hells can spit out. You know as well as I that those slaughtered in the initial wave will be the fortunate ones—those who remain will beg to share their fate.*
> *Order your whore to get the Saghred. Once she has it, bring her and the stone to me.*

"He didn't sign it," I said when I could find my voice again. "How uncharacteristically modest." I tried for sarcasm; the tremor in my hand holding the letter lessened the effect. I took a deep breath, and let it out slowly. Let go of the fear, Raine. It's not going to do you any good. Anger, now that's the way to go. Cold, hard, steel anger. You know what to do with anger.

"And this makes the third time he's called me your whore." The first time was under the elven embassy. I never did get full payback on that one. That crazy goblin wasn't going to get away with it this time. He wasn't going to get away with anything ever again.

"He says it to taunt you," Tam said. "And me. He knows it angers us."

"He's doing a fine job. I hope he enjoyed it. In my family, revenge may not be immediate, but we *will* get it; and when we do, it is sweet." I nodded my head toward Tam's bar in the corner of the room. "I could use a drink right about now."

"The usual?" Tam asked.

"And make it a double." I folded the letter. "What I want to know is why isn't he in the dark somewhere holding open a Hellgate?"

"What do you mean?"

"He said 'my associates will fully open the Hellgate.' Would Rudra Muralin need to stay at the Hellgate? Or once the door's cracked, so to speak, is he free to roam about the island?"

"That would depend on the strength of his allies."

I let my raised eyebrow ask my question for me.

"It is possible. Many of the most powerful mages in existence make their home here."

"That was everything I expected but didn't want to hear." I knew Rudra Muralin wasn't about to send one of his cronies to collect the Saghred and me. He'd want that satisfaction and pleasure for himself. "So in theory, he could be anywhere on the island."

Tam handed me a glass of liqueur so deeply red it was almost black. "A highly probable theory," he said.

I gave him back the letter. "So that's why you're standing in your own apartment armed for ogre."

Tam pocketed the letter and took a sip of his own drink. "I thought it a prudent precaution."

I snorted. "He's opening the Hellgate and we're taking the blame for his handiwork. That must make him one happy psycho." I paused. "Another thing I don't understand is that he wants me dead and the Saghred in his hands, not an island full of demons. Isn't opening a Hellgate like using a boulder to kill a fly?"

"He's a goblin, Raine—as much as it pains me, we are of the same race. You know how we are. A direct assault is not our way. The most successful plan isn't always the most direct."

"Great. He's nuts *and* a strategic thinker."

"And exceptionally good at being both. Chances are he's promised those like-minded dark mages a cut of any power he manages to grab. He would want allies magically talented enough to be useful to him, but whose greed blinds them into thinking he would share his power with them. And if he indeed has chosen to ally himself with the people I'm thinking of, even he—a master manipulator—will have his hands full. These people are far from stupid, but they are arrogant. They're waiting for Muralin to do all the work getting the Saghred, then they plan on taking it for themselves."

"Dangle the rock in front of their noses and they'd make friends with Death himself." I had to agree that it made perfect sense. "Rudra Muralin's been after the Saghred for hundreds of years. What's a couple more days? Though it is kind of an elaborate plan to throw together on the fly."

Tam was shaking his head. "Not on the fly, Raine. Carefully planned in advance. That's one thing you can always count on with Rudra—he has a plan and it's almost foolproof."

Tam and I had seriously screwed up Muralin's last evil master plan. I wondered what steps he'd taken to keep us from staging a repeat performance. One of those steps was named Carnades Silvanus; of that much I was sure. Carnades was a goblin pawn, if only indirectly. Rudra had to be thrilled that Carnades was gunning for Tam and me. It'd almost be worth getting in the same room with the over-bred elf just to tell him he was doing exactly what a goblin shaman wanted him to do and then watch his face.

But business before pleasure. Rudra Muralin in a Guardian containment cell first, then tell Carnades he'd been a goblin patsy.

"So, you got any ideas on how to flush out the bastard before this gets completely out of hand?"

Tam sipped meditatively on his drink. "We don't have to find Rudra; he will find us—before his next communication."

"If it's all the same to you, I'd rather not wait around for that to happen. Considering that he has *two* desires—the Saghred and my slit throat—I'd rather that first move be mine."

Rudra Muralin didn't just want me dead; he *needed* me dead.

About a thousand years ago, the goblin royal family had the Saghred in their arsenal, and Rudra Muralin at their right hand to wield it for them. Nothing could stop the goblin armies. They smote, conquered, and enslaved their way across the seven kingdoms—and most of those slaves were elves. On a challenge from the goblin king, Rudra Muralin used the Saghred to create the Great Rift in northern Rheskilia. The Great Rift was a mile-wide, nearly fifty-mile-long tear in the mountains of the Northern Reach. In one of the aftershocks that followed, Rudra Muralin fell off the highest edge into his newly created gorge, bringing an abrupt end to a notorious shamanic career. A couple of his more devoted disciples followed him like lemmings.

Rudra Muralin died in that ravine; but unfortunately, he didn't stay that way. Prolonged contact with the Saghred had extended my father's life. Prolonged use of the rock brought Rudra Muralin back from the dead. But in the instant of his death, Muralin ceased to be the Saghred's bond servant. My father led an elite team of Guardians charged with getting the Saghred out of goblin hands. My father was a mage, so when he took the Saghred, he unknowingly became the bond servant. Hundreds of years later, when the Saghred absorbed him, the stone considered him dead. So when I found the Saghred for the Guardians a couple of weeks ago, guess who got the job? For Muralin to get his old job back—and regain control of the Saghred—I had to die. He wanted to do the job himself, but any old death would do just as long as he was the first mage to reach the rock after my untimely demise.

Right now Rudra Muralin was somewhere on the island opening a Hellgate and playing political footsie with some of the local dark mages. Tam was right; he had his hands full. So if I'd gotten myself gummed to death by that giant yellow demon, his evil master plan might have gone right down the crapper. The Saghred was in the citadel, a fortress crammed full of Guardians and Conclave mages. The rock would probably bond itself to the first mage who got close enough. Rudra Muralin knew that little fact only too well. He had to control when I died. He'd love for Carnades to lock me up; the goblin bastard would know exactly where to find me when he was good and ready.

I didn't think I could be more motivated to remain a free woman. I was wrong. I took a not-so-healthy swig of my drink. The tang of Caesolian port burned with a cool fire.

"Well, neither one of us should go parading in front of local law enforcement—with the exception of Mychael—until we know how much trouble we're really in. That goes double for me. When Carnades said 'lock her up,' he wasn't talking to himself."

"Raine, prison guards can be bribed or killed," Tam warned. "You're as good as dead behind bars."

"Thanks, but I've come to that conclusion all by my lonesome. I'm a Benares, remember? We're allergic to iron bars. But Mychael needs to know about Rudra Muralin, and he definitely needs to see that letter." I paused. "And he needs to know about our . . . problem."

Tam scowled.

"Yeah, I know you don't like it, but after what just happened, you know we need help. But if you have a better idea, I'd love to hear it."

Tam's silence said he didn't.

"I've already told you that you're not on Mychael's list of suspects—and even though Rudra Muralin didn't sign it, that letter's just as good as a confession."

Tam laughed softly. "One letter's not going to change Carnades's mind. Mychael is probably about the only one who doesn't have me at the *top* of their suspect list. Part of Mychael's job is to know the names of the dark mages on Mid."

Tam grinned in a baring of fangs and teeth. "Most lawmen would stop at knowing names; Mychael makes the extra effort to personally inform these mages that he knows what they're up to, and if they break the law, they will pay the price."

"Bet that makes him popular with the black magic crowd."

"Over the years, several have gotten annoyed enough to try to do something about it. As a result of acting on their annoyance, Mid now has four less dark mages."

"Mychael killed them?'

"One got obliterated by his own spell. Mychael simply deflected it back at him."

I gave a low whistle. "Payback is hell." And deflecting something that big took even bigger magical mojo.

"The other three joined forces against him." His tone turned admiring. "Mychael took all three of them down. At the same time."

"Deflected spells?"

Tam shook his head. "No, just Mychael. There wasn't enough left for the watch to clean up."

I blinked.

"Those three had killed four students and injured nearly a dozen others. Mychael doesn't tolerate black magic anywhere near the students."

Students. Piaras. And Talon.

Damn.

Sarad Nukpana had done it, so had Rudra Muralin, and now Carnades Silvanus. They had used people we loved, threatened them with death and worse to get us to do what they wanted. It had happened to both Piaras and Talon. My lips narrowed into a thin, angry line. The demons wiggling through that Hellgate would be serving flavored ices back home before I let that happen again.

"Did you hear what Carnades said about Piaras and Talon in the watcher station?"

Tam's voice was dangerously soft. "No, I didn't."

I told him.

His long fingers clenched the glass in his hand. I expected it to shatter. "Carnades's prejudice will spread like a disease." His words were equally soft, and just as scary.

"Where's Talon now?" I asked.

Tam tilted his head, indicating a long hallway on the other side of the room. "In his room where he will stay until I can secure escorts that he cannot lose."

"Did he tell you what happened in the Quad?"

"I saw most of it through your eyes; so I had a good idea as to the rest. Talon doesn't know that, nor will he. Having four Guardians escort him home gave me the perfect excuse to get his side of the story, directly from him." Tam sighed wearily. "My son is, shall we say, creative in his evasion of blame."

I couldn't help but smile. "Like father, like son."

"In Talon's version, he played but a minor role. You and Piaras ended up with the credit for the demon's defeat."

"That was no minor role."

"I know."

"Your son has some major pipes." I hesitated. I didn't want to bring up painful memories, but if anything like the Quad happened again, I needed to know what Talon had in his vocal arsenal. "Talon's mother. What was her spellsinging specialty?"

"She was a nightclub singer. If she was anything more, she hid it well."

Just like Talon.

"Do you know anything about her family?" I asked.

"Nothing."

His answer was abrupt—and I knew Tam well enough to recognize it for the lie it was. Tam knew but he wasn't telling. I wasn't going to push him on it, at least not now. It was probably just painful memories of the woman he once loved, now dead. Probably.

"Does your family know about Talon?" No one other than Tam knew until last week. I didn't know if Rudra Muralin or any of the Khrynsani got a chance to send word back home of the new addition to the Mal'Salin family, but if they did, it could be trouble of the worst kind—for Talon and for Tam. Tam's only connection to the Mal'Salin family had been through his late wife. He'd told me that they hadn't had any children, so you'd think the Mal'Salins wouldn't care what Tam did—or who he did it with. Apparently once in the family, always in the family; especially when you'd been the goblin queen's chief shaman for five years. The Mal'Salins didn't let go of that kind of talent. I couldn't throw rocks; my family was the same way.

"They know," Tam said simply. "They have requested that I deny him."

I snorted. "Requested? The roundabout goblin way of saying 'do it or else.' "

"Precisely."

"What are you going to do?"

Tam smiled coldly. "What I've already done. Formally acknowledged Talon as blood of my blood, my son, and my heir."

I whistled. "That put you and the kid in the royal crosshairs."

"I was in the family's crosshairs before—and so was Talon. I've merely put my cards on the table. I will not deny what is mine."

"You can't be the only Mal'Salin with a half-breed child."

"I'm not, but the royal family keeps any dalliances—"

"Under the covers where they belong."

"Their opinion is not mine. And with Rudra Muralin still at large, and the Mal'Salins aware of Talon's existence, he has had an escort."

"I didn't see any guards."

"He has two, and this morning Talon eluded them. Though I'm certain he did it more out of a desire to rebel than any true desire to lose them."

"It's his way or no way," I said. "Again, sounds like you."

"Talon has assured me that it won't happen again. Many of the students who are of noble goblin blood have similar bodyguard arrangements. Talon doesn't stand out in the least."

I laughed. I couldn't help it. I knew what Tam meant by protected. "Oh, I'm sure your colleagues blend right into the woodwork. Other kids have muscle protecting them; Talon has a dark mage hit squad."

"Until the danger to my son is past—that is, until I see Rudra Muralin's cold, dead body for myself—then yes, my *colleagues* will remain here protecting my son. You have taken similar precautions for Piaras?"

Talon had dark mages. Piaras had pirates. A good choice if any potential attackers chose steel or clubs. Problem was, demons didn't favor either weapon—and neither did Carnades. Vegard was doing his best to keep me off of a slab in the morgue, or a cell in the citadel. I'd ask Mychael to make a similar arrangement for Piaras.

I tossed back the rest of my drink. "If Muralin doesn't get what he wants, how long will it take him to get that Hellgate fully open?"

"He's only completed the first steps to opening it," Tam said. "The types of demons spotted around the city today are nothing; they're just the beginning. It will take days to get a Hellgate fully open and stabilized. That's why it takes an obscene amount of strength to open one—that and stamina."

"So Muralin's somewhere on this island giving himself a psychic hernia opening a Hellgate."

"Unless he doesn't want it all the way open."

"Why?"

"Like you said, he wants the Saghred, not an island seething with demons."

"And because extortion works better that way," came Mychael's voice from the now-open door.

Chapter 12

Mychael looked at me with a mixture of concern and relief. "You're still here." He left out "with Tam," but his eyes said it clearly enough. "Vegard, allow no one in."

"Yes, sir." Vegard had the look of a man who knew a chewing out was coming. I knew it was my fault. What had happened between Tam and me wouldn't have happened if Vegard had been in the room with us. I owed my bodyguard an apology—and myself a swift kick for not listening to him.

Mychael closed the door.

"I asked Vegard to stay in the hall," I told him. "My fault, not his. So, if you're—"

Mychael held up a hand. "The last order I gave Vegard was to get you out of watcher headquarters."

"He did a fine job."

"I expected nothing less."

"After what happened in the Quad, I needed to talk to Tam, so I insisted that we come here."

"I assumed as much. I needed to find you, so knowing exactly where to look saved me some much-needed time."

Mychael's sea blue eyes went from me to Tam, searching, assessing, and knowing—but not judging. At least not judging me. He knew. How could he not sense the umi'atsu bond between Tam and me? Mychael was the paladin of the Conclave Guardians, duty bound to be the scourge of black magic practitioners everywhere. If what Tam and I had wasn't blooming black magic, I didn't know what was.

"Tam and I have a very big problem." I didn't care what my family said; confession was good for the soul—or at least the nerves.

"Umi'atsu," Tam said simply.

Mychael didn't even bat an eye. "How far has it gone?"

"Far enough."

I spoke. "He knows exactly how crappy my day has been." I tried for glib, all I got was ignored.

"She doesn't know, does she?" Mychael's voice was low and quiet.

Tam drew himself up. "I won't surrender to it, so I didn't think it necessary to tell her. She's been through enough already."

I looked from one to the other. "As fascinating as it is to listen to the two of you talk about me as if I'm not here, would one—or both—of you tell just what the hell is going on?"

Mychael's face was an expressionless mask. "You tell her, or I will."

"An umi'atsu bond does more than link two mages," Tam said. "It enables them to tap into each other's power."

"Like what we did under the embassy and in the Quad. I understand that. What's so . . . ?" Cold realization prickled down my back. "Back it up; did you say *each other's* power?"

He nodded. "Magically speaking, we are becoming one. You can focus and use my power now." He hesitated. "Eventually, I will be able to do the same with yours."

"Tam, my power's nothing to write home about. You're talking about the Saghred's power."

"Yes."

Just when I thought my day couldn't get any worse.

"As far as the Saghred is concerned, we will be one and the same," he told me. "Actually, I could probably tap the Saghred's power now." His expression was bleak and hard.

"Now?" Reality sank in, and lately my reality hasn't been pretty. "You could use the Saghred." Saying it out loud just made it worse.

"Or the Saghred could use him," Mychael finished for me. "Either way is just as dangerous. You were only a moderately talented sorceress until just a few weeks ago. Tam has been a master of the dark arts for most of his adult life. He would immediately be able to wield the Saghred's power to its full extent."

Tam spoke. "Raine, it won't happen, but the—"

"Damn right, it won't," I shot back.

"But the consequences would be dire if it did," he pressed forcefully. "So we have to face all possibilities. If the Saghred ever gained complete control of me, the only way to stop me—and to destroy what I would become—would be to kill me." He looked to Mychael like a man about to ask the ultimate favor of a friend.

"If it comes to that, I will be there for you," Mychael promised with quiet conviction.

Tam inclined his head in formal gratitude. "Thank you."

"Thank you?" I couldn't believe this. "*Thank you?* No, no, there'll be no thank-yous, no need to 'be there' for anybody, because none of this is going to happen."

My heart was pounding absurdly loud in my ears. The Saghred didn't want to use Tam; it wanted Tam to use *it*. Tam couldn't get his hands on the Saghred, but he'd just gotten his hands on me. Use me, use the Saghred. Oh *shit*. The rock was starving and it wanted souls. There was no way in hell that I was feeding the thing and the Saghred knew it, so it forged an umi'atsu bond between me and Tam. Since I refused to feed it, given enough time and temptation, Tam just might.

I turned to Mychael. "In watcher headquarters, when I

vaporized those demons, I didn't feel anything holding the Saghred back. Are the containments—"

"Gone," Mychael confirmed. "A few hours ago, I received a report from the citadel saying that the containment spells around the Saghred have failed, as have the wards on the room. The timing coincided precisely with what you did. I've ordered my men to guard the door to the containment room; it's no longer safe to be in the room itself."

That explained why Sarad Nukpana was able to put in a guest appearance in my dream—and why I couldn't get rid of him. No restraints on the Saghred meant no restraints on Nukpana. The Saghred was free and clear to do anything it could persuade, compel, or trick me into doing; and in a matter of days, hours, or even right now, it could do the same to Tam. What we'd done with each other and to each other was the Saghred testing the waters, seeing how much it could get away with. It was a test we'd both failed.

I took a shallow breath and pushed it out, trying to calm down. It didn't work, so I tried another. Calm wasn't happening. Screw calm. "None of that will happen," I repeated it like that would help make the nightmare any less real. "The Saghred can't be invincible; there has to be a way to destroy it."

"Raine, our top mages and scholars couldn't find a way," Mychael said. "Neither could the Guardians. The best of our order couldn't even scratch it."

I let the silence sit for a moment. "When was the last time anyone tried?"

"When your father brought the Saghred back to Mid."

"Anybody tried to whack the damned thing lately? All it's eaten in nine hundred years is my father and Sarad Nukpana. It's starving. And it's latched on to me, so we *know* it's desperate. That rock is vulnerable—and it knows it."

"It just tore through the strongest containments spells possible," Mychael reminded me. "That's not vulnerable."

"Sarad Nukpana told me before that the Saghred is conserving energy for important things, so apparently it doesn't have much to spare. But if that rock manages to get itself a decent meal, then we'll *really* be in trouble. Uncle Ryn's still alive because he doesn't wait around for his enemies to get stronger. He kills them right the first time."

"Raine, it repelled that Reaper," Tam said. "That was not the act of a weak enemy."

Mychael went very still. "Reaper?"

I waved a dismissive hand. "Yeah, one tried to suck all the souls out of the rock through me. It didn't succeed, and I'm hoping it won't come back for seconds." I pressed on before Mychael started asking questions, then making demands beginning with me going back to the citadel.

I ticked today's events off on my fingers. "I squashed that yellow demon, vaporized three of the blue ones, and held off a Reaper—all with the Saghred's help." I grinned and felt it turn fierce. "The rock's been working hard today."

"The most vulnerable enemy can also be the deadliest," Mychael noted coolly. "To survive, such an enemy will risk everything. The reward is great, but the consequences of failure are greater."

"So you're saying we shouldn't try?"

"Not at all, but I don't go into a battle without a strategy. And make no mistake, this would be a battle, possibly one we would not survive."

"So 'walk in, smash rock' isn't a strategy."

Mychael's lips actually curled into a grin. "It's not used very much."

"Sometimes simple is best," I countered. "The previous efforts to destroy the Saghred, they were all magical, right?"

"Mostly."

"Whenever Phaelan wants something gone, he blows it up. The Saghred looks like a cannonball; I say we use it like one. Put a big enough powder charge behind it . . . And if it doesn't work, some payback would feel good right about now. That rock has done enough to us; *it has to stop*."

"Raine, I—"

"Tam's not going to die, and you're not killing him." My words lashed out in anger and desperation. "The two of you

talk about it like it's some kind of twisted gentleman's agreement. Tam's just nobly going to stand there while you lop off
his head—all because of that damned rock."

"That is a worst-case scenario," Mychael said firmly. "I
don't want to kill Tam."

Tam smiled crookedly. "And I'm not keen on dying."

I ran a hand over my face. "Then let's stop talking about
what you say won't happen and find a way to make sure that it
doesn't." I looked at Mychael. "Tam says an umi'atsu bond
can't be broken—safely."

"It can't. And even with the few reported successes, the process was extended over weeks. We don't have weeks. The
Saghred links the two of you, and now with it unbound, you
may only have days, perhaps only hours. Tam, can you hear
Raine's thoughts?"

"No, only when she's really scared."

"I'm not scared; I'm pissed."

"Tam and I got that impression loud and clear," Mychael
said, smiling faintly. "No mind reading necessary."

"There are four stages to an umi'atsu bond," Tam told me. "I
believe we're halfway between the first and second stage."

I glowered. "What's stage two?"

"I'd know exactly what you're calling the two of us right
now."

"Before stage two," Mychael said, his expression distant.
"That's workable."

"You have something in mind." The tightness in Tam's voice
told me he already didn't like it.

"I do. I can't separate you from Raine, but I may be able to
slow the bond's progression."

I resisted the urge to take a step back. "To buy us some
time."

"But first I need to see how far it has gone."

"And you're going to do that how?" My mouth asked the
question; my feet thought it was a good time to run.

He saw it in my eyes. "Raine, I would never hurt you."

"I know that." And I did. But that didn't mean I wanted the

paladin of the Conclave Guardians carrying out a search warrant inside my head.

"What about the Saghred?" I asked. "I don't think it's going to like you trying to slow down its plans."

"No, I don't think it will."

"Mychael, I don't want to hurt you."

"That is a risk I'm willing to take."

"Because it's your job."

"It's more than my job, and you know it."

I did.

And so did Tam. The tension in the room went up a notch none of us needed.

I exhaled slowly. "I'm not willing to take that risk." My chest and throat felt tight and the Saghred didn't have a thing to do with it. "I don't want to hurt anyone—especially you or Tam."

Mychael's calm blue eyes held mine. "Raine, it is you who will be hurt if this bond is allowed to continue unchecked. I promise you that I will do whatever I can to keep that from happening—and I swear on my honor that I will not hurt you."

Unless it's necessary, my inner pessimist said.

Mychael's steadfast and reassuring gaze wasn't helping things any.

"Please, let me help." His voice was low and soft. It wasn't his spellsinger's voice. Mychael didn't want to compel my cooperation; he wanted that decision to be mine. But I knew if I said no, his duty wouldn't just let me walk out of here. One way or another, he was going to do whatever it was he felt he had to do.

I glanced at Tam. With our umi'atsu bond, Mychael going inside of my mind would essentially be him doing the same to Tam. This wasn't just my decision.

Tam hesitated and then nodded.

"You're just taking a look around, right?" I asked Mychael.

"Yes. For now."

I took a deep breath. "Do it."

He stepped forward, close enough to kiss me, and placed his

thumbs against my temples, his strong hands wrapping around my head, his fingertips a warm pressure against the base of my skull. Mychael held my face gently cradled in his hands, those tropical sea blue eyes gazing into mine, then the intensity of the gaze increased, and he looked inside of me—and he saw what was coiled there in the dark, waiting and growing, malignant. It hissed in anger and in warning.

The hiss wasn't only from the manifestation of the Saghred in my mind.

It was Tam.

I hadn't heard him move, but I felt him, standing directly behind me and in my mind, with me and with Mychael. Tam stopped just short of touching me, but even though my eyes were locked in a soul embrace with Mychael, I felt the heat of Tam's hands behind me, feverishly hot, eager to touch, his black magic desperate to take me away from Mychael. Beyond Tam was the Saghred. Neither one of them liked what Mychael was doing.

My breath suddenly came shallow and fast. Mychael in front of me, Tam behind me, both of them and the Saghred inside my mind. Our powers were brushing, touching, melding, flowing from me to them and back again in waves of ice and fire that left me gasping. My heart threatened to pound its way out of my chest. I couldn't breathe. It was too much.

It was not nearly enough.

It was the Saghred speaking, and more. It was my darkest self, the self who had enjoyed what I'd done to the demons, reveled in it, who wanted to do it again.

I tried to pull away from Mychael, but his strong fingers held me immobile; and behind me, Tam's hands went around my waist, tight and unyielding.

I heard Mychael's voice as if from a great distance. "It's moving too fast. I have to post a sentry."

"What is—" The question passed from my mind to Mychael's. My lips couldn't form words.

Tam clutched me tightly against him, and I felt the growl vibrate low in the goblin's chest. This wasn't Tam; it was his black magic fighting for survival.

"If I don't, you know what will happen to her." Mychael's voice was rough with exertion—and with something else. "Her link to the Saghred could be broken right now and it wouldn't make any difference. Soon you'll be too far gone, and you'll drag her down with you. Is that what you want for Raine?"

Tam didn't respond.

"Is it?" Mychael's eyes were blazing, the irises enormous, the white all but gone.

"You know I don't!"

"Then help me. Help her."

Suddenly the sense of Tam in my mind became less. My mind's eye could see the unbelievable effort it took for Tam to hold himself back, to contain his black magic. Mychael's essence filled me completely, overshadowing Tam, overshadowing the black magic—touching the Saghred.

Touching me.

I couldn't take it; it was too much. A scream rose in my throat. My body couldn't move, but my hands were free. I had to stop this. I put one hand on Mychael's chest, the other on Tam's, pushing them both away.

At the instant of contact, my breath caught and froze. White-hot light exploded before my eyes and inside my mind, and I saw everything, stark and clear as if outlined. I saw Mychael and Tam as if for the first time, completely, their souls laid bare to me.

I had seen Tam's magic before, under the elven embassy. It was a dark well of power, potent, rushing up from the deep, primal core of him. His black magic was like a caged beast, wild and untamable, tormented by its imprisonment, desperate to escape, its true nature denied for too long. The bars of its cage had been solid and impregnable, but no longer. Some of the bars had faded; a few had regained their power, glowing with renewed strength, a testament to Tam's efforts to control, to contain. The beast paced, eager yet patient, knowing it would be freed, and knowing it would be soon.

I had glimpsed Mychael's magic before, but never like this. His power shone like a burning sun. Bright, but not pure. I saw towering strength, felt the lethal magic of a warrior who had killed before and would kill again. There was no joy when he took a life, but a solemn acceptance, a sadness that tainted the fulfillment of his duty. Mychael Eiliesor glowed like an avenging angel, unrelenting, bloodstained and singed, beautiful and deadly.

That was the Tam and Mychael that the Saghred saw. It was what the Saghred wanted.

And through me, it was what the Saghred took.

Chapter 13

When I came to, I was on the floor, on my stomach, gasping to drag air into my lungs. I slowly raised my head. Mychael was stretched out on one side of me, breathing deeply, his pulse beating rapidly in his throat. Tam was on my left, lying on his side, lips slightly parted, the tips of his fangs visible, panting softly. He was looking at me, his black eyes enormous and gleaming. If he were a cat, he'd have been purring. Me? I felt tingly in places that hadn't tingled in far too long. I blew out my breath and rolled over on my back.

This was wrong in every way possible. An involuntary shiver ran through me. Wrong that felt really good, which made it even worse.

The three of us were fully dressed, but what we'd just done sure didn't feel like it. What we'd done gave whole new meaning to the word threesome.

Tam swore and pulled himself up to a sitting position and winced. *"Or foursome, if you count the Saghred."*

As if I could forget the rock.

"Raine," Mychael demanded, his voice worried. *"Are you all right?"*

I sat up. I was a little shaky, but I got there. *"What did you do?"*

Then I froze. I didn't just hear his worry, I *felt* it; a strong and tangible thing, concern real enough to reach out and touch. It was Mychael and Tam and me, all of us speaking in my head—and in theirs. Each of us could use mindspeak; most magic users could to one degree or another. This was different. Way different. Mindspeak was someone talking to you inside your head. Mychael and Tam *were* inside my head as if their thoughts belonged to me—and mine belonged to them.

I quickly turned to Mychael and my head swam. Too fast, Raine. Slow down. I reached a hand up to my forehead to steady myself. When I opened my eyes again, Mychael was watching me closely, seeing me as I could see him, inside and out.

"I was successful," he said, his blue eyes still huge and startlingly vivid.

I felt a wave of disorientation, and forced myself to stop looking at him. "At what?" I snapped out loud. I had to clear my head of the emotions and sensations still surging through me. Snapping helped. Saying to hell with mindspeak worked even better.

Tam leaned back against a chair, his breathing returning to normal. "He left a sentry."

Tam's face had no expression, but I could feel his emotions, all of them strong, so strong it made me dizzy. I fought it, taking one deep breath after another until it went away.

"I'm just a magically ignorant seeker." The woozies were gone, and my anger was arriving under full sail. I hadn't asked anyone to leave a damned thing. I had enough things that weren't me living inside of my head. "Just what the hell is a sentry?"

Mychael sat up slowly. "It means that I've left you with a part of my magic, my essence, if you will, to stand guard."

I didn't need to ask what his magical self inside my mind was standing guard over or against. He was guarding me against Tam, against the Saghred—and against myself.

"Basically, Mychael has joined our umi'atsu bond," Tam finished. "A three-way umi'atsu bond. I believe that's a first." He hesitated, his expression grim. "And forbidden for a paladin."

I froze. "Forbidden how?"

Mychael was silent for a little too long. "In posting a sentry, I have placed myself in direct contact with both you and Tam. While that contact remains, I am exposed to both Tam's black magic and your bond with the Saghred. For obvious security reasons, there's a law against that."

I didn't need to be told; I could see it. Mychael's essence, shining and steadfast, standing between Tam and me and that which sought to destroy us both. Mychael wasn't just standing guard over me.

He was protecting Tam.

Tam went utterly still, a statue encased in silvery skin. *"Why?"*

That single word, that one question echoed in my mind, in all of our minds. Anger, suspicion, confusion, and disbelief all contained within that one word. Another emotion stood out above all the others. Gratitude.

"Because you are worthy of saving, Tamnais." Mychael's voice was formal. "I will not stand by and watch you fall when there is anything that I can do to prevent it. You have come too far from who you used to be."

Tam hesitated and then inclined his head slightly. The thank-you remained unspoken but not unheard.

I wasn't about to ask my question out loud. *"And if someone like Carnades found out?"* I knew I didn't want to know the answer, but I had to ask.

"I would be stripped of my command, arrested, tried, and possibly executed."

Tam's voice in our heads was as hard as stone. *"No, you would definitely be executed."*

Mychael had just laid his career and his life on the line to protect me, to protect Tam—and he was a dead man if anyone on the Seat of Twelve found out.

"In nearly nine hundred years, your father never succumbed to the Saghred's temptations," Mychael reminded me. *"I do not plan for any of us to be connected to the stone for much longer. This is a temporary arrangement until we can find a permanent solution."*

It didn't matter if it was temporary or permanent, it was the most noble and selfless act I'd ever witnessed, and there was absolutely no way in hell that I would allow Mychael to go to his death because of me.

"Carnades believes that the two of you are working together," Mychael said, *"but he doesn't know about your umi'atsu bond."* There was fear in his eyes, not of Carnades, but for me. *"If he knew, he would immediately petition the Twelve to sign your execution order—and he would get it."*

One fanatical mage was enough, but I didn't need the Seat of Twelve lining up to take out Tam and me, or to imprison, convict, and execute Mychael.

"Mychael, you took one look at us and knew," I said. *"Could Carnades or the Twelve do that?"*

"If the three of us were in the same room with them . . . yes, they could."

I swore. "This is just getting better all the time," I said, and I said it out loud. "Can we stop with the mindspeak right now?" I rested my head in my hand. "It's too crowded in here, and disorienting."

"We can do that," Mychael said, using his speaking voice.

"Thank you." I slowly raised my head. "So if the three of us don't have a date night in front of Carnades and the Seat of Twelve, our problem should stay our problem." I realized something and froze, but not before I sucked in half the air in the room.

"What's wrong?" Mychael demanded.

"Uh, an umi'atsu bond is kind of like a marriage." I looked from Mychael to Tam and back again. "Does this mean I'm kind of married to both of you?"

Neither one of them made a sound, but I could literally feel the laughter—from both of them.

"To goblins, an umi'atsu bonded pair is considered the same as a married couple," Tam told Mychael solemnly. "What do elves think?"

"Officially, we defer to goblin law in such matters."

"Law?" I choked.

"Though I don't know how that would apply to an umi'atsu bonded *trio*," Tam mused, his eyes alight.

Mychael's mouth tweaked up at the corners. "I imagine it would set a new legal precedent, to say the least."

I couldn't believe my ears. "Mychael!"

He actually snickered. "Raine, the thought of the three of us legally married is the funniest thing to happen to me all week."

"Your funny could get us killed."

"Yes, it could," he agreed. "But that doesn't mean we can't see the humor in it. And believe it or not, I have been in far worse circumstances."

"There's worse than this?"

Mychael smiled like a man with a secret. "There was. And I'm still here."

"Well, I can guarantee you this isn't going to tickle Carnades's funny bone." And it wasn't doing much for mine, either. "It also doesn't get rid of the price he has on my head by now."

"There is no price on your head," Mychael assured me.

"But he said 'lock—' "

"What Carnades said and what he is willing to do are two different things. At least for now."

"Meaning?"

"Watcher headquarters was full of the wrong kind of witnesses—upstanding officers of the law. Dozens of watchers and civilians are alive right now because of what you did."

"And what I did made some of them throw up."

"You're a hero down at headquarters right now." Mychael looked amused. "Besides, Sedge doesn't think he has a cell that could hold you."

"I'm sure Carnades does."

"That's no longer an issue—at least not for the time being.

Carnades wouldn't dare touch you—at least not directly. There have been more demon sightings in the past hour. As much as he may want to, Carnades can hardly arrest the one person on this island who is now able to kill them. Carnades Silvanus is a political animal to his core. Arresting you now would be political suicide. He's desperate to portray himself as the leader Mid needs; such a leader could hardly stand by and let demons take over his island."

I scowled. "You're talking about him in the present tense. I guess that means the demon didn't get him."

"What demon?"

"The one you and Sora set loose on him. By the way, thank you."

Mychael pursed his lips against the smile that was trying to get out. "Carnades is being attended to by his healer."

Hope springs eternal. "The demon got him good?"

"Minor injuries, though it essentially ripped his robes to shreds. Professor Niabi caught it in one of her traps."

I nodded in approval. "So you and Sora let the thing go, but then catch it before it can take out Carnades. He gets some of what's coming to him; you keep your nose clean and get credit for saving him. Nice work."

"How did—"

"Phaelan saw what happened, right before he ran like hell." I had a thought and started to chuckle. Mychael was right; when you're in something deep enough, you could find humor in just about anything.

"What is it?" Tam asked.

"If Rudra Muralin wants the Saghred at his beck and call, in another couple of days, or hours, he'll have to kill all three of us."

Tam almost grinned. "I believe that is a possibility."

I chuckled some more. "And one hell of an inconvenience for him."

"Rudra Muralin?" Mychael asked.

"Is the one opening the Hellgate," I told him.

"With help from some of your local dark mages." Tam handed him the letter.

Mychael read it.

I felt his opinion of Rudra Muralin loud and clear. The goblin calling me a "whore" had only pissed me off; Mychael was enraged. I felt warmed all the way down to my toes. I wanted my hands around Muralin's throat, but maybe I'd let Mychael have a go at him first.

"May I keep this?" Mychael asked Tam.

"Of course." Tam hesitated. "You have a warrant out on Rudra Muralin, right?"

Mychael nodded. "I took the description you and Raine gave me and passed it on to Sedge Rinker."

"He can easily blend in with the students," Tam cautioned.

"I've made Sedge aware of that."

I hadn't thought of that. That'd be guaranteed to make an already tense situation worse. Most goblins and elves didn't get along in the best of circumstances. For years the goblin royal family had snubbed the Conclave college, until about ten years ago when goblin aristocrats started filtering into the college classrooms—and their gold started flooding into the college coffers, funding scholarships and teaching fellowships—all for goblins.

"Does Carnades or any of the Seat of Twelve know that Muralin could pass for a student?"

"Not yet," Mychael said.

"Are you planning to tell them?"

"I'd rather resolve the situation before it becomes necessary."

I knew what Mychael meant. If Carnades or any of his like-minded colleagues found out that a goblin grand shaman was responsible for opening a Hellgate, and that he also looked like a student, Carnades would order every male goblin student brought before the Seat of Twelve. He'd call it questioning, but it'd be an inquisition. And he'd lock up any likely candidate, which meant any goblin student with above-average magical skill would find himself in a warded cell. That would be a lot of students. Carnades would claim it was to ensure island security and safety—he'd do it because he wanted every last goblin out of the college and off of the island. Once the aristocratic parents of those students got word, ugly wouldn't begin to describe what would happen. Carnades would be better off with a demon infestation.

I had a sudden sinking feeling in my stomach. "Right now Tam and I aren't the most trustworthy witnesses to a lot of people. Ronan gave you his statement, too. Right?"

Mychael was quiet for just a little too long. "I asked Ronan for a description of Rudra Muralin, but he was unable to provide one. Apparently Ronan never saw him."

The sinking feeling in my stomach turned into a knot. "What?"

"Ronan was unconscious, and the spellsingers in the cell never saw Muralin, only the Khrynsani shamans he left to stand guard."

Tam swore. "Some of my men know him on sight, but they can't testify."

I knew why. A dark mage hit squad didn't exactly make for star witnesses. "So it's the two of us, and Piaras and Talon. That's it. If I didn't hate Rudra Muralin so much, I'd be impressed. We can't legally touch him, can we?"

"Let's get him in a warded cell first," Mychael said.

Tam frowned. "Mychael, he's got the Mal'Salin family behind him."

We all knew what that meant. The Mal'Salins wanted me any way they could get me, and the testimony of Piaras and Talon, because of their connections to Tam and me, wouldn't stand up to a light breeze in a courtroom.

Low, warm laughter bubbled up around me. Sarad Nukpana.

"An accused murderer, a Benares, a corrupted nightingale, and a wastrel half-breed," the goblin murmured in my head. *"Even if you found Rudra Muralin, you have no credibility, so*

you have no proof." The laughter continued. *"I guess you don't live a millennium and not pick up a trick or two."*

Mychael and Tam froze. They could hear Sarad Nukpana.

Through me.

Through the Saghred.

Oh no.

"Greetings, gentlemen." I could hear the slow smile in Nukpana's voice. *"I cannot tell you how good it is to be heard by someone other than Raine. Not that she isn't a sparkling conversationalist, but the three of you—all together like this—it's simply charming."* His next words came out as a resonant purr. *"And a death sentence for Paladin Eiliesor should anyone on the Seat of Twelve discover that he's in an umi'atsu bond with a dark mage and the Saghred's bond servant. I didn't think you were such a risk taker, Paladin Eiliesor. Or since we're all on such intimate terms now, may I call you Mychael?"*

"What do you want, goblin?" Mychael's voice was cold and hard.

"Such vehemence and disrespect to my race, elf." Sarad Nukpana made tsking sounds. *"No doubt Tamnais is mortally offended."*

"Not at all," Tam shot back smoothly. "I'm not your kind of goblin."

"I ask twice," Mychael demanded. "What do you want?"

"Why, to be of service, noble paladin. Although your boorish behavior makes me reconsider my generosity."

I put a finger to my lips. "Let's see . . . The containment spells are down, the Saghred is vulnerable, and Rudra Muralin's made a deal with Hell so he could get his hands on your little prison. I'd think you'd be asking for *our* generosity—and protection."

"But I am not the one needing protection." Nukpana savored the words, and I could almost see the smug glee on his face. *"There are many on this island who are in mortal danger of their lives—and their souls. And unless you act quickly, it'll be too late to save either one. Rudra Muralin has made a deal*

with the demons—they get the Saghred for him, and in return, all of the students and mages on Mid are theirs to do with as they will."

"Muralin wants me to get the Saghred for him," I said.

The goblin laughed softly. *"He is merely lining up an alternative plan should his other fail. A most enterprising young man, Rudra Muralin. Either way the demons will get all of those precious, magically gifted children."*

"We are listening, Primaru Nukpana," Tam said, his tone the very model of calm propriety, but his eyes were blazing.

The goblin's satisfied sigh floated through our minds. *"There, that's much better,"* he murmured. *"Was that so difficult? You should take note, little seeker. Polite respect for your betters can soothe almost any insult. Tamnais has not forgotten his courtly manners."* He paused meaningfully. *"Nor has the goblin court and royal family forgotten him."*

"I'm certain they haven't—nor I them," Tam shot back smoothly. "What do you require?"

"I require many things, but it would be rude to put my desires first. A better question might be what do the demons require—besides your students?"

"Spit it out, goblin," I said. "What do the demons want?"

"To be more precise, little seeker, I know what their queen desires above all else. With little else to do inside the Saghred, I've had the leisure to acquire knowledge from my fellow inmates. The queen wants her husband and king restored to her. Why else would the queen of demons lower herself to the indignity of dealing with one as vulgar as Rudra Muralin?"

"And how would consorting with Muralin get His Demonic Majesty back to home and brimstone hearth?"

"Rudra Muralin wants the Saghred. The demon queen wants what is inside the Saghred. Her lord and king was the Saghred's first victim. His queen desires his soul's release." Nukpana paused. *"I desire my release."*

"There is no escape from the Saghred," Mychael said. "The stone cannot be opened, cracked, or destroyed. Many have tried; none have succeeded."

"None of them had what the demon queen has her vassals scurrying all over your island searching for. So far they have been unsuccessful." He paused suggestively. *"I believe Mistress Benares can find what the demons cannot. That is the way you make a living, is it not? And with the enhancement the Saghred has given your previously mediocre abilities, I must admit that you have become quite proficient."*

"You need to work on your flattery," I told him. "And why would I want to find something to let you and a demon king out of the Saghred?"

I heard the smile in his voice. *"Don't forget about your father."*

"I haven't," I said once I'd unclenched my jaw. "Again, why would I want to do this?"

"Such a harsh daughter you are. I shall have to tell Eamaliel that his only child cares not what happens to him."

"Are you going to tell me, or do we play guessing games all night?"

"Forthrightness isn't a quality goblins embrace willingly. You should have learned this long ago from Tamnais. Where would be the anticipation, the sweet torment?"

"What if I tell you to go to hell? I'm sure Muralin's demons could help you make travel arrangements."

"You can tell me to go anywhere you like, little seeker, but we both know that I am not going anywhere—unless you find the object with which to free me before the demons find it. They will free their king, and I will be left behind. I would not like that at all."

"And you expect me to take on demons and free you from the Saghred out of the kindness of my heart? My family isn't known for kindness or having hearts."

"Oh, but you do have a heart, Raine. You will risk everything to protect those whom you love. Is my nightingale enjoying his foray into higher learning?"

"For the last time, Piaras is not your nightingale."

"Are you so sure about that, little seeker? You don't want to admit it to yourself, but you've contaminated young Piaras

with the Saghred. You're too close to him, and now it's too late." He paused. "*Closeness breeds familiarity, as you, Tamnais, and Mychael are discovering. Familiarity can take many forms.*"

Suddenly there wasn't nearly enough air in the room.

"*Yes, you're beginning to see now. You have asked yourself how Piaras was able to see that Volghul this morning when no one else could. And how he knew precisely what to do to hold the beast. He is certainly talented enough to do what he did—and as he said, Ronan Cayle is teaching him well.*" I could hear the slow smirk in Sarad Nukpana's voice. "*But young Piaras lacks experience—experience that coincidently I have. You may want to ask him if he has had any dreams lately. Or an inexplicable urge to do something that he really shouldn't.*"

"What are your terms?" Mychael snapped.

"*The seeker finds what the demons desire and frees me, or I will infect Piaras's mind to the point of madness, or compel him to do something so naughty that Inquisitor Taltek Balmorlan will have his legal excuse to take him back into custody. Either she helps me, or the inquisitor gets his excuse—and he takes her nightingale.*"

Tam hissed.

"*And Tamnais, I seriously doubt your half-breed spawn learned to do what he did this morning in a cabaret. The young are so easily influenced.*"

"If you touch my son, I—"

"*You are welcome to come and get me. Raine can tell you precisely where I am. Free me, and I shall release the songbirds.*" Nukpana sounded confident enough to start packing his bags now. "*But of course, the final choice is yours.*"

What choice did I have? What choice did any of us have? Son of a bitch.

"*I have been called much worse, little seeker.*"

Mychael's jaw tightened. "What is the object?"

"*The Scythe of Nen.*"

"Which is?"

"*A key to unlock the Saghred.*"

So much for what that purple demon who killed Professor Berel was trying to find.

"What does it look like?" I asked.

"I know not. But I strongly advise that you find out, and quickly."

Sarad Nukpana's voice trailed off and evaporated. There was none of the usual taunting laughter. He knew he had us. Laughter would have been redundant.

Chapter 14

Tam ran through the apartment to Talon's bedroom door. It was locked. Tam kicked it once and the lock ceased to be a problem— and so did most of the door. The kid was halfway out the window when Tam jerked him back into the room by his collar.

"Where the hell do you think you're going?"

Talon looked at his dad like he'd lost his mind. "I have a date."

Tam blinked. "A *date*?"

"You know, with a girl."

Tam gave him a shake, and I couldn't help but notice that the kid's boots weren't touching the floor.

"Okay, okay. Technically a woman." Talon grinned lascivi- ously. "Two women, actually."

Tam put him in a chair, but kept his hand right where it was. "I told you not to leave this room."

"Well, see, here's the thing. When you told me not to leave, it was *after* I'd already set this up. So technically my plans supersede—"

"Nothing!" Tam roared in his son's face. "Your plans supersede nothing!"

"You don't have to get so—"

"Yes, I do."

In a split second, Tam's voice went from a roar to a tight, hissing whisper. Talon's aqua eyes went wide as saucers. I think he wanted the roar back.

"I'm sorry?" Talon guessed.

With some effort, Tam unclenched his hand from the back of his son's neck. "You could have been."

Talon stopped just short of rolling his eyes. "Give me *some* credit. I take precautions; I always carry protection."

A vein I'd never noticed before was throbbing in Tam's temple. "That's not the kind of protection I mean."

"My bodyguards?" Talon shrugged. "They can come along; I don't mind. They just can't watch. I'm not into that."

If Piaras hadn't been in even more danger, I would have enjoyed watching Tam's attempts at parenting a goblin teenager.

I raced back through the apartment and flung open the door. "Phael—"

Phaelan and Vegard fell into the room from where they'd been trying to listen through the door.

"The damned thing's soundproof," Phaelan said indignantly, as if him getting caught eavesdropping was entirely the door's fault.

"We couldn't hear a thing, ma'am." Vegard managed to sound incensed and apologetic at the same time.

"I'm sure Tam had it built that way," I told them both. "Phaelan, Guardians took Piaras back to the *Fortune*. I need to know if he's still there."

"He should be."

I felt my own temple start to throb. "Does your crew know to keep him on board?"

Phaelan had to think about that one. "You would think so."

I couldn't believe my ears. "Dammit!"

"Dammit, what?"

I told them what Sarad Nukpana had said.

Vegard's next words blistered the air blue, and if I hadn't grabbed his arm as tight as I could, he'd have been running for the ship. As it was, he almost jerked me off my feet.

"You won't get there in time," I told him. "Phaelan, get hold of your ship's contact wizard. Tell him to keep Piaras on board. And if he's gone—Go. Get. Him."

"You have a contact wizard?" Vegard asked Phaelan, his tone somewhere between disbelieving and impressed.

"My one concession to magic."

Contact wizards could relay telepathic messages over great distances. I'd told Uncle Ryn about them years ago, and he saw the wisdom in being able to communicate instantly with any ship in his fleet. Within a year, all of his ships had a contact on their crew. Phaelan didn't like magic, but I'd never heard him complain about contact wizards. The stone in the ring Phaelan wore let him stay in communication with any contact in Uncle Ryn's fleet.

Phaelan had moved a few paces down the hall and was talking in low tones to his ring. Touching the ring's stone and projecting his thoughts was all he had to do, but that smacked too much of magic for Phaelan's comfort. He could talk to his right boot for all I cared, just as long as I could be assured that Piaras was still on the *Fortune* surrounded by pirates.

"Well?" I asked.

"Five Guardians showed up at the *Fortune* about a half hour ago and said that Mychael wanted to see Piaras immediately," Phaelan said. "They had a signed and sealed note from Mychael, and the kid recognized the one with the note, so he went with them."

My blood ran cold. "Mychael, did you—"

"No, I did not." The intensity of those four little words was frightening. "I want that Guardian's name, Phaelan. Does your wizard have it?"

Phaelan asked and smiled fiercely as he listened to the answer. "The Guardian didn't give his name, but Piaras did." He looked at me. "He said to tell you that he had gone with Sir Jari Devent."

"Who's that?" I asked Mychael.

"Knighted last year." The muscles worked in his jaw. "He's the younger brother to the defense attaché at the elven embassy."

Oh hell.

"Who reports to elven intelligence," I finished for him.

"Were the other Guardians elves?" Mychael asked Phaelan.

"He didn't say."

"Find out."

Phaelan did. "All elves," he reported. "All in Guardian uniforms. But this Jari person was the only one who came forward; the others stayed on the dock. Think we've got some fake Guardians?"

"Probably. One traitor is too many."

"My contact wizard said they looked real enough. Military bearing, the works."

I glanced sharply at Mychael. We were thinking the same thing.

Professional soldiers, like elven embassy guards.

"Carnades couldn't get Piaras this morning at headquarters, so Balmorlan's making his move now," I said.

Since we'd arrived on Mid, Piaras and his spellsinging voice had attracted the wrong kind of attention from the worst kind of people—people who recognized him for the dangerous weapon he was, and each one of them was determined to possess that weapon for themselves. Taltek Balmorlan, an inquisitor for elven intelligence, had Piaras kidnapped a week ago and imprisoned him in the elven embassy until he could get him off the island.

"Embassy guards?" Phaelan asked, his voice deathly quiet.

Last week, he'd seen embassy guards slaughter six Guardians and load an unconscious Piaras into a waiting coach—and he hadn't been able to do a damned thing to stop it. I wasn't the only Benares wanting payback. As embassy guards, Balmorlan's men had diplomatic immunity, and as a wanted criminal, Phaelan's testimony wouldn't have been worth the parchment it'd have been scratched on.

"Cousin, we need to do something permanent about Taltek Balmorlan," Phaelan told me.

"Agreed. Let's get Piaras first, then we can make Balmorlan sorry."

"My contact wizard said Piaras armed himself before he left the ship." Phaelan paused meaningfully. "Heavily."

I suddenly felt sick to my stomach. "Mychael, can you contact someone in the citadel to—"

Tam and Talon were looking down into Sirens' theatre, and from their expressions, they weren't admiring the view.

"Mychael, we've got unwanted guests," Tam said.

Two strides put Mychael at Tam's side. I went to the glass wall and peered down into the theatre two stories below. The only illumination was the pale flicker of lightglobes mounted along the walls to mark the exit aisles. Something was moving down on the floor of the theatre. I blinked. Cancel that. The floor of the theatre was moving. Shifting mist, with pale green motes of light winking beneath the surface. I didn't know what it was, but I knew it shouldn't be there, and we shouldn't stay here.

"Your wards?" Mychael's voice was tight.

Tam didn't take his eyes off of the swirling mist. "Meant to stop physical entry or magical attack."

I had a sinking feeling that the sparkly mist rolling around on the floor was none of the above. Thin threads of mist snaked upward from between the floorboards. Cold spots formed into columns of frosty air between the tables, frost that reached the window in front of my face. I felt the bone-chilling cold right through the glass. Below us, wisps of icy vapor swirled and solidified into things that weren't magical and sure as hell weren't physical.

At least not anymore.

They were dead, and from the looks of them, they'd been that way for a long time. They were armored and entirely too well armed. They drew new steel from moldy and rotting scabbards and sheaths.

The undead warriors appeared to be vaguely human, but unlike any human that I'd ever seen, unless those men had been dragged repeatedly through fire and then what remained of their bodies entombed and held together by the steel armor they wore. Runes and symbols were etched into the steel, glowing red from within.

Specters, ghosts, phantoms—call them what you wanted. Once they were through the boards, those sparkly bodies became entirely too solid. The really bad part was that since they were dead, us killing them probably wouldn't make them any more dead than they already were.

I hoped Uncle Ryn's men had had the time and good sense to get themselves back into the tunnels.

Talon swallowed. "I vote we go out my window."

As if on some perverse cue, Talon's window slammed shut down the hall behind us, and doors in Tam's apartment and on other floors started doing the same. The slamming was the only sound in the entire building. Some sicko sorcerer had a twisted sense of humor. My bet was Rudra Muralin.

"This isn't Rudra's work." Tam scooped up my thoughts like dice off a gaming table. That link of ours was coming in handy. Tam went to a massive cabinet that stood against one wall, placed his hand on the door, fingers spread. He hissed a few words in Old Goblin and the door simply vanished. Inside were an assortment of poled weapons; most of them taller than me. Some had a single, wickedly curved blade on one end; the rest sported a blade on both ends. They were monstrous and made the swords I carried look like toothpicks.

I wanted one.

Tam tossed a double-bladed one to Mychael, who expertly caught it. The moment he touched it, a brilliant blue-white light ran down the length of the weapon and blazed with white fire once it reached the curved blades.

"No necromancer on Mid can raise anything that old, and not in those numbers," Mychael told me. "And Muralin's got his hands full with a Hellgate."

"We think," I reminded him.

"I think her demonic majesty got tired of waiting," Tam said.

"But those aren't demons," Phaelan said.

I understood what Tam was saying. "No, they're not," I told Phaelan, "but they're dead. They're ghosts."

"But there's no such thing as ghosts."

"You want to go down there and tell them that?"

"No. But demons don't command ghosts. Do they?"

"Where do really bad guys go when they die?" I asked Phaelan.

"Hell?"

"And who's ruling Hell right now?"

"The demon queen?"

"Give that man a blade on a stick." I had a disturbing thought. "Will a blade on a stick work?"

Mychael spun the bladed pike once with practiced and deadly efficiency. "As long as they remain in their solid form, these should work. Bits and pieces don't fight back very well."

"What's the plan?" My question was for anyone who might have one. I wasn't exactly flush with experience dealing with dead people who didn't have the courtesy to act that way.

Mychael's response was pure, stoic paladin. "We go downstairs, destroy those things, and go after Piaras."

"Good plan. Simple and direct."

A ghostly face appeared at Tam's glass wall, right in front of me. I bit back a shriek. No body, just a floating armored head surrounded by mist. A floating, decaying, rotting head. Half of his face had been peeled back all the way down to the bone, skin and tendons dangling loosely from his jaw. Ruined eyes the color of curdled milk stared through the glass. A flicker of red flared to life in the center of each sightless orb. Those dead eyes shouldn't be able to see me, but I don't think anyone had told him that.

"Our lady sends her greetings and regards to the one who commands the Saghred." The words sounded choked with dirt and gravel, and flecks of decayed skin fell from the pallid lips as it spoke. "She would hold discourse with thee."

Mychael moved to step in front of me. I laid a restraining hand on his arm.

"Who is your lady?" My voice only trembled a little. Good for me.

"The queen of demons, the mistress of Hell, and the consort of our imprisoned lord."

Oh crap. That lady. Tam was right.

"You rejected our queen's first invitation. The Reaper's presence led us to you."

I took in a slow breath. "And why does she want to talk to me?"

"To request a boon."

A favor. The demon queen wanted a favor from me, and she'd sent her most winning and polite courtiers to ask me not so nicely. I glanced down at the theatre floor. Dozens, with still more squirming up through the boards. When they solidified, they stood motionless, as if waiting for some unspoken signal, probably from the big, bobbing head. My throat tried to swallow, either that or scream. I couldn't do either one.

"I will hear her request." When a platoon of ancient, burned, and mutilated undead seal my friends and me inside a building, I like to know why before they start killing us.

"Keep him talking, Raine," came Mychael's voice in my mind. *"We will clear the way."*

"And don't piss him off," Tam just had to add.

I was about to ask how the hell they expected me to do one without the other when I saw them out of the corner of my eye. One moment they were at the weapon cabinet, the next they'd literally blended into the woodwork. Vegard had likewise vanished. I'd seen Mychael and Vegard do it before, but it didn't make it any less spooky. I knew they weren't gone, at least not yet. It was an illusion that would enable them to move along the wall until they reached the door on the far side of the room. I imagine Tam had all kinds of hidden exits. And armed as they were, I knew where they were going. Downstairs. The three of them against a horde of undead warriors. Warriors who were waiting on the bobbing head in front of me to give them the signal.

And I had to keep him distracted. Wonderful.

"My mistress seeks the Scythe of Nen. She says that you know of its resting place."

"She heard wrong. Not only do I not know where it is, I don't know *what* it is. If you could tell me—"

"Dost thou call my lady and queen a liar?"

Way to go, Raine. "Not at all. She's merely misinformed. Happens to the best of us."

"You refuse to assist my queen?"

In my career, I've had some lowlifes try to hire me, but Hell set a new record for low.

"Not refuse," I clarified. "I'm merely unqualified to be of assistance—seeing that I don't know *what* this Scythe of Nen is, I can't possibly know *where* it is. If you would tell me what—"

"She said you would respond thus."

"Your lady is as wise as she is . . . uh . . ."

"Demonic?" Talon said helpfully.

Those red eyes fixed on him and the kid yelped. "I meant that in the most respectful and honorable and . . . and . . . Oh shit, I'm so dead."

The red flickering in the head's eyes dimmed and the ruined face actually managed to look like it was listening to a voice we couldn't hear. I had a sinking feeling I knew who he was talking to.

The eyes flared, enraged. "My lady says that it is you who are the liar. You *will* bring it to her."

I was losing what little patience I'd managed to scrounge up. Every second I stood here talking to an arrogant, floating head put Piaras that much more out of my reach. "Perhaps if you would tell me what it was, I could—"

"You insult our lady with your denial. She would question you herself."

"My schedule's a little full just now, but I'm sure we can set something up for next week when—"

"She would question you in person—and she will question you *now*." The lips spread in a smile, and more flakes fell off. Talon made a strangled sound.

I'd had enough. Apparently I couldn't talk to anyone—living, dead, or undead—without pissing them off. "I got that invite from her purple sidekick this morning," I shot back. "I told him no by stuffing him in a bottle. There's a full bar downstairs; maybe we can find something to fit you—if there's anything small enough."

The red in the center of his eyes spread until what had been milk white was blood-red. "Disrespect like that shall not go unpunished. My men and I are here to take you to where our lady waits."

I helped myself to one of Tam's blades on a stick. "Come and get me, shorty."

And he did, straight through the glass wall as if it weren't there. Apparently being undead lets you do all kinds of nifty tricks. Like move entirely too fast for a disembodied head. Not only was the head in the room with us, he'd brought his mist with him, mist that froze anything it came in contact with.

Like my leg. One swooping pass barely brushed me and I couldn't feel anything below my knee. It was all I could do to stay on my feet.

"Your queen won't like it if I'm frozen solid," I managed through pain-clenched teeth. "I can't exactly chat with her that way."

"You will thaw quickly where we're going."

Oh yeah, that would be Hell.

Phaelan came up directly under the head and impaled it on his sword. At least that was his plan. The head darted away, leaving Phaelan's blade sticking into thin air, and my cousin completely creeped out.

I considered a fireball, but I didn't think Tam would appreciate a fire in his nightclub.

The head swooped at Talon, the kid dove and rolled, and I swung the pike like a club, sinking the blade into the back of the thing's armored head.

And my blade got stuck.

Part of me thought this was progress; my blade was in the head. That was good. The other part wanted to drop the pike the blade was attached to and run. Some things were just too gruesome to stick around for.

Phaelan lunged again, and the head whipped around, jerking me with it. If I hadn't had a death grip on that pole, the thing would have flung me across the room. As it was, I had a head on a blade on a stick that was dragging me around Tam's living room like a rag doll. Phaelan was darting and weaving looking for an opening, and Talon was jumping around with no idea what to do.

"Grab Raine!" Phaelan yelled to Talon.

The kid stopped jumping around. "What?"

"Grab her! Keep that thing from moving!"

I saw where he was going with this. Goblin teenager as anchor. Talon wasn't that big. The only thing him grabbing me was going to do was get him flung around with me—or get his ass kicked if he "accidentally" grabbed me the wrong way.

Talon grinned at me. I glared at him.

The kid got the message and grabbed me around the waist. He was heavier than I thought, and stronger. The head was still for only an instant, but Phaelan was fast.

He brought his blade up in a slashing arc and severed the thing's ear, which fell with a wet plop to the floor. Black goo oozed and dripped out of the ear and the hole that was left in the head. Talon made a strangled sound. Phaelan followed his slash with a straight stab right between its eyes. More goo, also black.

Talon's grip on me turned to jelly and I actually felt the kid's skin go clammy.

"Not feeling good," he managed before fainting and dragging me down with him, his full weight landing on top of me.

A noxious vapor came from inside the helmet, and when it cleared, the helmet and head were gone.

I pulled in enough air to speak. "Get him off me," I gasped.

Phaelan looked down at us and grinned. "The kid's really gonna hate that he was unconscious for this."

I scowled up at my cousin. "Move. Him."

Phaelan dragged Talon off of me and tossed the kid like a limp doll across one shoulder.

We went downstairs—and saw a pair of masters at work. They didn't look like they needed our help or anyone else's.

Mychael and Tam were working as a team to take on the undead horde, with Vegard taking out any stragglers. They were doing a fine, workmanlike job. The phantoms could turn back into mist and rematerialize to fight again—that is if the glowing blades didn't get them first. Anything their blades put down didn't get back up.

I saw why Mychael was commander of the most elite magical fighting force in the seven kingdoms. I didn't impress easily. But damn.

Mychael and his blades glowed with a white light that blazed so brightly I couldn't look directly at him for more than a few seconds at a time. His blades sliced through and felled corporeal warriors, and the slightest touch of his light turned phantoms to harmless mist that sank back through the floorboards. Some turned to mist but retained their shape, their mouths moving in silent cries as they sank back through the floor. The phantoms were desperate to keep that light from touching them, but getting away from Mychael put them squarely in Tam's range. Tam's hands, blades, and entire body glowed red. What few attacks that made it past his blades to him glanced off in a shower of fiery sparks. They couldn't kill Tam, but Tam was decreasing their numbers with every spin of his weapon.

Soon there wasn't anything left of the demon queen's undead horde except more black goo that Tam was going to have a heck of a time getting out of his theatre floor.

Phaelan carried Talon over to the bar and laid him out on it. Tam was there in an instant, checking his son for signs of life.

"What happened?" His dark eyes reflected concern, relief, and rage all at the same time.

Talon groaned and started to stir.

"He's fine," I assured Tam.

The kid tried to sit up, weaving unsteadily. "Did I faint?"

"Yeah, you did," I told him.

"I don't normally have a problem with blood."

"That's okay; it wasn't the normal color."

Talon swallowed and looked like he might be sick. "That must have been it."

Phaelan tried to muffle a grin and failed miserably. "Next time I'm about to kill something that bleeds black, I'll warn you."

"I'd appreciate that."

Vegard was poking the floorboards with his boot. I guess he was making sure nothing else was coming up through it. "You're borrowing buckets of trouble today, ma'am."

"I don't have to borrow anymore; I've got plenty of my own, and so does Piaras." I checked the blades strapped across my back. "Now let's go get him."

Chapter 15

Outside Sirens, it wasn't completely dark yet, but it was close. I guess when you've either been in a tunnel or a theatre for most of the day, dark happens.

A couple of city workers were lighting the streetlights; though on an island of mages, they didn't use fire on a long pole—a whispered word and gesture got the job done just fine.

Phaelan looked around. "Time flies when you're not having fun."

Tam wasn't with us. He was staying with Talon. I think the kid's dating urges were gone—at least for an hour or two. When we'd been locked in Sirens, Tam's dark mage buddies had been locked out. When the last of the undead was sent back to where they came from, the doors and windows unsealed themselves, and Tam had all the dark mage backup he and Talon would need in the unlikely event the demon queen's minions put in a second appearance. Since I was leaving, I should be taking my trouble with me.

"Elven embassy or Balmorlan's yacht?" I asked Mychael.

Those were the two most likely places Jari Devent and the impostor Guardians would take Piaras. Balmorlan could be using a less obvious, temporary prison, but I was betting he'd go for quick over creative. I was a seeker; I could find Piaras, and I was going to, but it always helped to know the most likely direction.

"They're headed for the embassy," Mychael said. "Jari has four Guardian impostors with him. Sedge and I have the city covered with patrols, and they'll know those men aren't Guardians. Jari wants to get out of sight as soon as he can."

I felt my lips tighten into a thin line. "Meaning they already have Piaras knocked out, tied up, and carried off."

"I didn't say that."

"You didn't need to. What's between the *Fortune* and the embassy?"

"Conclave government buildings."

I snorted. "Now conveniently empty for the night. And if someone is working late, they wouldn't think twice about Guardians apprehending an unruly student outside their window."

"Unfortunately no."

"Can you track him?" Phaelan asked me.

"I can find him, but I have to be out in front," I told Mychael.

Mychael didn't like it, but he didn't have to. For me to find Piaras, that was how it had to be. Mychael was still virtually glowing from battling those phantoms. With interference from magic that powerful, I couldn't find my way out of a ripped fishnet, much less locate one abducted spellsinger.

When Balmorlan had Piaras kidnapped before, I'd been able to use my seeking skills to track him right to the elven embassy's front gates. I hadn't had an object then from Piaras to track him by, and I didn't need anything now. He wasn't related to me by blood, but that didn't stop me from loving him like a brother. Family knew their own, no tracking objects required. Conscious or unconscious, it didn't make any difference. I'd known

Piaras since he was about eight years old, long enough that my seeker self wouldn't even have to break a sweat.

"I'll alert Sedge and my patrols on this side of the city," Mychael said.

I nodded and watched for a moment as Mychael's gaze became distant. He almost instantly made contact. Show off.

I quickly crossed the street and stepped out of the lamplight into the shadows next to a building, resting my back against the rough brick. I didn't sense any magic users inside to get in my way. Good. The less talents between me and Piaras, the better. I closed my eyes and tried to relax, breathing deeply. Breathing I could do, relaxing took a few minutes that Piaras didn't have. I shoved that thought aside. When I'd calmed myself enough to work, I focused my will on an image of Piaras in my mind until it was almost real enough to touch. Then I reached out, down the streets, around the buildings, seeking, searching, methodically eliminating options.

Until I found him.

He was alive, he was conscious, and he was not a prisoner. But he was definitely afraid, though not of the men surrounding him.

Piaras was scared to death of what he was about to do.

I clenched my teeth against the flutter of panic in my own chest. I took one deep breath, in through my nose and slowly out through my mouth, repeating it until I had the calm, cool center I had to have to track him. Emotion was my worst enemy right now, not the men I could sense about to move on Piaras, not Taltek Balmorlan, or even Sarad Nukpana. Only I could screw this up.

I opened my eyes. Mychael was standing in the street, directly in front of me, but about a dozen feet away, giving me my space. "You have him?"

"I do." I described what I saw in my mind's eye. "White marble buildings on either side of the street, no windows on the bottom floors. Street's wide enough for two carriages; the cobbles are smooth. I smell . . ." My brow creased in confusion.

No, that couldn't be right. I closed my eyes. Those two smells shouldn't go together. "It's something sweet, almost like perfume; but there's this burnt-fat stench."

I opened my eyes to Mychael's fierce grin. "The candlemaker."

I blinked. "The what?"

"A candlemaker has a shop just off Bow Street. He mainly uses beeswax, but he still makes some candles with tallow. That stink goes a city block or more. The Conclave's been trying to get him to move for years, but he owns the building and won't sell."

"How far?"

"Six blocks. I'll let Sedge and my men know."

I told myself that Piaras was a smart kid, very smart. And if growing up around me taught him nothing else, it taught him to be suspicious. After what had happened to him over the past few weeks, the kid should be suspicious of his own shadow. The fact that he told Phaelan's contact wizard the Guardian's name and armed himself told me he was doing more than being cautious. My head wondered what the hell he was thinking; my gut knew.

Piaras wanted payback.

I doubted Balmorlan would have used the same guards as last time, in case Piaras had been conscious long enough to recognize them. But while they may not be the same men, they had the same intention—and Piaras was determined for the outcome to be different this time. I sensed it when I'd linked with him. He'd been planning what he was about to do almost from the moment he left the *Fortune*.

I had a sick realization. If Sarad Nukpana could influence Piaras, this was just the kind of thing he'd try to get Piaras to do.

"Piaras knows who those men are," I said to Mychael. "And he's getting ready to do something about it."

"Do you know what it is?"

"Just that it's violent. Piaras isn't violent—but Sarad Nukpana is."

Mychael swore and broke into a run. Vegard, Phaelan, and I followed.

I didn't think I'd ever seen Mychael that angry. Piaras wasn't the only one wanting payback. Elven embassy guards had murdered six of Mychael's Guardians in the alley behind Sirens so they could kidnap Piaras. And now one of his own men had turned traitor and four embassy guards were illegally impersonating Guardians. Mychael was entirely within his rights as paladin to kick their asses from here to the harbor then lock up what was left.

We'd gone a couple of blocks, and I didn't see anything out of the ordinary for past quitting time in the land of mage bureaucrats. Other than the candlemaker's place, I didn't smell anything but a low tide that took perverse pleasure in sending its stink as far into town as possible. I didn't even hear anything, other than Phaelan trying to breathe through his mouth. Mychael and Vegard were completely silent—and I do mean completely. Apparently Guardians were trained not to breathe while tracking.

That was what tipped me off. Silence. Way too much of it for my comfort or anyone else's. Mychael and Vegard stopped.

I already had.

In that silence I sensed Piaras—and something else.

I glanced at Mychael. I didn't know if he sensed Piaras, the men with him, or the something else that none of us needed tonight.

A roar answered all our questions.

I took off running. Behind me, Mychael spat a curse and was hot on my heels. Phaelan and Vegard had weapons out and were keeping up. Mychael stopped just before he reached the corner, and I thought it'd be a good idea to do likewise. I looked around the corner with Mychael and saw something out of a nightmare.

And Piaras had brought them to life.

The kid was spellsinging. Quick, sharp, and guttural. Piaras had conjured help, and he'd gotten a lot more than he'd bargained for.

He'd created monsters.

Piaras knew he couldn't take on five trained military professionals by himself, so he called for backup. I'd seen Piaras's spellsong conjurings before. They were good. But they were normal spellsong creature conjurings: all illusion, no substance. What I saw in that street definitely had substance. I thought I heard Sarad Nukpana's laughter, but with an embassy guard flying through the air and shrieking like a little girl, I couldn't be sure.

Piaras had conjured not one, not two, but three bukas—the nine-foot-tall, hairy, long-fanged, longer-armed mountain monsters of goblin legend. Not only were there three of them, they were solid (they shouldn't be), they could roar (conjurings shouldn't be able to), and they appeared to be enjoying themselves (I didn't know bukas could). One of them had armed himself with a guard's sword that the elf wasn't going to be using anytime soon—judging from his crumpled form lying against the curb—and was wielding it with what I could only call cheerful glee.

"Damn," Vegard said in awe and admiration.

Phaelan was grinning from ear to ear. "I love it. I hate magic, but I love this."

I didn't. Balmorlan would have told his men what Piaras was capable of. I imagine the fake Guardians had shielded themselves, but when you saw several tons of fanged and furry rage running at you, shields and discipline would be the first things to go, and your bladder could be next. While I was grateful that Piaras conjured something that could pound the crap out of those guards, I knew he didn't have that kind of power—but the Saghred did.

"Our nightingale has a rare gift," came Sarad Nukpana's voice and presence in my mind—and Mychael's. *"Don't you agree, Paladin?"* With a chuckle, he was gone.

While the bukas were playing with the embassy guards, Piaras was most definitely not playing with the two elves attacking him. Piaras knew how to use a rapier; Phaelan and I had taught him. He was a good student.

He wasn't this good.

One guard lay unmoving in the middle of the street, the streetlights illuminating the blood staining the area around his heart. No rapier lay in the street with him; Piaras had one in either hand. He'd taken it when he'd killed the elf. I could feel what he'd done. The guard's death lingered heavily in the air.

Piaras's first kill.

It was self-defense, I told myself. It had to have been. Piaras was not a murderer. He'd been forced to kill and it was my fault. Mine. Mine and the bastards who wanted me and the power I had. They were the reason why I was here; they were the reason Piaras had no choice but to come with me.

The reason he'd had no choice but to kill that embassy guard.

There was nothing awkward or hesitant in the way Piaras fought. Phaelan had taught him to fight with two rapiers, two men on one. Practicing with friends who didn't want to skewer you was one thing, fighting for your life against trained solders was something else entirely. I'd seen trained men panic in Piaras's situation. Not only did Piaras not panic, he fought like a sword master, not the student he was, moving like a hungry Nebian panther stalking dinner.

The embassy guards knew their business. They attacked together, then separately, one elf trying to get behind Piaras, the other intensifying his attack to force Piaras to focus all his attention on him. It didn't work. It was like the kid had eyes in the back of his head. He didn't, but Sarad Nukpana wasn't restricted by eyes. I hated that goblin shaman, but right now I was grateful. His skill was keeping Piaras alive.

The bottom dropped out of my stomach. That same preternatural skill would condemn him.

This might have started out as a kidnapping, but it'd turned into a setup. The embassy guards were no longer wearing Guardian uniforms. For anyone who saw them now, they were elven embassy guards under attack and defending themselves. One of the bastards was even standing off to the side, bearing witness to the whole thing. Balmorlan knew that Piaras was capable of defending himself. Taltek Balmorlan would call it an act of revenge and murder. Piaras was a subject of the elven crown attacking elven embassy guards. Balmorlan could have him arrested and extradited before the ink was dry on the paperwork.

The first squad of Guardians had arrived; their job was to deal with Piaras's bukas. I wished them luck.

Mychael and I drew blades. Before mine had cleared its scabbard, Mychael was halfway to the Guardian impostors.

One embassy guard risked a backward glance and Mychael's armored fist punched him squarely in the face. That was the distraction Piaras/Nukpana was waiting for. With a quick twist of his wrist and flick of his blade, Piaras easily disarmed the remaining elf and pinned him to the wall, the tip of his blade resting in the hollow of his throat. Both young men were breathing heavily, and Piaras's dark eyes were blazing.

"Piaras, stand down." Mychael kept his voice low and even.

Piaras didn't move.

The elf who Piaras had pinned to the wall swallowed, and a thin stream of blood ran down his throat where Piaras's rapier had pierced the skin. "Sir, I can explain," the elf whispered to Mychael.

"Jari, nothing explains or justifies this." Mychael's voice was tight with restrained fury. "Piaras, stand down. I've got him."

The tip of Piaras's blade was unwavering.

I slowly moved along the wall, closer to the young elven Guardian. I needed for Piaras to see me, to remember me. To remember himself.

"Piaras," I said. "Mychael can't question him if he's dead. If he dies, Balmorlan will never have to answer for anything he's done to you. Let him go. Please. Lower your blade; Mychael can take it from here."

I could see the struggle on Piaras's face, and I could feel the battle raging in Piaras's mind. He was fighting back, with everything he had he was fighting back. All Piaras had to do was extend his arm and that young elven Guardian would be dead, and this time it wouldn't be self-defense. It would be murder, cold and calculated. Sarad Nukpana wanted that murder, so did Taltek Balmorlan. Piaras wanted it to stop. He wanted to lower that blade, but he couldn't.

"Piaras, you're stronger than he is." I said it quietly, simply. I said it like it was the truth, willing Piaras to believe it. I was talking about Nukpana's strength, but the Guardian held captive at the tip of Piaras's rapier didn't know that; the Guardians within hearing didn't know that—and I didn't want them to. "Let him go; it's over."

Piaras swallowed, his breath hissing in and out between clenched teeth. His knuckles were white on the rapier's grip. Then he took a deep breath and let it out in a shuddering exhale, and with visible effort, lowered the bloodied blade.

Piaras was back with us and in control of himself. For now.

Mychael stepped up next to him, but made no move to disarm him. "Clean your blade and sheath your weapon."

Piaras did.

For Sarad Nukpana, this was just a demonstration, a taste of what he could make Piaras do—and how he could force me to find the Scythe of Nen and let him out of the Saghred.

"When the lower hells freeze over," I said in my mind. I was sure Sarad Nukpana heard me. To him, this was but the first move in a game he intended to play until he got what he wanted. Like I said, when hell froze over.

A pair of Guardians stood nearby, awaiting Mychael's orders.

"Take this traitor into custody." Mychael never took his eyes off of the disgraced elf.

The two Guardians chained Jari Devent's hands behind his back.

"My brother ordered me and I had no choice—" The elf's voice had an edge of panicked desperation.

"You had *every* choice," Mychael's voice slashed through the air. "You made the wrong one."

Devent's pale eyes flashed with defiance. Big mistake. "My obligations to my family—"

Mychael took two strides and was in the young elf's face,

his rage a living thing in the air, his voice low and furious. "As a knighted Guardian, you have duty and loyalty to the archmagus, the Conclave, and to me. You betrayed us all."

The elf's chin came up. "You're going to kill me." He was trying for brave, the tremble in his voice said otherwise.

"No, we're going back to the citadel, and we are going talk. I will ask questions and you will answer every one of them—truthfully and completely."

The Guardians took Devent away, and Piaras cleared his throat.

"Thank you, sir." Piaras's voice was quiet, but firm. "I don't know what happened to me."

"We do," I told him. "And we're going to fix it so that it never happens again."

"Sir!" An out-of-breath Guardian ran up to Mychael. The armor on his sword arm had been ripped away.

A buka's roar told us exactly what had done the ripping.

I swore. The Guardians and watchers couldn't kill those bukas, because even though they were solid, they weren't real. Piaras's voice had made them; Piaras's voice was the only thing that could unmake them. As if the kid hadn't endured enough tonight.

"You have to dispel them," Mychael told Piaras.

Another roar joined the first as a watcher and a Guardian tried a divide-and-contain tactic. It didn't work.

"I tried, sir," Piaras said. "When the second one materialized, I—"

"They're still here," Phaelan pointed out in a singsong voice, eyes wide and disbelieving, blades in both hands.

"I know that!" Piaras snapped in desperation.

Mychael was the calm in the middle of furry chaos. "What did you use?"

Piaras told him. I didn't know what the hell he'd just said, but Mychael did.

"That's not strong enough," Mychael said. Then he told him what to use; I didn't recognize those as words, either. "And be firm with them," he ordered.

"Got it. I think."

"Don't think, *do*!" Mychael barked like a drill sergeant to a new recruit. "You're banishing them! They're not going unless you force them. *Do it! Now!*"

Piaras did. He didn't think; he just reacted to that order. Mychael's voice gave him no choice. It wasn't Mychael's spell-singer voice. It wasn't magic. It was the voice of a commander of men, a leader on the battlefield, a voice you obeyed without question or faced consequences that might be worse than getting squashed by a buka.

Piaras squared his shoulders, braced his feet, and let the bukas have the full force of his voice. It rang like a bright battle horn in the night, the volume magnified by the marble buildings. It was majestic and compelling, commanding the bukas, forcing them to do his will.

I'm glad the kid wasn't aiming at me.

The bukas were becoming less substantial. One of them had a watcher by the leg and was dragging him closer; he lost his grip, his hand becoming translucent in the lamplight. The bukas were going, but they weren't going quietly. One roar shattered a row of windows on a pristine government building before becoming a mere echo, a distant cry. Then the monsters simply winked out of existence. Piaras's ragged breathing said there was nothing simple about it. He was bent over, hands on his knees, looking a little green around the gills. But he was still upright. Unbelievable. And the bukas were gone without a trace, not even a smell remained. Good work. Scary, but good.

And I think Piaras had done that all by himself. Sarad Nuk-pana had nothing to do with it. That was the scary part.

"Bravo, kid," Vegard whispered in awe. The big Guardian's grin was fierce.

There was a smattering of applause from the Guardians and watchers. The applause grew and with it came whistles.

Great. Once word got around, Piaras would be even more of a magical must-have than he already was.

I put an arm around his shoulders as he pulled himself

upright. "Raine, I couldn't stop myself," he whispered, looking down at the dead elf sprawled in the street. "Once I started, I couldn't stop."

"I know," I told him, resisting the urge to hug him. Later, not here, not now in front of dozens of Guardians and half the watchers in town. "It wasn't your fault."

Piaras's brow creased in confusion. "How?"

"Not now. Let's get off the streets first."

"Sir Jari said you needed to talk to me," Piaras told Mychael. "That's why I went with them."

"I know," Mychael said. "I didn't need to speak with you then, but I do now—and so does the archmagus."

Chapter 16

"You are not dragging him in front of that old man for judgment!" I was surprised at how vicious my voice sounded. I also didn't care. I was too tired and angry and scared and a dozen other emotions to care what I said or how I said it.

We were in Mychael's office in the citadel; Piaras was in the next room getting some cuts and scrapes taken care of by a Guardian healer.

"I'm not *dragging* him anywhere," Mychael told me. "And Justinius is not going to judge him. He's going to help him."

"The man's flat on his back and weak as a kitten. What help—"

Mychael's sea blue eyes were on mine. "Raine, trust me."

Trust was in short supply for me just now, as was patience and much-needed sleep. And I wasn't about to let go of perfectly good anger that easily. All the fighting I'd done today was with magic—sometimes a woman just needed to hit something. An embassy guard would have been perfect. But there wasn't one in the room with us, and if there had been, I was so tired I probably couldn't have made a decent fist.

I swore and sighed. "Sorry."

"About what?"

"Taking your head off. I just—"

Mychael's lips creased in a smile. "I think it's still attached, no apologies needed. You haven't been given much reason to trust anyone, myself included. When I asked you to come here with me from Mermeia, I told you there were mages here who could help. Apparently those mages are in a smaller minority than I thought."

"A minority of two," I said. "You and the old man. And seeing that the two of you are the strongest mages on this island—that is, when the old man gets back on his feet—that's two I'm grateful to have. Don't think that I'm not grateful for everything you've done for me—or at least tried to do."

"I knew there would be some who would want your power. I just didn't think it would be—"

"Damned near every mage on the island," I finished for him. I shrugged a shoulder. "Hey, I'm a Benares. If we're not on the receiving end of trouble, we're dishing it out. Trouble's nothing new for me; I've just got more of it than usual right now."

"I've been promising that I'll get you out of this entire mess." He paused. "I shouldn't do that."

I froze. "You shouldn't get me out of this mess?"

"No, make the promise to do it. I'm going to do everything I can to keep that promise—"

"But it might not be enough," I finished.

"No, it might not," Mychael admitted. He ran his hand over the back of his neck and winced, rubbing what I knew had to be some tired and tense muscles. It'd been over a week since he'd declared martial law. Mychael was burning the candle at both ends and had to be running out of wick. "You're still linked to the Saghred, and now you're linked to Tam."

"And to you," I said quietly. "Mychael, you shouldn't have done that."

His hand stopped midrub, and he looked over at me. "No

one forced me. I said I would do whatever I could to keep you safe; posting a sentry was one of those things. I swore to protect you." He paused, and when he spoke his words were softer. "More important, I *want* to protect you."

"And you could lose everything doing it. Literally. Your head included."

"It was my choice, and regardless of what happens, I know I made the right one." A shadow of a smile curved his lips. "That being said, I'd very much like to keep my head, and I have no intention of putting it on a chopping block. If someone wants my head separated from the rest of me, they'll have to fight me for the privilege."

"Uh, wasn't what you did against the law? And don't you uphold the law and all that?"

"Raine, I acted to prevent a worse crime from happening— actually it would have been a catastrophe. The Saghred cannot gain control of you or Tam. What I did to prevent that broke a law; but for the greater good some laws have to be broken. I acted for the greater good." He grinned. The man actually looked relieved. "My conscience is clear."

"Your record won't be if someone finds out," I shot back. "Mychael, listen to me. For your own good, at least distance yourself from me. Even a little bit might help. It's like they say: if you don't want to be accused to being a criminal, don't be seen with one."

A smile tugged at the corner of his mouth. "I'm afraid I can't do that. One, you're not a criminal. And two, I've found when it comes to protecting you, the closer I am, the better." He shook his head in amazement. "You can get into trouble faster than anyone I've ever met."

"It's a gift."

"Then you must be talented beyond measure. You almost got yourself killed how many times today?"

I did a quick tally and winced. It wasn't a good number. "Five definitely, but there might have been more." I tried an apologetic grin. "There were a lot of demons in that street."

"At least five." Mychael just looked at me. "Raine, a man

doesn't face certain death that many times on a battlefield, and today was just you walking around town." He took a deep breath and slowly let it out. "I'm going to do everything that I can to keep you safe; there's just the possibility that I may not succeed. When it comes to you, there's only so much a mere man can do. If I don't succeed, know that I did my best."

A slow smile spread across my face, then I chuckled. "It's about time."

Mychael looked completely baffled. "For what? Failure?"

"For finally letting the paladin get off of his white horse."

One corner of his mouth tipped upward. "He has to sometime. Risk of saddle sores."

"So, while he's being just as fallible as the rest of us, does he also put on his boots one foot at a time?"

"He does." Mychael's eyes gleamed, and he lowered his voice. "Just don't let that get around. It'd be bad for his reputation."

"His secret's safe. And by the way, tell him that he's the *last* person who needs to be sorry for anything. In case you've forgotten, I put that amulet around my own neck; you had nothing to do with it. And I've realized that my doing that was no accident—even then the Saghred was manipulating me. My father had the amulet made so he could hide the rock and still guard it without keeping it with him." I snorted. "I mean, what are the odds that nine hundred years later, his daughter ends up with the necklace?"

"Extremely remote."

"To say the least. I *knew* Sarad Nukpana wanted that amulet. If Nukpana wanted it, it stood to reason that it was a bad piece of jewelry. So I should stay away from it, right? Nope, not me. When I got my hands on it, did I do the safe and sane thing and put it in my pocket? No. I hung the damned thing around my neck. I didn't even think about it; I just did it. Then I couldn't take it off."

"Temptation is what the Saghred does best," Mychael said. "It can destroy cities—but it also possesses magic most subtle."

"And most potent." I tossed his words from watcher headquarters back at him. "Mychael, what happened between us in that conference room? Was that the Saghred laying the groundwork for bringing you into our umi'atsu bond . . . or was it something else? I'm almost hoping it was the rock; we don't need anything else."

Mychael studied my face for a long moment. "Did you feel the Saghred between us during what happened this morning?"

"No."

"I didn't, either," he murmured. "But it was there in Sirens, with the two of us and Tam. I felt it then, but not this morning."

I swallowed. "There was definitely a difference for me, too."

"Raine, whatever happened between us was triggered by me," Mychael said quietly. "The Saghred had nothing to do with it."

I stood very still. "What did you do?"

"I touched you."

He could say that again.

"Beyond that, I don't know," Mychael admitted. "I have more than a passing knowledge of all known magical bonds, contacts, links, or pairings. I've read extensively on the subject. What we experienced this morning didn't meet the criteria for any of them."

"So we're breaking new ground here."

"It appears we are."

"Any chances it was casual, garden-variety magic?"

"Did it feel casual to you?"

Most definitely not. I didn't need to say it; Mychael knew how it had felt. I'd never seen colors so sharp, scents more vivid, felt sensations so intense. I'd also never felt so completely alive.

"Any idea what it's done to us—or plans to do?" Then I thought of me and Tam, of searing kisses, and of feet off the floor. "Or what it plans to *make* us do?" My voice sounded small.

"None whatsoever," Mychael freely admitted.

I just stared at him. He didn't sound concerned, worried, or even mildly bothered.

"Raine, were you harmed by what happened between us?" he asked frankly.

"No." Quite the opposite. It'd felt really good. Too good.

"Then until we have time to investigate it, or until it proves to be a danger to ourselves or others, I suggest we solve the problems we know we have."

"We've got plenty of those."

"That we do. When the demons are no longer a threat, then we'll find out what we're dealing with." His expression turned grim. "No more demons have been sighted since early afternoon."

"You make it sound bad."

"It is. Dagiks are like scouts. Their task is to locate the nearest food source."

I felt sick. "This whole island is a demon food source."

"Exactly. Once the Dagiks knew that, they'd report their findings to their superiors." He hesitated. "Demons prefer to feed at night."

My stomach twisted. "College students prefer to party at night. Have you—"

"Dusk to dawn curfew," Mychael assured me. "The only people out on the streets right now are qualified to be there. Guardians, certain watchers, and demonology department faculty are patrolling the city in teams looking for demons. Sora, her faculty, and grad students are hoping to find that Hellgate before dawn by tracking a couple of demons when they go 'home.'"

I was incredulous. "Grad students? You've got to be kidding?"

"I wish I was."

"Talk about a final exam," I muttered.

"I didn't like the idea, but Sora reminded me that's the kind of job her grad students will soon be doing out in the real world. She assured me that they're trained and qualified for it, and she'd rather they had their first on-the-job experience with plenty of backup."

A college student facing down a hungry Volghul in the dark. Shit.

"Is there anything I can do to help?"

Mychael's silence was all the answer I needed.

"Wait. Let me guess. I've helped enough already."

"Raine, the demons want to open the Saghred, and for the foreseeable future, you and the Saghred are one and the same."

Gulp. "I see your point."

"I'm glad." Then he grinned slowly, like a little boy with a secret. "And I managed to get you back into the citadel without tossing you over my shoulder."

My mouth dropped open, then I drew breath to let him have it. "You—"

"It's too late for you to leave tonight, Raine. The streets to the harbor aren't safe."

I just glared at him. He was right and I knew it; and worst of all, so did he. "So if Piaras hadn't gotten into a fight with those guards, what were you planning on doing when we left Sirens?"

His blue eyes narrowed. "Whatever I had to. After what happened in Sirens with the demon queen, you wouldn't be safe on the *Fortune*. If you'd stayed there, you would have been putting Phaelan and his crew in the worst kind of danger. I don't know if you're completely safe here, but it's the best I can do."

I didn't like it, but I had to agree with it. Truth was I was too tired to do otherwise. "Thank you," I said simply.

"My job and my pleasure."

The silence stretched until I felt a twitch coming on. There was something I wanted to ask Mychael for, but awkward didn't even begin to describe how it was going to feel asking him for it.

"You're exhausted, right?" I asked.

He regarded me warily. "I'm still on my feet."

"Solidly on your feet or about to collapse on your feet?"

"I'm not going down for the count anytime soon," he assured me with a playful glint in his eyes. "What do you want?"

Just spit it out, Raine.

"The other week after I did that link with those kidnapped spellsingers to find out where they were being held—"

"And you were taken inside the Saghred by Nukpana, and you kept an entire stage full of mages from collapsing—all in the same day. How could I forget?" His eyes went from playful to gentle. "Do you have another headache you need for me to heal?"

"Actually, my head's the only part of me that doesn't hurt."

"I can take care of it." He took a step toward me.

I took a step back. "See, here's the problem. I really want you to. I ache and I'm so tired I'm about to drop where I stand, but what happened this morning might make the hands-on part of—"

"It won't be a problem," he said with quiet confidence.

"It won't?"

"When I was this close to you this morning, I could feel the pull of your magic. I'm not feeling that now."

"Probably because I'm so damned tired."

"Perhaps, but I don't think so." He extended his hand to me. "There's only one way to find out."

I looked down at his hand and then up at him. "Touching is necessary for healing, isn't it?"

"It is."

I swallowed hard and extended my hand until it almost touched Mychael's. He quickly stepped forward and enfolded my hand in his before I could pull away.

I let out the breath I'd been holding. The touch of his hand was a warm and gentle pressure. No fire, no surging magic, no urges. Well, maybe one or two urges, but magic didn't have a thing to do with those.

I blew out a couple of quick breaths. "Okay, that went well." I still expected the fire, but it still didn't happen. "Uh . . . since all of me hurts, what do you have to touch to make it not hurt?"

"I could work with just your hand, but it would be more effective with full-body contact."

My eyes must have gone as big as saucers.

"A hug would work nicely." He managed, just barely, not to smile.

Yes, it would. It'd also take care of one of those urges. Still, I felt a little flutter of panic. "Do you think it's safe?" I was talking really fast. "I mean, I could really use a hug, since I was five times close to death and all that, but what if you—"

In an instant, I was in his arms with my face smushed against his chest.

"And it helps if the patient doesn't talk."

I felt his words rumble deep in his chest against my ear. I turned my head and managed to look up at him; he looked down at me.

"Do you know how distracting you are?" he asked me.

"I wouldn't want you to be distracted."

"It's too late for that," he said quietly.

I meant talking. I don't think he did.

Mychael pulled me even closer and a slow warmth radiated from his entire body that was pressed full length against mine. A shiver ran through me all the way down to my toes as that warmth flowed through me as if my skin were no barrier.

My breath caught in my throat. "Maybe this wasn't such a good idea."

"Possibly not," he murmured against my hair. "But what I'm feeling tells me that you need it." Mychael's voice had dropped into that lower, velvety register, softer and more soothing than the barest whisper—his spellsinger's voice. I felt him smile. "And if your tomorrow's anything like your today, you'll need it to survive."

I nodded against his chest. "Survival is good."

"I thought you'd see it my way." He loosened his hold just enough to place his hands carefully on the small of my back. Then with agonizing slowness, he kneaded his way up the length of my back, past my shoulders to my neck, leaving a trail of tingling heat in his wake.

Oh. Yes.

I was intensely aware of the magic flowing out of Mychael

into me, and suddenly I saw myself lying on a powdery white sand beach, water that was the tropical sea blue of Mychael's eyes gently lapping against and over my body, the golden sun overhead warming my bare skin. Something inside me that I'd never known was there took what Mychael gave me and spun it into threads of flickering golden light, fed by that warm seawater and sunlight, and sent it back into him. I felt his breath catch in surprise as it flared to life and spread through his body. We stood pressed together as wave after wave of pulsing light warmed, healed, wrapped around us, joining us together. It intensified, faded, then it was gone. Mychael's breathing was ragged as he gazed down at me in wonder.

It was what had happened this morning and more, much more.

And the Saghred had absolutely nothing to do with it.

"Ever read about *that* in any of your magic books?" I managed.

"Never had the pleasure." Mychael's voice was a husky whisper. "I would have remembered if I had."

There was a quiet knock at the door. "Sir? Ma'am?"

Vegard.

I laughed quietly. "Vegard can knock. Who knew?"

"He learned his lesson from last time." I felt Mychael's warm breath against my temple. "Though his timing needs work."

Last time. I'd fallen asleep in the bathtub, and Sarad Nukpana had invaded my dreams. Mychael sensed something was wrong and knocked on my door. When I didn't answer, he essentially disintegrated the door. Vegard had seen me moments later in a towel. Mychael had gotten there first; he'd seen me naked.

Vegard's combination grimace and apologetic smile told us he knew what he'd interrupted. "The healer is finished with Piaras, sir."

"Show him in."

Vegard did and closed the door behind him.

Piaras's posture was ramrod straight, his chin up, ready to

face the consequences of his actions, to accept the punishment for what he did. But most of all he was scared to death and determined not to show it.

"How much trouble am I in?" Piaras was also ready to get it over with.

"You're not in trouble," Mychael told him. "Not from me or the archmagus. But you are in danger."

"Inquisitor Balmorlan." Piaras had to force his voice to say the words.

"Him, too," I said. "But mainly Sarad Nukpana."

Piaras was confused. "But he's—"

"Yeah, inside the Saghred," I finished. "Problem is the containment spells around the Saghred are gone."

Piaras looked at Mychael in disbelief. "They failed?"

"Eaten away from inside over the past few days," Mychael said. "And our best spellweavers haven't been able to repair them."

"Meaning that there's nothing between me and the souls inside the Saghred," I told Piaras. "I've spoken with my father—and with Sarad Nukpana. Through dreams at first, then in a more direct way, like a voice in my head."

"Piaras, have you had any dreams about Sarad Nukpana?" Mychael asked quietly.

Piaras swallowed hard, and the pulse throbbed in his throat. That told me all I never wanted to know. Sarad Nukpana was a master of lies, but he hadn't lied to me about Piaras. The goblin had been inside Piaras's head while he slept and influenced him while he was awake. He'd taken the first steps to carrying out his threat. He'd made his move, now he expected me to make mine. Get the Scythe of Nen, get him out of the Saghred. If I refused, Piaras's fate—and his blood—would be on my hands.

I forced myself to stay calm. "Do you remember any of your dreams?"

"Not really. I remembered that I didn't like them . . ." Piaras shook his head. "But I don't remember what he told me." He hesitated. "Or what he did." Hesitancy turned to horror, but not panic. "What did he do to me?"

Piaras was keeping his head, or at least trying. The next time Sarad Nukpana put in an appearance in my dreams, I *would* find a way to strangle him.

"He may be influencing your actions," Mychael told him.

Piaras was silent for a few heartbeats. "What I did tonight?"

"You're good with a blade," I told him. "Don't take this the wrong way, sweetie, but you're not that good. You were fighting two-on-one, and those embassy guards were doing their best to divide and distract. You didn't fall for it."

Piaras drew a deep breath; it shuddered as he exhaled. "In practice I still fall for it, don't I?"

I nodded reluctantly. "Yeah, you do. And when one of them attacked, you didn't drop your guard against the second one. You kept your vitals covered and your blade moving."

"But I've been working on that in lessons," he protested.

"And how is it going?" I knew and so did Piaras. As if what Sarad Nukpana had done to him wasn't enough, now I was making him admit that he wasn't a good enough fighter to have survived on his own tonight. But the first step to surviving Nukpana was for Piaras to realize just how much danger he was in. No doubt Sarad Nukpana had wanted him to kill that elven Guardian and all of those embassy guards. And no doubt Taltek Balmorlan and the elven ambassador would have come up with a perfectly good reason why their guards were wearing Guardian uniforms—and an even better reason to charge Piaras with five murders.

Piaras's jaw clenched. "I fought better tonight than in my lessons, didn't I?"

"A lot better."

His gaze became distant. "When I disarmed Sir Jari, I knew you were there," he told Mychael. "But I just couldn't let him go. Everything was blurry, like I was there, but not really. Some part of me *wanted* to kill him."

Change of plan. I was going to kick Sarad Nukpana in the balls, *then* I'd strangle him.

"There is a way to confirm that Nukpana was responsible," Mychael told him. "If you would allow me."

Piaras stood firm. "Do whatever you have to."

Mychael went to stand in front of him and put his hand on Piaras's forehead like he was checking for a fever. Mychael didn't close his eyes, and neither did Piaras. After a few moments, Mychael's lips tightened into a thin, tense line. I didn't have to hear the word to know what he'd just thought. My own vocabulary choice was even more colorful.

Piaras didn't move. "He's been in my mind, hasn't he?"

"He has."

Piaras didn't say anything else, but the emotions flowing over his face more than did the talking for him. Fear, helplessness, exhaustion, and rage were all there in spades. Piaras had been on the run with me since this whole crapfest had started. He wanted it to be over with, he wanted the people after him to leave him alone—the kid wanted his life back. All of those would work for me, too.

"But I was the one who killed that embassy guard," Piaras all but whispered. "Sarad Nukpana didn't have anything to do with it. I know he didn't. I'd just conjured the bukas. The guard was trying to kill me to make them go away. Sir Jari and the other two were coming at me. When a buka roared, the guard was distracted. I lunged." He looked like he was about to be sick. "I killed him."

"Before he could kill you," Mychael said. "It was self-defense. In another second it would have been three on one. You eliminated a threat to survive."

Piaras ran a hand over his face. "From live threat to dead in the street."

"You did what you had to do," I told him. "You did *nothing* wrong."

"The three of them rushed me; I had no choice." He said it, but he didn't believe it.

My gut twisted. "No, you didn't have a choice. Just because Balmorlan wants you alive doesn't mean those elves wouldn't have killed you and called it an accident."

I shot a glance at Mychael. I'd known Piaras for years, but I had absolutely zero experience talking a young man through the guilt of his first kill. As Guardian commander, I hoped Mychael did. He'd better.

"Piaras, do you still want to be a Guardian?" Mychael asked solemnly.

"More than anything, sir. But . . ." He closed his eyes for a moment, and when he opened them, they were glistening with tears he was determined not to shed.

Mychael gave no sign whatsoever that he noticed. I was glad Piaras wasn't looking at me.

"But what, Piaras?" Mychael asked.

"I don't think the Guardians still want me." He said it so softly I barely heard him. "I killed a man tonight; I wanted to kill a Guardian, I put half the Guardians in the citadel to sleep last week, and most everyone on the island probably still thinks I tried to assassinate the archmagus. People are afraid of me, and some of them are Guardians." Piaras looked like he was about to be sick. "They don't need to be afraid of me. I don't want them to be."

"Piaras, they were afraid of me, too," Mychael told him.

"Uh, you're their commander, sir. Aren't they supposed to be?"

"I said *were* afraid. Now I have their respect. Changing from one to the other took time. You've only been here two weeks." Mychael paused. "Piaras, look at me."

Piaras hesitated a moment and then met Mychael's eyes.

"The Guardians were established to protect the Conclave, defend the Isle of Mid, and administer justice to any mage who would use his or her powers to bring harm to others. The city watchers are qualified to deal with most cases." Mychael's smile was grim. "That leaves the nasty ones for us."

"Like Sarad Nukpana?" Piaras asked.

"Exactly like him. And one thing you can always count on is that every last one of them will fight back with any weapon at their disposal. Sarad Nukpana is inside the Saghred; that limits his options. He is incapable of physical attack, so he attacks the mind. As a Guardian, you would be trained not only to defend yourself against such attacks, but to strike back and defeat your adversary."

"But why did he want me to kill Sir Jari?"

"Nukpana's influence—"

I interrupted. "Mychael, I'm the reason he's attacking Piaras; I should be the one to tell him why."

Piaras looked at me in surprise. "You're the reason?"

I snorted. "I've been the reason for everything lately." I told him about the Scythe of Nen, and why Sarad Nukpana wanted me to find it—and then I told him what Nukpana had threatened to do to him if I refused. He needed to know; I wasn't going to keep him in the dark.

"I can't run from this." Piaras didn't ask it as a question. He knew the answer.

"Not when someone gets in your head," I told him. "That'd be like trying to run from yourself. And believe me, I've been trying to figure out a way to do that. No luck yet."

Piaras stood very still. "Is he in our heads right now?"

I felt my lips curl in a lopsided grin. "Honey, I'm too damned tired to have anything or anyone in my head right now."

Piaras almost smiled. "It's kind of quiet between my ears, too." The smile vanished. "How will I know if Sarad Nukpana is trying to tell me what to do?"

"I'm going to take you to someone who can help," Mychael said. "He can't keep Nukpana out of your head, but he can help you know when your actions are not your own. We can begin teaching you how to defend yourself, but that will take time. Meanwhile, if Nukpana does come after you again, you will be with Guardians whom I trust to keep you out of trouble."

"Vegard's been ordered to sit on me," I told him, trying to lighten things up.

Mychael grinned like a little boy, open and genuine. That one grin from the man he most admired did Piaras more good than anything.

"That's another thing Guardians get a lot of experience doing," Mychael told him, "keeping their brothers out of trouble."

Piaras bit at his bottom lip. "Brothers?" To Piaras, that one word meant a dream come true, something to change the nightmare his life was turning into.

Mychael nodded once. "The Guardians are a brotherhood, Piaras. We take care of our own. You have a rare and powerful gift. Our order would be honored to accept you for training. But the final decision is yours to make."

I saw a flicker of what may have been belief in his dark eyes. "Thank you, sir." Belief strengthened into resolve. "I want to be a Guardian, Paladin Eiliesor. Teach me how to fight Sarad Nukpana."

Mychael's smile was fierce. "It would be my honor and pleasure, Cadet Rivalin."

Mychael had his job to do, and I had mine. I knew exactly what I was going to do. There had never been any doubt in my mind. I was a seeker, one of the best. I was going to find that Scythe of Nen, whatever the hell it was, and I was going to find it before the demons got their claws on it. Finding valuables was what a Benares did best.

And double-crossing a goblin shaman who threatened someone I loved was what *I* did best.

Chapter 17

That someone who could help was Archmagus Justinius Valerian.

I had a whole list of reasons not to want to be seen by the most powerful mage in the seven kingdoms. I was under the impression—as was everyone else on Mid—that the old man was flat on his back and weak as a kitten. When I'd first arrived on the island, Justinius Valerian had looked at me and seen everything I had been, was now, and might possibly become. That last item on the list had just put the twitch back in my left eyelid. If the old man took a close look at me right now, he'd get himself an eyeful, and I'd probably be escorted to the closest containment room.

Right now there was a lot more inside of me besides me. The power generated by what had happened between me, Mychael, and Tam was still surging through my veins; the Saghred was seething below the surface. I was already linked to the Saghred, now I was magically attached to two of the most powerful dark and light mages, period. I was a demon-destroying, death-defying magical cataclysm waiting to happen.

We were still in the citadel. The Saghred was also in the citadel. I didn't want to be on the same island with that rock, let alone in the same building, but Justinius's apartments were in the citadel, so I didn't exactly have a choice. The archmagus's sickbed was probably one of the last places Piaras wanted to visit seeing that he'd been framed for trying to kill the old man. From the expression on Piaras's face, the only help he expected from Justinius Valerian was help turning into a slug.

Mychael, Piaras, and I stopped at a pair of massive doors flanked by four heavily armed and armored Guardians. Really big guys with no expressions whatsoever. Though I was sure if anyone tried to get past them without permission, those Guardians would be plenty expressive. And lethal.

If the Guardians didn't get you, the wards flowing across those doors would probably eat you alive and spit what was left across the room. I had no intention of putting it to the test. I'd be a lady and wait for Mychael to open those doors. Civilized behavior sometimes was a struggle for me, but I wasn't stupid—or in this case, suicidal.

Piaras ran a hand through his hair, trying to put his tousled dark curls in some semblance of order. He was determined to see this thing through, and as much as I hated the necessity of him being here, I was proud of him. I felt a little smile coming on.

Mychael nodded to the Guardians posted on either side of the massive door.

I couldn't understand the two Guardians' chanting, but I could feel what it was doing. The wards peeled back and the doors opened. I expected Justinius's apartment to be on the other side. Instead there was a long, wide corridor with a pair of Guardians every dozen feet or so. And more wards.

"Damn," I breathed.

"I'm not taking any chances," Mychael told me.

He could say that again. Nothing or no one could get through all that. Except you and the rock, the pessimist in my head just had to say. I told my pessimist to shut up.

Once we actually got inside Justinius's apartments, there were two Guardians, and an older woman wearing healer's robes. She respectfully inclined her head to Mychael. She was large boned and muscled like a Myloran sea-raider. Their men weren't the only ones who took to the seas for fun and profit. If anyone made it past all of the guards and wards, I think Justinius's healer could take them out all by her lonesome.

On the other side of the room was a large canopied bed with the curtains pulled back.

Archmagus Justinius Valerian was the supreme head of the Conclave of Sorcerers, commander in chief of the Brotherhood of Conclave Guardians, and the craftiest spellslinger in the seven kingdoms. And he didn't get there by being anything other than shrewd, manipulative, and brilliant, and that was just the start of his qualifications. I'd heard he was a foul-tempered, nasty old man. I'd heard right. But I liked the old guy anyway. Come to think of it, those things were probably the reason why I liked him.

Considering that he'd had a black-magic-induced heart attack only five days ago, Archmagus Justinius Valerian didn't look half bad. In fact, he looked pretty much the same as the last time I'd seen him. What once might have been lean had turned grizzled. What might have been a luxurious head of hair was now a fringe of downy, white tufts on a liver-spotted head. Only a pair of gleaming blue eyes gave a clue to the man himself. He was awake and those bright eyes were homed in on Piaras and me.

I smelled a setup and a half. Archmagus Shrewd and Manipulative was doing quite well, and when Mychael had said that he wasn't taking any chances, it appeared he wasn't taking any chances that anyone would find out the old man wasn't wheezing his last breath. A lot was going on here that I didn't know about. There was a reason for it, and I wanted to know what it was.

Then I was the sole object of Justinius's attention. I knew what he was going to do. With the strength I had now, I could have stopped him, but I didn't. Yes, one word from him could have me locked up or executed within two minutes, but since the moment I'd met him, my gut told me that I could trust Justinius Valerian. My gut had never been wrong, at least not yet. I didn't think now was going to be the first time. The old man was going to find out anyway, might as well be now.

Justinius Valerian's eyes never left mine, but they changed focus, and I felt the barest hint of the power that'd earned him his title. He was seeing me inside and out. Again. It was the type of seeing that'd earn any other magic user the business end of my fist. But until I could get rid of the rock and my umi'atsu bond with Tam and Mychael, I was what I was. There was no changing it or escaping it.

The archmagus's bright blue eyes were hard as agates as he looked from me to Mychael and back again.

"You've protected her," Justinius said.

"Yes, sir. I did." Mychael's voice, like his resolve, was unwavering.

I tried to pull a little air into my lungs past the sudden lump in my throat. To anyone listening, the archmagus was merely pointing out that the paladin was doing his job—not that he'd linked himself to the Saghred's bond servant to keep her from being consumed by an umi'atsu bond.

The old man nodded once. "And you did what you had to do."

"I did, sir."

Justinius paused. "You're protecting the other one, too."

I knew who he meant. Tam. I also knew the reason Justinius didn't say his name out loud wasn't due to any prejudice that Tam was a goblin, or distaste that he was a dark mage. Even though the other people in the room listening were probably trusted ears, the old man was smart; he didn't get and keep his job by taking chances.

"I thought it necessary." Mychael paused. "And worthwhile," he added with quiet conviction.

Damned smoky fireplaces, making my eyes water.

Justinius kept his eyes on Mychael. The only sound was the pop and crackle of the burning wood.

"You're going to need help, son," Justinius said in Mychael's mind. *"And soon."*

Since Mychael heard it, I heard it. And Justinius knew it. He'd meant it for both of us—for all of us.

"*I know, sir,*" Mychael responded.

Mychael had gone leagues beyond his job and the old man and I both knew it. No one else needed to. And Justinius Valerian wasn't going to tell them. I had to resist the overpowering urge to hug the old man's neck. I settled for taking my first decent breath in five minutes and giving Justinius the slightest nod of gratitude. If the old man had blinked, he'd have missed it. He didn't miss it.

"You're looking well, sir," I said.

Justinius smiled slyly. "And feeling better than I look."

I didn't move my head, but my eyes indicated the healer and two Guardians.

"Other than Mychael here, those are the three people on this island that I trust the most," Justinius told me. "Hugh and Farold have been my personal bodyguards since I took this miserable job, and Dalis does more than just look good. She's my eyes and ears outside the citadel. If I need to know information, Dalis knows where to find it and who to ask."

Piaras had been standing there the entire time in complete confusion and stunned disbelief.

I said what I knew he wanted to. "You faked an assassination attempt." I kept my voice calm and level; it wasn't easy, but I managed. And I didn't ask it as a question; it was obvious to anyone with working eyes that Justinius Valerian wasn't going to his great reward anytime soon. I was sure the old man had a perfectly good reason for his little charade, but that didn't change the fact that Piaras had gone through a living hell thinking that he'd killed Justinius. Taltek Balmorlan had tried to trick Piaras into signing a confession. The inquisitor wanted a legal way to take Piaras off the island, and trying to kill Justinius had given him just what he needed. He'd damned near gotten away with it—and Piaras.

The old man pulled himself up on his pillows. It took more than a little effort, and I almost felt a twinge of guilt. "I faked nothing. I knew I was being attacked and I protected myself. Some of that spellsong got through; most of it didn't. I've waited years for this chance."

"For what? To lay in bed and let Carnades run amok?" My voice felt the need to snap, and I let it. The old man—or his twin Guardian behemoths—would probably make me regret it, but right now I was more angry than smart.

"To lay in bed and watch my enemies slither out of hiding," he said smoothly. "Thanks to that goblin trying to spellsing me to death, I'm finding out who my enemies really are." A shadow of pain that wasn't physical flowed across his face. The old man had been betrayed and he was hurting. "It's been an eye-opening experience."

There had been another attempt on Justinius's life on my and Piaras's first day on the island. "The Nightshades at the welcoming ceremony," I murmured.

Justinius nodded once.

Nightshades were elves—they were also assassins, kidnappers, blackmailers, or whatever they had been given enough gold to do. You pay and they'll play. And someone had given them enough gold to try to kill the archmagus and Mychael. I had a feeling Justinius now had a couple more names on his list of enemies.

I was still mad at the old man, but I had to admire the simple beauty of his plan. "Nothing flushes out predators like wounded prey," I said.

The old man's eyes flashed dangerously as he brushed his finger past the tip of his nose, confirming my theory.

I looked at Mychael. "You didn't tell me." I glanced at Piaras. "Or us." I know the kid had to feel betrayed; I was getting used to it.

"It was necessary that information not leave this room." That was the paladin talking, not Mychael. "For his own safety, I can't allow the archmagus to leave this room until he is physically and magically recovered."

"One sign of weakness and Carnades would claim he was still incapacitated," I said.

"Exactly."

"What he means is that I can't leave this room until I can

kick Carnades's lily-white, patrician ass," Justinius said. "I've told Mychael here that I just have to be strong enough for one kick." He grinned evilly. "I'll get it right the first time."

I didn't doubt that. Secrecy was critical for the old man's plan to work, but that didn't mean I had to like it. I didn't, and neither did Piaras. But any hurt, disappointment, or anything else he felt was well hidden.

"Archmagus Valerian, I am glad you were not seriously injured," Piaras said. He looked at Mychael uncertainly, and kept his voice down. "Sir, is my being here a good idea?"

Piaras didn't mean hearing something he shouldn't, though I was questioning the wisdom of that. Piaras didn't want Sarad Nukpana to suddenly possess him and compel him to kill the old man for real this time—or feel a sudden urge to go running to Carnades and blurt out the old man's plan.

"It's necessary," Mychael told him. "And you don't need to be concerned." He looked at Justinius and a quick, unspoken communication passed between them.

The old man muttered a rather crude obscenity. Mychael had just relayed what Sarad Nukpana was up to: the Scythe of Nen or Piaras's sanity.

"Hugh, Farold," Justinius said to the Guardians by the door. "Since Mychael's here, why don't the two of you take a break. Say half an hour. Dalis, you, too."

The Guardians immediately did as ordered; the healer gave him an openly disapproving look.

"Dalis," Justinius said with surprising gentleness. "I'm quite well, and perfectly safe."

The healer reluctantly left with the Guardians, who closed the door behind them.

The archmagus regarded Piaras in silence for a few squirm-inducing moments. It took everything Piaras had not to run out after the old man's bodyguards. Not for fear of the archmagus, though no doubt Piaras thought the old man was just as scary as Sarad Nukpana, maybe more. Piaras was afraid of what Nukpana might suddenly make him do.

Justinius spoke. "Master Rivalin, you can't hurt me—and you won't."

"Hurting you is the last thing I want to do, sir."

The old man chuckled. "With the wards on this room, Sarad Nukpana can't reach you here; and even if he did, I can take out one scrawny goblin black mage bastard on my worst day."

Piaras swallowed. He knew exactly what the old man just said. If Justinius took out a scrawny goblin, he'd be taking out a scrawny elf.

"Just laying my cards on the table, young man."

"Yes, sir. And an impressive hand it is."

That comment almost earned Piaras a smile from the old man.

"Master Rivalin, I told Katelyn only this afternoon that I wasn't at Death's door." Pride shone in his eyes. "The girl damned near took my head off. Can't say that I blame her." His voice softened slightly. "I heard what you did for my Katie— this morning and under the elven embassy. As a grandfather, you have my thanks and gratitude."

That's what his mouth said. His eyes were saying in no uncertain terms that the kid had best behave himself around his grandbaby. Piaras's feelings for Justinius's granddaughter were well on their way beyond casual infatuation. He'd rescued Katelyn Valerian from that purple demon this morning and from Rudra Muralin's clutches last week—and they'd spent a lot of time together in between.

Piaras flushed until the tips of his ears went pink. "You're welcome, sir. I'm glad I was able to help."

Those blue eyes regarded me. "This morning Dalis told me that Carnades threatened you down at watcher headquarters."

I shrugged. "I'm starting to get used to it."

"I heard what all you did today, girl. You've made quite an impression."

"It wasn't exactly what I had in mind when I got out of bed this morning."

"There's no one on this island who can hurt you now—and Carnades and his yes-mages know it." Justinius lay back on his pillows, paler than before. "This would all be more fun if I felt better."

Mychael spoke. "Rest and you will."

"Carnades's whispered threat to you at headquarters wasn't as quiet as he thought it was." The old man's eyes gleamed. "Lets people hear all kinds of interesting and incriminating things. He was in here just last night."

"So I heard, sir." Mychael didn't sound happy that he'd only been told and not been here himself.

"Mychael, the son of a bitch would hardly incriminate himself if he thought I was listening to every word. Hell, he doesn't even think I'm conscious yet." The old guy winked slyly at me. "I'm saving that for a surprise."

"I would love to see that."

"I'm getting stronger every hour. Dalis says I'll be sitting in a chair in a day or two. The day after that I plan to be on my feet and back in charge. Then Carnades gets to see me with my eyes wide open, and my bootprint on his backside."

"Other than myself and Phaelan, the only people close enough to hear Carnades this morning were the fancy-robed mages with him," I told Justinius. "And I know for a fact that my cousin hasn't paid you a visit."

"No, he hasn't. And once Mychael here deems me well enough to lift a pint, I want to rectify that oversight. And I understand his father is in the harbor."

"With warships."

"And me in a room without windows." He threw an accusing glare at Mychael. "My bloody harbor is teeming with pirate ships, and I don't get to see a damned one of them."

Mychael sighed. "No windows are for your protection, sir." It sounded like he'd uttered that phrase a couple dozen times. And until the old man was back on his feet, he'd probably say it a few dozen more.

"You have ears in convenient places," I told Justinius.

"Any more convenient, and they'd be in Carnades's robes right along with him."

"They?" Sounded like some of those fancy-robed mages

might be with Carnades, but they were working for Justinius.
Nice.

"I don't do anything halfway, girl."

"No, sir. I don't imagine you do." I felt my lips curl in a grin.
"Don't take this wrong, but you'd make a fine Benares."

Justinius laughed, a dry wheezing sound. "Nicest thing anyone's said to me in days." Those sharp eyes were on Piaras.
"However, I will not have Carnades threatening my students."

I swore silently. I hadn't told Piaras about Carnades because
we were doing all we could to prevent anyone acting on his orders.

Piaras shot a glance at me. "He threatened me, sir?"

"Just the usual—that you're 'tainted by my influence,'" I
assured him. "He threatened all of us; you just got added to the
list." It wasn't exactly the truth, but it wasn't a lie. "Don't
worry; he can't act on any of it."

Piaras looked at me as if to say what had happened tonight
wasn't bad enough.

"Okay, we won't *let* him act on any of it."

"Who's we?"

"Me, Mychael, and my entire family."

"Add me to that list, girl," Justinius said. "Mychael and
Ronan have told me what you're capable of, Master Rivalin—
without Sarad Nukpana at the reins. You're the most gifted
spellsinger to come through here since the two of them. And
Katelyn told me everything you did this morning. You have
my word that I will not lose you to Carnades's ignorance, the
Seat of Twelve's arrogance, or Inquisitor Balmorlan's greed."
His eyes narrowed. "Or Sarad Nukpana's manipulations." He
pursed his thin lips. "I understand you've been doing more than
studying."

The old man could have meant any number of things by
that, and Piaras was smart enough to keep his mouth shut until
his brain had a chance to work through it. One, it wasn't a question. Two, it wasn't specific. Sleeping wasn't studying, but the
kid knew that wasn't what the archmagus was getting at. And

three, Piaras had been around me long enough to know the first rule of the Benares family: don't confess to something you ain't been accused of doing yet.

"Yes, sir. I have."

Honest, yet admitting to nothing. Maybe my influence wasn't all that bad.

Justinius's bright eyes narrowed. "I understand you have used a containment spellsong against a class ten demon; a Volghul to be precise. And that you held it immobile, unable to summon reinforcements, or cast your song back in your face. And I understand that you did so until Miss Benares here could cram the purple bastard in a bottle." He regarded Piaras in silence. "Do I understand correctly?" The old man's voice sliced through the silence as smoothly as razor-sharp steel.

Piaras was almost too stunned to respond. "Yes, sir. You do."

Justinius's next questions came rapid fire. "And do I understand that you did all this to defend your fellow classmates— and my granddaughter?"

"Yes, sir."

"After giving little or no thought to your qualifications to act as you did, the consequences of your actions, your chances of success, or the danger to yourself or others?"

Piaras blew out a little breath and shifted from one foot to the other, finding a simply fascinating spot on the floor by his right boot.

"That was a direct question, Master Rivalin." Justinius's voice cracked like a whip. "I require a response."

"Yes, sir. I know." Piaras raised his head and met the arch-magus's intense gaze. "And no, sir, I didn't."

The old man's eyes glittered like sapphires. "Didn't what, Master Rivalin?"

"Think about any of those things, sir. I just acted."

"And why did you 'just act'?"

Piaras stood a little straighter. "No one else was doing anything, and if I hadn't acted, more people could have been hurt or killed." He paused and cleared his throat. "I did what I thought was right, sir . . . And I would do it again."

The archmagus sat in silence, unmoving. "And you would do it alone," he said quietly. "Just like you did this morning." His next words were slow and precise. "There was no Sarad Nukpana in the Quad with you this morning—just your talent and foolhardy bravery." The tiniest smile curled the corner of the archmagus's thin lips. "You're noble to the point of suicide, boy." He glanced at Mychael. "Just like a certain paladin of my acquaintance."

Piaras's eyes flicked to Mychael, and he bit the corner of his bottom lip to stop a smile.

Justinius spoke. "Master Rivalin?"

"Sir?"

"Look at me."

Piaras did.

I could feel Justinius doing the same kind of gaze with Piaras that he'd done with me.

After a few moments, the old man broke his gaze and chuckled. "Bukas. Brutal savages. A fine choice, Master Rivalin." He looked at Mychael. "And you said they were solid, complete with roars?"

Mychael nodded. "Roars that took out all the first-floor windows on the Judicial Building."

Justinius laughed, a bright bark. "Nicol and his office lackeys will have a hell of a cleanup in the morning. I'd like to see that."

"I only meant to conjure one, sir," Piaras hurried to explain.

Justinius waved his hand dismissively. "You got carried away with all the excitement; happens to the best of us."

"But I've never done anything like that before."

"Have you ever been attacked by elven embassy guards disguised as Guardians?"

"No, sir, but I—"

"Just because you've never done something before doesn't mean you can't do it, and do it well. There's a first time for everything. It appears that the more you're challenged, the more you're capable of. Maestro Cayle told me the same thing about you."

"He did?"

"I said so, didn't I?"

"Yes, sir, but I didn't know he thought I could—"

"When Maestro Cayle wants you to know what he thinks, and what he thinks you can do, he'll tell you." The old man grinned impishly. "Unless I tell you first."

Piaras flushed slightly with well-earned pleasure. "Yes, sir."

"In the meantime, I'm inclined to trust his assessment."

Piaras didn't respond. I could virtually see the wheels turning in his mind. "So Sarad Nukpana didn't have anything to do with the bukas?"

"Not. One. Thing. Once again, it was just you and yours. Nice work, young man."

Piaras looked like the weight of the world had just dropped off of his shoulders. "Thank you, sir."

"Though apparently Nukpana was involved when you took on those elven embassy guards." His expression darkened. "Disguised as Guardians. How many survived?" he asked Mychael.

"Two, sir. Jari Devent and an embassy guard by the name of Kasen Aratus."

"Isn't Devent's brother the defense attaché at the elven embassy?"

"Yes, sir."

"And his uncle is with elven intelligence."

Mychael's distaste was obvious. "Correct."

"And Aratus . . . Isn't that General Daman Aratus's son?"

"Yes, sir."

"Shit," the old man spat.

"My thoughts exactly."

I looked from one of them to the other. "What?"

Mychael answered me. "Taltek Balmorlan receives much of his funding from General Aratus."

"One hand washes the other," Justinius said. "And rumor has it that General Aratus can't take a crap without permission from his new boss."

That wasn't exactly enlightening. "And this is bad how?"

Mychael sighed. "Raine, General Aratus reports to Markus Sevelien."

Chapter 18

My mouth fell open and stayed there.

Normally news like that would have me blistering the air blue, or looking for something to throw or hit. Right now I was too shocked to do any of it.

And I felt too betrayed.

Duke Markus Sevelien was the elven intelligence agency's chief officer in Mermeia. I'd done some work for him over the years that mostly consisted of finding abducted elves—diplomats, intelligence agents, aristocrats who'd gotten involved in something over their highborn heads. It was gratifying work and I was good at it. Markus had recruited me, and I'd only worked with him. And he'd made no excuses about why he wanted to me to work for him. Markus thought my being related to criminals helped me know the criminal mind. I wasn't proud of it, but he was right. If it could be picked up, pried off, or in any way pilfered, my family would make off with it.

I liked Markus; he'd always been up-front and honest with me. And if I'd been standing face-to-face with him right now, he'd probably still be honest—his loyalties were to elven intelligence, not to me. He'd put any friendship we had to the side as an impediment to him doing his job. And I knew from past experience that Markus would do his job at any and all costs. Whatever was going on wasn't personal; it was business.

It was the Saghred.

And since the Saghred had attached itself to me, that made *me* his business. I could almost understand that; the Saghred was a weapon that elven intelligence wasn't about to let fall into goblin hands. That meant he couldn't allow me to fall into goblin hands. Hell, I didn't want to be in anyone's hands.

But that didn't explain the chain of command that led from Markus to Taltek Balmorlan to what had happened to Piaras. Markus had always made it his business to know what all of his people were up to. I was sure that included me. If General Aratus was one of his people, and Balmorlan his lackey, Markus had to know about Piaras.

And Markus had to know what Piaras meant to me.

Some last part of me refused to believe that Markus had ordered Piaras kidnapped for agency use. Piaras was just a boy. Okay, a young man. But Markus wouldn't order one of his own people taken against their will.

Or would he?

I felt the rage building and did nothing to stop it.

"Girl, we don't know that Sevelien ordered anything."

Justinius had been following my every thought. I knew Mychael had. Good. It'd save me explaining why I was about to put my fist through the nearest wall.

"We don't know he didn't," I said through clenched teeth.

"He's the one you know, isn't he?" Piaras asked quietly. "The one you've worked for."

I swore silently. I'd never told Piaras about Markus because I didn't want him involved in any way with the agency. The kid was entirely too good at listening when he wasn't supposed to. Apparently my efforts at secrecy didn't work. I took a deep breath, half hoping that it'd calm me down. That didn't work, either. No sense denying it now. "Yes, he is."

"I'm sorry," Piaras said.

I waited a moment for that statement to make sense. It didn't. "What for? None of this is your—"

"That's not what I meant, Raine. I'm sorry that someone you trusted betrayed you." His expression reflected controlled anger. A man's anger. "No one should treat you like that. You don't deserve any of this."

Piaras wasn't worried about his own safety or why Markus might want him. Right now all of his concern was for me. My vision blurred again. The old man's fireplace was too damned smoky.

"Thank you." It was all I could manage to say. I waited a few seconds until I was sure I had myself under control. "Mychael, let's operate under the assumption that the general and Balmorlan took their craps because Markus told them to." My voice was hard, my words clipped. "I want to know the instant Markus Sevelien sets foot on this island. I don't think he'll come, but if he does, I want to know about it. Immediately. I'll be telling the same thing to Phaelan and Uncle Ryn. If Markus does show up, I *will* know about it, and we will have a talk."

"Raine, I don't think that's a—"

"Good idea?" I snapped. "No, it's not. Markus having anything to do with what happened to Piaras wasn't a good idea, either." My voice dropped to a hissing whisper. "And if he was involved, I will make him realize just how bad his choice was."

"Son, you don't need five hundred Guardians," Justinius told Mychael. "Just point this one in the right direction and set her off."

I couldn't get my hands on Sarad Nukpana, but Markus Sevelien was flesh and blood. My reaction was violent and primitive, but I was a violent and primitive kind of woman and Mychael knew it. His eyes stayed locked with mine for the span of a few heartbeats. I had to force my breathing back to normal.

"Sir," Mychael said, slowly taking his eyes from mine, "do you have enough strength to ward Piaras's mind against Sarad

Nukpana? I'll be assigning four Guardians to help him resist any impulse that may get through, but Piaras needs to know when he's being tampered with."

The old man snorted. "Of course I have the strength. Which four Guardians?"

"Herrick, Arman, Drud, and Jarvis."

Justinius whistled and shook his head. "You're not taking any chances, are you, son?"

"No, sir, I'm not."

Piaras paled. "Who are they?"

"They're the men who will prevent you from doing anything Sarad Nukpana tells you to do." The old man's eyes gleamed. "They've done this before—and they're good at it."

"Good at it, sir?"

"Exceptional."

"What about spellsongs?"

"What about them?"

Piaras winced apologetically. "I'm kind of fast—"

The old man chuckled. "You're not that fast, boy."

Piaras gulped audibly. "This sounds painful."

"Not if you stop when they tell you to."

I couldn't believe what I was hearing. "He can't use any magic? Just how the hell is he supposed to defend himself?"

"Those four Guardians will defend him," Justinius told me. "And should they require any assistance—and that is highly unlikely—they'll know the difference between Master Rivalin's magic and Nukpana's. They'll stop the goblin, not Master Rivalin. They're four of Mychael's best."

Mychael spoke. "I have the same hopes for Cadet Rivalin."

The archmagus smiled in genuine pleasure. "Cadet? So you want to be a Guardian?"

"More than anything, sir."

"Ronan told me as much." He looked to Mychael. "That means an induction ceremony." He grinned slowly. "Considering present circumstances, it would need to be public, wouldn't it?" His grin broadened. "And it would need to be soon." It was obvious that the old man was hatching something.

"And it would be best if you did the induction yourself," Mychael said. "My men need to see that—and so do the Seat of Twelve."

"To let everyone know that I didn't try to kill you?" Piaras said.

"That, too. I'd hardly induct my own assassin, now would I? This way I kill two birds with one stone, so to speak."

"You'll be using Piaras to show you're back in power," I said quietly.

"You see anything wrong with that?"

"Not a thing. The sooner you get out of that bed, the better."

"Everyone who needs to know that I'm back in command will be there. Do it once, and do it right—prevents any rumor or doubt as to my condition."

"I'll have the papers brought for your signature," Mychael told Justinius. "That will make it official in case our hand is forced before the ceremony; and I'll tell Herrick and the others. Since they'll be guarding Piaras, they need to know that he's one of ours."

I held up a hand. "Hold on a minute. If Piaras is a Guardian cadet, he answers to Carnades until Justinius is back on his feet. I don't want Piaras under Carnades's control for one second."

"Which is why we'll be keeping his new status quiet until the ceremony," Mychael said.

"When I will be back in charge." The old man sounded like he couldn't wait to clean house once he was.

"Raine, I consider Taltek Balmorlan the greater evil right now," Mychael told me. "He—and the people above him—are the ones pulling Carnades's strings whether Carnades is aware of it or not. Piaras being a Guardian cadet protects him against arrest, prosecution, or extradition." Mychael looked at Piaras. "Once you become a Guardian cadet, you will no longer be a subject of the elven crown. You'll be subject to Guardian law and under our protection."

"I really like the sound of that, sir."

Yeah, it sounded good, but the agency wasn't known for giving a damn about anyone's laws. Like certain members of my family, if they saw something or someone they wanted, they just took it or them. Mychael glanced at me. He knew it, too. But right now, getting Piaras into the Guardians was the best he could do. I had to agree; anything was better than nothing at all. Besides, it was what Piaras had always wanted.

"We'll go ahead and have you fitted for your uniform," Mychael was telling Piaras, "but you'll wear civilian clothes until then."

"How long, sir?"

"Two days at the most, and I'll be on my feet and back in charge," Justinius said.

"At least three," Mychael countered.

"Two, with no arguments." The old man's bright blue eyes narrowed in challenge.

"We'll see."

"Mychael, you can prop me up with a stick if you have to, but come hell or high water, in two days I will be robed and in the Great Hall tapping Cadet Rivalin on the shoulders with a sword."

"Sir, I—"

"Son, you know as well as I do that I needed to be on my feet yesterday. That's not possible, but in two days, I *will* be making a speech and lifting a sword. I will show myself to be completely in command of this island. I have no choice. *We* have no choice, and you know it."

Mychael's silence said the old man was right; the scowl said that he didn't like it one bit. I didn't want Justinius to hurt himself, either, but the quicker Carnades got booted out of the big office, the better off we'd all be.

"Good. Since that's settled, how about I plant a little surprise for Sarad Nukpana." Justinius crooked a bony finger at Piaras and indicated the chair next to his bed. "Contact is necessary for this, Cadet Rivalin."

Piaras looked as if getting within touching distance of the archmagus was the last thing he wanted to do. Though with the alternative being Sarad Nukpana roaming around in his head, the kid quickly got over his squeamishness.

It just looked like the old man had his hands on either side of Piaras's head. From the sweat starting to bead on Justinius's forehead, there was a lot of hard work going on. After at least five minutes, the old man released Piaras, leaned back on his pillows, and took a couple of deep breaths. Warding Piaras had taken more than he could really spare. He glared at Mychael like he defied him to say one word about it.

"There," the old man said when he had his wind back. "That'll take care of it. And I left a little something extra for the goblin. The worse the impulse he tries to plant in Cadet Rivalin's head, the worse the shock that goblin's going to get." He winked at Piaras. "A little negative reinforcement."

"Will *I* get shocked?"

"Nope, though you might feel a twinge."

"Oh boy," Piaras muttered.

Justinius's eyes narrowed. "What was that?"

"Thank you, sir."

"That's what I thought you said." He leveled his gaze on Mychael. "So, are you any closer to finding the Hellgate-opening son of a bitch who tried to spellsing me to death?"

"Not yet, sir."

"Most of the best mages alive are on this island," Justinius snapped. "Make them earn their keep and go slam that Hellgate shut; the work will do them good."

"Unfortunately, sir, we suspect some of our most qualified mages are helping Rudra Muralin open it. At least six of them. And I'm certain he has more allies among the Conclave and/or our faculty."

"Do you have names?"

Mychael nodded. "They're all on your list."

"Would those be the same enemies he's watching slither out of hiding?" I asked.

"The very same." Mychael handed Justinius a familiar folded parchment. "This was delivered to Tamnais Nathrach this morning. It's Rudra Muralin's demands."

The old man took it. "Why Nathrach?"

I thought I'd answer that one. "He hates Tam more than anyone else on this island—besides me."

Piaras gave me a questioning look.

"Rudra Muralin wants the Saghred," I told him. "He's made a deal with the demons; they get the Saghred for him, and in return, they get all of the students and mages on the island."

Piaras stood straighter. "Sir, where's Katelyn?"

"She's safe," Justinius told him, never taking his eyes off of the letter. He finished it, carefully folded it, and calmly handed it back to Mychael. "This Rudra Muralin. Exterminate him."

I liked the old man's choice of words.

"Now, what are you doing to find and close that Hellgate?" he asked.

Mychael told him the same thing he'd told me. Guardians, watchers, demonology faculty, and some grad students taking the ultimate final exam.

"That's one problem and hopefully a solution," I said, "but we have another one. A bigger one. Rudra Muralin wants the Saghred, and he's opening a Hellgate to scare us into giving it to him. But the demon queen wants to release what's *inside* the Saghred. I don't know if Rudra Muralin knows about the Scythe of Nen and the queen's plans. The cocky bastard might know and just not give a damn. But those demons do. The only thing we need less than Rudra Muralin and rampaging demons is a demon king freed for the first time in a couple of millennia— along with anyone or anything else that can squeeze out of the Saghred with him. There are no containments on that rock in your basement. If the demons get their claws on that Scythe of Nen, reach the Saghred, and open it—"

Mychael interrupted me. "Potentially thousands of souls looking for bodies to possess, and my Guardians will be first ones they find. Yes, I know. My men are aware of the danger and are taking measures to defend themselves."

"I need to find out what this Scythe of Nen is and get it," I told him. "Quickly."

Mychael frowned. "You?"

"Yes, me. You know anyone else better qualified than a seeker *and* a Benares to find and make off with something valuable?" I turned to Justinius. "You wouldn't happen to know what the Scythe of Nen is, would you?"

"Not a clue."

I had no idea what time it was; my body was telling me it was way past time to get some sleep. I blew out my breath and gave the old man the shortened version of the demon queen's demand delivered by her undead warriors at Sirens.

"So the demon queen and Sarad Nukpana both want this Scythe of Nen," he said.

I nodded. "Right. Nukpana doesn't know what it is, but the demons do. And to add a sick twist on this whole mess, the demon queen—or that bobbing, talking head thing she sent to Sirens—wouldn't tell me. She thinks that I know what it is, where it is, and that I'm lying to keep her from getting it."

"A scythe would indicate a blade of some kind," Piaras offered. "Or so you'd think. But aren't scythes large and used to harvest wheat or something?"

"Size is relative," I said. "The Saghred is its own self-contained world. The smallest dagger would be massive if seen from inside."

"Every type of steel, stone, and spell has been used to try to destroy—and open—the Saghred," Mychael said. "Obviously none have succeeded."

"Professor Berel was killed because the demons believed he had it," I reminded them. "He was screaming that he didn't *have* it—not that he didn't know what it was." I liked this train of thought; it might actually lead somewhere besides a dead end. "Professor Niabi said she didn't know what Berel could have been carrying that the demons would want, but she did tell me that demonologists have all kinds of talismans and trinkets. She just might know what this Scythe of Nen is. If so, it'd save us time that we may not have. If not, I'll just do it the old-fashioned way. Have the locations of the demon sightings been reported to you or the chief watcher?"

Mychael's brow creased. "Both." He didn't know where I

was going with this, but I finally did. At least I felt as if I knew something; it was a welcome change.

"It stands to reason that if the demons were sent to look for something, they'd pop up as close as possible to where they thought it was. Those locations just might help us do more than find that Hellgate."

Justinius Valerian's eyes were brilliantly bright. The old man hadn't heard my entire idea, but he liked what I'd said so far—a lot. In an instant, Mychael's solemn expression turned forbidding.

I held up my hands defensively. "I'm looking for the Scythe of Nen, not a pack of dark mages bent on world domination. Yes, I would love to get my hands around Rudra Muralin's throat. All I've managed to do to him so far is leave my teethmarks in his ear."

Justinius grinned impishly. "Your what?"

I told him about my tussle with Muralin on the catwalk above the stage at Sirens right after the goblin had tried to spellsing him to death.

Justinius laughed, a dry wheeze. "He tried to kill me, and you bit him."

"*And* used my knees, elbows, and fists anywhere on him I could get to. Unfortunately, that's all I could do."

"Sounds damned gratifying to me."

"I didn't get nearly as much out of it as I wanted."

"A dead goblin."

I nodded. "Would have been the ideal conclusion. And if I could have done that then, we probably wouldn't be doing all of this now." I rubbed my eyes. "What time is it?"

"Probably a little after two bells."

The sun would be up in a few hours. "I don't have time to sleep, but I need it," I said.

"Yes, you do." Mychael glanced at Piaras. "You both do."

"Cadet, I have a spare room down the hall," Justinius said. "Until Mychael can get your big brothers on guard duty, you need to sleep somewhere warded. Sarad Nukpana can't reach you here. And Miss Benares, I have a guest room right next to this one that you're more than welcome to." He winked. "Don't worry. Your virtue's safe with me."

I snorted. "Because you don't have the strength right now to get out of bed."

"Sadly true."

"Thanks for the offer, but I don't want my sleep warded. I *want* Sarad Nukpana to come looking for me."

Chapter 19

I think I fell asleep somewhere between the bedroom door and the pillow.

I was back in the citadel guest room I'd occupied before I'd moved onto the *Fortune*. Mychael didn't like what I was going to do. If I wouldn't accept a ward, he at least wanted me guarded. I told him I was perfectly capable of having a nightmare by myself, but I conceded to the guard. This earned Vegard the mind-numbingly dull job of watching me sleep. He'd guard my physical body; protecting my dream self was my problem.

When I opened my eyes—or more accurately when my dream self opened her eyes—I wasn't in my bedroom back home in Mermeia. I wasn't really anywhere that I could determine. Part of my brain wondered if I was so exhausted that I couldn't even conjure a decent setting—the other part of me didn't give a damn because I had gotten what I wanted.

Sarad Nukpana was waiting for me.

The goblin made a show of looking around. There was no

one but the two of us and he knew it. "Apparently your father is unavailable." His eyes glittered brightly. "So much more intimate this way, don't you think? Though it is unfortunate that your bed is missing."

"I'm not here to see my father. I'm here to talk to you."

"Why, little seeker, this keeps getting more delicious."

"Don't excite yourself, goblin. I'm not your midnight snack—and neither is Piaras."

Nukpana shrugged elaborately. "You didn't believe me. What happened to Piaras tonight was entirely your fault. You forced me to stage a demonstration of my control. Though I would think you would be more grateful. Without my influence, your songbird would have never survived. Only my skill with a blade kept him alive."

"Maybe, maybe not," I said. "Either way, your little show bought us time to stop Piaras from killing that Guardian, traitor though he is."

Nukpana negligently waved an elegant hand. "My point was made; I needed to do nothing more. So I released the boy. Have you come to submit to my request? Or do you require further demonstrations?"

I smiled and didn't say a word. My smile was genuine and I could virtually feel the evil twinkle in my eyes. I trusted Justinius's work; better yet, I trusted the old man's viciousness. If he said he had a nasty surprise in store for Sarad Nukpana, I believed him. Hell, I wanted to watch it happen.

"I'm not submitting to anything, but I am going to find the Scythe of Nen."

Nukpana was utterly still. "And release me."

I shrugged. "That's what you want, but it's not my first order of business."

"I dislike your games, seeker."

My voice dropped, low and angry. "I dislike you, and I don't play games. So let's save us both time and aggravation and just cut the crap. I don't know what the Scythe of Nen is. You *say* you don't. The demons do—and your fellow inmates include at least one demon. Either ask him or get close enough to find out."

"We all want something. Ask him yourself, seeker."

"See, here's the thing. I can't. You're in the Saghred; I'm not. You want out of the Saghred; I couldn't care less if you rot. But if you don't want to do business with me . . ." I shrugged. "Your continued imprisonment would be, in your own words, entirely your fault."

The goblin's narrow-eyed silence told me I had him by the short hairs, he knew it, and he did not like it. Tough. None of this was my idea of a good time, either.

"You gamble with your nightingale's life."

"I only bet on sure things."

Nukpana's gaze went distant. I knew what he was doing—or what he was trying to do.

"Having a little trouble finding him?" I asked innocently.

The goblin's lips were a thin, angry line. "His mind is warded."

"It seemed like an obvious solution."

"A solution that needs reinforcing to maintain its effectiveness. Or did the archmagus fail to mention that?"

He didn't. And I didn't respond. Nukpana had lied before and he could be lying now.

Or not.

"I'll take that as a no," the goblin said. "Perhaps he was too weakened from his initial effort. Reinforcing such a ward would drain a healthy man. For one in such a fragile condition as Justinius Valerian . . . No doubt he hopes I will abandon my efforts when I spring the trap he has laid for me in Piaras's mind. Your archmagus did not take into account my motivation. I am a desperate man. Pain lasts mere moments—existence in the Saghred is an eternity. Piaras's mind cannot remain warded forever, but forever is all I have." Sarad Nukpana's gracious veneer had cracked, reminding me that not only was he a sadistic monster, he was now a desperate sadistic monster. "Rethink your impertinence, seeker."

"Rethink your cooperation. Do you want the Scythe in my hands or demon claws? I need that information."

"From the demon king."

I nodded once. "That's him. If the demons get this Scythe of Nen first, you *know* you're going to get left behind. So you have to ask yourself who do you trust more—me or the demon queen?"

Nukpana sneered. "You or a queen of demons. You present me with a most difficult choice."

"I never said it'd be easy."

"I do not know what the Scythe of Nen is. I did not lie when I told you that. But even if I did, you will never find it without my help. You need me, seeker."

"And that would be because . . ."

"You lack, shall we say, a certain necessary quality. You could be in the very room with the Scythe of Nen and you would not recognize it for what it is."

"If you don't think I have what it takes, why don't you get someone else to run your errand?"

"Because I believe you to be one of the few individuals on this forsaken island who could survive long enough to get what I require. It is quite simple: I have the knowledge you need; you have the freedom I want. Mychael said it himself: the Saghred cannot be contained. That means that *I* cannot be contained. Piaras isn't the only desirable target. I can plant suspicions and questions in the minds of certain highly placed mages, questions that Mychael, Tamnais, and yourself do not want asked. Or I could confirm that which Carnades Silvanus already knows— that you and Tamnais are in what he would call an unholy alliance. And the knowledge that your paladin has joined you both in your bond would make Carnades, quite possibly, the happiest mage on Mid."

"You're lying. You can only communicate with me because of my link to the Saghred." I said it, but I didn't know it for a fact.

"Communicating with those outside of your realm of influence would be difficult, but not impossible. It will require substantial effort on my part, but the reward will more than compensate for any discomfort I may suffer. And if you doubt that what I say is true, ask your father. He spent hundreds of years with the stone. Ask him if he ever heard whispered voices in the still, secret hours of the night." Sarad Nukpana was finished playing. "Find a way to release me, or prepare to spend the rest of your life imprisoned—or walking to the executioner's block to join Tamnais and Mychael."

"Tell me why I can't find the Scythe myself."

"I will share my knowledge, but only because it benefits me. The Scythe of Nen is of demon make. They made it; they can find it." His smile turned sly. "But as with any demon-crafted object, it will react to that which it is not. When it reacts, you will recognize it for what it is."

"Is it too much to ask that just once a goblin would give me a straight answer?"

"Anything a demon crafts or uses absorbs their corruption, their evil, their impurity. To counter that, and to find the Scythe of Nen, you will need the help of someone pure." His eyes glittered wickedly. "And as untouched as freshly fallen snow."

I knew what he meant. "You have got to be kidding."

He smiled. "Would I lie, seeker?"

In a heartbeat. But I knew in my gut that he wasn't lying, at least not this time. To find the Scythe of Nen, I first had to find possibly the most elusive quarry I'd ever had to locate in my entire seeking career: a virgin on an island full of college students.

"But know this, seeker—I do not make idle threats. Fail me in this and I will destroy you, but first I will destroy those you love." His voice dropped to a low purr. "Yes, seeker. I know whom you love—and who loves you. You would protect them at any cost, even if you will not admit it to yourself except in your most private thoughts. Tamnais. You find him seductive, yet vulnerable, wounded by his past, wounds you want to heal, a past you secretly yearn to help him forget. He cannot forget his past." Nukpana laughed softly. "And believe me, his past has not forgotten him. It's coming for him; *they* are coming for him. And Mychael, the gallant knight, the noble protector of the people—and of you. He protects you for reasons you know, and for reasons he has only begun to acknowledge. I will twist his strength into his undoing." The goblin's eyes were the flat black of a shark. "I will destroy them first, then the nightingale; and after all of them are gone, and your pain and loss has become too much for you to bear, only then will I come for you."

He faded into the gray void.

"Fail me not, seeker," came his voice from far away.

The goblin was gone. I told myself I could stop shaking now, but apparently I wasn't finished yet.

Sarad Nukpana was gone, but I was still here. Just me. All alone. By myself.

And not waking up.

I desperately wanted to wake up, but I couldn't.

"Raine," came a distorted whisper from behind me in the mist.

I spun, my hand going for a dagger. It wasn't there. I couldn't believe this; my dream self was completely unarmed. If I survived, I needed to have a serious talk with my dream self.

"Daughter," said the same voice, closer this time.

My shoulders slumped in relief. "Why the hell didn't you say that the first time?" My hands were still clenched in fists ready to fight. I think they were stuck that way.

Eamaliel came out of the mist; or more accurately, the silvery mist formed into my father.

"Bravo, daughter. It is dangerous to toy with one such as Sarad Nukpana." He smiled. "Though you do it exceptionally well."

I held out my hand and looked at it. It'd stopped shaking. Almost. "Under different circumstances, it could have almost been fun. Though having me and mine threatened with torture, death, and eternal torment kind of took the shine off the whole experience." I paused. "You heard everything?"

"Every word."

"Is he lying?"

"About what part?"

"Me needing a virgin to find the Scythe of Nen."

"No, he did not lie."

I was so screwed, no pun intended. "I have to use something that doesn't exist to find something I don't know what it is."

My father's gray eyes twinkled with mischief. "Sarad Nukpana doesn't know, but I do."

I couldn't believe my pointy ears. "The Scythe of Nen?"

"The very thing. But knowing may not make finding it any easier."

"I don't care. I'll take anything at this point."

"It's a dagger."

I couldn't believe my ears again. "A dagger?"

"It was forged by demons to open the Saghred. When the demons found the stone, it already contained trapped souls. The demon king wanted to open the Saghred to consume the souls inside."

I grimaced. I had an entirely unwanted image of using a knife to pry open an oyster.

"So did the demon king get a chance to use the thing?"

"He did; and since he's in here, let's just say it didn't go as well as he planned."

"How the heck do you know all this?"

"The demon king isn't the only demon trapped inside the Saghred. There are others; one of them was the demon who forged the Scythe. He's really not a bad sort for a demon, and he's quite talkative. The king ordered him to open the Saghred for him so he could have the first pick of the souls inside."

"So if they're in here, that means the Scythe doesn't open the Saghred?"

"Unfortunately, it works all too well. The king plucked out quite a few souls before the Saghred plucked back. The Scythe's forger had plunged the dagger into the stone, the stone was open, the king was holding it in his hand . . ."

I grimaced. "A pair of sacrifices waiting to happen."

"Exactly. The Saghred does not like to part with that which it has consumed."

I remembered that all too well from the Reaper. I had myself a head-to-toe shudder. "No, I don't think it likes that at all."

I had a thought that I didn't like at all. "There have to be thousands of daggers on this island."

"But only one of them is the Scythe of Nen."

I blew out my breath. "Okay, what does it look like?"

"I have never seen it myself, but from what I've gathered, it's a small dagger with a curved blade. The scabbard is ornately carved with cavorting demons."

I felt my lip curl up. "Cavorting?"

"Unfortunately, yes. You'll know it when you see it."

I added a stomach roll to my lip curl. "That's something to look forward to."

"As to size, the entire weapon is no larger than my hand."

"So it could be hidden literally anywhere. Wonderful. I'm on an island with probably five virgins and thousands of daggers. Needle, haystack. Need I say more? Those aren't my kind of odds."

"They could be better," my father agreed.

"And to liven things up, a demon horde is looking for the same thing, and they don't need a virgin." I had a really bad thought. "Or do they?"

"Do you believe that they are close to finding the Scythe?"

"Doesn't look like it. We've got demons popping up all over the island, and the demon queen herself wants to have a heart-to-heart chat with me, if she has a heart," I muttered. "She thinks I know where the Scythe is but just won't tell her."

My father winced. "When you wake up, you may want to have Paladin Eiliesor take steps to protect the island's virgins."

"Demons can sense that sort of thing?"

"They can. Some claim that virginity even attracts them."

I groaned inwardly. I might not beat the demons to the Scythe, but I suddenly thought I knew where I could find a virgin. "I won't be searching haystacks. I think I know someone."

"You don't sound happy about it."

"And neither will he."

I really needed to sit down. In my next dream, there *would* be a chair. Too much had happened since I rolled out of bed this morning, and none of it had been good. I wasn't the only one in danger; I could handle it if I were. Okay, at least I could handle it better. But because of me, because of the Saghred, some of the people I cared for the most were about to be at the mercy and whims of men who had no business wielding that kind of power. Overwhelmed pretty much covered how I felt. And scared. Definitely scared.

"Raine?"

"I'm scared, Dad."

He gently laid his hands on my shoulders. I didn't know if I was imagining it—this was a dream after all—but his hands felt warm and strong.

"Scared sounds like the right thing to be," he said softly. "You're in a bad situation—"

"It's my friends—"

"Your *good* friends."

I nodded once and took a little breath. It shook just like the rest of me. "My *very* good friends."

"You fear for them."

"More than for me."

"Sarad Nukpana is a threat to you, a very real threat. But know this, daughter. I am a very real threat to Sarad Nukpana. There are others like me, and he knows it."

I remembered what I'd seen the last time I was in the Saghred. Shadowy figures just waiting for Sarad Nukpana to give the word. "There are others like him—and worse."

"Makes life interesting." Eamaliel grinned. "Or whatever it is we have in the Saghred."

"I want to get you out."

"No." His gray eyes were like twin thunderclouds.

"What do you mean, no?"

"If you find the Scythe of Nen and try to release me, others will follow—others who should not be loose in the world. I am still a Guardian, and I still guard the Saghred from those who would abuse its power. I do the same thing, only now from the inside. As to Sarad Nukpana, leave him to me." Those gray eyes went from grim to sparkling. "Or the demon king."

"What about the demon king?" I asked.

"What about him?" My father's expression was the very picture of innocence.

"You're smiling," I said.

"Am I? I wasn't aware of it."

"If it's something good, tell me. I could use a laugh."

"The demon king has an unspoken rule. We stay away from him; he doesn't eat us. We feel it's a fine arrangement."

I felt myself begin to smile along with him. "Let me guess. Nukpana's the new kid on the block, and no one's told him anything."

My father grinned from ear to ear. "We thought we'd let it be a surprise."

Chapter 20

I woke up in the same place where I'd fallen asleep. I loved it when that happened.

What I didn't love, and couldn't believe, was that Piaras had actually gone to class this morning. I didn't care that the four Guardians who'd become the kid's new shadows could squash flat anything that Sarad Nukpana tried. And even worse, Mychael had to leave the citadel only an hour ago to deal with what Vegard called a sizable demon outbreak in the center city. Sora, her faculty, and the grad students hadn't been able to find the Hellgate.

And my loyal Guardian bodyguard had let me sleep through every last bit of it.

"Why didn't you wake me up?"

"The boss ordered me not to."

I stifled a growl—and some four-letter expressions of my displeasure—and strapped on my weapons. There was no use starting an argument. It wouldn't change the fact that Piaras was somewhere on campus, Mychael was somewhere in the center city, and demons were all over the freaking place.

I armed myself as fast as my sleep-induced grogginess would let me, which wasn't nearly fast enough for me. Then I was out the door and down the corridor. I was almost running, and Vegard kept up. He was getting used to it.

"Sizable meaning a lot of demons?" I asked. "Or one really big one?" I had a flashback to the big, yellow, and ultimately squishy demon that'd virtually taken apart watcher headquarters, and hoped nothing like that was rampaging through the city right now.

"Sizable as in more than one."

That didn't make me feel better about anything. I told Vegard some of what Sarad Nukpana had told me and all of what my father said about the Scythe of Nen and the only way to find it.

I'd never seen the big Guardian look so completely baffled. *"Virgins?"*

"Yeah, virgins. You know, people who haven't had sex yet."

"I know what they are, ma'am."

"You just don't know any here."

He barked with laughter. "In the citadel? Hell, no."

"I mean on the island."

"Well . . . I guess some of the students could possibly—"

I waved my hand, cutting him off. "That's what I figured. We're going to see one of them now. I think. I hope."

"Which one?"

I told him.

Vegard chuckled. "No real surprise there. Though he's not gonna like why you need him to help."

I'd come to that uncomfortable conclusion all by myself. For teenage boys, virginity didn't exactly give them bragging rights. It was more like a disease they wanted to cure as soon as possible.

I'd rather fight demons with Mychael.

"Mychael probably doesn't have time for this now, but Dad said that the demons might be looking to get themselves a virgin guide, too."

Vegard swore. "Though how many students could that apply to, realistically speaking?"

"One student in demon claws would be enough," I told him.

"I'll send a runner to the boss."

Or I could tell Mychael myself. Right now.

I really trusted Vegard, trusted him with my life, but the fewer people who knew about my bond with Mychael and Tam, the better. And it would be safer for Vegard. If Carnades went into inquisition mode, I'd rather Vegard not end up on his list of interrogation subjects. Though after carrying me out of watcher headquarters yesterday, Vegard was probably the first name on Carnades's list.

"What is it, ma'am?"

"Can you contact him?" I asked. "With mindspeak?" Mychael had contacted his men that way last night as backup for Piaras. Hopefully Vegard could do the same thing.

"Normally I could, ma'am. But for some reason there's too much distortion. It's the same way all over the city. Must have something to do with the demons. Everyone is having to use runners."

I took a deep breath. Well, it couldn't hurt to try. Maybe an umi'atsu bond could cut through demonic magical distortion.

"Mychael?"

Static. And no Mychael.

Crap.

Piaras had gone to Ronan Cayle's tower for his morning voice lesson. I guess his way of dealing with everything that had happened last night was to do what he was supposed to be doing this morning.

The kid was doing his job; I was doing mine. I had to find the Scythe of Nen, which meant I had to find a virgin. A demon would know instinctively whether Piaras was a virgin or not. I wasn't a demon, so I wasn't sure. I was actually going to have to ask the kid for confirmation.

Now I'd *really* rather fight demons with Mychael.

Ronan Cayle's tower was only about a quarter mile from the citadel walls. I guess when you trained all of the Guardians' top spellsingers it paid to be close to your best source of income. Uncle Ryn had often said the same thing about his homeport's proximity to the eastern kingdom shipping lanes.

There was a pair of Guardians at the door to Ronan's tower. Good. Even better, they let us in when Vegard asked them the first time.

I looked up through the center of the winding stair that spiraled toward infinity and hopefully the top of the tower.

Dang.

Vegard looked up with me. "Yeah, this is why I'm glad I can't carry a tune."

And Ronan's spellsinging students had to haul themselves to the top in less than three minutes.

I was almost certain there was a top, even if I couldn't see it. Ronan Cayle's tower didn't look that high from the outside. But I'd discovered that people weren't the only things you couldn't trust on Mid; you couldn't trust your eyes, either.

There was no impatient, toe-tapping maestro waiting at the top measuring our speed, but Vegard and I hustled anyway. Time was something none of us had. When we reached the top, we weren't the only ones in Ronan's reception area. Vegard exchanged greeting nods with a pair of huge Guardians who I assumed were two of Piaras's new big brothers. I was wheezing like a punctured bellows; Vegard was trying to breathe normally and still get enough air to stay conscious. I guess he didn't want his brothers to see him winded. I didn't give a crap and kept right on gasping. The Guardians weren't alone. Two goblins were standing in the shadows against the wall, armed and armored in more ways than one. I recognized them. Apparently Talon also had a voice lesson this morning, as well as guards of his own, courtesy of his dad's dark mage school buddies. It made sense to me; who better to protect Talon against Sarad Nukpana's black magic? This pair probably knew every dirty trick in Nukpana's book and had a few of their own. The Guardians and the goblins were keeping a wary eye on each other, but keeping their steel and spells to themselves. The boys were playing nice—for now. Unless one of them had to scratch, there shouldn't be any fatalities.

Vegard passed his hand over a crystal set into the wall next to the door. The crystal flashed once, and after a minute or so, Ronan answered the door.

If you were a magic user, you'd heard of Maestro Ronan Cayle. The spellsinging master. The legend who only taught future legends. The maestro who turned out the finest spell-singers the Isle of Mid and the Conclave had to offer. The snappiest dresser I had ever seen.

His robes were a riot of silk and color. Red, orange, amber, gold—every color that flame could be at one point or another in its capricious existence—Ronan managed to wear them all at once and wear them well. It was nothing short of a stunning fashion achievement.

I was about to say as much when Ronan quickly held up a hand to stop me and put a warning finger to his lips. I shut up and froze, and so did Vegard.

I cautiously looked over his shoulder. Ronan's music room was filled with a profusion of cushions and rugs and furniture carved from exotic woods all topped with more cushions, all in sumptuous, brightly colored and gilded fabrics. A Nebian pasha's throne room would have looked drab in comparison. Piaras and Talon were there along with another pair of large and highly watchful Guardians. Everyone was standing perfectly still, and the Guardians weren't watching Piaras. They had their eyes on something else entirely and had glowing weapons in their hands. I looked where they were looking.

Hellfire and damnation.

A knee-high, naked, yellow, potbellied demon was sprawled like a Nebian pasha on a pile of silk cushions. His eyes were closed, and his fleshy lips stretched in what looked like a contented smile on his flat and ugly face.

I'd squished his big brother yesterday.

I sucked in my breath and went for my daggers.

Ronan held up both hands. He wanted me to stay put; I

wanted to move. If I was going to be a demon target, I was going to be a moving target.

An armored goblin dark mage slipped silently between the Guardians; he had an ornate and open bottle in his hands. One hand held the bottle; the other had the stopper. Tam and I had done the same thing in the Quad yesterday. I stayed put and let the mage do his work.

The little yellow demon snorted, rolled over, and started to snore.

After a hissing incantation from the goblin dark mage, the demon was doing his snoring from inside a sealed bottle.

We all started breathing again.

"I used an ancient Caesolian love song with a lullaby twist to put him out," Ronan said with satisfaction. "He seemed to like it."

"Looked like a bored stupor to me," Talon muttered.

Ronan's amber eyes fixed him with a look. "What was that?"

"Nothing, sir."

"Are you both okay?" I asked Piaras and Talon.

"Sure," Piaras said. "It was just a little one."

Talon shrugged and grinned. "A little ugly never hurt anyone."

I looked at Vegard, he looked at me, and we decided not to enlighten either one of them.

"Don't demons wear clothes?" Piaras asked, clearly grossed out.

"No demons wear clothes," I told him.

Talon looked at the bottle and made a face. "Some demons should."

"How did that thing get in here?" I asked Ronan. I didn't ask what it wanted; I had a good idea. Maybe I wasn't the only one virgin hunting.

The maestro pulled back a section of silken drapes to reveal a mirror, a big one, easily the height of the room and at least six feet wide. After what had happened last week, I would have thought Ronan would have been the last man to have a mirror anywhere near him. I was about to ask Ronan how many different kinds of insane he was, when I saw the ripples rolling just beneath the mirror's surface. It was warded. Nothing could get through a warded mirror.

Nothing, apparently except for demons.

Dammit.

Last week, spellsingers had been kidnapped through mirrors. This week, every big mirror on the island was still warded. If one demon could get in, so could hundreds or thousands of his brothers, sisters, or whatever.

Mirrors could be used to translocate people, manifest creatures, or move objects from one place to another. Mirror mages needed a crisp, clear image to do their thing. The surface of a warded mirror reflected an undulating wave, its pattern constantly changing. Seeing someone or something step out of my reflection was one of the reasons why I owned only one mirror and it was just big enough to see my face in. Anything that popped out through that mirror would be small enough for me to stomp on.

My expression must have spoken volumes. "It's been warded since my students were abducted last week," Ronan assured me.

"Your mirror mage must have missed a section." Or done a piss-poor job.

"She didn't miss anything. After she left, I checked her work myself."

I indicated the bottle and its snoozing contents. "And potbelly still got in."

"Obviously," Ronan said. He pulled the curtain back over the mirror.

My stomach was grateful; looking at a warded mirror made me dizzy.

"Though I wasn't aware that demons could come through a warded mirror," he added.

Mychael wasn't aware of it, either, and the same applied to almost everyone else on this island—everyone except for Rudra Muralin and his dark mages directing traffic down at the Hellgate.

"Vegard, where's Mychael?" Ronan asked.

Vegard told him. The maestro scowled.

"Get word to him about this," Ronan said. "He needs to know."

Vegard shot a questioning glance at me.

"I'll be fine. Ronan and I can take out anything that comes in. And we've got plenty of backup."

"I'll go find another message runner," Vegard told the maestro.

"Another?"

"Don't ask, sir." Vegard gave me a look that said he'd really like it if I didn't budge from the exact spot where I was standing. "I'll be right back."

"I'll be right here."

He left and I turned to Ronan. "Are you finished with Piaras's lesson?"

"I am now. Talon, you're excused as well."

I didn't think I'd ever felt more awkward in my life. And I knew it was just going to get worse. "Piaras, can I talk to you in private?"

"Why? What's wrong?"

"Just more of the same stuff that's been wrong since we got here."

"You can use my office," Ronan offered.

"Any mirrors in there?"

"None."

"I'll take it."

Piaras's new guards started to follow. I stopped and blocked the door. "Gentlemen, this won't take long, and it is highly personal. If Piaras suddenly gets possessed, I'll yell. Good enough?"

They hesitated. They didn't like it, but they did it.

"Thank you," I said, and closed the door.

I'd never been inside a genie's bottle, but Ronan's office was what I imagined one would look like. The pasha's throne room decorating theme carried over from the music room. Silk, velvets, gilt and gaudy. Ronan liked his creature comforts. A lot.

Piaras wasn't having a good day; yesterday had started off the same way, and by last night, it had slid downhill into a cesspool. Today was showing all the signs of doing the exact same thing.

There was no easy way to ask what I needed to ask. Sure, I could just come right out and say it; it was a simple enough question, but the words just refused to come out.

"You and Katelyn like each other, right?" Yeah, I know. It was the cowardly way in, but at least it was a related topic.

Now the kid was completely confused. "Yes, we do."

"A lot?"

"Yes, a lot. Why do you ask?"

"The two of you haven't . . . done anything about really liking each other, have you?"

Now he was confused *and* concerned. "Not yet. I . . . That is, we want to . . . We think . . . But . . ."

"But what?"

"Before I came to class, the archmagus and I had breakfast together."

I pressed my lips together so I wouldn't snicker. Oh, I knew what was coming. Uncle Ryn had done the same for me. Any boy—or a couple of years later, any man—who wanted to see me socially had to go through the Talk. One of my hopeful suitors said going through the Talk was like being forced to walk through fire, except without the fun parts. You tried to get through it as quickly as possible and told yourself the pain would be over soon. To the best of my knowledge, Uncle Ryn had never actually laid hands on one of my suitors, but he'd always made it plain and clear what behavior he expected, and what actions would be taken if he was "disappointed" that the boy/man's behavior fell short of those expectations. Needless to say, I didn't date all that much.

Piaras was looking at me. "What?"

I swallowed a snort. "Nothing. Go on."

Piaras glanced at the door; it was closed, but he lowered his voice anyway. "Archmagus Valerian said he would know if Katelyn and I . . . you know. Raine, I'd like to live long enough to graduate, or at least graduate in this form. He can't really turn me into a squid, can he?"

"Is that what he told you?"

"And a couple of other things."

"He can't do it, at least not the squid part."

"You're sure?"

"Positive."

Piaras let out a relieved breath. "That's good." His look turned suspicious. "Why are you asking about me and Kat?"

I really didn't want to come out and say this. "I need to find the Scythe of Nen. And by the way, you weren't too far off the mark. It is a dagger."

"What's it look like?"

I told him what my dad had told me.

"Something that small won't be easy to find," Piaras noted.

"No, it won't. And apparently a certain type of person is helpful for finding this kind of thing."

Piaras's eyes narrowed. I had a sinking feeling he'd figured out where I was going with this.

"What type of person?" he asked.

I winced. "Uh . . . a virgin type of person."

His lips narrowed into a thin line to match his eyes. "And when you found out you needed a virgin, you immediately thought of me."

"Not immediately."

"What, so you had to wait two seconds?"

"More like five actually. Don't feel bad about it."

"You think I'm the only virgin on this island! How's that supposed to make me feel?"

I grinned hopefully. "Special?"

Piaras gave me a look. You know the one.

I threw my arms up. "Okay, I'm sure there are other virgins on this island, but I don't have time to find them. I was pretty sure you were qualified—"

Piaras glowered. "As a virgin."

I held up a hand. "No, no." I was just getting myself in deeper. "I knew you were qualified in other ways to help. Levelheaded, good in a fight, that kind of qualified."

Piaras arched an eyebrow. "Nice try."

I hung my head and sighed. "Kid, just help me out here, will you?"

Silence. I looked up. Piaras was grinning.

"What do you need me to do?" he asked.

I told him.

"One question," he said when I'd finished.

"Shoot."

"This virgin thing, does thinking about it count? Just because I haven't done it doesn't mean I don't think about it." He lowered his voice again. "A lot."

Chapter 21

Piaras and Talon needed to go to their next class. I needed to talk to Sora Niabi. Both destinations were conveniently located in Starke Hall, also known as the demonology department. I had Vegard, Piaras had four grim Guardians, and Talon had a goblin dark mage hit squad.

Good thing I wasn't trying to be inconspicuous.

Vegard's messengers had hopefully reached Mychael by now, and hopefully he'd taken steps to protect the virgins and break the mirrors. If it were me, I'd have every mirror on the island broken. I was sure Mychael had a better solution, but big demons would have a tough time wiggling through an itty, bitty shard of glass. In my opinion, the solution for the virgins was obvious. Get laid now. I muffled a smile. The lower hells would freeze over before Mychael would issue *that* order.

Knowledge about demons came in three varieties: legend, rumor, and fact. Demonologists knew the facts; the rest of us floundered with legends and rumors; none of them were pleasant, and each of them was more gruesome than the one before.

The rumor that would probably be making the rounds on campus within the hour—if it wasn't already—would have nothing to do with fact and everything to do with horny college students looking for an excuse. Whether demons liking virgins was fact or fiction didn't matter. I'd be willing to bet that the number of virgins among Mid's student population was suddenly going to skyrocket. And every last one of those kids would be desperate to lose their apparently forgotten virginity as quickly as possible to ensure protection against the demons. I wondered what new pickup lines they'd be using. Help me; I'm a virgin.

With the impending increase in fake virgins, I was really glad I'd already secured the help of the real thing.

I think.

Piaras still wasn't happy about his role in our little expedition. And I didn't think his opinion was going to change anytime soon. Especially since Talon had already heard the one about demons and virgins.

Talon's grin was full of fang. "Well, I'm safe," he was telling Piaras. "I'm probably one of the safest people on this island. Hell, I'm probably demon repellant." His grin broadened. "Are you safe?"

It was obvious that Piaras didn't want to answer that question. "Not exactly," he finally said.

"Piaras, either you're safe or you're not. There's no gray area here. Which is it?"

I'd listened long enough. "Everyone is safe. Regardless. The island is crawling with armed Guardians. Everyone will be safe."

Talon's grin never wavered. "But are you sure of that?"

"Yes."

"Absolutely positive?"

I glared at him.

"When there's a danger, shouldn't you take *every* precaution?" he asked innocently, his aqua eyes wide.

I added a growl to go with the glare.

"I'll be helping Raine," Piaras said between clenched teeth.

"Helping?"

"Because I'm . . ." Piaras really didn't want to say the word.

"Not safe?" Talon said helpfully, grinning from ear to pointed ear.

"No, I'm not safe!" Piaras snapped. He turned on me. "Now everyone's going to know!"

Talon snorted. "Everyone already does."

Piaras actually snarled at me.

Talon clapped him on the back. "Not a problem. I know some ladies who can get you safe real quick. Though if you're looking for a freebie, you and Katelyn could help each other out. She's definitely not safe."

Piaras blushed scarlet. I smacked Talon in the back of the head.

Topic closed.

*Demonologists could make a lot of money in the private sector. Law-*enforcement agencies were the natural choice for postgraduate work, but it didn't pay worth a damn. City governments expected their citizens to be protected but only paid a pittance for the privilege. The more money-minded demonologists worked for themselves—if you had demon problems and enough gold, a freelance demonologist would gladly take both of them off of your hands.

So while Mid was on its way to becoming hell on earth—a freelancer would have called it paradise.

We didn't have freelancers, or time to call any in. We had students and faculty. Hopefully the old adage "those who can't do, teach" didn't apply to the demonology department faculty. If so, we were all seriously screwed.

Starke Hall, which housed the Conclave college's demonology department, wasn't chaos, but it was close.

The students were either grim-faced and determined or wide-eyed and excited. The former were probably graduate students or upperclassmen who knew what was happening; the latter were merely young and clueless. Those grad students knew that during the next few hours or days, they were going to get a nasty taste of what working in the real world was like. The young ones would be told to hide.

The sight of me, Vegard, four massive Guardians, and four leather-clad goblin dark mages in the corridor didn't help the situation. If anything, grim turned grimmer, some of the wide-eyed ones added open mouths to their expressions, and several students decided they needed to be somewhere else.

But most of them were looking at me. From the looks I was getting, they knew who I was and what I had done at watcher headquarters.

The crowded corridor suddenly got a lot less crowded.

Professor, and now demonology department chairman, Sora Niabi was standing at the far end.

I was armed for ogre. She was armed for everything else.

The professor had a couple of bladed and blunt weapons that I could see, but it was the talismans I sensed on her that would ensure the instant regret of anyone or anything who had the poor judgment to mess with her. If what I sensed was any indication, anything they started, she could finish. Permanently.

Talon saw the professor. "Damn." He sounded disappointed.

"Damn what?" I asked.

"We have to go to class and you and the prof are off to kick demonic ass."

"You *want* to kick demonic ass?"

"Anything's better than Demons for Dummies."

"What?"

"Demonology 101," Piaras clarified. "It's an introductory course. It gives the non–demonology major some practical experience. It's a general college course, so everyone has to take it."

Talon snorted. "After what we did yesterday, you'd think we'd get bumped up a level or two."

"Master Nathrach, do you know the name, type, and classification of the demon that by some miracle you actually managed to hold on to for two minutes?" It was Sora Niabi, her arms were crossed, and her expression severe.

"No, ma'am," Talon said. "But we—"

"It was a Volghul, Master Nathrach. I would advise that you look it up in your textbook. And while you're at it, you may want to pay special attention to a Volghul's preferences in terms of captives/food, and precisely how they play with, and eventually prepare and consume that which they have caught." She leaned forward and lowered her voice. "You meet every last one of its preferences, and no doubt it would have enjoyed you immensely. So before you mistake the miracle that enabled you to survive your encounter as skill, and think that it qualifies you to move up to a more advanced course, you should think again."

Talon swallowed with an audible gulp. "Thinking's good."

"It's very good. In fact, we highly encourage it here. Now you and Master Rivalin are dismissed."

"With your guards," I added firmly.

"Guests are always welcome in class," Sora murmured. She glanced at the four dark mages. "Especially those who have practical experience to add to a lesson."

"Piaras, I'll probably be in Professor Berel's office," I told him. "When you get out of class, come and find me. We have work to do."

Piaras nodded. Talon's snicker ended in an oof when Piaras elbowed him in the ribs.

Sora didn't say a word until Piaras and Talon were safely in their classroom with their guards.

"Work?" she asked. "Something I should know about?"

I told her about the Scythe of Nen, why I needed it, and how Piaras was qualified to help me find it. And I told her that I wanted to start that search in Professor Berel's office.

Sora smiled and nodded. "Virgins and demons, an oldie but a goodie. I've overheard the students talking. It sounds like they've put defense plans of their own into motion."

I grinned crookedly. "Working together to make sure everyone's safe?"

Sora grinned back. "Damn fine work if you can get it. It's good to see the student body working together."

"The kids are going at it like rabbits, aren't they?"

Sora chuckled. "That's what I hear."

"Is it true?" I asked. "That demons like virgins?"

"Raine, demons will eat anything, male or female, virgin or not. Some do have preferences, but they'll all take what they can get."

"And they're capable of taking anyone on this island."

"If what we've seen is any indication of what's coming, they can take *everyone* on this island. I don't care how much demon fighting experience someone has, myself included. Outnumbered plus overwhelmed equals eaten." She looked through one of the partially open classroom doors at the young students inside, and I saw concern and maybe even fear reflected in her dark eyes. "Or worse."

"Well, if you have any idea where this Scythe of Nen is, Piaras and I won't have to go looking for it. It'd be a lot safer for both of us."

"The demons obviously didn't find it in Professor Berel's town house."

"How about his office here?" I asked.

"I've been in there. Nothing in there matches that description, though you're more than welcome to look. Laurian Berel didn't like knives, daggers, or any edged weapons. But colleagues and visiting academics kept giving him the things as gifts. I guess they thought a demonologist would like weapons."

"Demonologists can't be easy to shop for," I said.

Sora smiled. "We're not, though most of us will take a couple bottles of good whiskey. Since Laurian didn't want to admit that he was afraid of daggers, he gave every last one of them away. Only a few of us knew of his fear."

I had an unpleasant flashback. The Volghul claws that ripped out his throat definitely qualified as edged weapons. Killed by what you feared the most. Oh yeah, everybody wanted to go like that.

"Apparently the demons didn't know that daggers weren't his thing," I said.

Raised voices came from the classroom with the partially open door. I could see a man, presumably a professor, cross his arms and lean against the front of his desk.

"Let me get this straight—a demon ate your homework?" the man asked dubiously.

"Yes, sir." The response sounded like it came from the front row.

"You mean dog."

"No, sir. Demon. A Crog."

The man raised an eyebrow. "You're sure?"

"Positive, sir."

"You don't want to change your story?"

"I can't. It's the truth. It was in my bookbag."

"Where is it now?"

"It jumped out and ran off when I unbuckled the bag." The boy made a face. "I really didn't want to chase it, sir. It didn't take anything else, and Crogs are really disgusting."

Sora pushed open the door. "Was the Crog brown with blue stripes or green?" she asked the startled student.

The boy sat up as straight in his chair as possible. "Blue, Professor Niabi."

"You're positive?"

"Unfortunately positive, ma'am. I got a really close look at it."

Sora turned to me. "Crogs like any kind of paper, parchment, or ink."

I made a face. "Ink?"

"They'll drink the stuff if they can find a bottle. You usually find Crogs in libraries or bookstores." She turned back to the wide-eyed student. "Were you in the Scriptorium last night?"

He nodded. "I was finishing a research assignment."

"You must have picked him up there. The Scriptorium staff sets traps baited with outdated textbooks," Sora told me. "This one must have had a taste for fresher paper."

"There hasn't been a Crog in the Scriptorium in years," the student insisted fearfully. "Chief Librarian Kalta would never permit it. He has wards in place to keep everything out."

And everyone. I'd had an up close and unpleasant encounter with Lucan Kalta last week.

I stepped forward. "And how do you know about the Scriptorium's wards?"

The student looked questioningly at Sora. She nodded.

"I have a part-time job in the Scriptorium," he told me.

That would make Lucan Kalta his boss. The kid must have needed the money real bad.

"Excuse accepted," Sora told the student. "In the immediate future, check your bag before leaving the Scriptorium."

"Definitely, ma'am."

Sora left the room; I followed. Vegard had waited outside.

"Demons are turning up everywhere," he muttered.

Sora strode purposefully down the hall. "Not just any demon, Vegard. And not just any place."

What I knew about demons wouldn't fill a hat, but I'd gathered from Sora's reaction in that classroom that blue stripes were worse than green. "Blue stripes are bad, I take it?"

"They are. Greenies are as common as rats in a warehouse. Officially they're not even demons. They closely resemble Crogs, so most people just lump them together, most demonologists included."

"So blue-striped Crogs are significant how?"

Sora kept walking, but her lips curled in a satisfied smile. "They're not summoned."

"Let me guess: they came through the Hellgate."

"Correct. And they stay close to it." Her smile broadened. "Very close."

Chapter 22

"The Hellgate's under the Scriptorium?" I asked.

"Maybe, maybe not," Sora said. "The Scriptorium is in the center city, and under the city are—"

"Tunnels." My lack of enthusiasm was evident.

Sora nodded. "Hundreds of miles of them, I understand. Never felt the urge to go exploring myself. Though it's ill-advised to open a Hellgate in a tunnel. You'd need a chamber. Fairly large, definitely stable, and if you don't want to get caught while you're opening it, easily defensible."

"Anything like that under the Scriptorium?"

"Too many to count. Though with very few exceptions, the center city is where most of the sightings have occurred."

"Under the campus."

"Unfortunately, yes. The largest area to cover and also the most densely populated."

"How far is the Scriptorium from here?"

"Just two blocks."

I looked down, wishing the Saghred had given me the ability

to look through floors and rock. "Tunnels and chambers right under our feet."

Sora lowered her voice. "Quite possibly."

I swore silently. I hated tunnels. I especially hated tunnels probably seething at this very second with demons and dark mages—or Reapers. Thankfully, I had work to do up here. "Can I see Professor Berel's office?"

"Follow me."

Laurian Berel's office was what you'd expect a department chairman to have. Spacious corner office with a window. At least it would have been spacious if it'd been cleaned out in the past couple of decades, and there was probably a window with a nice view behind those heavy and closed drapes. Permeating the place was a smell I couldn't identify and quite frankly, I didn't really want to. I was tempted to pull back those curtains and open the window to let in some fresh air, but something on a long table in front of the window made me reconsider that. Several somethings, actually.

Demons in miniature. Dead and otherwise. The dead ones were either preserved in jars or stuffed and mounted. The others were alive and in clear cases faintly glowing with containment spells. A couple of them were glowing a little too faintly for my comfort.

"Pets," Sora told me.

I blinked. "What?"

"Most of us faculty feel the same way."

Vegard's expression was somewhere between appalled and just plain disgusted. "That's creepy as hell, Professor," he said. "No pun intended."

They were all looking at us, and one looked uncomfortably similar to the yellow latrine demon, except this one was green. I didn't want to ponder what caused the color difference. Its lips curled back, showing me several rows of needle-sharp green teeth. He glared at me. I stared back. Then I realized something and looked away—you can't win a staring contest with something that doesn't have eyelids.

"I don't even want to ask how he fed them," I muttered. "Or what."

"Sometimes he did a better job of it than others," Sora told me. "One time he was having a faculty meeting in here while he fed them. He got distracted, and Green Teeth there got a surprise treat. Laurian was certainly surprised. Did you notice he was missing two fingers on his left hand?"

My stomach did a little barrel roll. "I must have missed that one."

She waved a dismissive hand. "You were face-to-face with a Volghul. You had more important things to do. Laurian always said that these little ones were bound and could do him no harm."

Yeah, where had I heard that one before?

"If we're all still alive next week, I'm sending these things back where they came from," Sora told me.

Berel's pets compared to what would be coming through that Hellgate were like house cats compared to lions—giant lions that were damned near impossible to kill. I looked down at the now chittering demon in the cage. I'd take Green Teeth here anytime.

I didn't feel comfortable turning my back on the late Professor Berel's pets, but I couldn't exactly search the office while staring at a lidless mini-demon.

From the looks of things, Berel had been department chairman and had occupied this office for a long time. You just couldn't get that kind of clutter overnight. There wasn't room for one more book on Berel's shelves. When he'd run out of horizontal space, he started stacking books vertically on top of other books. The shelves were floor to ceiling with a ladder on rollers that could slide down the entire length of the wall. That told me the shelves weren't likely to fall on me, but I didn't want to push my luck. Besides, I wasn't looking for a book.

"Do you mind if I search?" I asked Sora. "I promise not to trash the place."

"Search away. Anything I can do to help?"

"I know he hated daggers, but if he had kept one that he'd been given, where would he have put it? Did he have a safe, strongbox—"

Sora was shaking her head. Not the response I'd hoped for.

"Not that I'm aware of," she said, "but I'll look."

"Thanks."

"What can I do, ma'am?" Vegard asked me.

I nodded toward a row of file cabinets next to the table with the mini-demons. I smiled apologetically. "Check those, please."

He gave me a flat look. "Professor Niabi?"

"Yes?"

"Permission to stab anything that escapes and jumps on me?"

"Feel free, Vegard."

Before I started knocking on the walls to check for hidden compartments, I thought I'd eliminate the obvious. Berel's desk. It was old and massive. I'd seen mages' desks that had more hidden drawers than real ones.

The second drawer I searched had more of the usual desk contents—and a pair of small leather boxes, trimmed in gilt filigree, about the size of a man's hand. I froze. My present problem didn't start by my finding the Saghred or the amulet; my problem had started as a result of a thief friend of mine finding said amulet in a pretty little box much like these. That one had been closed with a black wax seal; these boxes were closed with latches. Still, there was no way I was touching them without asking a few questions first.

I took one step back. "Sora?"

"Yes?"

I leaned forward just enough to pull the drawer open wider. "Any idea what's in these?"

"These what?" She came over and looked. "The boxes?"

"Yep."

"I don't know. Feel free to open them."

I swore. "Gee, thanks."

"What's wrong?"

I told her.

Sora whistled. "I wouldn't want to open any more boxes, either."

Vegard came over. "Ma'am, maybe I should—"

I held up a hand. "I found them." I sighed. "I'll open them."

"I'll stand here," he said, his hands now faintly glowing.

Vegard had a spell ready to launch; I muttered a shielding spell into place. Not that either would do any good if there was something truly nasty in those boxes, but events of the past couple of weeks had made me cautious, if not downright paranoid. I picked up the first box; it was covered in midnight blue leather. I held it at arm's length and gave it a little shake. It didn't sound like there was anything in there. Only one way to find out. I put it on the desk, flipped the latch, and opened it. Inside was a star-shaped medallion; it looked like an award or something.

"The Order of Goulous," Sora said as if that explained everything. It didn't.

"Which is?"

"An academic award for excellence in research," she explained. "Laurian was widely published."

I took out the other box, flipped the latch, winced, and looked inside. It was empty, but there had been something in there, nestled in the dark velvet lining. Something that had left an indentation like a curved dagger no larger than my father's hand.

Just an imprint, no dagger.

I made no move to put my hand anywhere near that imprint. "Okay," I said carefully, never taking my eyes off of that box. "Theoretically the Saghred and I are one. So it would stand to reason that the rock wouldn't be too fond of the Scythe of Nen—and possibly anything that had held it."

Vegard didn't move. "Ma'am, I think you should put the box down." His voice was tight. "Slowly would be good."

I kept my eyes on the box. "Vegard, we have to know for sure."

"Are you feeling anything from just holding it?"

"A little tingle maybe, but that might be my nerves." Before Vegard could stop me—or before I chickened out—I threw caution to the wind and reached out to touch the velvet indentation with my fingertips.

I really shouldn't have done that.

The next thing I knew, I was on my ass, and the box was across the room. I'd never been struck by lightning, but this had to be what it felt like. I wanted to say something, my mouth was opening and closing, but words weren't making it out.

Vegard and Sora were doing my cussing for me.

"I . . . think that . . . was it," I finally managed. I couldn't imagine the Saghred being that pissed off at any other piece of cutlery. Vegard started to reach for me and got one hell of a shock for his trouble.

"Don't touch . . . Wait a . . . minute."

"Laurian did have it," Sora said.

I grabbed the edge of the desk and hauled myself off the floor. The desk didn't catch fire, so I thought I was safe for contact. Vegard thought so, too. He grabbed my arm and helped me the rest of the way to my feet.

"Who else has access to this office?" I asked Sora.

"Just Laurian's secretary. But he didn't take it."

"How do you know—"

"Daggers didn't stay in Laurian's possession long enough for anyone to steal them."

I was confused. "If he gave it away, why would he keep the box?"

"The mage he gave it to collects daggers." Sora said it like she knew I wasn't going to like it. "He has display cases and didn't need the box. Over the years, Laurian has given him a lot of daggers. He called them gifts; I called them bribes."

I didn't move. "Who?"

"Carnades Silvanus."

That wasn't the name I wanted to hear.

"Carnades collects exotic daggers," Sora told me. "Laurian hated the things. Laurian also hated Carnades."

"Sounds like he was a good judge of character."

"Carnades is the chairman of the funding committee," Sora explained. "They decide how much money each department gets. Guess which department Carnades thinks should be eliminated because any moral person wouldn't want to study demons?"

"No guess needed. I see why you turned that demon loose on him yesterday."

Sora grinned. "Mychael and I wanted to give Vegard a chance to get you out of there, but I will admit to a more personal reason."

"Payback's hell."

"Literally."

I chuckled. "And those blue demons were on him like—" I stopped, thought, and realized in the span of about two seconds. Then I felt a sudden and entirely justified urge to bang my head against Laurian Berel's bookcases.

Vegard stepped forward. "Ma'am? What's wrong?"

"Carnades had it." Saying it out loud just made it worse. "Carnades *has* it."

"What does—"

"Carnades actually had the Scythe of Nen on him yesterday at watcher headquarters," I said. "He had a small, curved silver dagger tucked in his sash. I saw it—and those demons knew what it was; that's why they attacked him." I suddenly felt like the biggest idiot on the island; then my Benares instincts put in an appearance. "When Carnades was out cold; I could have swiped the thing."

"Ma'am, you didn't know."

"I do now, a lot of good it does me."

I imagined myself tackling Carnades and wrestling that dagger away from him. Fun, but hardly practical. I pulled my bottom lip between my teeth and bit it while I thought some very Benares thoughts that would have made Phaelan proud.

"Ma'am, no." Vegard was adamant, firm, and he knew he wasn't going to change my already-made-up mind.

"Vegard, we have to have that dagger. We don't have a choice."

"We could go to the boss. He could talk to Magus Silvanus."

I just looked at him. "Do you honestly believe that Carnades will hand over the Scythe to Mychael for safekeeping?"

"Hell would freeze over first," he admitted.

"Exactly."

"You can't break into and rob Magus Silvanus's town house."

"I never said I was."

"You didn't have to say it; I know what you're thinking."

I half smiled. "And because I'm a Benares, you assumed that I'd opt for the larcenous approach."

"No, ma'am." He grinned. "Because you're you."

I crossed my arms over my chest. "How long have you known me, Vegard?"

"A little over two weeks."

I chuckled. "Damn, but you're a quick study." I turned to Sora. "You didn't hear any of this."

"Any of what?" she asked innocently.

"Thank you." And I meant it. There were too few people I could trust on Mid, and I really wanted Sora Niabi to be one of them.

There was actually paper and pens on Laurian Berel's desk. I scribbled a quick message and folded it tight. Then I pressed my thumb to the fold and muttered a sealing spell. No one could open that note except for its intended recipient. The thing would go up in flames if anyone else tried to take a peek.

"Do you have a student you can trust and spare to deliver a message?" I asked Sora.

"I do."

"Do you have a student who can go to the gangplank of the *Fortune*, ask for Captain Benares, give this to him, and not crap their pants?"

Sora chuckled. "I train demonologists, Raine. They're up to it."

"Good." I pointed at the Scythe's box, still on the floor. "May we borrow that?"

"You can have it."

Vegard looked baffled.

"It still has the Scythe's residuals on it," I said to his unspoken question. "If I knew for a fact that the thing was in Carnades's town house in a display case, I could find it myself. I know what it looks like, so I wouldn't need to drag Piaras into this with me. However . . ."

"The Scythe probably won't be out in the open," Vegard said.

I nodded. "That's the thing. We don't know. So Piaras can probably use that box the same way I use an object for seeking. I can't touch that box again, and I know the Saghred's not going to help me find that dagger."

"So we still need a virgin."

"Unfortunately."

"What if Carnades is wearing it again today?" Vegard asked quietly.

"I'll cross that bridge when I come to it," I told him.

Or tackle that mage.

Piaras's class would be over in another ten minutes, so Vegard and I waited around the corner from his classroom. Waiting for Piaras also gave me more time to think. I couldn't exactly walk up to Carnades's front door, knock, and ask nicely. But at the same time, Vegard was right. I didn't need the real crime of breaking and entering added to the list of imagined crimes on Carnades's arrest warrant. The little Benares voice in my head whispered that breaking and entering could only be added to the list if I got caught. I told the little voice to hold that thought while I tried to come up with something less risky. Problem was I was having absolutely no luck. Perhaps my family urges were too strong for my law-abiding efforts.

"And this is Starke Hall, home to the college's demonology department," said a familiar voice.

Vegard and I looked at each other in utter shock. His eyes went wide; my mouth dropped open.

Carnades Silvanus.

What the hell was the acting archmagus doing playing tour guide?

"I promise not to linger for long, Magus Silvanus," said a melodious voice, smooth and seductively beautiful. "It would be unspeakably rude to be late for my own reception luncheon."

I sucked in my breath and held it. I didn't mean to hold it, but at the sound of that voice, my mind forgot to tell my lungs to breathe. It had other things to do. Like panic.

I didn't have to look to see who it was. I knew who it was.

Rudra Muralin.

Chapter 23

My mind raced, logic and reasoning struggling to keep up and fail-
ing miserably. What I was hearing was impossible. Rudra Muralin was under the island somewhere opening a Hellgate, or
in hiding. And if he wasn't in hiding, he sure as hell wouldn't
be touring the campus with Carnades. I peeked quickly around
the corner, Vegard's head doing the same thing above mine.

It was Rudra Muralin, all right—young and perfect like fine
sculpture, and just as ageless. His beauty was no glamour, no
spell to trick the eye; it was all him. The goblin's waist-length
hair was so black it shone almost blue, and his black eyes were
bright with entirely too much intelligence.

And he was evil incarnate, responsible for the enslavement
of thousands of elves and the sacrifice to the Saghred of thousands more. He'd done it before and he couldn't wait to do it all
again. He was standing not twenty feet away from me with at
least six black-robed Khrynsani shamans and there wasn't a
damned thing I could do about it.

Vegard pulled me back into the side hallway.

"Professor Niabi," Carnades was saying. "Ambassador Mal'Salin would like to meet you."

I sucked in air between my teeth in a stunned hiss.

Ambassador Mal'Salin? What the hell?

"I have looked forward to it." I could hear the smile in Rudra Muralin's words.

Sora saw us as she walked past, but gave no outward sign that we were there. The goblin bastard could probably smell fear, so I made myself stop feeling it. Easier said than done, but I did it.

"My condolences on the loss of Chairman Berel," Rudra Muralin murmured smoothly.

"On behalf of our department, I thank you," Sora said, her voice formal and frosty.

I smiled. Sora was a demonologist; she knew evil when she met it.

"I have come to offer my assistance," Muralin said. "I have mages who have come with me from Regor who are highly experienced in demon containment."

I bit back a snort. Yeah, Khrynsani shamans would know all about demons, especially conjuring. Either some did survive the cave in, or Muralin imported more. Probably both.

"I assure you, Ambassador Mal'Salin, that we have the situation in hand," Sora said. "But your gracious and generous offer is much appreciated, and I will keep it in mind."

"As you wish. When I have the means to help, I cannot stand by and not act."

I didn't know how Rudra Muralin had managed to become an ambassador *and* a member of the goblin royal family in the few days since he tried to kill me, and right now, it didn't matter.

Carnades had been turned away from me. I couldn't see if he had the Scythe of Nen on him or not. My little Benares voice told me that it wouldn't do any good to ransack his house if a mugging was needed instead.

If he was wearing it, I had to get it. If he wasn't wearing it, I had to get out of here.

Then I remembered that I couldn't go anywhere. Any moment now the classroom door not five feet down the hall from where Carnades and Muralin were standing was going to open and Piaras, Talon, and their combined eight bodyguards were coming out. As acting archmagus, Carnades could order those Guardians back to their regular duty, and probably find some reason to have Talon's dark mages arrested.

And do the same thing to Piaras and Talon.

The boys could get away if someone kept Carnades's and Muralin's attention.

I was someone. And I knew I'd grab their attention, to say the least.

I stepped out into the corridor before Vegard could get his hands on me, a smile on my face and concern in my eyes. Rudra Muralin wasn't the only one who could act.

"Magus Silvanus, I'm glad to see that you're unharmed from yesterday. I heard about that demon escaping and feared the worst."

I got an all-too-brief moment to enjoy the sight of Carnades Silvanus's highbred mouth hanging wide open. I saw something else that I liked even more—Carnades was wearing a dagger in his sash, but it wasn't the Scythe of Nen. Ransacking a house was a lot less risky than mugging a mage, especially that mage.

Rudra Muralin looked like he'd just gotten the best gift of his life, grinning until his fangs showed. I felt Vegard step up behind me. I didn't turn around, I knew the expression he'd chosen for the occasion—touch her and die. My smile rivaled Muralin's.

The goblin's smile went from delighted to confident. He knew I couldn't touch a hair on his head. I knew he wouldn't kill me in public.

Rudra Muralin leaned over and spoke in hushed tones to Carnades. The elven mage's lips tightened so much they almost vanished entirely. He took two steps toward me, no more.

"Mistress Benares, the goblin ambassador would like to be formally introduced." Though the disdainful curl of his lip said he couldn't imagine why. "Ambassador Rudra Mal'Salin, may I present Mistress Raine Benares."

Rudra stepped forward and extended his hand. I stood my ground and ignored it, opting instead for graciously inclining my head.

He lowered his hand. "How insensitive of me. You're the Saghred's bond servant; physical contact with you might endanger me. You are too courteous."

"I'm sure Magus Silvanus wouldn't appreciate me accidentally vaporizing the goblin king's new representative to Mid."

"He's been a splendid host, as my king longs to be to you." Rudra's beautiful black eyes glittered. "But you have spurned his advances."

"And his lawyers."

"An unfortunate necessity."

"I take it King Sathrik felt his former ambassador wasn't getting the job done?"

"Considering the state of affairs on Mid at the present time, His Majesty felt that a change of administration was called for."

Now we couldn't lock him up because he not only had diplomatic immunity; he was now the voice of King Sathrik Mal'Salin on Mid. I didn't have to think hard to know exactly how Muralin had booted the previous ambassador out of office. The Saghred. Muralin thought he was close to getting his hands on it, and no doubt he promised to share the power bounty with the goblin king. Just like old times.

In one swift move he gained power, influence, and protection from prosecution. I had to admit that it was brilliant. It was probably going to get me killed or worse, but it was brilliant.

The goblin turned his attention to Sora. "Tell me, Professor Niabi, is Mistress Benares here to lend her unique talent to help with the demon infestation?"

"I'm hardly an expert," I told him. "Unlike yourself."

"That's not what I've heard, Mistress Benares. I heard that you killed, captured, or crushed numerous demons yesterday. Who else but an expert could have accomplished such feats of daring? I eagerly await seeing what you have planned for an encore."

"You'll have a long wait, Ambassador. I'm not in that business."

"What a pity. Especially since I understand that you are a seeker by trade, a quite proficient seeker. Magus Silvanus, it would be a shame not to take advantage of such skill. Finding a Hellgate is nearly impossible under the best of circumstances."

I felt the barest hint of Rudra Muralin's voice doing its thing. He was a spellsinger, one of the best, and at a thousand years old, he'd had a lot of time to practice. He was trying to influence Carnades, but he was wasting his breath. Carnades already wanted me dead; Muralin had just proposed a quicker alternative. The bastard.

My smile and polite demeanor never faltered. "I know enough about the shortcomings of my own skill to acknowledge a true professional like yourself, Ambassador Mal'Salin. From what I've heard, your expertise in all matters demonic is unparalleled. As is your modesty."

He smiled, showing his fangs to everyone within seeing distance. People started backing off. "May I have a few moments alone to speak with Mistress Benares?" he asked Carnades. "I assure you I will be quite safe," he added when the elven mage started to protest.

The mage inclined his head, but his eyes were arctic ice on mine. "But of course."

Rudra Muralin held out his arm to me. I wasn't about to take it.

Vegard started to follow me. I shook my head. He didn't like it, but he stayed put.

I indicated a doorway about a dozen feet from where we stood. Rudra Muralin nodded and walked slightly ahead of me.

"You do not wish to be alone with me, Raine?" he whispered.

"That wouldn't be good for either of our reputations," I shot back smoothly.

I stood on one side of the door, Muralin on the other. There wasn't nearly enough distance between us for my comfort, but it was far enough to keep him from slipping a dagger in my ribs. But it wasn't a dagger that I was in danger from. It was his voice.

"I assure you that I will not try to bend you to my will," he murmured. His voice dropped into a low, seductive register. "Unless you want me to."

"Maybe next time."

His smile was slow and mocking. "Though it would be amusing to watch Silvanus's reaction if you suddenly wanted nothing more than to walk out of here with me. It would certainly save me much effort over the next few days." His black eyes started at my boots and worked their way up—and took their sweet time doing it. "But some prizes are worth the wait."

My eyes took in the not-quite-healed teeth marks in his right ear. My teeth marks.

"Nasty bite you have there, Ambassador Muralin . . . Excuse me, Mal'Salin. You should have that looked at."

The goblin's smile vanished. "I keep it to remind me of unpaid debts."

"So did the former ambassador get a chance to clean out his desk, or did you just bury him in the basement?"

"I told His Majesty that I would prefer to quietly retrieve that which I came to Mid for. Your interference—along with Tamnais, his half-breed spawn, and Piaras—forced me to use a different approach. Do not think for one moment that I have forgotten their involvement. I repay *all* of my debts."

I wasn't going to be goaded into going down that road. "At least Sathrik let you keep your real first name." I glanced over at the Khrynsani. "Keeps your minions from getting too confused."

"Considering my youthful appearance, His Majesty thought it best to give me the use of the royal surname. He thought it might smooth the transition from the previous administration and open a few doors that might otherwise be closed to me." He winked. "And my own name is rather notorious."

"And no one would dare question or deny a Mal'Salin."

"Precisely." His black eyes glittered. "As you are well aware, I dislike being denied anything."

"Get used to it, goblin."

Genteel threats, all delivered under our breaths with amiable smiles for curious onlookers. I could fake nice, too.

"You take a great risk, Raine. As long as you and the Saghred remain on this island, it will be a target for those who desire power—and there are many who desire power. The last time the Saghred was on Mid was nearly a thousand years ago. Your father brought it here for protection. He realized the danger and fled with the stone. Now there is a college here with eager, young students, hungry for knowledge—and vulnerable. And thanks to you and Paladin Eiliesor bringing the Saghred here, now there are mages hungry for power. And demons hungry for students. My allies want power on this island and beyond. Your paladin stands in their way. They want him gone. I want the Saghred. You give it to me and they get disappointed."

"I give you the rock and you'll go away?"

Muralin snapped his elegant fingers. "Just like that."

"Right. And I'll bet you have a bridge in Laerin you want to sell me."

The goblin laughed, vibrant and wantonly seductive. "We are not so different, you and I. When we want something, we will do whatever necessary to attain it."

I felt the pull of his voice, the power that had been running under his words. Softly coaxing, gently probing at my will.

I pushed back.

I intended a psychic slap; it landed more like a jaw-shattering punch thanks to Mychael and Tam's combined power inside me. I hadn't meant to do it, but seeing the goblin flinch sharply in pain made it all worthwhile.

Muralin went utterly still. "You are stronger than before."

"I've been working out."

"I need that strength, Raine. And I will have it—and I will have you." He didn't wait for a response, but turned and went back to where Carnades waited. "I believe I am finished here, Magus Silvanus. Whenever you are ready, we will go."

I swallowed and forced the shaking that had started to stop, right now. I didn't want to do what I was going to do next, but I had to. I needed to know if Carnades was in this up to his pointed ears, or if Muralin had duped him. I was betting for the latter. So I'd do the right thing and try to enlighten the pig-headed jerk. That way, when Muralin dropped the civilized act, Carnades couldn't say that I didn't warn him.

"Magus Silvanus, may I have a brief word with you?" I was pretty sure Carnades would take the bait. I didn't think he could resist some semipublic posturing and threats.

The elven mage paused and regarded me, searching for any sign of trickery. I didn't move, but he did, right over to where I was standing. I took a breath and tried to force any emotion out of my voice. I kept my voice low, my eyes on Carnades.

"I don't suppose you'd believe that His Excellency over there is Rudra Muralin, Saghred wielder, elf slayer, and evil incarnate, would you?"

Carnades's smile had zero humor. "That would make him nearly a thousand years old."

"He is."

"He died at the bottom of the Great Rift."

"He didn't stay that way."

"I can add slander to your list of offenses."

I shrugged. "Suit yourself."

"Mistress Benares, please refrain from trying to convince others that your Saghred-induced delusions are anything other than manifestations of your deteriorating mind."

I couldn't believe the next words actually came out of my mouth. "Be careful with him." They came out from between clenched teeth, but they did make it out.

"He is a goblin and a Mal'Salin, that goes without saying." Carnades said "goblin" with the sentiment normally reserved for something you scraped off your boots.

That did it; Carnades deserved everything he got.

"I am open to the possibility that you may not have called the demons," Carnades said, a cold light in his pale blue eyes. He raised his voice so those standing nearby could hear. "You are a seeker. Our chief watcher and Paladin Eiliesor have said that you are one of the best they have ever encountered." His smile was bright and beautiful. "I want you to find the Hellgate, Mistress Benares. Find it and close it. The demons fear you; the task should be quite simple."

"Or I'll be quite simply dead."

He lowered his voice, but the smile stayed right where it was. "An unfortunate risk. Your loss will be mourned."

"Right. I'll bet you want to deliver the eulogy yourself."

"The pleasure would be all mine. Should you by some slim chance survive, I might be willing to discuss your continued freedom. If you fail, the demons will save the Conclave the trouble of a trial and execution."

"And if I find it and can't close it, I get ripped apart by demons or dragged through a Hellgate."

"Either option would be a fitting end for you."

"Let's see, topside with you and your mage politicians; or at a Hellgate, risking life, limb, and soul with demons." I didn't have to think for long about that one. "Demons or politicians?" My smile was a baring of teeth. "I'd rather go to Hell."

Piaras stepped out into the hall, saw Rudra Muralin, Carnades, and me and immediately stepped in front of Talon, blocking him from sight. Talon's breath exploded in an oof as he walked right into Piaras's back. My hand went to a throwing dagger concealed in my doublet. Muralin made no move toward Piaras; he inclined his head in greeting. Piaras hesitated and then coolly returned the gesture.

Carnades and Rudra Muralin left, their entourages in tow.

In my family, we believed that you couldn't just let your archenemy brazenly walk around in public. It was bad for the family reputation, aside from being just plain embarrassing.

Rudra Muralin looked back. I knew he couldn't resist seeing if his threats had left me shaking in my boots. When he did, I did what Uncle Ryn had used to great effect many times. Uncle Ryn was huge and imposing. I was little and pissed and scared. But when it came to payback, size didn't matter, and anger won out over fear anytime.

Rudra's dark eyes gleamed in triumph. I gave him my most winning smile. To everyone else, it looked like I was just being friendly. Whenever Uncle Ryn threw in a wink and a chuckle, it meant: "Your ass is mine. I know how I'm going to do it, and you won't know a thing until it happens. Have a nice day."

I threw in the wink and chuckle.

The goblin got the message, and I saw a flicker of doubt in his black eyes.

My grin broadened and I gave him a little finger wave. It was always nice to have my efforts appreciated.

Killing Rudra Muralin the ancient Saghred wielder would be extermination. Killing Rudra *Mal'Salin* the goblin ambassador would be an assassination. One was welcomed with gratitude; the other with a noose. Big difference. Careful thought was called for. Just because Rudra Muralin had cleverly maneuvered around me didn't mean he was getting away, not by a long shot. Sure, I was scared, I was angry, but most of all I felt challenged. Challenges could be fun; it was all in how you handled it.

Vegard joined me.

"Muralin has the goblin king's blessing for anything he does," I murmured. I looked up at Vegard. "You know what I have to do."

"Yes, ma'am. I know." He scowled at the now-closed door Carnades and Muralin had left though. "Let's go get that dagger."

Chapter 24

Housebreaking wasn't just about breaking into a house. Any street thief could break a window and crawl in. The trick was to get in, get what you came for, and get out without breaking anything—all without getting caught.

And without setting off the house wards of one of the most powerful mages in the seven kingdoms.

Normally I loved a challenge, but this was one that I could do without. So I brought in a professional. While I felt perfectly capable of handling it myself, I was a firm believer in qualified backup.

Phaelan was waiting for us two blocks from Carnades's town house. Naturally he was in the shadows, and of course he had two of his crew with him. They could keep watch outside, but they were not going in. I was going to burgle a house, and burgling was best done either alone, or with one or two other people at the most—*professional* people. Any more than that and it wasn't burglary; it was crowd control.

When Talon's dark mage bodyguards had caught sight of

Rudra Muralin, Talon's school day was officially over. He was going home, under full guard, and one of the mages assured me that the kid was going to stay put. From the look on his face, sitting on Talon had not been ruled out as an option. And I knew when they got back to Sirens, the first thing they'd tell Tam was not only was Rudra Muralin on the surface, he was having lunch at the faculty club. Yes, there were Khrynsani with him; and yes, it was broad daylight, but I had a feeling that these boys lived for challenges like that. I knew Tam did. Muralin had to leave that faculty club sometime, and when he did, he'd better watch his back—and his front and his sides. I hated I was going to miss it.

Carnades wanted me to find the Hellgate, but he'd have to get in line. I smiled. I had a house to rob first. His house. I knew Carnades had no intention of discussing my continued freedom; so I had no intention of hunting for a Hellgate. In my mind, Carnades had just joined Sarad Nukpana on my list of people to double-cross. There were others much more qualified to find and slam a Hellgate; besides, there was a demon queen at that Hellgate and she was pissed at yours truly. I wasn't going demon hunting.

Though at the moment, demons and daggers weren't my biggest problem. My biggest problem was standing right next to me with four behemoth Guardians. I'd decided that Piaras wasn't going with me.

"Okay, last chance, Piaras," I told him. "Leave this to me."

The kid shot an uncomfortable glance back at his Guardians. "You said you needed a you-know-what to find this thing. Magus Silvanus collects daggers. That means he's got a lot of them. You know what it looks like, but what if he has more than one dagger with cavorting demons on it?"

"Then I'll take them all."

"And what if it's hidden, not in a display case in plain sight? How will you find it then? Do you want to risk that?"

"I don't want to risk you."

"You're doing this because of me and Talon." His eyes were

dark and intent—and looking down at me. Damn, when had he gotten so tall? "I won't stand by and let you put yourself in danger—*again*—for me. Raine, I'm not being stubborn about this, you need me and you know it. Yes, I'm in danger; we both are. And that danger's not going to go away without risk. I won't let you take my risks for me anymore."

"You'll be breaking the law. If we're caught we—"

"Then we won't get caught." He sounded confident about that; I'd like to have shared his optimism.

"I know what will happen if the demons get that dagger," Piaras continued. "If they reach the Saghred, they'll let the demon king out, and people who might be even worse." He paused. "I'm sure Sarad Nukpana will be second in line. There's no question of what I have to do."

I stood there, looking at him. Then I hugged him. Guardians and pirates be damned; I didn't care who saw it. Piaras hugged me back; it looked like he didn't care, either.

Then came the fun of negotiating terms with Piaras's Guardians. When the dust settled, three of them had agreed to wait outside, wait close to the house, but definitely outside. If any nosy neighbors were looking out their windows, Guardians on duty outside the acting archmagus's town house wouldn't be suspicious in the least. If Piaras was going inside, he'd need protection from outside as well. And if we needed help, we'd yell. Phaelan and I were good at that.

One of Piaras's Guardians was going in with us. Mychael had told Herrick to stick to his future little brother like glue, and stick he would. The huge Guardian wasn't going to let a little thing like treason to an acting archmagus keep him from doing his guard duty. The chance of capture and being charged with treason didn't faze Vegard, either. His response when I told him I wanted him to stay outside was, "No, ma'am, and no arguments." Truth was I wanted him with me, and I think he knew that without me saying a word.

Phaelan sauntered over. "We've scoped it out." He paused. "No one on guard."

Warning bells went off in my head. "What?"

"Not one highborn elven goon in fancy livery. The place looks deserted."

Come right on in, said the spider to the fly.

I swore. "Maybe Carnades took them all to the faculty club." I said it but I didn't believe it, not for one minute. They could be waiting inside. Or worse, Carnades had such kick-ass wards that he didn't need any guards.

"Is the kid going with us?" Phaelan asked me.

"The kid is," Piaras told him.

My cousin looked at me with no expression whatsoever.

"He is," I said.

Phaelan solemnly put out his hand and Piaras took it. Right now, Phaelan wasn't my cousin. He was Captain Benares, scourge of the seven kingdoms, and we were about to break a double armload of laws. "Welcome to the family, Piaras."

Three of Piaras's Guardians staying outside left only Justinius's wards and Herrick to keep Sarad Nukpana out of Piaras's mind. Nukpana had told me what he thought of the old man's efforts. If those wards failed, Herrick was the only barrier keeping the goblin from taking over Piaras—the only barrier except for Piaras himself. I looked over at him. While Phaelan and Vegard took one last look at the back of the house to locate the best way in, Piaras hadn't moved. He was completely silent and still, ready and waiting—the perfect future Guardian. Herrick loomed like a protective shadow behind him. If Sarad Nukpana was smart, he'd keep his manipulations to himself.

I didn't think Nukpana would try anything; he needed for me to find the Scythe of Nen. The demons sure as hell weren't going to let him out, at least not intentionally. Problem was, I was pretty sure Nukpana trusted the demons more than he did me. I had to hand it to the goblin; he was a good judge of character.

Phaelan and Vegard came back to where Piaras and I were waiting.

"There's a door by the kitchen, probably for deliveries," Vegard said. "The wards aren't quite as sophisticated there, probably so the kitchen staff can let delivery people in and out."

Vegard didn't have to spell it out for me; I could read between the lines. If Carnades had wards on the kitchen door, and kitchen staff talented enough to use them, that didn't bode well for what we'd run into in the rest of the house. It went without saying that Carnades valued his dagger collection and the rest of his worldly goods. I bet those wards packed a punch. Maybe we'd get lucky and he left the Scythe on his bedroom dresser from when he wore it yesterday. You'd think that Luck had to start speaking to me again sometime. The pessimist inside my head told me not to hold my breath on that one.

"No kitchen staff?" I asked Vegard.

"No signs of anyone being in the house, period."

"It's spooky," Phaelan added.

It was worse than that, but I didn't need to say out loud what all of us knew—it sounded like a trap with our names on it. Nothing that I had done since I had arrived on the island warranted arrest, regardless of what Carnades said. However, if I got caught in his house, Carnades would have every right to toss me in prison along with my accomplices.

"We're not going to get caught," I said to no one in particular.

Phaelan's grin was crooked. "Damn straight we're not. Our family pride is at stake."

And our heads.

Phaelan's preferred method of theft usually involved a ship, forty cannons, and an overenthusiastic crew. As Guardians, Vegard and Herrick hadn't been trained in the more subtle points of building entry. If a door or gate was in their way, Guardians would simply get rid it. As a seeker, I've had to retrieve objects or people from behind locked and warded doors or cells. I had been taught lock picking by a retired cat burglar. She was retired because she never got caught; as a result, she retired very comfortably.

The locks and wards on the delivery entrance weren't easy to disable, but they didn't make me break a sweat, either. That bothered me, a lot. Before turning the latch, I carefully reached out with a searching spell. No alarms, magical or otherwise, had warned anyone of our arrival. Maybe since Carnades was an arrogant jerk, he thought his reputation and position on the Seat of Twelve would protect him and his valuables. Or maybe I wasn't good enough to sense what he had in place. Only one way to find out. I turned the latch and slowly opened the door. Nothing.

Except a stomach-turning and familiar stench.

Oh no.

Phaelan was wrong, there were people in the house. Dead people. Not just dead, butchered. There were plenty of knives in Carnades's kitchen, but the staff had been the only ones who had tried to use them. The things that had sliced them to ribbons, eviscerated them, or both, didn't need knives. Demons had claws, horns, and teeth. I went in, Vegard and Phaelan on my heels, then Herrick with Piaras. I forced myself not to look too closely at what was left of a cook slumped over a chopping block.

The blood was still fresh; these people had been dead an hour, probably less. I looked at Vegard, and the Guardian nodded. I felt him reaching out, careful and silent, searching for signs of life, demonic or otherwise. I did the same in the opposite direction.

Not one breath. Whatever had been here had come, killed, and gone. I got a sick feeling that had nothing to do with dead bodies. If the demons were gone, chances were good that the dagger was gone right along with them. The smart thing would be to get out of here. Now. I was smart, but I was also desperate. Vegard was looking at me, his question unspoken but obvious.

"We have to search." I said it on an exhaled breath, audible only to those around me. If there was any chance at all that the demons didn't find the Scythe of Nen, we had to look. We all put our weapons in our hands where they belonged.

I turned to Piaras. He was staring steadfastly ahead and breathing through his mouth. He looked down at me and nodded once, tightly.

Vegard gave Piaras the box that had held the Scythe of Nen.

Piaras opened it and laid his hand flat against the velvet lining inside. Unlike myself, he didn't get kicked across the room. Piaras looked at the lining, concentrating. Normally, closed eyes worked best for this kind of thing. I didn't blame Piaras; I wouldn't close my eyes in this slaughterhouse, either. After half a minute, he closed the box and gave it back to Vegard. His brown eyes were distant and focused, though not on anything the rest of us could see.

Piaras indicated an open door on the other side of the kitchen. Even though neither Vegard nor I had sensed anything still among the living in the house, none of us wanted to say anything out loud. The things in Sirens hadn't been alive, and they'd caused plenty of trouble.

Vegard and Phaelan went to check the door, and more important, what was on the other side. When they'd finished, Vegard looked back at us and nodded.

Beyond that door was a hallway in the back of the house. There were several doors leading off of it and one staircase, leading up, presumably into the main part of the house. Everything was plain and practical; it had to be the servants' section. I'd expected Piaras to make a beeline for those stairs and Carnades's study or bedroom. He indicated a door that led to what must have been a common room for the servants. Thankfully, there were no bodies in there. Lamps were lit, but light didn't make it any better. There was something on the floor that I'd seen before and didn't want to see again.

Black goo. Undead horde black goo. Along with it was a yellowish, green slime that shone in a thin trail across the room and ended at a closed door. None of us wanted to open that door, but at least one of us had to. I took one step toward it, but Vegard was there first. One hand held his battle-ax, its blade glowing blue in the dim light. His other hand reached for the doorknob. I felt a brush of cold air coming from beneath that door. I swallowed, braced myself, and nodded to Vegard.

There weren't any demons or undead warriors on the other side of the door, though what was there was just as bad.

Stairs leading down into pitch darkness.

"Why is the spooky shit always in the basement?" Phaelan muttered.

"Piaras, are you sure?" I asked.

He nodded. "What was in this box went down those stairs."

And it didn't get there by itself. The demons found it, the demons had it, and now the demons had gone into the basement. And we had to follow them. No choice, no option.

"Let's get some lights," I said. "I want it bright as noon down there."

Down there was packed dirt walls and nothing else. Leave it to Carnades not to have a basement full of junk. The only thing that was there was a fresh hole dug into the wall, about four feet tall. The hole was fresh; the stench was not. Vegard took a whiff and scowled.

I smelled brimstone. I felt something else.

I stood motionless and let the residuals flow over me.

It was black magic, thick and vile. It had been done here, and recently. Raising an undead horde would definitely qualify. It was fetid and dripping with raw hatred. Evil. I felt it through my clothes, crawling on my skin, slick and cloying. I immediately started breathing through my mouth to keep myself from gagging.

The glow increased on Vegard's ax. "What is it?"

"You can't smell it?"

"Brimstone?"

I shook my head. "Black magic."

"You can *smell* it, ma'am?"

"More like sense, probably through the Saghred. I guess evil calls to evil."

"You're not evil."

"Thank you, Vegard. Tell that to Carnades. Or better yet, save it for my trial."

"There won't be a trial."

"You're right," I said, staring down into the darkness where

I had to go. "If the demons don't get me, Carnades will skip the trial and go straight to the execution."

Vegard opened his mouth to protest and I held up a hand. "That's his plan—that's not what he's going to get."

"That's my girl, ma'am."

I looked at him. "Vegard, when are you going to stop calling me 'ma'am'?"

He grinned. "When I don't respect and admire you anymore."

My throat went tight. "That hasn't happened yet?"

His eyes shone with unabashed pride. "Not even close."

I shone my lightglobe into the hole. I wasn't worried about anything jumping out at me. Whatever had been here had gotten what they came for and was running back to the Hellgate that spawned them.

"Phaelan, you and Piaras are leaving," I said. "Herrick, take—"

"I'm not going anywhere." Phaelan's dark eyes flashed in anger.

"Yes, you are and you're taking Piaras with you."

"I'm not going." Piaras stepped up beside me and looked into the dark. "You need me to—"

I turned on him. "You say the Scythe went down there. It didn't go by itself. The demons have it, and they're taking it back to the Hellgate. If I can't catch the little sons of bitches first, I can at least track them far enough to locate the Hellgate and report back to Mychael."

Piaras went to the hole and leaned inside before I could stop him. "I can feel the Scythe from here. Can you?"

I squatted down beside him; the only thing I felt was stinking air. "You're not just saying that so you can go?"

Piaras sighed. "Raine, none of us want to go down there; but yes, I can feel the Scythe. It's like something tugging at me, like there's a cord attached." He pointed to the center of his chest. "Right here."

Dammit. That was exactly what he should feel; it was a classic seeking response. I needed the kid and the determined look in his eyes told me he knew it. That Guardian nobility crap must be rubbing off on him. If we lived until the end of the day, I was going after the kid with a scrub brush.

"You're still leaving," I told him.

"I'm staying."

"You're—"

An explosion from upstairs shook the ground beneath our feet.

"That wasn't gunpowder," Phaelan said.

"It was magic." Herrick was halfway to the stairs.

Enraged shouts in elven and the pounding of booted feet came from upstairs. Carnades's guards. Lunch must be over, and guess who was home. Oh shit.

"They're still in the front of the house," Herrick said. Unspoken communication passed between him and Vegard. Herrick nodded grimly and bounded up the stairs.

"In the hole!" Vegard ordered. "Now! Herrick will keep them off us."

In the hole with the brimstone, black magic, and demons.

I'd told Carnades that I'd rather go to Hell.

Me and my big mouth.

Chapter 25

The dirt tunnel hadn't extended far, only about thirty feet or so. That was good. The only way we'd managed to squeeze through was hunched over and scrunched up; wide shoulders need not apply. Vegard had gotten stuck twice. It had taken a lot of grunting and quick shoving, but Phaelan had gotten the big Guardian moving again. We were certainly motivated to keep moving; there were demons in front of us and possibly Carnades's guards behind us.

We wiggled out of the demon-dug hole in the wall and into tunnels that I was more familiar with; I didn't like them, but at least they were familiar. I shone my small lightglobe around. Nothing but a lot of dark and cold air in both directions. But on the upside, there were no demons waiting to eat us. Vegard's lightglobe joined mine, crackling with what looked like lightning inside. Light *and* an incendiary device for demons. I liked it. I beefed up my own to match.

I sent my globe down the tunnel a few feet in each direction and swore silently. No demons waiting to bite our faces off, but the black blood and green ooze extended in both directions.

Phaelan saw what I saw and nodded in grudging approval. "You can't fault the bastards' tactics," he whispered. "When you steal something, split up now, meet up later."

Demons were strategic thinkers. Wonderful.

"But isn't Hell supposed to be down?" Phaelan asked.

"We're headed for a *gate* to Hell," I reminded him, "not the actual place." I looked at Piaras. "Which way?"

Piaras was standing quietly, unmoving, unblinking. Then he turned his head toward me, his dark eyes glittering like twin onyx orbs.

Oh no. Not now.

My hand dropped to the blackjack I had tucked in my belt; Phaelan shifted slightly behind me. His blackjack was the twin to mine. Vegard had silently moved to cover Piaras's right side—his sword arm. I didn't want to hurt Piaras; but I would knock out Sarad Nukpana. Piaras the virgin would lead us to the Scythe of Nen. Sarad the psycho might have other ideas first.

"Piaras?" My voice was calm, and I never took my eyes from his. Phaelan and Vegard would deal with Piaras's hands if need be. I'd heard that the eyes were the windows to the soul; I needed to be sure Piaras's soul was home alone.

Piaras blinked and shook his head, as if waking up from a brief nap. Then he saw me and froze, his now brown eyes wide. "What?"

"You tell us, little brother," Vegard rumbled.

"Did you just get a visit?" I asked quietly. "You looked like you left us there for a second."

"We just came out of the hole, didn't we?" Piaras stopped and swallowed. "What did I do?"

"Nothing," I assured him. I lightened my voice. "It's okay; just a trick of the light. My mistake."

Piaras wasn't buying it. "Are you sure?"

I looked up into his obviously brown and definitely scared eyes, and gave him a reassuring smile. "Positive. There's no one in there but you, sweetie. Which way do we go?"

Piaras stood still as if listening. I couldn't hear anything, but neither could he. The kid was concentrating; I was still shaking. Sarad Nukpana had come and gone, literally in the blink of an eye. It was a message for me, subtle and damned effective. The goblin had found a way around Justinius Valerian's wards, or else he'd just muscled his way through. Either way, those wards weren't keeping him out. Nukpana was watching, keeping an eye on his investment. If I didn't get the Scythe for him, he'd instantly make Piaras pay—and probably have the kid try to take one of us down with him.

"Down there," Piaras said, indicating the tunnel to the left. He looked over my shoulder at Phaelan. "And yes, I'm sure."

"I didn't say a thing," my cousin protested. "Far be it from me to question a man's purity."

I didn't want to say anything out loud, at least not yet, but I was more than confused by our direction. I was concerned. Not that I doubted Piaras's ability to track the Scythe. Piaras said this was the direction, and the trail of black goo and green slime confirmed that something demonic or undead had been this way recently. But that didn't mean I had to feel all warm and fuzzy about it. There were a lot of things wrong right now, and our direction was just the most recent.

There were no signs, sounds, or sensations of pursuit from behind us. That was good. Maybe. I didn't know what had happened to Herrick, but true to his promise, he'd kept Carnades's guards off of us. That brought up problem number two—there were no sounds or sensations of anything in *front* of us. But it was as if the demon queen had ordered her minions to bleed and/or ooze to give us a trail that no one could possibly miss. And last, but definitely not least, Sarad Nukpana could now come and go as he pleased. Like I said, no warm and fuzzies for me, but I was jumpy and twitchy in spades.

My experience with demons had all been of the bad kind. I didn't know of anyone who'd had a happy demon encounter. The only happy camper was usually the demon because it got a meal out of it. The mortal they grabbed ended up dead and eaten, and sometimes not in that order. I decided it was better to be jumpy than some demon's lunch.

The tunnel was definitely sloping upward. Up conceivably meant out of the tunnel. Vegard put his hand on my shoulder, and I damned near jumped out of my skin.

"Ma'am, I think I know where we're going." Vegard's voice was so quiet that I could barely hear him and he was standing right next to me.

Vegard never whispered without a reason. A soft voice usually equaled a bad place or bad guys. I responded with a single nod; movement might not be a good idea, either. I shot a quick glance at Piaras. Brown eyes; check.

"The Assembly." The sound barely made it past Vegard's lips.

"Which is?" I mouthed.

"Where the Conclave met before the citadel was built."

"That's bad?"

"It ain't easy. Crumbling ruins, five floors of offices under the main Assembly chamber."

Phaelan spoke. "Let me guess: we're under the bottom floor."

Vegard gestured up ahead with his eyes. "We're coming up on it now."

"And those five floors are probably a bureaucratic maze of halls and tiny offices," I said.

"Yes, ma'am."

With potentially a demon around any or every corner.

"Still straight ahead?" I asked Piaras.

He nodded, looking as nervous as the rest of us. That was good; it meant he was still himself. Sarad Nukpana would have been having the time of his life sending us on a stroll amongst demons.

"We'll know for sure when we get closer," Vegard told us, "but the Hellgate's probably in the Assembly chamber. Huge room, vaulted ceiling."

And plenty of space to stage demon hordes for an invasion.

I didn't want to take Piaras anywhere near a Hellgate. If the demons from Carnades's town house had gone to the Assembly—and it was looking like they had—Piaras's work was done; it was time for him to leave.

"Any quick way to the surface from here?" I asked Vegard. I flicked my eyes toward Piaras. The Guardian saw, but gave no indication. He knew what I wanted—a way to get Piaras out of here. Now.

Vegard's lips narrowed into a thin line.

Not the answer I wanted. "No way out but up," I said.

He nodded. "Or back the way we came."

"Do you know where the other end of this tunnel comes out?"

"No clue, ma'am."

So, no choice but to take Piaras with us. If the demons had taken the Scythe of Nen to the Assembly, then that's where we had to go.

"Well, I've never stormed the gates of Hell before," Phaelan muttered sarcastically. "If we don't die horrible deaths, who knows, it might be fun."

In a matter of minutes, the tunnel turned into a deserted corridor. Stone. Hand-hewn. Man-made. And other than our muted lightglobes, pitch-dark.

Welcome to the Assembly, bottom floor, nowhere to go but up to Hell.

Apparently the demon queen's command to bleed and ooze had ex-pired some time ago. Not one drop of anything broke the ac-cumulated dust in the hall we were now in. It looked just like the last half dozen halls we'd walked through. There weren't any foot- or claw prints, either. That told me the demons might have taken a different route up to the Assembly. I really didn't want to look, but I had to. I shone my lightglobe on the walls and up to the ceiling that was only a few feet above our heads.

Oh shit.

Intersecting lines showed where dozens of tiny claws had

gouged the stone along the walls and straight up to the ceiling. The little bastards could run on the freaking ceiling.

Piaras looked where I was looking and said a word I didn't think he knew. "Are those what I think they are?"

"I wish they weren't." I had an unpleasant flashback to the Volghul scuttling along the sides of the buildings that lined that street, brick chipping and flying as his claws dug in. I really didn't want to have a swarm of tiny needle-fanged and razor-clawed demons drop on top of me out of the dark. Damn, why didn't everything have to walk on the floor like the rest of us?

I took a steadying breath and let it out. "Vegard, could you—"

"Covering the ceiling, ma'am." A second lightglobe flared to life above Vegard's open hand. It crackled with cobalt fire as it floated above our heads and just below the ceiling. The fire extended beyond the confines of the globe, hungrily licking the ceiling as it traveled ahead of us. Anything in its path would probably find itself fried.

"Nice work," Phaelan said. "I like it."

"The demons won't," the big Guardian told him.

"Even better."

We kept going.

Piaras was still on the Scythe's trail like a hound on a strong scent, and Vegard knew the layout of the place. Phaelan and I felt like hired blades along for the trip.

I knew better. Even if she already had the Scythe of Nen in her hands, claws, whatever, I had a sinking feeling that the demon queen still wanted to have that chat with me. And here I was walking straight into her waiting clutches. I just wanted the Scythe; I had no intention of taking on a demonic horde or slamming a Hellgate. And even if I wanted to, I didn't know how. But we needed to get close enough to confirm that the demons had the Scythe, and I was sure Mychael and Sora would appreciate knowing where the Hellgate was. I swore silently. Mychael. He had no idea where we were and what we were doing; maybe Sora had gotten word to him that Rudra Muralin was topside playing goblin ambassador, with Carnades as his clueless host and tour guide. I wondered if Rudra had roped Carnades into showing him around town so the elf mage wouldn't be in his town house when Rudra's demon allies went after the Scythe.

With my next step, I felt a crunch followed by a squish. I jumped back and stifled a squeal; it came out as a squeak. I grimaced and raised my boot; Phaelan saw what was on the bottom before I did. The last time I'd seen him look that sick was after a business rival sealed him in a brewing vat and Phaelan had the bright idea to drink his way to freedom.

I flexed my ankle and looked down. The goop on the bottom of my boot was blue, which was a healthy color for a demon, but flat wasn't a good shape. I tried to scrape it off, then froze. I sensed it before I heard it. Scuttling, sibilant hissing, straight ahead.

And right behind.

Above and all around us, glowing eyes peered out of abandoned offices. They were small, but when there were that many, size didn't matter.

Phaelan had a wickedly curved blade in each hand. "Let's hope these bleed and die."

Vegard's lightglobes flared bright as day, showing us things that made me want to scream, run, and not stop doing either one until I was back in the middle of Carnades's kitchen. Tiny demons, no taller than my hand, scurried like mice. That is if mice were blue and spindly and looked like legs with teeth. Really, really sharp teeth. I'd just squished their sibling; they probably weren't happy about that.

A swarm of demons, no room to fight, and we all had blades out. No good could come of this. Magic would be best; fire would be better—both would make the tiny demons seething around us scream, which would bring bigger demon reinforcements from upstairs.

"If we skewer the little bastards, they're gonna scream," I warned in a singsong voice through clenched teeth.

"If they jump on me, *I'm* gonna scream," Phaelan shot back. "Can't the kid sing them to sleep?"

Piaras grimaced. "I don't think they have ears."

He was right. With that many teeth, the only other things they had room for on their misshapen heads were yellow eyes.

Phaelan went back-to-back with me. "If we just stand here, they're going to eat us."

"Shield and torch," Vegard said calmly.

"Phaelan can't shield," I hissed.

"Mine aren't that good," Piaras added quickly.

"And I can't torch," I told Vegard. He knew why. No containments on the Saghred meant no containments on me. If I used the tiniest fraction of what I'd used in the watcher station, the demon queen herself would be down here in nothing flat. We needed a quick, quiet, hot burst, not a volcanic eruption.

"Can you shield them?" Vegard asked me.

"Yes, but I have to drop my blades."

Vegard couldn't believe what he just heard. *"What?"*

"I need a hand on each of them, bare palm."

"Can't you—"

"No, I can't!" I snapped. "I'm a seeker, not a soldier!"

"If we survive this, I'm teaching you how—"

"Whatever! I'll shield; you roast!"

I slowly sheathed my blades with dozens of hungry demons within touching distance and grabbed hold of Phaelan and Piaras and pulled them close.

Vegard did his thing. A wave of ice-blue flame rolled off of the Guardian and engulfed the demons. It didn't burn them—it froze them. The ones on the ceiling started falling to the floor like fanged icicles. Once the last one hit the floor, I let Phaelan and Piaras go.

Vegard took a couple of deep breaths. War magic like that was like lifting weights, and he'd just lifted more than his share.

"Ma'am, when we get out of here, I'm going to teach you how to—"

The shadows shimmered and parted, revealing a Volghul that had probably been there the entire time. I didn't know if all

Volghuls looked alike, but this one could have been the twin to the one Tam and I crammed into that bottle.

The demon looked straight at me and smiled, his teeth pointy and sharp, handy for things like ripping throats out. His claws seemed to be flexing with a life of their own and were similarly practical. Others flowed out of the offices ahead and behind us.

My steel was sheathed; I reached for my magic.

A Volghul's claws whipped out, wrapping themselves around Phaelan's throat. The tip of one razor-sharp claw rested confidently against the big vein in my cousin's throat. Phaelan wasn't going anywhere.

And neither were we.

"Our queen wants the Saghred bearer alive." The Volghul's smile broadened, showing me all of his teeth. "As do I."

Chapter 26

I wanted to get to the Assembly chamber as quickly as possible, but this wasn't what I had in mind.

Fate was a bitch with a warped sense of humor.

"No resistance and this one lives," said the Volghul holding Phaelan captive. The demon looked down at my cousin with confused distaste. "This one has no magic; it is a waste of skin."

Phaelan opened his mouth to say something he shouldn't. The demon's hooked claw penetrated his skin just deep enough that a single drop of blood welled around the claw's tip. "You wish to contradict me, little mortal?"

I shot Phaelan the mother of all shut-up looks. I'd seen what those claws could do. My cousin was not going to die in a pool of his own blood.

The demon queen wanted me alive, but I suspected that distinction was only temporary, and it applied only to me. The Volghul that had Phaelan's entire neck in his hand wanted to play—and he was looking for an excuse. In our family, snarky one-liners came as naturally as breathing. But if Phaelan wanted to continue breathing, we both needed to keep our big mouths shut.

Phaelan was a hostage, the rest of us were prisoners. My cousin had no magic to defend himself, and now he had no weapons. And in a matter of moments, neither did the rest of us. I'd gotten my cousin into this; I'd get him out. I'd get us all out. Piaras was being treated like a prize. I knew why, and so did he. Phaelan was a hostage; Piaras was going to be a royal gift.

With an escort of nine Volghuls that I could see, and more that I could sense, we weren't going anywhere but where our captors wanted to take us. And I couldn't see them going anywhere but the Hellgate. We'd be there in minutes. Any plans I'd come up with until now had centered on getting in, locating the Scythe, stealing it if possible, then getting out, preferably without being seen by anyone. Capture by demons had put a major crimp in those plans. Not that the finding, stealing, and escaping parts of my plan couldn't still happen. A master thief might be able to snatch the goods out from under their mark's nose.

But their mark wasn't the queen of demons. And I wasn't a master thief.

Phaelan and Vegard weren't going to die, and the demon queen wasn't getting her hands on Piaras. The only way either would happen would be over my dead body, and I'd take as many demons with me as I could.

Our captors led us up the last flight of stairs and the heat hit us. A broad hall curved in both directions—my guess was we were in an entrance hall to the Assembly. A sickly green glow, like some sort of fungus, had been smeared along the walls at irregular intervals, dimly lighting a space big enough to hold hundreds of mages. The heat was stifling; but it wasn't a dry heat, this was like walking into a greenhouse. Directly across from us were a pair of massive doors that must have been at least three times my height. They were closed and were guarded by more Volghuls.

All of that registered in the only part of my brain that wasn't screaming.

The floor was covered with eggs.

We were in a demon incubator.

I didn't want to meet the demons that had laid these things. The eggs were oval and almost came up to my knees. Some kind of sticky goo held them upright on the floor. Half of the eggs had hatched, the rest were glowing softly, their shells nearly translucent. Things were squirming inside, things that wanted to be outside. With us. In the middle of several of the already hatched clutches lay pale bones and what looked like the remains of shredded robes. The newborn demons' first meals had probably been Rudra Muralin's now-deceased allies. No wonder Muralin was topside playing ambassador. He wasn't in control down here anymore. No one was—at least no one from around here.

No wonder he wanted me to come down here to close the Hellgate.

The Volghul that had my arm clutched in his claw saw where I was looking and knew what I had seen.

"Yes, the mortal spellcasters made fine food for our children. They grow quickly and eat much. There is no more food here, so they have gone to the surface to hunt."

My stomach knotted. Newborn demons. That was what we'd run into downstairs, hatchlings on their way to feed. Swarming through dark tunnels that emptied all over the city. Except the demons weren't going all over the city, at least not yet. First they'd take what food was closest.

Campus. Hundreds of students.

I remembered the terrified chaos in the Quad yesterday that had been caused by one demon. These were swarms, nothing but teeth and starving stomachs, small enough to go anywhere, ravenous enough to eat anything.

I saw Vegard out of the corner of my eye. His face was an expressionless mask. Guardians protected the Conclave mages and students. Mychael would defend a student before a mage anytime, and Vegard thought like his commander. He needed to get away; we all needed to get away. Now. Someone had to warn those kids. Sora and her faculty were expecting Volghulsized demons and larger—not hundreds, maybe thousands of piranha with feet and endless appetites.

"Your young ones will be sweet." The demon's sharp black tongue flicked across his lips in anticipation. "Our young will feed first, then we shall join them."

I felt the pull of the Hellgate through the closed doors. Actually it was the Saghred doing the feeling; I wanted to be doing the running. What lay beyond those doors was the entryway into our world for a horde of demons. In the midst of my growing panic, it dimly occurred to me that I had absolutely no clue how many demons were in a horde.

The Assembly was huge. Row after row of crumbling stone tiers that had once held chairs fanned up and out from the massive round stage with steps leading up to a dais that dominated the chamber. Seven columns rose from the edge of the stage to meet the vaulted ceiling.

The Hellgate was on the dais, and it was only a gate in the loosest sense of the word. A slickly wet membrane was suspended between two of the columns like a spiderweb, opaque around the edges where it touched the columns, and increasingly transparent as it neared the center, with a narrow opening that looked more like a slit than anything else. A demon slid through and landed with a wet plop on the stone floor. It looked up, quivering in its eagerness. Demons only got that excited over one thing. Food. It scrambled to its feet, claws, whatever, and with two bounds disappeared through one of the five man-height mirrors set up at the base of the other columns. Depending on where the receiving mirrors were on the island, the demon might not have to go far to find what it wanted.

"Oh shit," Vegard breathed.

I couldn't have said it better.

As fascinating as incoming demons from Hell were, my attention was riveted to a stone slab to the right side of the Hellgate opening, a slab that bore a disturbing resemblance to an altar. Or more to the point, I was riveted to *who* was on that slab.

Carnades Silvanus. Chained, gagged, and laid out in a white robe like a demon snack.

Rudra Muralin stood at the head of the altar, and at the sight of me, what was a confident smile twisted into a smirk. He was one happy goblin. My goal—with my dying breath, if necessary—was to ruin his day.

I wanted to yell out "I told you so" to the elf mage, but I looked around me at an uncountable number of yellow, green, and red eyes shining out of the darkness—and every last pair of those eyes were staring unblinking at us.

We were newcomers, prisoners, playthings.

We were food.

I couldn't see the stairs beneath my feet all that well, but it didn't really matter since my feet didn't touch them but once or twice. The two Volghuls who gripped my upper arms decided that I was easier to lift and carry.

We were nearly to the stage before I saw the demon queen. She was tall and slender with opalescent skin that was a near-perfect match for the Hellgate's membrane. She wore an intricate headpiece set with pale jewels. That was all. The queen of demons was naked. It took me longer to realize this. I was a Benares; I looked at the jewels first. But from the collective intake of breath from behind me, her nudity was the first thing—and probably the only thing—that Phaelan, Vegard, and Piaras had noticed.

She had an unearthly beauty that was spoiled somewhat by her red eyes with vertical black pupils, and the twisting claws on the end of tapered, but otherwise elegant fingers. Aside from that she was flawless, and quite obviously female.

"The Saghred bearer comes to me at last." Her voice was lush and full, like overripe fruit on the verge of rotting. "You are too late to bring me what I wanted." She paused, and her lips curled as if from a private joke. "But you are just in time to give me what I require."

As she spoke, she negligently twirled something between her fingers; it was silver, slender, and curved. I was sure there were cavorting demons carved into it, but I didn't feel the need to move in for a closer look.

The queen of demons had the Scythe of Nen.

I had a feeling of impending doom.

She smiled fully. Her teeth were more or less human—more if you just considered the number, less if you noticed that every last one was fang sharp.

"Nice knife," I managed through a suddenly tight throat.

"It is a pretty little thing, isn't it? I thought you would appreciate it, considering that it was acquired through no effort of your own."

I didn't mention that I'd made every effort to get to it first. She knew that as well as I did.

Her voice dropped to a resonant purr. "Come closer, elfling."

I didn't move. The Volghuls clutching my arms simply lifted me straight up and carried me. It was hard to look tough and be defiant when your feet didn't touch the floor. They put me down about five feet in front of their queen and right next to Carnades's altar. I looked down at the elf mage, sighed, and just shook my head. From the flare of rage in those arctic eyes, I think I got my message across. I'd warned him; he didn't believe me, and now here he was. I'd imagine his abduction had resulted in some halfhearted searching and a lot of silent cheering.

Beyond the stage were shadows and restlessly shifting shapes. Large shapes that were moving in closer to get a better look at us—or a better sniff and probably hoping for a taste. From what I could see, a couple of them were large enough to have been responsible for the population explosion upstairs. I was sure I'd been in worse places, but I couldn't think of one right now. My brain was too busy running back and forth between mere panic and basic terror.

The black magic Rudra Muralin had used to create and open the Hellgate was still there. A brimstone stench seeped through the Hellgate from what lay beyond, but hanging over it all was terror, pain, despair, death—all the ingredients for inviting hell on earth. People had suffered and died here. And the smarmy goblin not five feet in front of me was responsible for it all.

I slowly looked around at the horde moving restlessly in the darkness around us. "Is this more or less what you had in mind?" I asked Rudra Muralin. I was going for cool, calm, with a touch of cocky. I didn't quite get there, but my voice didn't crack once. I was nothing short of stunned.

He flashed a grin full of fang. "I'm anticipating much more. And now that you're here, the real fun can begin." Muralin turned to the demon queen and inclined his head respectfully. "Your Majesty, when we have the Saghred and it is time to kill this one, may I use the Scythe of Nen and do it myself?"

The queen kept her eyes on me. "Patience, young one," she told Muralin. "The elfling has yet to be truly useful to me. You would carelessly waste a valuable resource."

"The elf will only be useful when she is dead," Muralin countered adamantly.

"That is your opinion. It is yet another that I do not share." The demon queen's lips curled in the faintest of smiles. "I have found that males are best used, not trusted," she murmured in my direction.

The goblin's black eyes flashed in anger. "But I have—"

The queen's smile vanished and she held up a single, taloned finger. Wisely Muralin swallowed his next words. The goblin was insane, not stupid. He was cautious, maybe even afraid of her. Smart of him.

And good to know.

"Curb your tongue, goblin," the demon queen snapped. "Or you may find yourself without it." Her ruby eyes settled on me. "Silence is another admirable trait in males. Unfortunately, so few possess it."

I grinned. It was probably a bad idea, but I just couldn't help it.

"You find my words amusing, elfling?"

"Just highly perceptive, Your Majesty. Particularly when it comes to him." I nodded toward Rudra Muralin.

"Ours is a business relationship, nothing more. Trust never entered into it."

"Trust and business can be a dangerous combination," I agreed, tossing a meaningful glance in Muralin's direction. "It can blow up in your face at the most inconvenient times."

The goblin stood utterly still, his black eyes promising murder, but interestingly, he made no move to deliver. In fact, I felt nothing from him. No presence, no magic, nothing. If I hadn't been standing there seeing him with my own two eyes, I wouldn't have known he was there. The open Hellgate distorted all of my senses, and if there was ever a time that I needed all of my senses on high alert, it was now.

The demon queen's ruby eyes met mine and I couldn't look away. "You I trust less, but I like more." She looked past me and smiled slowly. "Do you wish to barter for the elfling's freedom as well?" she asked someone behind me.

"I do."

My mouth fell open. I tried to jerk around to look, but my head was all that could move thanks to my twin Volghul anchors.

Tam stepped up on the dais, giving the Volghuls no more consideration or notice than the columns surrounding the stage.

I hadn't sensed a thing. I still couldn't, even with our umi'atsu bond, and Tam was standing right next to me. All I could hear was a crackling white noise from the Hellgate, distorting my thoughts, filling my head. Focusing was an effort. Magic was . . .

. . . Oh no.

Magic wasn't possible. I couldn't use any magic, and neither could Rudra Muralin.

And neither could Tam.

The distortion from the Hellgate was too strong, and the tangible proof was chained to that altar—and standing right next to me. The manacles holding Carnades weren't the magic-sapping variety. They were just iron. Just iron was holding down one of the strongest mages there was.

Then there was Tam. His leather armor was slashed across his chest and back, by both claws and steel, and more than a few of those cuts had reached Tam's skin. He didn't have a single weapon on him—at least not any that I could see. Tam's long hair was down and disheveled, the queen was all cold beauty and confidence. There was no sign of Tam's dark mage hit squad. They were either dead, or they were the ones Tam was bartering for. Oh, this was not good.

Tam wasn't a prisoner, but he wasn't a guest, either.

The queen was looking from me to Tam and back again, thoughtfully tapping the tip of the Scythe's blade against her lips.

Then she made a low, pleased sound from deep in her throat, part purr, half hiss. "You know the elfling."

"We've met," Tam said dryly.

"Oh, I think it is much more than that. You barter prettily, goblin; but I require more than sweet words. You know this."

"I have told you that I cannot procure what you want."

"Cannot procure? Oh, but I think you can. You simply refuse to get it for me. If you require an incentive, I would greatly enjoy providing it for you. You brought many other goblins to fight beside you. I could torment them one at a time before your eyes, if you make it necessary. I assure you that there is no limit to my creativity. Eventually you will do what I want."

The demon queen was playing with Tam, and I had a sinking feeling she had only begun her games. Eggs were hatching, demons were rampaging, her enemies were magically helpless or chained before her, and she had the Scythe in her hands. She could afford a little time to indulge herself. I resisted the urge to step in front of Piaras. It would just attract her attention that much faster.

The demon queen gazed down at Carnades. "And I thought this one would be my only source of amusement. Release her," she told my demon guards. "Release all of them; they cannot escape."

They immediately did as ordered. When they let me go, I felt a cool rush of blood into my lower arms and flexed my fingers to restore the circulation. Not that I could do anything, at least not yet, but it always paid to be prepared. I wondered how

far the no-magic zone extended. My legs wanted to find out;
my head knew I wouldn't make it two steps.

"By all means, elfling. Try to escape." The queen looked out
into the shadows. "My subjects are forbidden to be on this side
of the columns. It pains them to see you thus, you and your
friends, since I have not yet released them to feed. Their hunger
is quite overwhelming them." The queen's red eyes sparkled
with malevolent glee, and her voice dropped to a sibilant whisper. "By all means, take a walk in the dark."

"I'll pass."

I couldn't see into Tam's mind, but apparently the demon
queen could see into mine. Then again, maybe she couldn't.
Escape was the obvious thing to do when a pair of demonic
thugs let you go. But I wasn't going to take the chance; if by
some miracle I got a plan worth pursuing, I'd do everything I
could to keep it to myself.

The queen looked over my other shoulder. Piaras. She'd
spotted Piaras.

Dammit.

"You bring me treasure," she murmured in approval, her
eyes bright. The demon queen cast the barest glance at Rudra
Muralin. "This one brought me nothing. No gifts, no tribute."
Her full lips narrowed in regal displeasure. "Arrogant."

"Not even flowers?" I said before I could stop myself.

The queen laughed, silvery and cold, a calculated sound,
probably practiced to duplicate the real thing. She showed Muralin her teeth. He had only two fangs; she had a mouthful.

"I gave you the inhabitants of this island," Muralin reminded
her.

"You gave? I take what I want, goblin." She gestured distaste-
fully at Carnades. "You have given me nothing but a poor substi-
tute for what I truly desire. And you were so very foolish to think
that I would be satisfied with mere entrance into this world." The
demon queen moved toward him with liquid grace, sensual, mes-
merizing. Rudra Muralin didn't move. He couldn't—or he didn't
want to. The queen reached out and brushed Muralin's flawless
cheekbone with the tip of the Scythe, leaving a thin trail of blood

against his silvery skin. "You know not how helpless you truly are." Her smile broadened and her eyes gleamed. "I should like to see true fear in your eyes. And I think I shall."

The goblin swallowed. "You have my respect and loyalty, Your Majesty." He stood frozen to the spot like a mouse with a large and hungry cat standing over it with twitching tail.

"Loyalty," she purred. "We shall see."

She turned to Carnades and ran the tip of one taloned finger lightly down the elf mage's chest, parting the pristine white linen robe as she did so. "My poor husband is a soul without a body. This beautiful one will make a fine royal vessel, albeit a temporary one."

Carnades Silvanus with the soul of the king of demons. I was wrong; this *was* the worst situation I'd ever been in.

Chapter 27

Tam didn't bat an eye.

"So, Carnades gets to be the demon king," he commented mildly. "What's in it for you?" he asked Rudra Muralin.

"The Saghred, once Her Majesty frees the king." His eyes were the flat black of a shark. "Then I'll have anything I want, beginning with some long-overdue revenge—starting with you, Tamnais."

Tam looked at the goblin queen and raised one flawless brow. "He gets his choice of toys? Simply for opening a door for you? Your rewards are more than generous, Your Majesty."

"Those who serve me are *appropriately* rewarded."

Tam didn't bat an eye, but Rudra Muralin did. The smarmy punk suddenly got a tad less smarmy. "I kept my end of our bargain, Your Majesty. The sacrifices, a Hellgate large and strong enough to admit your legions, and the breeders to make more."

There was rustling and low, throaty growls and grunts coming from the darkness around us. I kept my eyes straight ahead.

There were some things I absolutely did not want to know about.

"I allow my servants their pleasures," the queen told Tam. "My husband and king was taken by the Saghred while dining from it. I will not risk losing him again. This goblin has agreed to become the Saghred's bond servant and wield it for me."

"And once your elf whore is dead by my hand, I will again be the bond servant," Muralin gloated.

There was that word again. I felt a growl growing in my chest and stifled it. It'd almost be worth the risk of getting my own throat torn out to get my hands around his. Tam was probably having similar thoughts, but he'd always had more self-control than I did.

Tam looked at Muralin, his lips curling into a grin, and then he actually chuckled. "So once again you'll be taking orders from someone else. For eternity. And in Hell, no less. Appropriate and delightfully ironic at the same time." He shook his head in amusement. "Rudra, you've merely traded a goblin king for a demon queen. Have you forgotten that a Mal'Salin king was the cause of your first death? Do you truly think the outcome will be different this time? You're not known for being likable. It's only a matter of time until you've annoyed her enough to chain *you* to a slab."

The demon queen scowled down at Carnades. "I might have been more favorably disposed toward the goblin if he had brought the correct elf to me. Though his power is impressive, this was not the one I desired. The elven paladin is the most powerful of his race that I have ever seen."

I froze. Oh no. Mychael. She wanted Mychael.

The demon queen stretched a languid hand toward Rudra Muralin, stopping just short of touching him. The goblin's black eyes widened, his expression a twist of fear and desire.

"The young elf will make a fine songbird for your majesty," Muralin said quickly. "And he will be useful to secure Raine's cooperation. The dark-haired elf is her cousin. She would do anything to keep either of them from harm." I could see the tension ease out of the goblin's body. To save your own ass, put someone else's in the sling. Bastard.

"Cooperation is more easily gained when the subject is motivated," the demon queen agreed. "So the elfling would do anything to keep her loved ones safe." She looked at Tam, her eyes lingering appreciatively. "And her soul twin," she said softly. "Not lovers. No, not yet." The queen paused thoughtfully, reaching out with her mind, feeling the air between us, touching, sensing. Knowing. "But the bond that links them is even more intimate than mere flesh." She went to stand before Tam and gracefully bent her head to his throat, taking in his scent. Tam didn't flinch, but it took every bit of his control not to. His lips pulled back from his fangs in a silent snarl.

"Delectable," the queen murmured. "Your black magic clings to you like exotic perfume. And to make you even more exquisite, your scent is blended with the elfling's power." One corner of her full lips curled into a secretive smile. "Or should I say the power of the Saghred?"

There was silence, then Rudra Muralin laughed in sheer, mad delight. "An umi'atsu bond? With an elf? This is too much. Did you hear that, Silvanus? The only one to attempt to help you this day is in an umi'atsu bond with a goblin dark mage."

"And they are not alone," the demon queen said, her words soft and for our ears only, Tam's and mine. "One who is equal in power to you, my delectable goblin. Perhaps even greater. One whose power is light to your dark. I thought to use the elfling to go through the mirror to fetch the Saghred for me, but she will be more valuable as a lure." Her ruby eyes bored into mine, and I felt myself falling into them. "The one I desire must care for you greatly to do what he has done to protect you. His efforts to prevent you from falling will seal his fate." She raised her voice slightly; she wanted Rudra Muralin to hear. "And I have the two of you here with me now, bonded to each other." Her smile was slow and horrible. "And to the Saghred."

Muralin paled. He knew what the demon queen was saying. So did I. It took everything I had to keep from running into the dark with the monsters.

"The Saghred is already bonded to the elfling." Her words were for Muralin, but she kept her fiery eyes on Tam and me. "You claim that by killing her the Saghred will again accept you as its bond servant." She slowly turned her head toward the goblin. "I have no proof of that, only your word. And your word has proven less than reliable. The elfling can wield the Saghred now; her goblin bondmate will be able to do so soon—and he is also a master of the dark arts." She paused thoughtfully. "What is it that you mortals say? Two for the price of one. My servants for eternity, wielding the Saghred for me. There will be no further need of Hellgates; I will be able to come and go as I please."

Muralin's black eyes glowered in barely controlled rage. "You swore that I—"

The queen turned on him, her words slicing like the Scythe she held. "I swore *nothing*; you presumed everything." Her long-taloned hand shot out toward Rudra Muralin, lifting the goblin off his feet and sticking him like a bug into the Hellgate membrane. He struggled, but just worked himself in deeper.

And the Hellgate's glow flickered and diminished briefly when she did it.

"Now you are a part of your own creation," the queen said with smug satisfaction. "A fitting place for you to think and remember who is ruler here and who is the servant. My husband will require food when he arrives to claim his new body. Do not try my patience any further, or you shall be that first meal."

Her gleaming eyes fell on Tam. "Consider that a warning, lovely one. Do you still wish to defy me?"

Tam's will, like his stance, was cold and unmoving. "Mychael Eiliesor cannot be acquired, Your Majesty—regardless of the lure."

The demon queen placed the tip of one talon against her lips. "You will not assist me even if one hundred lives on this island are spared?" she murmured, her voice like molten honey. "Including your beautiful son. One hundred lives of *your* choosing. Untouched, unmolested, unharmed. They will be allowed to live and leave this island when no one else will." Her eyes brightened. "All for a single elf. If this Mychael Eiliesor is as infected with nobility as I have heard, he would agree to my proposal and sacrifice his life without hesitation. I wish to negotiate with you, goblin. Not persuade. My persuasion is always fatal; by the time a mortal is broken and willing to do what I require, they are no longer in a condition to do so. All that effort wasted. Pity."

The demon queen wanted Mychael, and Tam was her choice for his kidnapper. Tam wouldn't do it; I knew he wouldn't. I glanced at him and saw his black eyes glittering in the dim light, his profile expressionless. As with the Volghuls, Tam gave me no notice or regard. With Tam and the trouble he often found himself in, to ignore was to protect. He was ignoring the Volghuls; he was protecting me, or at least he was trying.

All I heard was the Hellgate's thrumming distortion. Tam's thoughts were his own, and he was determined to keep them that way.

That was fine; I knew what he was thinking. Tam wasn't going to betray Mychael, regardless of the offer. However, if the queen forced his hand, he would go along—up to a convenient point of betrayal. Tam was a goblin to his core. Manipulation was his kingdom's national sport. As for the demon queen, I knew that tall, naked, and nuts had no intention of keeping her word. As a Benares, I'd been told that our word wasn't worth the air it was spoken into unless we wanted it to be. Demons probably weren't much different.

But the demon queen wasn't lying when she predicted that Mychael would take her offer in a heartbeat. And that heartbeat would be the last one he had without the demon king's soul in his body.

The thought of Mychael's soul helpless and imprisoned in his own body kicked every last bit of panic and fear out of my head. Rage replaced it, and it felt good. A tight, searing knot blazing in the center of my chest. It fed the Saghred, and the stone's white heat joined my own. Seething, scorching, eager for a way out.

Except there wasn't a way out, for either it or me.

Magic wasn't an option. Even the Saghred couldn't get in on the action as long as I was on the dais. Beyond the columns, I would have my magic back. But beyond the columns there were monsters. Cavorting monsters. Going there would be a bad idea; it'd also be the last idea I'd ever have.

"If you do not convince the paladin to return with you within an agreed length of time, I will begin to persuade the elfling that she desires nothing more than to assist me in any way that she can. Tell me, lovely one, can you feel the elfling's pain? Has your bond become that strong? Defy me and we will find out together."

"Perhaps there is an easier way, Your Majesty," said the Volghul behind me. "The elfling's bodyguard is a Conclave Guardian."

The queen's eyes lit with renewed interest. "A Guardian?"

"Of the highest order. He reports directly to Paladin Mychael Eiliesor. It is said that they can communicate with each other over great distances. We can take him into the hall where he will be able to contact Eiliesor, and you will not have to relinquish any of your captives." The Volghul's smile showed every last one of his razor-sharp teeth. "Or perhaps you can use the Guardian's mind to reach Eiliesor yourself. This way there would be no need to damage the elfling since you will have need of her later."

I'd had my life threatened before, many times. I'd even had people threaten to slice and dice me up. It scared the hell out of me every single time. Especially when it came from the ones who were serious. The demon queen was serious, eager even. The enthusiastic ones always wanted to get started before the time was up.

But no one was going inside Vegard's head.

I tried to do some fast thinking.

Something besides the brimstone didn't smell right. The demon queen had Carnades and Rudra Muralin on the dais where the Hellgate distortion was the strongest. I was brought here. Tam was brought here. None of us could use our magic. She kept sending flunkies after Mychael instead of going herself. This thing was the queen of the freaking demons; she was beyond ancient, with enough power to do anything, slaughter anyone. I could feel it. I knew it.

I suddenly knew something else. I put on my best poker face. There was a reason for the flunkies, the minions.

She couldn't leave.

Every ounce of her raw power was the only thing holding the Hellgate open. Attacking Rudra Muralin had broken her hold on it. Only for a moment, but it had happened.

Move the queen. Close the Hellgate.

And probably kill us all.

Brilliant idea, Raine. And if you don't end up vaporized, why don't you hand her the Saghred on a silver platter, and set her up on a date with Mychael?

Tam said it took days to get a Hellgate open and stabilized. Somehow I didn't think closing one was as easy as slamming a door. Doors didn't have black magic backlash that could turn us all into piles of ash—or do the same to every living thing on the island. But it wasn't like I was exactly flush with options. And if Tam had any brilliant ideas, he wasn't sharing them with me; and thanks to the Hellgate distortion, our bond was worthless. I knew he was plotting something, and since he'd opened a Hellgate before, I thought it safe to assume his thinking was running in that direction. But I'd found out the hard way on more than one occasion that a wrong assumption could very well be my last assumption.

I'd counted five mirrors at the base of the columns behind me. Each was linked to another mirror somewhere on the island. One of those mirrors had to be inside the citadel. The demon queen said as much. The Saghred was there, the demon king was there, a mirror had to be there. Mychael already had one Guardian who had betrayed him to elven intelligence. Selling your soul to the demon queen might actually be a moral step up. Someone had to have put a mirror in the citadel, and it was as close to the Saghred as they could get it. There were hundreds of cells and containment rooms in the citadel's subterranean levels. The one and only time I'd been down there, all of those doors had been closed. Oh yeah, there was definitely a mirror in one of those cells. A big one.

I needed to know which mirror *here* led to that mirror *there*, because we sure as hell couldn't get out the same way we were brought in. We needed an exit, a fast one, preferably to the citadel teeming with heavily armed Guardians. I hated mirror magic with a passion, but better to jump through a mirror than to be a demon queen's Saghred-powered plaything for the next eon or two.

With the queen pondering how best to use Vegard's mind, I raised my hand level with my ear, like I had an itch. Tam saw what I was doing. The Volghuls couldn't. With the barest movement, I inclined my head in the direction of the Hellgate, then slowly brought my thumb and forefinger together until they touched. Then I turned my head ever so slightly in the direction of the mirrors, and raised one eyebrow in a silent question. Was it possible?

Close the Hellgate. Jump through a mirror.

Out of the corner of my eye, I saw Tam's lips form a word that not only told me what he thought of my plan, it perfectly described what the grunting demons were doing in the dark. I clenched my jaw and squared my shoulders, my body language telling him that if he didn't like my idea, he'd better come up with something better, and quick. Tam had to know why the queen hadn't gone more than a few feet away from the Hellgate. He'd opened a Hellgate before; he knew how to close one. And if there was any chance that he could close this one, we needed a way out.

Or we needed the mother of all distractions.

I couldn't use magic right now, and I couldn't fight the demon queen, at least not on her terms. I'd leave the Hellgate to Tam. I had to find out which mirror led to the citadel. And I'd do it using a tactic that had gotten members of my family killed about as often as it'd saved our asses. I drew a ragged breath to do what I did best.

I knew how to piss people off. What can I say? It's a gift.

"Excuse me," I said to the demon queen.

"Raine," Tam growled in warning. Bond or no bond, he knew me too well.

"How long has your husband been in the Saghred?" I asked her.

Wary replaced smug on her flawless face. "Why ask you, elfling?"

"I have a reason, a reason that would concern any woman." I was trying for calm; my heart was trying to beat itself out of my chest. "How long has it been?"

"Millennia."

"You have had access to . . . uh . . . amusements." I paused and forced myself to breathe. "He hasn't. I've been inside the Saghred twice. There's nothing in there but a lot of gray void and rotting wraiths. I imagine His Majesty has been doing a lot of sitting and waiting. Believe me, there's nothing amusing about that."

The queen's red eyes narrowed. "What are you implying?"

I spread my hands defensively. "I'm sure it's nothing. I don't know all that much about mirror magic, but I do know that your husband can't get back here through whichever one of these mirrors leads to citadel without a body."

She didn't glance toward one of the mirrors. Dammit.

"Then he will take a body," she said.

I nodded. "Chances are he'll grab himself a Guardian body, seeing that they're guarding the Saghred. A big, strong, manly body. With manly urges," I added meaningfully. "Urges that he hasn't indulged in a long time."

The queen's full lips curled into a sensuous smile. "Then I shall welcome his return."

Again, no glance at a mirror. Double damn.

I played my last card. "I'm certain your husband has no problem with impulse control. His only desire will be to come home to wife, dinner, and brimstone hearth." I hesitated thoughtfully. "*However*, he'll have the Saghred, a Guardian body, and all the nubile coeds he can . . . whatever. The seven kingdoms at his mercy, the works. He's been penned up in the Saghred. I've been in there; it's not a resort." I jerked my head toward Carnades and Rudra Muralin. "You've set the table, but do you honestly think he's coming home?"

"You have a point, elfling." The queen contemplated something over my left shoulder. I casually turned and looked where she was looking.

Mirror number two was escape route number one. I gave a little silent cheer and bit my lip to keep from grinning.

The demon queen gestured and at least a dozen chittering purple demons scrambled up onto the dais from the dark. Volghuls in miniature. She bent to speak to the mini-demons. "The citadel air passages, my children. Use them quietly and use them well. Go."

The little demons leapt through the mirror to the citadel and were gone.

"They will bring me the Saghred," the queen told me. "Instead I will release my husband once the stone is here."

The bottom fell out of my stomach.

Last week, Piaras's voice carried through an air duct into the Saghred's containment room and put the stone to sleep. Now tiny demons were scrambling into those same ducts on their way to the Saghred, and the demon queen hadn't budged an inch.

That could have gone better.

"Satisfied?" Tam muttered.

Chapter 28

I didn't know how much time we had until the mini-demons grabbed the Saghred and came back through that mirror, but depending on how close the exit mirror was, we might only have minutes.

There were no Guardians in the room with the Saghred. The containments on the rock had all failed, so Mychael had pulled his men back. And if the mini-demons managed to keep their chittering to themselves, they could get back here with the rock before any Guardians were the wiser.

Here. Right here. We'd be in the same room with an un-shielded Saghred and a demon queen who had the key to open it. And once she did, the demon king might not be the only one to escape. Sarad Nukpana was in there, as were thousands of other things that should never be allowed to leave.

But my father was also in there.

Every last one of them was a soul without a body. And here we all were, lined up like sheep for slaughter—or in this case, possession. Sarad Nukpana could possess Piaras for real this time.

I felt a growl starting in my chest and I let it grow. I figured I couldn't be scared out of my wits and growl at the same time.

If the queen was using all of her strength to keep the Hellgate open, that meant she couldn't spare any magic to obliterate me. She could stick me up there next to Rudra Muralin, but she wouldn't kill me; she needed me. And if she did get off a shot, her concentration would waver, and the Hellgate would flicker. I'd have to trust Tam to act when that happened. He'd never let me down before, and I had to believe now wasn't going to be the first time—and the last. I dug deep into my rage, trying to scrape up some courage to go along with it. To do what I was going to do, I'd need every last bit of both and then some.

The queen's nails were all twisty; I told myself they'd never last in a real fight. And that was what I was going to give her— a fight like she'd never had. If I died doing it, fine. At least I'd die; it'd be a damned sight better than being a Saghred-wielding demon slave.

I was a Benares. If I was going out, I was taking that bitch with me.

Of the five of us, I was the closest to her and she was mine.

I looked over at Phaelan. He smiled, showing me all of his teeth. Whatever I had up my sleeve, he wanted to be in the middle of it.

Vegard was like Phaelan; he'd wanted to kill something ever since we'd been grabbed. If he died doing it, not a problem. He was a Guardian; it was his job. Piaras's eyes were determined— and warm brown. There was no sign of Sarad Nukpana. The goblin was probably too busy shoving his way to the front of the line to get out of the Saghred.

I felt Tam's eyes on me. I turned just enough to see the barest nod. I let out the breath I wasn't aware that I'd been holding. When I moved, so would he.

I shifted my weight, ready to spring. The demon queen was within range. As she turned toward Rudra Muralin, it was as though everything went into slow motion. She was turning to taunt him, and it was like I had all the time in the world. I bared my own teeth. I didn't need all the time in the world, just two seconds to get her on the ground and get that dagger.

The queen froze, then spun around, her eyes glowing and locked not on me, but on the back of the Assembly.

I heard it. Voices coming from beyond the doors, in the halls with the eggs and their Volghul guards. Mortals and demons shouting, screaming, struggling.

"Children!" The demon queen's voice rang out. "I release you to feed!"

A deafening roar went up from the demons in the darkness, and shapes and shadows surged up the stairs and through the massive doors surrounding the Assembly chamber. Their triumphant roars and starved shrieks added to the din.

"Go with them," she ordered the Volghuls standing on guard around the columns.

I took a look and did the math. Only one Volghul was left for each of us. One on one. Now that's what I called better odds. Yes, they were demons and we were unarmed mortals who couldn't use our magic, but I knew for a fact we had something going for us that they didn't—the desire to survive at any and all costs.

I felt a pressure building, and the air in the room contracted, tightened, as if something in the hall beyond was trying to suck all the air out of the Assembly. I covered my ears with my hands, trying to stop the stabbing pain against my eardrums. Everyone else did the same, demons included. Then the pressure stopped, suddenly and painfully. I lowered my hands, half expecting to see blood on them. All around us, the Assembly doors began slamming with resounding booms until they were all closed.

Beyond the doors was silence. On the dais, no one moved.

The doors didn't open. No demons appeared to report victory to their queen. No mortals stormed the Assembly to rescue us. Nothing.

That was either really good or very bad.

"Kuitak!" the queen snapped at a Volghul.

"Your will, Majesty?"

"Take the Scythe and go free my—"

Oh, hell no.

My shoulder took the demon queen in the midsection with a satisfying thud. The Scythe flew out of her hand and skidded across the dais, disappearing over the side onto the floor below. We both scrambled for it, but not before the queen's foot gave me a solid kick in the head, and black flowers bloomed on the edge of my vision. I shook them off and threw myself on top of her, grabbing for her throat, my weight and momentum taking her to the floor. The demon queen hissed and twisted sharply, putting us face to fangs with her on top. One of my arms was pinned between us, but the other got in two solid punches to the side of her face and she had a few less fangs.

The second punch snapped her head to the side and gave me enough leverage to flip her onto her back. Problem was I'd miscalculated how close we were to the dais stairs. I think I hit every bone in my body rolling down those stairs entangled with the demon queen. She was hissing; I was snarling. Her claws were going for my eyes; I was going for anything I could knee, elbow, or punch.

Everything was pretty much a blur while we rolled down the stairs, but from what I could hear, the boys were giving as good as they got. From the stench of burning demon flesh, I guessed that Vegard had gotten clear of the Hellgate distortion and was lobbing fireballs. Piaras's voice rang out in a single, imperious word, and a Volghul flew by overhead, arms and legs desperately flailing. Tam's sibilant incantations from the dais above us were tight with effort, fighting for control. I'd taken on the queen, leaving Tam to replace the void of her power with his own, to single-handedly try to keep the Hellgate from exploding, imploding, or whatever it was that a loose Hellgate did.

Tam was powerful, but he was mortal. His power had limits, and time was not on our side.

The queen and I rolled to a stop as a needle-thin shaft of white light exploded the head of the nearest Volghul. I didn't move. It didn't seem smart with skull-piercing lightning bolts flying around.

My mistake. A big one.

The demon queen got her hands around my throat and dug in. I screamed, searing pain following the hot wetness of my own blood running down my neck. I'd been right, her nails hadn't survived the fight, but broken nails left jagged edges, and they were razor sharp.

A dot of blazing white light appeared in the exact center of the queen's forehead. The fighting around us immediately stopped. The only sound was Tam's unbroken stream of incantations and hissing, labored breathing.

The light remained where it was, unwavering.

"Her death will be your doing!" the demon queen shouted into the darkness.

A strong, deep voice came from the shadows just beyond the columns. Mychael's voice. "Release her or share your guard's fate."

Just what I didn't need—a hostage situation and a standoff all rolled into one.

Mychael's statement was a warning; his words were raw power given voice. Demanding, compelling, those words gave the demon queen a choice, and one choice only—obey or die.

The queen swayed as if from an unseen breeze, but her hold on me never lessened. Mychael's voice had gotten to her, and for a brief instant he had controlled her.

Her fiery eyes blazed with renewed rage. "Show yourself, mortal!"

I heard the sharp echo of Mychael's boots as he stepped up on the stage and into the light, but he didn't pass between the columns. He knew better. Mychael's left arm was extended; the light beam coming from his index finger was leveled like the deadly weapon it was, never wavering from its target. In his right hand, his sword blazed with pure, white light. His entire body was surrounded by a glowing nimbus.

When the demon queen saw him, her full lips curved in a satisfied smile. "You. I should have known. Come to me, and I will allow the elfling to live." Her words had power of their own, not the magical compulsion of a spellsinger, but the smoothly seductive tones of a temptress with millennia of experience.

"Release her and you will not die." Mychael's voice was calm, but unyielding.

The seductive smile twisted into a sneer. "You think you can destroy me? I will rule when you are dust. Come closer, paladin."

"Sir, no!" Vegard shouted.

"I can feel the distortion from the gate," Mychael assured him, keeping his eyes on the demon queen. "I need not come any farther. And neither do your brothers."

Backup. Guardian backup. Now that was some much-needed good news.

"More flesh for my children," the queen said in approval. "More gifts for me."

Mychael's beam flared in intensity, searing a blackened circle into her forehead like a brand. The queen screamed in pain and fury, and her claws contracted. I clenched my teeth against the pain. I wouldn't scream again.

"My children will feast on you!" she shrieked at him.

"Your children are prisoners." Mychael's voice was relentless. "Release her."

"Impossible, there were hundreds."

"Now they are captives."

"You lie!"

"Then where are they?" he asked quietly.

The demon queen didn't have an answer for that, and neither did I. But I had connected some dots, and I knew she wasn't going to like the picture it made. When I told her, she'd either let me go or finish the bloody job she'd started. Anything was better than a naked demon queen on top of me.

I tried to speak without moving my throat, which was easier said than done. "You have no Scythe," I rasped. "Saghred coming here . . . Guardians already here . . . Only I can touch the rock." I swallowed, or at least I tried to. "And you have a beauty mark that's about to become fatal."

The demon queen smiled, sure and confident. "Not all of my servants are here."

Several things happened more or less at once.

The demon queen half jumped—but mostly flew—straight up into the shadowed vaults of the ceiling like she'd been shot from a cannon.

Then she vanished.

It had to be a cloak, one so complete that it left no sign that she still existed. I knew better; she wasn't leaving without everything she'd come for. If she could cloak, it meant she was outside of the Hellgate distortion.

It also meant that she could do anything magically speaking; and from up there, she could do it to anyone.

I scrambled for the last place I'd seen the Scythe. I was bleeding, but it wasn't life threatening, at least not until I collapsed from blood loss and woke up on the wrong side of that Hellgate.

Both of Tam's hands were sunk into the Hellgate membrane on either side of the slit. All around him, forms writhed and pushed against the milky surface—big forms, hulking; one hand trying to press its way through was twice the size of Tam's head. Tam saw that massive hand and his incantation sounded more like a snarled string of goblin obscenities. There were bigger, meaner, and more dangerous things desperate to get through that Hellgate before it sealed.

If Tam could seal it.

I ran up the stairs to the dais, and to Tam.

"What can I do?"

The demon queen's voice rang out from the vaulted beams supporting the ceiling. I didn't know the words, but I knew what it sounded like.

A call to arms.

Volghuls poured like purple tides through four of the five mirrors.

Tam's black eyes blazed. "Get the Scythe!"

I didn't want to leave him there.

"Now!"

I jumped over the side of the dais to where the Scythe hope-fully still was. There it was, gleaming in the dark, the first thing to go right all day. I snatched it up and a mini-Volghul came with it. I shrieked; I couldn't help it. The little bastard sunk his teeth up to the gums in my leather sleeve, his claws raking my bare hands.

My shriek gave way to swearing, which led to stabbing. The thing was trying to eat me from the fingers up. The Scythe was a knife, and I used it. A couple slashes and a stab later, one less Volghul was going to reach adulthood.

Mychael and his Guardians were battling the Volghuls com-ing out of the mirrors. Piaras had joined his soon-to-be broth-ers. Those mirrors needed to be shattered. Anything thrown through magically linked mirrors would go in one side and out the other. But if something were coming through at the same time, it'd be like two people trying to come through the same door from opposite sides. Except in this case, the thrown object would break the glass.

Broken glass, no more Volghuls.

I desperately looked around for something, anything. The Assembly was a ruin, there had to be chunks of stone, some-thing. I spotted one. It was close to the mirrors, but I had one shot at it, so I needed to be as close as I could get. I scooped up the rock, saw a demon head coming through, and threw it with everything I had.

The mirror shattered, leaving one less demon door, and hopefully a demon with a concussion on the other side.

"Raine!"

It was Phaelan. My cousin was in the safest place a non–magic user could be in a room full of magic-flinging mages and demons—behind Carnades's stone altar.

You know the saying "I wouldn't wish that on my worst enemy"? I did, and I wished I didn't. If Carnades Silvanus wasn't my worst enemy, he was at least in the top five. I'd have liked nothing more than to have left him right where he was, but I couldn't. I wasn't a particularly nice person, but I wasn't a murderer.

I'd unlock his manacles, but first I'd take what I needed from him.

The Scythe was good and sharp. Carnades's white linen sacrificial robe was nice and clean. My throat needed a bandage. I grabbed the hem just above the elf mage's ankles, plunged the blade through the material, and slashed my way around the robe.

Carnades screamed in appalled rage through his gag and tried to kick me with his bare, manacled feet. If he could have made some coherent words, I'd probably have been turned into a slug.

"I'm not trying to kill you," I snapped.

I wrapped the cloth around my throat a couple of times to try to stop me from getting any more light-headed from blood loss than I already was.

I flipped the Scythe point down and reached for Carnades's ankle manacles to pick the lock.

Phaelan couldn't believe what he was seeing. "What the hell are you doing?"

"We have to let him go."

"No, we don't."

"Yes, we do. We're not killers."

"Speak for yourself."

I ignored him and kept working. A second or two later, Carnades had free ankles.

A pair of spells collided, ricocheted, and sent a comet of green flame shooting straight for us.

"Incoming!" Phaelan yelled. He ducked behind the altar and pulled me down with him.

The flame smashed into the stone tiers behind us, blasting a hole that was big enough to sit in. I popped back up and went to work on Carnades's wrist manacles. They clicked open just as another green comet blazed toward us, twice the size of the first. Phaelan swore, I added to it, and we both grabbed handfuls of robe and hauled Carnades over the side of the altar. He landed hard and face-first.

I didn't mean to do that. Really.

Carnades sat up and tore off his gag in fury. "You planned this from the very—"

That did it. I didn't hear the demons; I didn't hear the explosions. It was just me and a mage who had blamed me, degraded me, and pissed me off for the last time. I got in his face.

"Let's try this again," I said between clenched teeth. "I am saving your life for the *second* time in *two* days. I tried to warn you, but you didn't listen. I don't like you, I don't believe in *anything* you stand for, but I don't stand by and let people get killed. If I can help, I will. That's the kind of person *I* am. You can believe it or not; right now I don't give a damn!"

Carnades was speechless. Phaelan was checking out his robe.

"White robe, chained to an altar—what are you, some kind of sacrificial virgin?"

"I am *not* a . . . virgin."

Carnades almost choked on that last word. Highborn elves were notoriously uptight when it came to sex. It was a wonder there were any of them left.

"I bet you don't even wrinkle the sheets," I muttered.

The next explosion made all three of us duck and cover. That was way too close. As the blast faded, I heard tearing or peeling or . . .

. . . Oh crap.

I looked up and saw a Rudra-shaped indent in the Hellgate. The goblin was gone. Escaped.

Phaelan and I swore and scrabbled away from that altar. It was cover but it was also a death trap if Rudra Muralin was crouched on top. He had weapons; between Phaelan and me, we had one knife. Carnades stayed put. Fine.

An explosion shook the Assembly, and the stage floor buckled from underneath, slabs of the stone jutting up at sharp angles. Phaelan and I were already on the floor, and after that, so was everyone else. Two mirrors toppled and shattered. That left only the citadel mirror and one other. We had to reach that mirror.

My mouth was bone-dry, my body was determined to bleed

to death, and breathing was entirely too much work. "Phaelan, I need you to—"

A Volghul slammed into me from behind and tore the Scythe out of my hand.

Carnades had to have seen it coming and the son of a bitch didn't say a word. Phaelan was right; I should have left him on that altar.

In a flash of opalescent flesh, the demon queen dropped from the ceiling attached to what looked like a spider's web. I didn't want to know what part of her it had come from.

She landed in a crouch at least twenty feet from the citadel mirror. The distance didn't matter; she covered it in two leaps and dove through, the Volghul with the Scythe right behind her. Rudra Muralin dashed out of the shadows where he'd been hiding and was right on their clawed heels.

The demon queen, Rudra Muralin, and the Scythe of Nen— all in the citadel, close to the Saghred.

If she got to the rock and opened it, the disembodied souls of the demon king, Sarad Nukpana, and the worst that could ooze out of the Saghred would possess the first bodies they could find, and those bodies would be Guardians. They would turn the most elite magical fighting force in the seven kingdoms into the most elite and *evil* magical fighting force.

All under the command of the king and queen of demons.

Chapter 29

"Mychael!"

It was Tam, he was up to his elbows in Hellgate, and the damned thing still wasn't closed.

It was trying to open farther.

And it was no longer milky white. It was stretched so thin it was almost transparent. A riot of color pressed from the other side; faces and limbs and misshapen bodies surged against it. The tips of multiple and impossibly large claws punched repeatedly at the membrane, trying to puncture it and tear their way through. If they succeeded, it wouldn't destroy the Hellgate.

It would destroy the *need* for a Hellgate.

The barriers between our world and theirs would cease to exist and the way would be open. Permanently.

Tam's shout was for Mychael. His eyes—and his thoughts—were for me.

His thoughts. I could hear them. Tam was telling me all this. I knew nothing about Hellgates, but Tam did, and his thoughts were in my head.

He could use his magic again.

But only if he touched the Hellgate.

Tam needed Mychael and me. Rudra Muralin hadn't been able to control an open Hellgate, or the demon queen that came with it. And the queen had to stay within inches of the thing to keep it under control. Together, we might be able to control it, possibly close it—unlikely, but possible—but it would take the three of us and everything we had.

It would take the Saghred.

In that instant I knew true fear. The paralyzing kind. Icy terror that freezes your blood and clenches your heart in its fist and won't let go. I couldn't move, and believe me, I wanted to. In the next few minutes, I was going to die by demon or Saghred, or maybe even both. Horribly, painfully killed. If it was death by Saghred, the rock would kill me first, then it would take Mychael and Tam.

After our failure, the demons would be free to take everyone else.

And they would start with Piaras, Phaelan, and Vegard.

A roar came from beyond the Hellgate and an impossibly large head thrust its gaping maw against the membrane with such force that I could see every curved fang, each longer than my hand. It wanted out. And unless we closed that Hellgate, it was coming out. People I loved were going to die—or pray for death.

That was not going to happen.

I might fail; I'd probably die. But every living thing on this island was going to die if I didn't get my ass moving and do something to stop it.

I ran to Vegard's side. "Take Piaras and Phaelan and get through that mirror. Now!"

Vegard's face was the calm of the soon-to-be martyred. "I'll take them, but I'm coming back."

I didn't believe this. Nobility was a disease around here. "Why? So you can—"

"And leave you with *him*?" Phaelan jerked his head in Carnades's direction. "You're better off with the demons."

"I'm staying," Piaras insisted.

I clenched my teeth and I tried for calm; all I could muster up was barely controlled infuriation. Why wouldn't anyone just do as I said?

"There's nothing you can do here," I told Phaelan and Piaras. I'd given up on Vegard. "I'm not sending you to safety; the citadel's a war zone by now." I blew out my breath. "Piaras, just *please* go to your brothers and do what you can. Go save some lives." I felt myself smile, fierce and feral. "And Phaelan, go make Rudra Muralin pay for this—and make it *hurt*."

Mychael barked orders and about a dozen Guardians ran out of the dark beyond the stage, armored for battle and armed for Hell. I thought I'd seen every weapon that could be forged from steel, but I was wrong. The Guardians' weapons had sharp hooks and curved jagged blades—and the metal was green. If it was steel, it was no steel that I'd ever seen. Those blades had been made for a purpose, and from the black demon blood coating them, they and the grim-faced Guardians who wielded them had been doing their jobs.

A pair of them stopped in front of the only other remaining mirror. The tide of Volghuls had slowed, but not stopped. The Guardians had to wait less than two seconds for another horned demon to emerge. When it did, the Guardians impaled it as it was coming through, shattering the mirror. The men extracted their blades with a quick twist, and the upper half of the dead demon fell out of the mirror's frame along with shards of shattered mirror. Severing the magic that linked the mirrors severed the demon coming through. And people thought mirrors were harmless.

Six of the Guardians charged through the citadel mirror in pursuit of the demon queen and Rudra Muralin—and hopefully to keep anyone from breaking the mirror from the other side and trapping us here. The remaining Guardians formed a protective circle around the mirror, steel in their hands since spells were worthless this close to the Hellgate.

In the dark beyond the stage, flashes of blue flame and

demonic screams told me that the rest of Mychael's men weren't limited to steel. An intense volley of fireballs lit the entire Assembly as bright as day, and I saw what was out there.

Our situation just went from critical to unsurvivable.

Volghuls were everywhere. I had no idea how many there were, but there were too many, and they were too fast. While I was freeing Carnades and dodging green comets, those mirrors must have been belching Volghuls. Either that or some had survived whatever had happened out in the halls. The demons weren't winning, but they weren't dying, either. The Guardians were holding their own. Barely.

Volghuls weren't our worst enemy; that distinction went to the elf standing entirely too close to the citadel mirror. Phaelan was right; I'd be better off with the demons.

Carnades Silvanus was a mirror mage, and he hated Tam and me and wanted to get rid of Mychael. I couldn't read minds and in his case, I didn't need to. I knew what the highborn SOB was thinking. Get through the mirror, destroy the one on the other side, and leave us all here to die or worse.

Take care of the Hellgate first, Raine; deal with the self-righteous jerk later.

Mychael took the stairs four at a time to Tam's side, and I was right behind him.

Tam's breathing was ragged, and his bottom lip was bleeding from where his fangs had bitten through in his effort. He tried for a weak smile. "This isn't going as well as I planned."

"There's a lot of that going around." I looked up and up some more. The Hellgate had grown taller, or maybe it was my terrified imagination. Taller, wider, longer—it didn't matter. The damned thing was a Hellgate. Smaller wouldn't make it any better, and bigger couldn't make it worse than it already was.

"Mychael, how do we do this?" My voice sounded incredibly small.

He was calmly inspecting the Hellgate. The same things that gave me the shakes Mychael coolly analyzed for weakness and possible courses of action that would culminate in a brilliant plan. At least that was what I hoped he was doing. I was in so far over my head, I'd forgotten what the surface looked like.

"We banish it," he said.

I blinked. "What?"

"Those demons want to be here. We make it unbearable for them to stay."

I had no idea how Mychael planned to roll up the demonic welcome mat, but Tam and I needed to know, and quick.

Mychael removed his steel gauntlets, baring his hands. "Tam, when I tell you, pull your hands out of the Hellgate."

Tam was incredulous. "But I'm the only thing holding—"

"You're feeding it, Tam. Your body's blocking the opening, but your black magic is feeding that frenzy."

More monstrously huge faces thrust themselves against the membrane, stretching it so thin I saw the outline of an eyeball the size of my head.

I blanched. "If Tam moves, everything in there's coming out here."

"It's too strong now to be closed by the same magic that made it," Mychael told me.

"Then how the hell are we supposed to close it?"

"White magic." Tam sounded like he'd been handed a worse death sentence than he already had.

Mychael nodded once, tightly.

Call it what you would—light to their dark, good to their evil, white magic to their black. We needed nearly limitless amounts of it and we needed it now. Too damned bad we didn't have it.

"Tam's a dark mage," I reminded Mychael. "I'm an evil rock's bond servant. That makes you the only goody-two-shoes mage around here. You got enough juice for that thing?"

Mychael's expression was grim and determined. "No, but the three of us do."

There it was. The ultimate testing of a three-way umi'atsu bond. A type of bond that had never existed before, now had to do something that had never been done.

"Carnades can't see this," Tam told us.

Dammit. Carnades.

If we didn't get the Hellgate closed in the next few minutes, we were dead. If we closed the Hellgate, we'd still be dead; it'd just take a little longer for Carnades to push through the paperwork.

What sounded like a muffled explosion echoed through the Assembly as one of the enormous doors was flung open. A phalanx of Guardians cleared the way for a slender figure followed by six men carrying what looked like a coffin. A flash of fireballs showed them to be Sora Niabi and six of Uncle Ryn's crew. The elven pirates put down the coffin and ran like hell, slamming the massive door behind them. Sora stayed.

"Trap open!" she roared.

The Guardians battling the demons stopped battling, shielded themselves, and hit the floor. On the stage below, Vegard shielded Piaras and Phaelan. Mychael put one bare hand on the Hellgate, and wrapped the other around me, pulling me tight against his chest. He went back-to-back with Tam, and I felt his shields encase the three of us. The same eardrum-bursting pressure tightened the air and compressed my lungs like a vice. I felt Mychael's chest expand and contract with rapid, shallow breaths. I tried to do the same.

The Volghuls closest to the trap were the lucky ones. They were instantly jerked inside. The screams of those farther away became shrieks as their bodies were stretched impossibly thin as the trap caught and pulled them across the chamber. When the last demon was inside, the lid closed with a resounding boom.

"Mychael, that's my last trap," Sora shouted.

So much for what had happened to the demon queen's court.

"Understood." Mychael lowered his shields and loosened his arm around me, but he didn't let me go. "You can't do any more here, Sora. Knights," he called to the Guardians who'd been fighting the Volghuls. "Go protect the people."

When Mychael touched the Hellgate and pulled me to him,

the distortion lifted and I felt my magic. When he leaned against Tam to share his shields, our combined power was palatable and we weren't even doing anything yet.

Carnades was staring at the three of us standing together. His arctic blue eyes widened for a split second in realization, then all expression vanished from his face. I didn't need to see it on his face; I could literally feel the elf mage's revulsion— and triumph.

He knew.

I was the enemy, Tam was evil incarnate, and Mychael was his last obstacle to ultimate power.

"Paladin Eiliesor, I order you to step away from that Hellgate." Carnades's voice was deathly quiet.

Mychael couldn't believe what he'd just heard. I not only believed it, I was expecting it.

"Sir?" Mychael stood utterly still, a dangerous stillness. I felt the power he was barely holding in check.

Carnades's power flared in response. "A goblin opened it; a goblin can stay here and close it." The elf mage cast a disdainful glance at Tam. "*If* he is able. Protecting the Saghred and myself as your archmagus is your only duty. We will return to the citadel. Immediately." He looked from Mychael to me. "Mistress Benares, consider yourself taken into custody. Paladin, bring our prisoner."

Mychael released me and came down those stairs even faster than he'd gone up them. Carnades didn't flinch, but he squared his shoulders and stood his ground.

"That was a command, Paladin. To disobey me is treason. The penalty for treason—"

Mychael didn't stop until he was nose to patrician nose with Carnades.

"I am well aware of the penalty." Mychael's whisper lashed like razor-sharp steel. "*Your* duty is to the people of this island. The archmagus is the protector of the people, defending them from any and all danger—even unto death. You *will not run* from that danger. If you require more clarification of your duties, I will be glad to provide it—*after* I close this Hellgate."

"You will pay for this," Carnades hissed.

"For doing my duty to our people? Gladly." Mychael turned his back on Carnades to come back to Tam and me.

The elf mage's face turned livid with outrage. "You will pay *now*!" His voice was thunder, his eyes blazed with self-righteous fury, his rage lashed like—

Phaelan hit Carnades over the head with a rock.

I saw it coming; I could have warned him. But I'd warned him once today. He ignored me, so I ignored Phaelan's rock. I felt vindicated somehow.

Vegard bent over the out-cold Carnades. "Still breathing," he reported. He sounded disappointed.

Phaelan tossed the rock in his hand. "You can arrest me later," he told Mychael. "You're kind of busy right now."

"How long will he be out?" I asked Phaelan.

"Let's see . . . Weight of the rock, angle of the hit, point of impact—at least ten minutes. That give you enough time? Or should I hit him again?"

"That won't be necessary, Captain Benares." Mychael looked at his men. "Knights?"

Those six Guardians had heard and seen everything, and they hadn't budged or lifted one finger to defend Carnades or stop Phaelan. Mychael had ordered them to guard that mirror. If they protected Carnades, they'd have disobeyed Mychael's order. Were these men Mychael could trust, or traitors in waiting?

"That demon came out of nowhere, sir," one of them told Mychael.

"Not a thing we could do to stop him," another added. "And we didn't see the rock until it was too late. Sorry, sir."

Loyalty. It's a beautiful thing. Carnades sprawled on the floor was even better. And if we were lucky, there'd be some short-term memory loss to go with his concussion.

"Thank you," Mychael told them, and he meant it. "Take Magus Silvanus back to the citadel and guard him well." His meaning wasn't lost on his men. "Vegard and Cadet Rivalin, escort Captain Benares."

No one moved. I knew why. Their paladin was staying, and so were they.

"Knights, there's nothing you can do here," Mychael told them. "We'll follow you when we're done."

Or not. He didn't say it, but his men knew it. He also didn't want them to see what we were about to do.

In my family, that wasn't just exercising authority; it was getting rid of witnesses.

Mychael trusted his men, at least most of them. But there was a breaking point for every man's trust, and seeing their paladin join with a goblin dark mage and the Saghred's bond servant might test their loyalty or lose it altogether. Mychael couldn't afford either one.

They reluctantly went through the mirror. Piaras had to give my magic-phobic cousin a push, but he went.

Vegard stayed.

Mychael studied the Hellgate while removing the steel encasing his forearms. He didn't turn to look at Vegard. He knew he was there.

"Vegard, go with them."

"I can't do that, sir."

Mychael pulled out a dagger and slit the quilted sleeves of his arming jacket, exposing his leanly muscled forearms. "That's a direct order, Sir Knight."

"I know." Vegard's voice was steadfast.

"You're disobeying me."

"Yes, sir. I am. I'm staying to watch your back, sirs—and ma'am. And to defend this mirror for you."

Mychael finally looked at him, a sad smile curling his lips. "You're a good man, Vegard. Thank you."

"I do my best, sir."

The shrieks and wails continued from behind the Hellgate, louder because they were closer—and there were more of them. The demons seethed en masse against the membrane, feeling its weakness, knowing that in mere moments they could have what they had wanted for countless ages—the end of our time, and the beginning of theirs.

Hell on earth.

And we were in the front row.

Tam spoke without moving. "Mychael, I've got a problem with your suggestion to take my hands out of the Hellgate."

"That wasn't a suggestion."

"Take a look at my problem."

We did. A demon that was little more than fangs with legs was attached to Tam's chest with only the Hellgate's thin membrane separating them. The thing was gnawing at the membrane, mewling eagerly.

"If I step out of the opening, this thing bites a chunk out of my chest—the chunk with my heart in it."

"Why don't you stay where you are," Mychael told him.

"I thought you'd see it my way."

"You'll have to take one hand out. Raine needs it."

I blinked. "I do?"

"Yes."

Tam laughed once, without humor. "Mychael's going to use our power to blow sunshine up the demons' collective ass."

Mychael raised one eyebrow. "In a crude manner of speaking, yes."

I got it. This place was evil central. Rudra Muralin started with black magic rituals and sacrifices, and once the demons arrived and started setting up housekeeping, the walls in this place were literally smeared with evil. I remembered my vision of Mychael when he'd joined our umi'atsu bond. Power shining like a blazing sun, deadly and unrelenting, an avenging angel. And with our combined strength, Mychael could very well be a Hellgate-banishing angel.

Our combined strength included the Saghred.

"You'll be using the Saghred," I said.

In response, Mychael took my hand in his, his fingers interlacing with mine. His large hand was warm and strong, and the pressure was reassuring. Through that simple contact, I felt the bright core of his magic through his palm. His sea blue eyes were calm and steady.

"We'll work together. At watcher headquarters, *you* controlled the Saghred."

"Until I lost control."

"You didn't lose control; you focused that power and used it."

And a giant yellow demon went squish.

I tried to swallow, but my mouth was bone-dry. "Mychael, I don't know what to do here."

He gave my hand a gentle squeeze. "I do. I'll show you how."

Tam pulled his left hand from the Hellgate and held it out to me. I expected it to be dripping Hellgate goo, but it was dry. I took his hand in mine; it was deathly cold. Tam gasped at the contact, and a shiver ran through him.

"You're warm," he breathed.

"Still being alive will do that." I tried for a smile; it didn't make it. I pulled the back of Tam's hand against my chest, sharing what warmth I could, while I could. Tam's power, his deep well of strength flowed into me and through me to Mychael, and it was my turn to shiver.

I felt a deep thrum of power run through us and down into the stone beneath our feet. The floor vibrated with it. My fear and exhaustion was washed away, a calm certainty taking its place. For the first time, I actually believed that this could work. My power, Tam's power, Mychael's power and guidance.

"Ready?" Mychael asked us.

I nodded.

Tam blew out his breath in a hiss.

We touched the Hellgate.

My magic flared, and my chest caught fire. Freed from the distortion's restraints, my magic and the Saghred's power flared and twisted until what was me and what was the Saghred became a white-hot cyclone. It filled me to overflowing, but it wasn't like with the yellow demon, when its uncontrollable power felt like a wall of water crashing down on me. This water lifted me, like giant sea swells. Unfathomable depths of power surged beneath me, but it also held me up, supported me. I rode the power, flowing with it.

It was my magic. Mine. Not just the Saghred. The power that had magnified my magic had come from the Saghred, but the seed that it had grown from, the core of my strength, was all me. My father had been right. What I did with that power, how I used it, was up to me. My decision. My choice.

Tam's power coursed like liquid fire through my body, red-hot and searing, my magic and his power erupting into an inferno that blazed through me and into Mychael, wrapping and entwining, joining the three of us together.

Mychael slammed all of that power against, into, and through the Hellgate.

Screams, agonized roars, and wails from a thousand nightmares rose around us as the light pierced the Hellgate to the other side, bright as a newborn sun. The light blazed and fed, an unrelenting and consuming flood of white fire, searing the darkness, cleansing the evil, and immolating the demons pressing against the Hellgate and beyond.

The blinding light exploded, and our screams joined the demons'.

Then darkness and blessed silence. I welcomed both with open arms.

Chapter 30

I opened my eyes and raised my head—and *was nothing short of* stunned that I was alive to do either one. The only thing left of the Hellgate was the stink. I could live with that. Better yet, so could everyone else on the island.

Mychael was on his feet, but barely. Tam was on his knees. Apparently, at some point, I'd decided that facedown on the floor was the way to go. Needless to say, no one was holding hands anymore. I rolled over and concentrated on breathing. A smoky haze lingered in the air where the Hellgate membrane had stretched between the two columns. That had to be the source of the rotten-egg stench. Other than that, there was no sign the Hellgate had even been here.

I loved it when something I thought was going to kill me didn't.

The remnants of Mychael's and Tam's magic still rolled in waves through my body, but the intensity was gradually decreasing to calm, flowing ripples. That sensation brought on one big head-to-toe shiver—the good kind.

I sat up; past experience had taught me to take it slow. I had only minimal swirlies and no urge to be sick. A nice surprise for a change. But I did feel really, really light-headed.

Vegard ran up the stairs and knelt at my side. From the look on his face, I must have looked like I had one foot wedged in Death's door.

"Ma'am, please don't move. Sir!" he called to Mychael. "Blood loss. A lot."

That might account for the light-headed feeling. I looked down at myself. No blood there. I couldn't see the linen I'd wrapped around my neck, but I could feel it, and it was heavier than it should have been. The blood soaking it should have been flowing around in me.

Mychael knelt beside me and began carefully, but quickly unwrapping my soggy, makeshift bandage.

"Mychael, I'm fine," I insisted. I tried to get to my feet; Tam's hands on my shoulders pushed me back down. I think I growled at both of them, or at least I tried. "We don't have time for this. We've got to get through that mirror to—"

"*After* I stop the bleeding." Mychael's voice said no arguments.

I drew breath to give him one.

"Carnades knows," Tam said from behind me.

Oh shit. Carnades. The first thing he'd do after he could stand up would be to look for a pen to sign our collective death warrant. *That* took the rest of the wind out of my sails.

I heard a sound out in the darkness of the Assembly, like the scuff of boots on stone. Tam was instantly on his feet, panther-quick and just as silent. Vegard drew steel and planted himself in front of Mychael and me. Tam's dark eyes were alert to any movement out in what was supposed to be an empty chamber.

"*What is it?*" I asked Tam in mindspeak. With no Hellgate distortion, all of our magic was back.

"*Someone.*" He scowled. "*I think.*"

"*You think?*"

"*They were there; now they're gone.*"

"*Who?*" Mychael asked.

Tam hesitated a little too long. *"No one I know."*

"Human, elf, or goblin?"

"Couldn't tell."

Now I *knew* Tam was lying. Goblins had legendary night vision; if something was out there, Tam would have seen it as clear as day. Just what none of us needed—a witness to everything we'd done who knew Tam. People who knew Tam weren't people we wanted to see what we'd just done.

Mychael's blue eyes narrowed. He knew Tam was lying, too. *"Keep watch,"* he said tersely.

Tam nodded once and didn't take his eyes from the spot. He'd closed his mind to us, but not before I felt something that I'd rarely sensed in Tam. Fear.

"Raine first," Mychael said, back to business. "Then the Saghred. Then I will deal with Carnades."

"Not if I get to him first." Tam said it like a vow. And I knew Tam; if he vowed to do something—especially if it involved much-needed vengeance—the object of said vengeance better leave town, or in this case, the island.

"Phaelan's following him around with a rock," I reminded him. "You might not get the—dammit!"

Mychael's palm felt like a branding iron on the side of my neck.

"Battlefield healing," he told me, holding me still. "We don't have time for fancy."

I grimaced. "Do what you have to," I managed through pain-clenched teeth. I did my best not to move—or scream. "I have payback due to some people on the other side of that mirror, too."

The citadel was quiet. Way too quiet. Either nothing had happened yet, or everything already had. Or in my family, silence didn't mean the fight was over; it meant everybody was catching their breath—or sneaking up on somebody to stab.

Tam swore to himself. I heard him in my head, and couldn't

have agreed more with his word choice. There was no demonic welcoming committee waiting to slice us to ribbons when we'd stepped through that mirror, but there weren't any Guardians, either. As I'd guessed, the mirror was in a containment room, but the room was empty, and the door was standing wide open. Under normal circumstances, that'd be downright inviting. But I wasn't about to stroll through that door and find demon hospitality at the end of a skewer.

Once we were through the mirror, Mychael shattered it. There wasn't a Hellgate for the demons to escape through anymore, but Mychael didn't want them leaving the citadel, at least not alive.

Mychael held up a hand for me and Tam to stay put, and he and Vegard took up positions on either side of the door. Mychael nodded once and they made their move. When Vegard's shoulders relaxed, I knew the hall was clear. Suspicious as hell, but clear.

At least of men or demons.

The air was literally vibrating with magic. It was coming from all around us, but mainly from the floor beneath our feet. Tam clenched his dagger in his teeth to free his hands and quickly tied back his long black hair in a tail.

"We're one level above the Saghred's containment room," Mychael said in mindspeak. *"There should—"*

Screams, shouts, and demonic roars damned near deafened us, like someone had opened a soundproof door to a madhouse. That someone had used a sound veil, a good one. Apparently they didn't need to be quiet anymore—my money was on the demon queen.

Mychael ran down the hall and all but threw himself down the stairs; Vegard, Tam, and I were hot on his heels. It suddenly occurred to me that my hands were empty. I didn't have a weapon to my name, and no one I was with had one to spare. I silently swore a blue streak. I was running full-speed and unarmed into a nest of demons. Usually I'd get what I needed from the first bad guy I could knock down and pilfer, but this time the bad guys were demons—naked demons. No sword belts there. Though when you had claws, horns, and a mouth full of fangs, steel was redundant.

No one had been upstairs, because everyone was down here.

Too many Volghuls and not nearly enough Guardians. The only Volghul I'd seen go through the mirror was the one with the demon queen. The number of Volghuls down here didn't bode well for the number of Guardians left alive up in the citadel. Where was Sora and a demon trap when you needed them?

Open space was at a minimum, which made for ugly, close-quarters fighting.

And Piaras was in the middle of it.

He had his back to the Saghred's containment room door with a pair of long daggers in his hands. The blades were glowing. Not the white of Mychael's magic, but like polished silver infused with pure light. I didn't know Piaras could do that. Like Justinius said, the kid could rise to the occasion. He wielded those silver blades with feline grace and, hell, even with flair. Piaras couldn't move like that—but Sarad Nukpana could.

However, Piaras was killing demons, not Guardians. Nukpana would have been doing the opposite. Piaras's lips were moving in spellsong incantation. I couldn't hear the words, but the Volghuls that got too close to him obviously could. They screamed and staggered back, and when they went down, they didn't get back up.

Piaras's eyes were wide and terrified, but determined. They were his eyes, not Nukpana's. What abilities the Saghred had enhanced in me, I'd kept. It looked like the same was true for Piaras. The goblin's sword skills must have rooted themselves deep in Piaras's reflexes. Creepy as hell, but anything that kept him alive was good.

Helping Piaras stay alive was Archmagus Justinius Valerian.

The old man was kicking demonic ass and having the time of his life. It was beautiful.

He'd staked out ground in the hall near Piaras, and the

forces of Hell literally couldn't budge him from that spot. He vaporized a knot of demons trying to overrun him and Piaras. That move alone went a long way toward evening the odds, and it boosted the heck out of Guardian morale. The men redoubled their efforts and more Volghuls died. Justinius was flushed, but he was grinning like the spell-happy maniac he was. The archmagus was back, and I didn't see Carnades anywhere. Maybe Phaelan and his rock had another talk with him.

Mychael jerked his gaze up toward the ceiling. He heard something, and so did I. It wasn't coming from the ceiling; it was coming from *inside* the ceiling. Scuttling, scratching, and moving fast.

Running *away* from the Saghred's chamber. The little purple bastards had gotten their claws on the rock.

"They're taking it to the queen," Tam said. Like their elven counterparts, goblin ears did more than just look good.

Mychael shot a glance back at Justinius. His duty was to protect the old man, but the old man didn't look like he needed or wanted any help. It'd just piss him off. As six more demons went down in blue-flamed death, I knew I never wanted to piss him off, either.

"Where does that air duct go?" I asked.

Mychael actually growled. "All over the damned citadel."

I felt a tugging in my chest and grinned in fierce determination. The Saghred wanted me to follow it, and I was only too happy to oblige. The rock had been stabbed with the Scythe once, and it didn't want it to happen again.

"I can track it," I said.

No one asked how I could; they knew. I took off running down the hall in the opposite direction of the Saghred's containment room with Mychael, Tam, and Vegard right behind me. The tugging led up, so up the stairs I ran. Up was good; up meant out. I was sick and tired of being stuck underground. The tugging led to a dark hall with a pair of doors about twenty feet ahead. I stopped. There were lightglobes set into the walls, but they were as dark as everything else. I was impulsive, occasionally dim, but never suicidal.

"What's through those doors?" I asked Mychael in mindspeak.

"Our gym."

The gym. The place where Guardians worked out, trained—learned to kill.

"It's packed with weapons." My lack of enthusiasm was evident.

"Yes."

"Is there another way in?"

Mychael nodded once.

A room with weapons was good for me since I didn't have any; but it would be bad for all of us if the demons got to them first, which they probably had. Just because they had claws, fangs, and horns didn't mean they wouldn't take anything hanging on the walls—like those demon-slaying, green-bladed, hooked spear thingies. I swallowed. Killed by demons with weapons that were made to kill demons. Irony sucked.

A faint clinking came from the darkness, not just inside the doors, but farther into the room—much farther than I wanted to go without knowing exactly what was in there.

"Chains," Mychael said before I could ask.

I arched a brow.

"Attached to punching bags," he clarified.

Oh.

I wondered if the demon queen knew that we'd destroyed her only way home, and now her situation was all or nothing, do or die, kill or be killed. She was cornered and we had no choice but to go in after her and however many Volghuls were sharing the dark with her. The queen had the Saghred and the Scythe; and if she managed to stab the former with the latter, she'd have all the backup she needed, and we'd have Hell on earth—thousands, maybe millions of souls looking for new bodies, and the inhabitants of Mid would be just the beginning. And the four of us would be at the front of the line. It was up to us to stop it all, and my hands were as empty of blades as the day I was born. We didn't want to rush in, but it only took a second for a demon to stab a rock.

The whole situation had suicide mission written all over it.

I didn't need to project my thoughts to Mychael and Tam; I was sure they'd arrived at the same gloom-and-doom conclusion.

"Stay here," said Mychael's voice in my head.

I didn't have to say or think "like hell"; my expression said it perfectly.

Mychael gave me a look; you know the one. Then he handed me the best gift I'd ever gotten from any man—a knife. Actually it was more like a short machete. I loved it. It didn't increase my confidence level in where we were going, but it went a long way toward making me feel better about not dying immediately when we went in.

"Tam, you and Vegard go in through the locker rooms," Mychael said.

I felt Tam's magic power up. *"Veils?"*

"The best you've got. Whoever gets to her first takes her down."

Tam grinned in a flash of fangs, but there was death in his eyes. *"Race you."*

"Raine, you're with me," Mychael said.

If Tam didn't like that arrangement, he didn't say or think anything. I didn't care who went with whom; I didn't like the idea of splitting up, period. Demons with an evil rock of power and the means to open it didn't seem like the best time to divide forces. But Mychael didn't get to be paladin by being a crappy tactician, so until something jumped out of the dark and started killing us, I'd go along with his plan.

Mychael gave Vegard and Tam half a minute to get to where they were going. Then looked down at me, his eyes dark and unreadable in the faint light. *"Can you veil?"*

Damn. I had a feeling he was going to ask that. I'd never done it before, but thanks to the Saghred, I could do pretty much anything I put my mind to. Problem was, I'd never put my mind to wrapping myself in a veiling spell, and now wasn't the time for a screw up.

Mychael took my hesitation as an answer. He reached out

and took my hand, and once again, his magic ran up my arm and into every part of me. Instantly, it felt as though I were still there but not quite. I looked down at myself and up at Mychael. We were both still there.

"No one can see us," he assured me. *"Including demons."*

"You sure?"

"I've done it before."

We slipped silently—and hopefully invisibly—around the corner into the gym. The hand-holding thing worked out well. I was right-handed and Mychael was a lefty, so our respective weapon hands were free. I was holding the knife Mychael had given me; Mychael's weapon hand was empty. Though considering what he'd done to the demon queen earlier, his empty hand was a lethal hand. But if anything came at me, veils and hand-holding were history.

We weren't alone. I couldn't see the proof, but I sure as hell sensed it. The room smelled like a gym was supposed to, with two notable and gut-wrenching exceptions—blood and brimstone. Blood in a gym wasn't unusual, but this was fresh, and it hadn't come from a demon. Brimstone meant we were in the right place with the wrong people.

The demon queen didn't want to kill us. Usually someone wanting to keep you alive was a good thing—unless that someone was the queen of demons. In that situation, given a choice between taken dead or alive, I'd go with dead. And if I died, I was taking as many demons as I could down with me.

We moved into the room, Mychael intent on any shadow, brush of air, or sense of movement. Considering recent bad experiences, I was checking out the ceiling. Just because we didn't hear clicking or scraping didn't mean Volghuls weren't dangling from the rafters like giant bats waiting to drop on us.

We didn't have to look far to find the demon queen. She was waiting for us in a picture straight out of a nightmare.

Illuminated by a pool of sickly green light, the demon queen held the Scythe of Nen tightly against the throat of a captive Guardian, and a young blond elf lay dead at her feet—an elf in a Guardian uniform who couldn't have been much older than

Piaras. His eyes were open and fixed, and the blood pooling on his chest said how he'd died. The bloody Scythe in the demon queen's hand said who had done the killing.

And clutched in the captive Guardian's white-knuckled hands was the Saghred.

Oh no.

I froze and held my breath. He might as well have been holding a bomb with a lit fuse. If one drop of blood fell from the Scythe onto the Saghred, he was worse than dead.

He'd be a Saghred sacrifice.

"Do you desire this, elflings?" Either she could see us, or the bitch just knew we were there.

The Guardian she held captive hadn't been cut. The blood on the Scythe's blade was from the dead elf. She'd wet the blade in preparation for plunging it into the Saghred. I knew this as sure as if she'd told me—or as if the Saghred had told me.

I dropped Mychael's hand. She knew we were here, and I wanted both of my hands free.

"Yes, elflings," the demon queen purred when we materialized, pulling the Guardian closer. He gasped and shuddered; I didn't blame him. Some things you just didn't want touching you. "You all appreciate the helplessness of your situation. Soon you will experience helplessness as you never have before. The soul of another violating your body, pushing your soul aside, taking you completely. I have heard it said that you will remain aware through all of it—the taking, the possession—for the rest of your lives." She smiled at us, pleasant, almost human, as if she'd just given us the best news in the world. "And you will be helpless to stop anything your new master or mistress wants your body to do."

Just when I thought I couldn't be more scared, someone came along and redefined the word for me. Killed by what you feared the most. Laurian Berel had been killed because of a dagger; he'd been terrified of daggers. I wouldn't be that lucky. I wouldn't be killed by what I feared most—I'd get to live with it, and wish I were dead. No control, helpless, completely at the mercy of another. Sarad Nukpana would love to have the job. He'd love to have me. I glanced down at the Saghred held tight in the Guardian's hands. Colors swirled just beneath the surface, flowing, circling. Souls waiting and eager to get out.

"A sacrifice to use it; a sacrifice to open it." My voice only shook a little. Good for me. A lot better than I'd expected. Fear, mixed with an urge to run, blended together with a desire to bloody my own blade with royal demonic black.

The queen inclined her head in a single, regal nod. "One must die, so that my lord and king may live again." She gazed down at the dead elf. "He gave himself for a noble cause. Isn't that what you teach your young ones, Paladin? Nobility and self-sacrifice?"

"He *gave* nothing." Magic spun in the air with Mychael's words. "You took." He was a step closer to her; I hadn't seen him move. "And you will pay."

The queen laughed, bright and brittle—and nervous. She stepped back, pulling her prisoner with her. "And you will make me? I think not. You will not risk losing another of your own. That is a great weakness in you—you're unwilling to lose even one, even when you have no chance of preventing it. Defiance in the face of futility. It is a weakness that my husband's soul inhabiting your body will cure you of." Her gaze turned lascivious. "You will be cured of many such weaknesses—and inhibitions."

There were a few Volghuls around her that I could see; I was sure there were more in the dark. When it came to bad guys, there were always more in the dark.

"Kuitak?"

"Your will, my queen?" said a Volghul from the shadows at her right shoulder.

"If the paladin moves or uses that magnificent voice of his again, tear out his Guardian's throat."

In the blink of an eye, the Volghul had the man's throat in his claws, and the demon queen held the Scythe poised above the Saghred.

"I have everything I need." Her smile spread as she looked at Mychael. "A strong and desirable body for my husband to inhabit, and the elfling to wield the Saghred for us." She spoke without turning to a pair of Volghuls standing behind her. "Find the goblin. He is here; I have caught his scent." She inhaled in pure pleasure. "Still delectable," she breathed. "Bring him to me; do what you will to the human with him."

One of the Volghuls ran a quick black tongue over purple lips. "We hunger, Your Majesty."

She dismissively waved her free hand. "Then feed on him, but be quick about it."

My power was free to do with as I willed. No Hellgate distortion was holding me back, and the queen knew it. But the captive Guardian held the source of that power clutched in white-knuckled hands. If I tapped my Saghred-spawned power, would the Saghred take him? Would it take all of us? I had no idea what the damned rock would do.

I knew what I wanted to do, what I had to do. That Guardian wasn't going to die. Mychael wasn't going to be possessed by the demon king and then had by his bitch bride. I didn't care what I had to do to save him, but he would walk out of here alive, soul intact. We all would.

She had the Saghred, but I *was* the Saghred. And I was really pissed off.

Mychael's hand lightly touched my arm, telling me to wait. He was buying time. We didn't have any time; the Guardian had even less time, and the smug demon not a dozen feet in front of me was acting like she had all the time in the world. She wanted Tam here to watch.

Tam.

He wasn't here. That was what Mychael was waiting for. And from the silence, the demons hadn't found him or Vegard. We would have heard that. All we heard was silence. Deadly silence. Killing quiet. I'd seen Tam do it before, and I was sure Vegard was equally qualified, and both of them couldn't be more motivated. I put on my best poker face and kept it there—and I kept my thoughts on the captive Guardian and the sweetness of payback.

Tam was fast.

He rose up behind the queen's guards like Death himself, and with one sweep of his demon-killer blade, two Volghuls lost their heads. From the surprised hisses and thumps in the dark, Vegard was having similar success.

Mychael's voice rang out, and the Volghul's claws clenched in rigid paralysis at the big vein in the Guardian's throat. The queen snatched the Saghred from his hands and plunged the Scythe into it, slicing through the stone like living flesh.

My flesh.

I screamed. The Saghred and I were one. Flesh of my flesh. My screams turned to agonized gasps. No air. So cold. I tried to stay on my feet. I had to; I had to get that rock. I felt myself sinking to the floor. You're not bleeding, Raine. You haven't been stabbed. Get up!

Tendrils of multicolored light writhed their way out of the Saghred. I felt each soul flow up the blade as if it were coming out through my own skin. Elongated shapes of dark shadow and mist, breaking free into the air around us, circling, searching.

The demon queen saw it and laughed, high and wild, and utterly insane.

Until the light from Mychael's hand took her in the chest and flung her backward, slamming her against the far wall. Tam was waiting for her.

Mychael caught the Saghred as it fell.

No. Oh please, no.

I heard Tam's shout, Vegard's roar, and everything slowed until time barely moved at all.

"Drop it!" It was my voice screaming at him, but I sounded so far away. Too far to reach him in time.

Mychael didn't drop the Saghred; he didn't even shield himself. He couldn't do what he had to with shields in his way. He held the stone tightly against him and pulled on the Scythe with everything he had.

It didn't budge.

Only for you, Raine.

It was a voice and not a voice. It could have been the rock; it could have been me. I was the bond servant; Mychael wasn't. I had blood on me where the queen had slashed my neck. I was a Saghred sacrifice waiting to happen. Another wraith flowed up the Scythe to freedom. Maybe the Saghred was too busy spitting out souls to suck mine in. Maybe.

It didn't matter. Mychael wasn't going to die or worse because of me.

I was the Saghred; and the Saghred was mine.

I dragged myself to Mychael's side and put my hand over his, over the Scythe. Something in the Saghred responded to my touch.

Or someone.

Mychael felt it. He moved his hand from the Scythe to grip the Saghred in both hands, holding it for me. I pulled on the blade.

And someone inside the stone pushed.

My father was pushing the Scythe out. When the blade was out, the gash would close. He knew this; he was telling me this. He would remain inside, giving up his chance for freedom.

My father was sacrificing himself.

My vision blurred with tears. Sobs I couldn't stop came between gasps for breath.

Please don't. Don't do this. You can survive; we'll find a way. I need you. Tears streamed down my face and onto the Scythe, onto the Saghred.

I need you, Dad.

The Scythe jerked in my hand, like someone had grabbed hold of the blade.

Dad.

It felt like he was holding my hand, holding on tight. I desperately pulled air into my lungs, put both hands on the Scythe's grip, and pulled with the last bit of strength I had, pulling like I was dragging a drowning man from a flood.

The Scythe quivered weakly in my hand. A thin sliver of silvery mist flowed up the blade and into the air above us. It hovered there, flickering with pinpoint motes of light, before gently settling into the dead elven Guardian. The body took a shuddering breath and his now-living eyes looked directly at me.

"Daughter," he whispered.

The Scythe came free, and the Saghred sealed.

I quickly crawled to his side and took his hand, holding it tightly in mine. Deathly cold was surrendering to life-giving warmth. The body was a young elf; the soul looking out through his eyes was my father. He smiled and weakly squeezed my hand. As he closed his eyes, his chest continued to rise and fall.

And heal.

"What's his name?" I could barely get the words out.

"Arlyn Ravide," Mychael told me.

"Does . . . Did he have family?"

There was a smile in Mychael's voice and tears in his eyes. "He does now."

Chapter 31

My new leathers arrived just in time for Piaras's induction ceremony.

The citadel's Great Hall wasn't filled to capacity; about a fourth of the Guardians were still out demon hunting two days after we'd closed the Hellgate. Between the Guardians and Sora's faculty, most of the demons had been trapped or killed, but Guardian patrols were still out in the city hunting down what was left.

But Archmagus Justinius Valerian had made sure that everyone who needed to witness Piaras's induction into the Conclave Guardians was here.

Except Carnades Silvanus.

Protocol demanded that he be invited, even though I didn't know of anyone who wanted him here. So the invitation had been extended, and Carnades had refused, politely of course, citing injuries sustained while a prisoner of the demon queen. The only injuries he'd sustained were from my rock-wielding cousin, but no one was lining up to tell him that. The elf mage had earned himself one heck of a concussion, but no doubt the memory of what he'd seen was quite intact. His absence confirmed it.

Carnades was holed up in his town house. He hadn't had contact with anyone—including the Seat of Twelve, whose signatures he'd need on any arrest and/or execution order. Uncle Ryn had taught us that a quiet enemy is an enemy to be feared.

It was a lesson I'd learned only too well over the years, and I didn't need a refresher course to tell me that I'd better watch my back.

At the moment, my back was firmly against a wall in an alcove to the left of the Great Hall's dais. There were chairs, but I didn't want to sit down. The alcove was a place usually reserved for dignitaries or special guests who didn't necessarily want to be seen by everyone in the main audience. I didn't care who saw me, but I went along with Mychael's precautions. Besides, everyone's attention should be on Piaras where it belonged. This was his moment, and he'd more than earned every second of it.

On the dais was the archmagus's throne, and Justinius Valerian looked right at home. His lean and grizzled body didn't stand a chance of filling that chair, but the old man's presence more than made up for it. Justinius was wearing formal robes that must have weighed as much as he did; and if they didn't, the massive sword he lifted to tap the kneeling Piaras on the shoulders had to make up the difference. It was nothing short of a towering testament to the old man's stubbornness and determination to show that he was back in charge. He wasn't even breaking a sweat.

Piaras was splendid in his dove gray Guardian cadet uniform. It was identical to the uniform that fully knighted Guardians wore, with the exception of color. Cadets wore dove gray; knights' uniforms were the color of dark steel. The short, quilted tunic was cut to accentuate broad shoulders, muscled chests, and narrow waists. The formfitting leather trousers did the same thing, but to other places. Piaras and the other cadets who stood in the front ranks still had a little bit of filling out to do, but no doubt those uniforms still did a fine job of turning coed heads on campus. One coed's head was being turned right now. Being the archmagus's granddaughter had earned Katelyn Valerian a front-row seat; being Piaras's girlfriend put an appreciative gleam in her bright eyes. I knew that look. That girl had intentions, serious intentions. If Piaras didn't already know, I wasn't about to tell him. He was going to have to figure out things like that for himself.

"You're smiling," said a new, yet familiar voice.

Standing next to me was the father I'd never known, in a body that until two days ago, I'd never met.

Vegard had himself a partner in crime—and I had a second bodyguard. Arlyn Ravide's brother Guardians thought the kid was a glutton for punishment for requesting the assignment. I knew he was a father with a lot of catching up to do and with a daughter he was determined to protect.

I was a daughter determined to protect him.

"Yeah, I am," I admitted. I was so proud of Piaras that I could burst, *and* I had a father. Those were two of the best reasons I'd had to smile in a long time.

In my mind, the absurdly young blond elf by my side was Eamaliel Anguis, my father; but I'd called him nothing but Arlyn in the two days since his body and my father's soul had become one. And I'd tried my best to think of him only as Arlyn Ravide. On an island full of mages, they didn't just listen with their ears. No one could know his true identity. Mychael had convinced the Guardian who had been the demon queen's hostage that Arlyn hadn't died. He'd been critically injured, but Mychael and the archmagus's healer had been able to mend his chest wound. Arlyn had stayed secluded until this morning to make the story more believable. No one could suspect that he was really Eamaliel Anguis. There was no statute of limitations on Saghred stealing. If certain people found out, Arlyn Ravide would be put on trial as Eamaliel Anguis, charged with theft, treason, and abandonment of his post. He'd just gotten his life back; no way in hell was anyone taking that from him.

No one was taking him from me.

Mychael was standing at Justinius's right, wearing his steel gray formal uniform. Vegard had told me once that Mychael was responsible for the uniforms he and his knights wore. If I didn't know Mychael was humble, modest, unassuming and all that, I'd say that he'd had those uniforms made for the express purpose of leaving no doubt that he was completely irresistible. I smiled. Then again, I'd only known Mychael for a little over two weeks. There was lot about him that I didn't know.

Mychael was still an enigma, wrapped in a riddle, coated in yum. Only now the enigma was a little less mysterious; I was a few clues closer to solving the riddle—but damn, that man would always be coated in yum.

"A fine man, your Guardian," my father commented.

"He's not mine."

Now it was Arlyn's turn to smile. "That's not what your eyes are saying."

"What's that supposed to mean?"

"Precisely what I said."

"He's a Guardian; I'm a Benares—never the two shall meet."

Vegard cleared his throat meaningfully behind me. Mychael and I had more than met.

"You know what I mean," I told him.

"Ma'am, the boss doesn't care what anyone thinks."

Until the Saghred and I came along, Mychael's reputation was spotless and his position secure—and his neck wasn't in danger of leaving his shoulders. "Maybe he should," I murmured.

"Or maybe *you* shouldn't," Vegard countered.

One side of my mouth quirked in a quick grin. "You sound like your boss."

He winked at me. "Why, thank you, ma'am."

At Justinius's command, Piaras arose to thunderous applause. Arlyn and I joined in, and Vegard added some loud whistles. He wasn't the only one. The Guardians in the audience were enthusiastically welcoming their new little brother. Between what Piaras had done with the bukas and his display of courage at the

Saghred's containment room door, he was well on his way to gaining the respect and admiration of his brother Guardians that he'd always wanted. I didn't think I'd ever seen Piaras that happy. The kid was virtually glowing. Dreams coming true had a way of doing that.

Now all we had to do was stop the nightmares from becoming real.

Six souls had escaped from the Saghred.

Sarad Nukpana was one of them.

The demon king was still inside. But to tell you the truth, if I'd had a choice between the demon king and Sarad Nukpana, I would have picked the demon. His demonic majesty just wanted to raise hell. Sarad Nukpana wanted vengeance: slow, sweet, and personal. Then he wanted the Saghred and all the power that came with it.

I didn't think it could get any worse than demons. I was wrong.

My father had told Mychael and me that Sarad Nukpana and the others would possess one body after another, keeping themselves corporeal until they could find the perfect hosts—people with enough magical power and influence to be useful to them.

"Sarad is still body jumping," Arlyn said, his voice low enough for my ears only. He could still read my mind. I wasn't surprised. And considering that we had to hide who he was, it could be a literal lifesaver. "If he remains in the same body from one sunrise to the next, it's permanent. He doesn't want that—at least not yet."

It was the "not yet" part that had me waking up in a cold sweat for the past two nights. I could *feel* the son of a bitch; I knew he was out there. And he wanted me to know it; he wanted me to wonder when and where he would finally show himself. The goblin wanted me, but first he wanted me terrified. His cat-and-mouse game had only just begun. He could be anywhere—and inside of anyone.

I don't play cat and mouse. And I don't do terrified—at least I was trying really hard not to. Not being scared out of my skin was easier said than done. Sarad Nukpana wasn't just stalking me, he was haunting me. He wanted to drag out the game as long as possible. I was determined to end it before he got started. I knew where he had to be—the goblin embassy. Problem was, getting in would be next to impossible; getting out would take nothing short of a miracle. Quite frankly, I wasn't chomping at the bit to take a stroll into enemy territory to go ghost hunting.

Rudra Muralin had come through that mirror into the citadel, and he hadn't been seen since. Tam's source in the goblin embassy said their new ambassador had come home. What I needed to know was had he come home alone. I was betting he hadn't.

"What will happen to the people he infests?" I asked Arlyn.

"When he leaves them, they'll be disoriented for a day or so; or insane if they weren't emotionally stable to begin with."

I could see where being possessed by Sarad Nukpana could do that. And Rudra Muralin was already nuts.

"No trail of dead bodies to follow?"

My father shook his head. "Sarad will be careful. He has everything to gain, and too much to lose. He will be cautious until he is ready to make his move."

And when he made that move, we would all know about it.

I looked back up at the dais where a line had formed to welcome Piaras into the Guardians.

"Piaras is safe," Arlyn assured me.

"How do you know that?" It came out a little sharper than I'd intended.

"Sarad would possess Piaras for spite, but it is too great a risk for him. As a cadet, Piaras will be living in the citadel, and he will be closely watched. Sarad will not risk capture to satisfy a petty vengeance."

He was right, and I knew why. Sarad Nukpana wouldn't waste time or strength on anything petty, most of all vengeance. No doubt Nukpana thought that revenge was best served in cold blood and up close and personal. And when he came for me, I wanted to have a fitting welcome waiting for him. I said I wanted to; I didn't have a plan yet. I told myself that brilliant retaliation takes time. Too bad my time was running out.

Mychael was walking toward us, and I knew it wasn't for a casual hello. We hadn't had much time to talk in the past two days and had had absolutely no time alone. Mychael had the Guardians' best spellweavers secure the Saghred as well as they could, and they'd done a fine job with no objections from the rock. The Saghred had been cut open; apparently it needed some time to heal. The spellweavers had likewise secured the Scythe of Nen, which was being kept in an undisclosed location. Undisclosed was good; hopefully spellweavers were good at keeping secrets—and hopefully elven intelligence hadn't recently bought itself a Guardian spellweaver.

When Mychael got close enough, I asked the inevitable question. "Your office?"

"Please."

The Guardians we passed in the wide corridors had smiles and salutes for their paladin. They'd heard that Mychael had closed the Hellgate. That was the story we'd told, and that was the story we were sticking to—and with Mychael's report, that version had become official. It wasn't a lie. It was more like a simplification of an entirely too complicated truth. Mychael had been the one to hit the Hellgate and the demons on the other side with more white magic than they could survive. My and Tam's roles had been reduced to no role at all. Officially, I'd been too injured from my catfight with the demon queen, and Tam's strength had been exhausted keeping the Hellgate stable until Mychael could take over. It *was* Mychael's magic that had closed the Hellgate—that Tam and I had helped fuel that magic didn't bear mentioning.

Vegard and Arlyn walked a few paces behind us. They were my bodyguards, but Mychael was their commander. I knew it had to feel strange beyond belief for Mychael with my father's soul being in the body of one of his junior knights, but he handled it well, better than I would have in his place. I had to hand it to Mychael; he would have made a fine actor. No one watching or listening to him would suspect that Arlyn Ravide was anything other than one of his young knights.

Mychael told Vegard and Arlyn to stand guard and see to it that we weren't disturbed, and then he closed his office door behind us.

Blessed silence, and no sense of anything outside of the room. Mychael's office had always been warded, but he'd recently laid on a couple of fresh layers. Very recently.

"Just being careful," he told me.

"There's no way we can have too much of that."

Mychael almost laughed. "You? Careful? I would say I couldn't believe you broke into Carnades's house *and* attacked the demon queen, but I can believe it. The last one I saw with my own eyes."

"It wasn't like I had a choice."

"I will admit that even if he hadn't already been kidnapped by Rudra Muralin, Carnades would never have turned over the Scythe to anyone. But attacking—no wait, that would be too dignified—*tackling* the demon queen was not—"

"Again, I had no choice. Tam needed a distraction, so I—"

"Tam is perfectly capable of causing his own distractions."

"So I *wanted* to take down the bitch," I snapped. "She sent her spawn to feed on students. The kids they would have eaten would have been the lucky ones." I stopped and exhaled slowly, forcing myself to calm down. I spread my hands. "You do your job; I do mine," I said in as much of a level tone as I could manage. "I'm a Benares. I can go places and do things that you can't. Since you had no prior knowledge of my actions, your nose is clean. And since we weren't caught at Carnades's house, so is mine."

"You could have been caught."

"But I wasn't."

"What happened to sending for help? I could have gotten a search warrant."

"I didn't have time to wait for help, backup, a cheering section, or anything else. The fact that the Scythe had just been snatched only confirms it."

Mychael gave me a look; you know the one. "You didn't have time to wait, or you just didn't want to?"

Coming clean is good for the soul—and sometimes the temper. I managed a crooked grin. "Both."

"I assumed as much." Mychael shook his head, the barest shadow of a smile on his lips. "I should arrest you, if just to save you from yourself. Worse yet, you talked five of my best men into going with you."

I held up a hand. "Only two came into the house with me. Vegard and Herrick insisted. Vegard wasn't going to leave me; Herrick wasn't leaving Piaras."

"That's another thing—you took Piaras."

"He's a virgin. I had to."

Mychael blinked. "Excuse me?"

I told him about virgins and the Scythe, purity finding evil, and all that.

Mychael didn't laugh; but he didn't need to, those blue eyes of his were doing a fine job of both. And it did an even better job of taking the tension right out of the room.

"Then it was a good thing that you knew about Piaras," he admitted, trying to keep from smiling. "Finding a virgin on this island on short notice would have been a challenge."

I snorted. "To say the least. And I *suspected* about Piaras; I didn't know for sure."

"How did you—"

I winced. "I had to ask him."

"I hate I missed that."

"I don't."

"Sora told me you had gone to Carnades's and why," Mychael said. "And Herrick told me you'd gone into the tunnels under the house. I'd just received confirmation that the Hellgate was in the Assembly. Knowing where those tunnels led—but mostly knowing you—I assumed the worst and went straight to the Assembly."

"I'm glad you did," I admitted. "Things weren't going quite as I planned."

Mychael raised one eyebrow. "What I witnessed was the culmination of an actual plan?"

"More like a loose gathering of possible actions." I picked at the expensive fabric on the back of one of his guest chairs. "Please tell me you have a better plan for Carnades."

Carnades knew about our umi'atsu bond, his word carried weight, his accusations would be believed, and if Mychael, Tam, and I were forced to appear before the Seat of Twelve, there would be no doubt. And since the Saghred was involved, even Justinius Valerian wouldn't be able to save us.

"Carnades knows and so does Rudra Muralin," I said. "One of them is going to act on that knowledge. Soon."

Mychael's face was somber. "It won't be Carnades."

"You say that like it's not good news."

"Carnades has had one visitor. Markus Sevelien's ship came in with the high tide, night before last."

"Dammit, Mychael, you said you'd tell me!"

"You demanded; I never promised. I needed to know who Sevelien saw first. That would be difficult with one of your daggers sticking out of his chest."

"I just want to talk to him." My words coming out from between clenched teeth said otherwise.

"And if he didn't answer correctly, he would have been sporting your steel—or more likely, his security detail would have killed you before you got the chance."

I froze. "Security detail? Markus has never had one of those before."

"He does now. Mages, heavy hitters."

"Which of your men followed him?"

"I did."

I blinked. The paladin of the Conclave Guardians didn't follow; he delegated. Then I knew why Mychael trailed Markus himself. Me. Mychael trusted his men, but no doubt some things he wanted to do himself. Because of me.

"Carnades had a meeting scheduled with three of the Seat of Twelve," Mychael said quietly.

"You have names?"

"I do." He paused. "After seeing Markus Sevelien, Carnades canceled that meeting. He hasn't seen anyone since."

The implications of that kicked an already bad situation into the realm of catastrophic. "Markus told him not to do anything," I heard myself say. "Yet."

Given enough time and motivation, I could usually get into someone's mind. Not literally, but I could observe them enough to know how they would respond in a given situation. It was a knack that had come in handy on several occasions, saving my life in at least two instances. I'd never been able to read Markus Sevelien to save my life—and I just might have to.

"Justinius has two sources inside Carnades's household," Mychael was saying. "They said that Sevelien stressed most strongly to Carnades the need to rest, remain at home, and see no one."

"Sounds like an order to me."

"It was."

While I loved the idea of Carnades staying home and keeping his mouth shut, I didn't like that Markus Sevelien in all probability knew everything that Carnades did. And my blood ran cold at the thought of Markus being the one who was ultimately pulling Carnades's strings.

"Where's Markus now?" I asked, though I knew. He wouldn't be anywhere else.

"The elven embassy," Mychael confirmed for me.

"And Rudra Muralin is in the goblin embassy."

"And neither one has left since they arrived."

"Plots and nefarious deeds are best brewed in one place." I tried for a quip; it didn't quite make it.

"Raine, promise me you won't try to see Sevelien."

I answered with silence.

"I will be meeting with him myself," Mychael told me. "As I do with every dignitary or official who drops anchor in our harbor."

"It sounds like you've already set it up."

"I have."

"I want to be there."

"Absolutely not."

"Why?"

"For every obvious reason."

And every last one of those reasons involved me.

"Where are you meeting him?" I asked.

"Here in the citadel."

That made me feel marginally better. Markus wouldn't try anything on Mychael's home turf—at least the Markus I knew wouldn't. I had no idea what the Markus who could order Carnades Silvanus around was capable of.

"Think he'll be straight with you as to why he's here?"

One side of Mychael's lips curled in a quick smile. "Of course not. They never are. With some it's like verbal chess. Getting information from Markus has always been more like verbal fencing."

"Has always been?" I was incredulous. "You've met him?"

"On several occasions, either business or politely social."

"I take it I'm business."

The crooked smile came back. "I certainly wouldn't call you politely social."

"Touché." I was silent for a time. "Markus knows me, but he's kept it a secret until now. Though for all I know, he still might not have told anyone. People like him don't associate in public with people like me. You'd have been better off if you'd done the same thing. I'm a lot of things you don't need to have anywhere near you, now or ever."

Mychael leaned back against the closed door and crossed his arms over his chest. "And what kind of things would those be?" he asked, his blue eyes sparkling.

I was stunned. He actually thought all this was funny. "Infested with an ancient rock of evil should be reason enough. But if you need another: you uphold the law; my family doesn't."

"Raine, you aren't your family," Mychael told me. He thought for a moment, then let out a little laugh. "Most of us aren't like our families, and some of us don't want to be." He leveled those eyes on me. "You, Miss Raine Benares, are impulsive, trouble personified, you defy me at every turn, and to order you not to do something is a waste of my breath." He stepped away from the door and slowly came toward me. "But you're also brave to the point of being damned near fearless, unwaveringly loyal, fiercely protective of those you love, and have literally stormed the gates of Hell to keep them safe." Mychael stopped directly in front of me; amusement and sincere admiration shone in his eyes. "You're the most challenging woman I've ever had the pleasure to meet." His voice lowered to a bare whisper. "And yes, I did say pleasure."

I looked up at him. "Don't you think 'misfortune' would be a better word?"

He laughed. "And you would argue with a fence post." He reached out and brushed one finger down the side of my face and lightly hooked it under my chin. "Meeting you was not a misfortune," he said softly. "I meant what I said." He paused meaningfully. "I always have and I always will."

"You're in an umi'atsu bond with me and Tam. Considering who and what we are—"

Mychael lowered his hand from my chin, brushing my arm on the way. "What I did was necessary. And I've sent for A'Zahra Nuru for help."

I just stood there, stunned. "You've what?"

"She is well versed in umi'atsu bonds," Mychael said firmly. "If help is to come from any source, she's it."

Primari A'Zahra Nuru was a powerful goblin mage, and she was the one teacher Tam would admit to having. I'd only met her once, but from what I'd seen she was brave, noble, and definitely not a dark mage. A'Zahra Nuru had been strong enough to help Tam pull himself back from the black magic abyss. Though it was her present position that raised the small hairs on the back of my neck.

"Is she still chief counselor to Prince Chigaru?" I asked.

"She is."

"And if you've sent for her, chances are he'll come with her."

"Probably."

I snorted. "Definitely. He knows the Saghred is on Mid. You

just invited his counselor to come to Mid. I don't think his highness is going to stay home."

Not that he had a home to stay in. Prince Chigaru Mal'Salin was the younger—and exiled—brother of the goblin king. Chigaru wanted his brother's throne and wouldn't mind having his brother's head on a platter while he was at it. And he saw both of these as being a heck of a lot easier to get if could get his hands on the Saghred first.

"The Conclave has secure accommodations for guests such as Prince Chigaru," Mychael assured me.

"A containment room on the other side of the island?" I asked hopefully.

"A very secure and well-guarded inn. The prince and his retinue have stayed there before, and I recall that he was pleased with his accommodations—and I was more than satisfied with the security."

I blinked. "He's been here?"

"More than once. Since Mid is politically neutral, exiled heads of state know they will be safe here."

"Last time he was here, the Saghred wasn't," I pointed out.

Mychael looked down at me, his smile cheerfully serene. "Raine?"

"Yes?"

"Leave the prince to me. Leave his retinue to me. Handling visitors with questionable motives is one of the things I do best."

I gave him an apologetic little grin. "Sorry about that. It's your job, isn't it?"

"It is."

"And I'm trying to do it for you."

"Again."

"You're really good at your job."

Mychael inclined his head graciously. "Thank you. If I weren't, I wouldn't be standing here to agree with you."

I knew no one was in the room with us, but I lowered my voice anyway. "Were you also going to ask A'Zahra Nuru about our . . ."

"Situation?" he provided helpfully.

"That's the one. Does she know about magical connections that you don't find in books?"

He knew what I was talking about. Our link, our connection. A very deep sense of connection on a very personal level.

"A'Zahra Nuru is considered an expert in magical pairings of all sorts," Mychael said.

"A pairing." I said it, wrapping my mind around the words, what they implied, and what they could potentially mean for us.

"And it's getting stronger," Mychael said quietly. "I can feel it."

I could, too.

A pairing. Mychael and me.

A bond. Tam and me—and now Mychael.

A tangled knot. What my life had become.

"The paladin of the Conclave Guardians has gone and gotten himself 'paired' with a Benares." I felt laughter bubbling up and let it. I'd earned it. "You know, to some people on this island, you paired with Raine Benares might actually be a worse offense than getting cozy with the Saghred's bond servant."

A corner of his mouth quirked upward. "I wouldn't be surprised."

Considering what I'd done over the past few days, I wouldn't be surprised, either. I grinned crookedly. "We did storm the gates of Hell, didn't we?"

"We most certainly did."

"I squashed demons, vaporized demons, and was crazy enough to get into a catfight with the queen of demons."

Mychael chuckled. "Crazy. I couldn't have said it better myself."

I ignored him and continued. "You know, when you look at it that way, one little fist-sized rock doesn't stand a chance against me," I said brightly. "While Carnades is still 'resting,' Markus is still plotting, and Prince Chigaru hasn't gotten here yet, what say we do something about that rock? Given any more thought to blasting it out of one of Phaelan's cannons?"

"While that idea is appealing on many levels—"

"You don't want to risk the rock getting pissed off and blowing up the entire island."

"Precisely."

"Okay, fine. No turning the Saghred into a cannonball. I'm open to any and all ideas. But while we have a little breathing room, let's confront the problem head-on. I'm past ready to roll up my sleeves and get to work."

Mychael shook his head, smiling. "And the fact that the finest magical minds couldn't destroy it means nothing to you."

"Oh, it means something. It means they weren't as motivated as I am." I met his smile and raised him a grin. "Or as you would say, as stubborn. Until two days ago, no one thought the Saghred could be opened, either." I jerked a thumb toward the hall outside the office. "But no one has had my dad as a consultant before. He's been with the Saghred for centuries; and for the past year he's been *inside* of it—so he knows it literally inside and out. He's free now. With what he knows, and what we can find out, if there's a way, we'll find it. Tam thinks that the Saghred caused the umi'atsu bond between us. I agree with him. And a three-way umi'atsu bond is a first, right?"

"I've never heard of one before."

"Then maybe we're linked in a different way since the glue that's holding us together is the Saghred and not each other. Get rid of the glue, get rid of the bond. Get rid of our problem." I looked at him expectantly. "What do you say?"

"I say you're right."

I think my mouth dropped open a little. "You do? I mean . . . I am?"

"I can't agree with you?"

"It's just not something I expected."

Mychael smiled slowly, his eyes lit with a dangerous sparkle. "I can do the unexpected, Raine. It's not just my job that I'm good at."

Chapter 32

It was bright and sunny on the Fortune. *It was edging toward late* afternoon, so the sun had finished baking the wooden decks for the day, and a cooling breeze was coming off the harbor. I was sitting on a bench, working on my third ale, or was it my fourth? I hadn't bothered to keep count. I'd hauled the small keg up on deck with me to save myself the walk down to the galley, though now it'd probably be more like a stagger.

I'd left Mychael's office feeling confident enough, but the closer I got to the *Fortune*, the more my enthusiasm started to wane under the weight of reality. Carnades wouldn't stay at home forever, Markus would make his move soon, Sarad Nukpana's soul was out body shopping, Rudra Muralin was in the goblin embassy plotting my death, and the Reapers could find me anytime, anywhere.

Then there was Mychael and Tam—and me with Mychael and Tam. So far I hadn't had any time to really consider the consequences of our predicament, and I'd been avoiding to the point of denial the fact that a large segment of goblin society considered me married to both of them. Part of me rather liked the idea and felt deliciously naughty about the whole arrangement. The other part of me went with a time-honored Benares solution—if I drank enough, my problems would go away, probably along with my consciousness, but I'd deal with that when I found myself facedown on the deck.

And all of my problems and predicaments were courtesy of a fist-sized, soul-sucking rock.

Where I was sitting, anyone who wanted to spy on me—or take their best shot—could do so to their heart's content. I didn't care about that, either, and cared less after each tankard. Vegard and Arlyn had strongly suggested that the safe place for me to do my drinking would be belowdecks. I strongly refused, and in emphatic and colorful terms told them that I was staying precisely where I was and that I wanted to be left alone. They were still on deck with me, but guarding me from a respectful distance. If I fell over—either from ale or a crossbow bolt—I was sure they'd pick me up. I took another long drink. I knew I was behaving like an ass, and I'd have to apologize to them later, but for now I wanted sun on my face and a keg by my side.

I'd never been good with feelings. Don't get me wrong; I was on a first-name basis with fear and anger, but feelings of the romantic kind . . . Well, let's just say our paths hadn't crossed that often. I've never been what you'd call datable. When a man found out my last name was Benares, all I had to do was watch his face and know how that relationship was going to go—or not go. It was all in the eyes; they either bugged out in sheer terror, or narrowed in anticipatory greed. Unfortunately, there wasn't much of a middle ground.

Mychael and Tam were two notable exceptions.

So far all my romantic encounters with Mychael had been for diverting enemy attention, for healing, or for relief that I wasn't dead—at least those were his excuses. But after what he'd said, not said, and implied in his office a few hours ago, I had the feeling that Mychael's excuses were turning into intentions. And regardless of what Vegard said, or Mychael might think, or I might want, the top lawman in the seven kingdoms could hardly get involved with a member of the top criminal family. Talk about a career-destroying move. Though with the Saghred involved, career-destroying was also life-threatening. But that hadn't stopped me from pondering some intentions of my own. What had happened when he'd touched me wasn't a feeling or a sensation; it was an experience of the once-in-a-lifetime kind. And I'd already been treated to it twice in two days.

Then there was Tam. I knew what Tam wanted from me—the same thing he'd wanted since the night we'd met. And during the time that I'd known him, those black, bedroom eyes of his made sure I didn't forget it. I was pretty sure his feelings for me went beyond what would no doubt be an amazing time in bed—or on the floor, in the tub, or against the wall—I just didn't know how far those feelings went, and Tam hadn't seen fit to tell me. And in any romantic encounters with Tam, my good sense had left the room. Tam could do that to a woman, and he certainly did that to me. Then there was Tam's past. Normally a man's past wouldn't bother me, as long as it stayed in the past where it belonged. But Tam's notoriety, indiscretions, sins, and assorted crimes weren't just chasing him, they were catching up.

Two gorgeous, sexy, dangerous, and downright delicious men. And now the Saghred was playing matchmaker for me with both of them, making it a bad situation with even worse timing, and I didn't even want to think about the ending. But what if we got rid of the rock, and the bonds, and no one was trying to arrest and/or kill us anymore? What if it was just Tam and me, or Mychael and me? What would I do then? And who would I want to be doing it with?

I drained my tankard and reached for the keg's tap.

"You might want to rethink that," Sora Niabi suggested. "Or at least admit the reason for it."

The demonologist was standing close enough to talk, but far enough away not to get hit with anything I might possibly throw in her direction. Apparently she'd seen her share of mean drunks in her time.

I bristled. "Why?"

"Draining that keg isn't going to make whatever's wrong any better, and pickling your brain never helps anything."

"So you've never gotten pickled?"

She let out a snort of a laugh. "Plenty of times. I hunt demons for a living."

"Since you're here, does that mean the demon hunt's over?"

"It does."

"Wanna join me?"

"Love to."

I looked around, seeing nothing but my tankard and one keg. "We'll have to get—"

Sora flashed a grin and pulled a dinted metal mug from her robes. "I always carry my own."

"That's convenient."

"And ensures I never go thirsty."

Sora sat down on the deck next to the keg, filled her mug, and with a sore and weary sigh, slowly eased back against the mainmast.

"There's plenty of room on the bench," I told her.

"I'm good right where I am." Sora took a long drink and nodded appreciatively. "A fine brew. My compliments to your cousin."

I pushed on the tap and started refilling my tankard. "Phaelan thinks a happy crew is a loyal crew."

"This would certainly help. And you're sitting here getting yourself happy because . . . ?"

"I'm scared and I'm confused, and I'm overwhelmed by what I'm scared of and confused about."

Sora's brow creased in concentration. "That almost made sense."

"Thank you."

"And will emptying that keg make you any less confused, scared, and overwhelmed?"

"No, but—"

"Let's see . . . One, you're alive. And considering present circumstances, you used up half a dozen miracles making *that* one happen. Two, so you've got people after you." She dismissively waved her hand. "They're all assholes."

"Powerful assholes," I reminded her. I think my words were starting to slur.

Sora took another healthy swig. "All that means is they can blow more gas."

I had to laugh, even though it hurt my head. "I don't think Carnades blows gas."

"You're right. Too tight-assed." She paused with a knowing grin. "Third, and the main reason you're trying to drown yourself in a keg, you've got man problems."

I saw no reason to deny it. "On top of all my others. And it's not a man problem—it's a *men* problem."

Sora nodded. "Ah. Let me guess—two men, one you, and a lot of confusion in between. Seen it before."

"Not like this, you haven't. And it's not like I've had time to sit around and make a list of pros and cons."

"You don't need a list. What's your gut tell you?"

I grimaced and burped. "That I should have stopped two tankards ago." I leaned forward and dropped my face into the hand not holding the ale. "And being anywhere near me is going to get them both killed."

"Both meaning Mychael Eiliesor and Tamnais Nathrach?"

"That would be them." My words were muffled against my hand.

"First of all, I'd like to congratulate you on some damn fine taste in men."

"Thank you."

"So you're saying that you're not interested in either one of them?"

I lifted my head and regretted it. "I'm saying that I *can't be*."

"You can tell yourself that until you're blue in the face." She indicated my ale mug. "Or in your case, throbbing in the head. All the ale on this island isn't going to change how you feel here." She took the hand that wasn't holding her mug and poked herself twice in the center of her chest. I think she was swaying, or maybe it was me. "I take it that's the source of your confusion?"

"Uh-huh." I couldn't tell her that it was also the source of my fear. Sora didn't know about the Saghred's foray into matchmaking, and it was safer for her if she stayed that way. Sometimes, ignorance wasn't just bliss, it was survival. But I could tell her about Mychael's excuses turning into intentions, and Tam's lust turning into . . . well, serious lust and more. My love life had been mostly famine, but soon I might be confronted with a feast—and a choice.

I told her, and she listened.

"Being a demonologist gives you a certain perspective on life," Sora told me. "I went up against I don't know how many demons in that dark hall, with nothing but a handful of backup and half a dozen old and overused demon traps. By the way, that backup was some of your uncle's crew."

"I saw."

"When you and Captain Benares went missing, the commodore went to Mychael and demanded to help find you. The paladin and I knew where you were by that time, and with the Guardians protecting the students, I needed some strong backs to haul in my big-ass demon traps."

"Looked like a coffin to me."

Sora flashed a grin. "For a demon, that's what they are. My own invention. Once we got them spaced out around the Assembly outer hall, we opened them up and sucked the bastards right off the face of the earth."

"So what kept us from getting sucked in?"

"Shields and the fact that you're not a demon."

I chuckled and shook my head, slowly this time. "Some would say that's open for debate."

"Earlier models couldn't tell the difference between demon and mortal." She paused and looked a little embarrassed. "Design flaw."

"That's some flaw."

"Especially to the poor demonologist who got sucked in there with them; I had a hell of a time getting him out. Your uncle's crews hauled the traps in and then stayed to pose as lunch to lure the demons into range. Your Uncle Ryn and his officers took on a pack of Volghuls that arrived before we were ready to start the party." Sora smiled fondly. "The demons were actually afraid of your uncle. He and his crew are a fine bunch of men."

Now that was something Uncle Ryn and his crew had never been called. But I had to agree with Sora, any man who'd act like demon food, even for a few seconds, was worthy of any and all kinds of admiration.

"Your family's good people, Raine."

"They're pirates."

"Doesn't mean they're not good people."

I smiled. Sora was good people, too. "All of your students are okay?" I asked.

Sora's smile spread into a grin of fierce pride. "Every last one of them. And after what some of my grad students did in the Assembly, they'll be graduating with honors. Two of them didn't have the best grades in their class, but exam scores don't mean shit when you've got a ten-foot-tall demon trying to have you for a snack. It's what those two kids did to that demon that mattered. I'm proud of my students." She looked me squarely in the eyes. "And having demons trying to eat you reminds you real quick what's important and which things just don't matter. It seems that our fine paladin's acknowledging that he has some strong feelings for you. And I gather that you've known for some time how Nathrach felt. And you telling them that you can't be with either one of them won't do a damned thing to change their minds once they've made them up." Her dark eyes sparkled appreciatively. "In case you haven't noticed—and I'm sure you have—our paladin is a grown man."

I raised my tankard in salute. "Noticed that many times."

"And before Talon enrolled in the college, Tamnais Nathrach dropped by my office for a talk. Likewise, a grown man—a very well-grown man. And since they're both big boys, they don't need anyone to protect them from their choices—especially the woman it seems they've set their sights on."

"No one's set their sights on me."

"I study demons, Raine. But deep down, I'm a hunter. I recognize my own kind. Mychael and Tamnais are hunters to their core." She smiled slowly. "From what you tell me, and from what I've heard on my own, they've deemed you worthy of pursuit." Her dark eyes twinkled. "Girl, you'd better watch your back. Though you might have more fun if you didn't."

"Sora, I'm trouble to *my* core. I don't want them to die because of me."

"Because you love them, or at least that's the direction you're heading. If you won't say it, I will."

"I don't know what I—"

"Yes, you do. You're just too stubborn—or afraid—to admit it yet."

I didn't answer. I didn't have to; we both knew what that answer would be.

"Your not wanting them to die because of you won't change how they feel," she said. "The only thing you have to decide is what you're going to do about it. Personally, when a class twelve demon finally catches me with no spells, no trap, and no hope in hell, I don't want to have any regrets. How about you?"

I leaned forward and rested my elbows on my knees, letting my tankard dangle loosely from my hand, and stared down at the deck. As paladin, Mychael faced death every day. As a former member of the Mal'Salin family, Tam knew that death was hot on his heels right now. Both of them lived their lives like that, and they enjoyed living. I knew for a fact that Tam didn't let anything get in the way of his having a good time. Yes, knowing me could get them both killed; it could get us all killed. But if they could live like that, so could I.

I raised my head—slowly this time—and grinned up at Sora. "You're right. You're absolutely right."

Sora shrugged. "It happens from time to time. Though I can't blame you for tying one on; you've literally been to Hell and back."

I sat up straight and looked out over the harbor. The sun was lower in the sky. It'd be setting in about an hour; it looked as if it was going to be a beauty, and I was going to be sitting right here to enjoy it.

"I can't let what might or might not happen keep me from living my life," I said. "And I have no right whatsoever to tell anyone else how to live theirs—or how to feel. I won't let Carnades and men like him ruin however long any of us have left." I looked down in my mug; it was about half full. I set down beside me. "I'm done. I need what wits I've got left intact." I sighed and grimaced. "I've got some thinking to do, but first I've got a rock to destroy."

"Beautiful women getting drunk," Phaelan said from behind me. "Mind if I join you?"

"Pull up another keg, Captain," Sora told him. "This one's about empty."

"Is my cousin regaling you with stories about her exploits with the demon queen?"

Sora stretched her legs out, crossing them at the ankles. "I haven't heard that one."

I shot Phaelan an exasperated look. "Because there's nothing to tell."

"Nothing to tell? It was the best part of the whole day. Well, next to what I got to do." He lowered his voice and grinned slowly. "But that's highly classified information." He winked at Sora. "Mine was more satisfying, but what Raine did trumped it for sheer entertainment value."

I snorted. "For you."

"Let's let the professor decide. Raine started a catfight with the demon queen," Phaelan said gleefully.

Soras's brown eyes went wide. "A *what*?" Then she started to laugh. "Please tell me he's kidding."

"Afraid not."

Phaelan chortled. "Two beautiful women, one of them naked, both rolling around on the ground. What's not to enjoy?"

"That was insane," Sora told me, incredulous.

I shrugged. "I know; but sometimes insanity works."

"You won?"

"Not really."

"You're here; she's not."

"Uh, that was Tam's doing." I made a slashing motion across my throat. "With one of the Guardians' green demon blades."

"That'd certainly do it. But *you* attacked *her*?"

"Yeah, I did."

"With her bare hands," Phaelan chimed in.

"Hey, I had a reason. I had to get the Scythe."

Sora's brow furrowed. "I don't think I've read or heard of anyone attacking the queen of demons before."

"She did seem kind of surprised," I admitted.

Phaelan draped an arm around my shoulders. "When word of this gets around, do you have any idea how this is going to enhance the family reputation? The one who isn't even in the family business kicked the demon queen's shapely ass."

I raised a brow. "Shapely?"

It was Phaelan's turn to shrug. "Call 'em as I see 'em. And thanks to you, I got to see everything." His grin turned seven times wicked. "And with all that rolling around, I got to see everything at least twice. I've never been more proud to call you my cousin."

I felt a presence brush my skin like fingertips. I stood, Phaelan's voice fading into the background. I knew he was there before I could see him. I walked over to the railing and looked down at the dock.

Tam was standing alone, no dark mage hit squad, just him. His cloak blew back to reveal leathers and at least one blade at his hip. I was sure there were more. No battle braid contained his hair. It was down and blowing in the evening breeze. Sora was right; I had some damned fine taste in men.

Phaelan stepped up behind me.

"Permission to come on board, Captain Benares?" Tam asked formally.

Phaelan blew his breath out through his nose. He wasn't going to like it, but he was going to do it—for me. "Permission and welcome," he called out.

"Thank you," I whispered.

He smiled faintly. "Who am I to judge?"

Sora nodded in greeting to Tam and then went to join Vegard and Arlyn. Tam sat on the bench next to me. I leaned back against the mainmast.

Tam glanced down at the keg. "You've been drinking."

"Extensively."

"May I ask why?"

"You can't guess?"

Tam didn't say a word as his dark eyes gazed out over the harbor. "Piaras's ceremony went well?" That was one thing you could always count on with a goblin—when a topic wasn't to their liking, they'd change it.

"It was perfect," I told him.

"I'm glad; he deserves it. I would have liked to have been there, but . . ."

"The three of us together in a room full of Conclave mages isn't the best idea right now," I finished for him.

I didn't need to say out loud who was the third one of "us." Heck, with our umi'atsu bond, Tam and I didn't have to talk out loud at all. But to use the bond would be to acknowledge it. Until we could do something about breaking that bond, denial was working just fine for me.

"People could see us here," Tam said.

"I don't give a damn who sees us."

"You might tomorrow."

"Then I'll deal with it—and with them—tomorrow. *You* came here alone," I said accusingly. "Anyone could have seen you, or worse." I stopped and cringed. Way to go Raine. The demons probably ate his dark mage school buddies; he doesn't have any guards anymore, and you just—

"Four of them are recovering at Sirens," Tam said, plucking my thoughts like grapes. "The rest stayed there to protect them and Talon." His face was set like stone. "If anyone had attacked me on my way here, they would have paid dearly for the privilege."

I didn't doubt that.

"Raine," Tam said quietly. "Dark magic will always be a part of who I am."

"I know. Even if I could pound the Saghred into dust right now, what it's given me will always be with me, too."

We sat for a while without speaking, in an awkward yet companionable silence. The *Fortune* rocked gently beneath us as the tide came in.

Tam shifted slightly and laid his hand on the mast's smooth wood. "Remember the last time we were here together?"

Like I could have forgotten. Now there was a good-bye a woman could remember. When I'd left Mermeia, and Tam had stayed, he'd come down to the *Fortune* to see me off. Tam's idea of saying good-bye had been slamming me against the mainmast and kissing me passionately enough to curl my toes.

"I didn't want you to forget me," he said.

"No chance of that, with or without that kiss."

More than a kiss joined us now.

Tam's voice was a bare whisper. "Raine, if there was no Saghred, no umi'atsu bond, no Carnades or anyone like him . . . would there be any chance for the two of us, knowing what I am, what I've done?"

"Tam, I don't know everything you've done, only what you've told me. And I'm getting the impression that it's just the tip of a very big iceberg."

"If you knew, you might not want to see me again."

One corner of my lips curled in a tiny smile. "Don't be too sure. I'm a Benares. Our standards of proper behavior are a little different from everyone else's." I pushed at my mug with the toe of my boot. "You've changed since then." I didn't look at him, but kept my eyes on the ale sloshing in the mug. "And you're doing the best you can to stay that way, and you're confronting your past as it comes at you. You have to be strong to do that, and brave. I admire you for both."

Tam laughed once, without humor. "Neither one has been easy." He paused. "And my best might not be good enough."

I nodded. "Especially with me around."

"You have always been a delectable temptation." Tam's voice caressed the words like dark silk.

A delicious shiver ran down my spine. Tam was no spell-singer, but his voice could do all kinds of things that had nothing to do with magic and everything to do with seduction. And attraction. Don't forget attraction, Raine. Like a moth to a flame.

"And the Saghred's power makes me that much more desirable," I said bluntly.

"Raine, I don't want the Saghred. I want you."

There it was.

"For the foreseeable future, we're a package deal," I said, my throat tight. "Wanting me will get you killed; the Saghred will get you damned. You can't have one without the other."

"Then I'll take both." His voice had a raw edge. It wasn't Tam's black magic talking; it was all Tam. I could almost feel his need, his desire to take what he wanted and damn the consequences.

Tam's hand was between us, and I reached down and took it. With our bond, I could feel the blood surging through his veins, quickening at my touch. Tam wanted to touch me; he wanted to take me in his arms and make it all go away.

I didn't look at him. "Mychael's asked A'Zahra Nuru for help."

"I know. I suggested it." He sat in silence, until the tension was as thick as the mast at our backs. "Raine, I want to share an umi'atsu bond with you, but not if it would harm you. With the Saghred connecting us, it would do more than harm, it could destroy you. I won't risk that."

I looked up sharply. "You're going to risk separating us?" And risk losing your magic and your life. I didn't have to say it; we both knew it.

Tam nodded once. "It has to be done."

"Maybe that's a risk we don't have to take."

He looked at me. "What do you mean?"

I told him my plans for finding a way to destroy the Saghred.

"Those are long odds, Raine."

"I've seen worse. You're a gambling man. How about it?"

"The rock has the best cards," he countered, but I could see a trace of a smile and a peek of fang.

I met his smile and raised him a grin. "Then we'll cheat."

Tam squeezed my hand. "Then deal me in. But we'd better play our hand quick. There are new players coming to the table." He took a deep breath, slowly let it out, and didn't say anything for a couple of heartbeats. That didn't bode well. "Imala Kalis is on the island," he said quietly.

"Who—"

"She's the chief of goblin intelligence." Tam hesitated. "She was in the Assembly after we'd closed the Hellgate."

"The one you saw?"

Tam nodded.

And the one he'd lied about.

"How much trouble will she be?" I asked.

"Possibly more than we can handle."

"I take it that you know her."

"I do."

Tam didn't elaborate, and I didn't really want to know how well Tam knew her. He had been the goblin queen's magical enforcer; Imala Kalis was the chief of goblin intelligence. I imagine they'd worked together. Very closely together.

My ale and my stomach suddenly didn't agree with each other. "Okay, so the chief of goblin intelligence saw what we did. What will she do about it?"

"Nothing, for now. Imala doesn't believe in wasting good information. She will wait until revealing it is the most advantageous for her."

"What a sweetheart. Has she contacted you?"

"Not yet, but it's only a matter of time."

I thought of Markus Sevelien telling Carnades to sit tight. Markus horded information like a miser horded gold. But unlike a miser, Markus didn't keep what he horded; he used it. And like Imala Kalis, he used it when it would have maximum effect.

"I have a source in the goblin embassy," Tam said. "I received one report, but I haven't heard from him since."

He calmly stated it as fact, not what it probably was—his source was dead or worse.

"I've heard that Rudra Muralin is in the embassy," I said.

"He is."

I scowled in frustration. "Muralin kidnapped Carnades when he was the acting archmagus and we *still* can't touch him. Diplomatic immunity sucks."

"And to go in after him would be an act of war."

"I'm betting Sarad Nukpana has already gone in after him."

"Rudra would be a good catch for him," Tam agreed. "He's powerful, influential, and has the full backing of King Sathrik Mal'Salin; but most important, he has been the Saghred's bond servant before. Rudra would be the perfect body for Sarad to possess. And if Sarad has taken him, we will be finding out soon enough."

"And both Muralin and Nukpana know about our umi'atsu bond," I said. "If we move on them, they'll move on us—if they haven't made their first move already."

I told Tam about Markus Sevelien.

"It's starting." Tam's expression was as dark as his eyes.

"What?"

"Sathrik is sending those closest to him; your government is doing the same. They're getting directly and openly involved."

"They want the Saghred." I knew that fact only too well.

"And in all probability, you to wield it for them. Before your father took the Saghred from King Omari Mal'Salin, the goblins had been waging a campaign of complete extermination against the elven people—and they nearly succeeded. For the past nine hundred years, neither goblin nor elf has had a tactical advantage."

"By tactical advantage, you mean a rock that will suck out your enemies' souls."

"Yes."

"As far as our governments are concerned, the Saghred is back on the market," I said.

"Precisely. The goblins want to reclaim it—"

"And the elves want payback."

This was about more than Tam and Mychael and me. This went much further than simple prejudice and centuries of racial hatred. It was about control over your enemies. The Saghred had become a symbol, a reason for the powerful and bloodthirsty to take those first steps toward something worse.

They were starting a war.

About the Author

Lisa is the editor at an advertising agency. She has been a magazine editor and writer of corporate marketing materials of every description. She lives in North Carolina with her very patient and understanding husband, one cat, two retired racing greyhounds, and a Jack Russell terrier who rules them all.

For more information about Lisa and her books, visit her at www.lisashearin.com.

P.O. 0003542391

M15G0907